OLD WORLD, NEW WORLD

a novel
MARK DINTENFASS

WILLIAM MORROW AND COMPANY, INC.

New York   1982

Library of Congress Cataloging in Publication Data

Dintenfass, Mark.
  Old world, new world.

  I. Title.
PS3554.I5O4   813'.54   81-14044
ISBN 0-688-00811-9   AACR2

Printed in the United States of America

First Edition

1 2 3 4 5 6 7 8 9 10

BOOK DESIGN BY MICHAEL MAUCERI

For my parents

OLD WORLD,
NEW WORLD

I

What is there between us?
What is the count of the scores or
hundreds of years between us?

—WALT WHITMAN,
"Crossing Brooklyn Ferry"

ONE

COME, MEET THE FAMILY. Begin with Jacob Lieber, the sire of the brood. There must still exist somewhere in one of the family albums that singular old photograph of the man, the only image of him his grandchildren would have. It shows him posed stiffly, clutching a fat book, in front of a tangle of vines and leaves and flowers, a kind of cheap bower effect rigged up somehow out of paper and tricks; and after one has absorbed a quick, vague impression of his white beard, his long black coat and derby hat, his air of gloom and exhaustion (which the grandchildren would probably mistake for saintliness), the incongruity of the backdrop—the simple artifice of it—leads the eye astray. The next thing you know, you are imagining the photographer, bald and sweating beneath his black cloth; and the antique box and tripod of the camera; and the darkroom, with its chemical smells and dripping faucet; and a pot of magnesium powder, ready to explode: all of these assembled in a Brooklyn storefront studio in the balmy and hopeful springtime of 1919. But that was years after the family arrived in America. The grandchildren would have to envision for themselves Jacob Lieber as he was in the early days, in 1906, 1907, 1908—so long ago anyway that the years in retrospect seem to shimmer and merge and lose their precision—when his beard was still black, and his soul was in torment, and the strange uncertain grace of his old age had not yet fallen, like the softest of snows, upon him.

He was, in those days, a sallow, potbellied man with weak, damp eyes and bad lungs. He had a long bent nose, from which in winter a drop of water seemed perpetually suspended, and a droning voice, which echoed even in ordinary conversation the old tones and rhythms of talmudic singsong. Though he had acquired from his father the subtle craft of bookbinding, he was stupid about money and clumsy with his hands. Back in the old country—back in that muddy and ramshackle village, the very name of which the family would later conspire to forget—he had spent most of his time in the study-house reading the laws and commentaries. Even in America he felt most at home at the synagogue, and would continue to wear to the end of his life the skullcap and ritual fringes of the Orthodox. He was, depending on your point of view, too proud or stubborn or honest or ignorant to adjust. If you told him the world was round, he might try to prove to you, quoting ancient authorities, that actually it was as flat as paper. He was shy, unworldly, pious (at his funeral the rabbi would suggest that he was, perhaps, one of the ten good souls for whose sake God preserves the universe), the sort of man who never would have decided on his own to come to America. One must suppose that chance and circumstance and his wife's ambitions had driven him here. He had been twice Sophie's age when their marriage was arranged, and probably had never considered, this study-house innocent, that there follows inevitably from marriage and its fumbling rituals hungry mouths to feed; and he was already past forty when he found himself plucked out of his accustomed life and set down again, puzzled and blinking and reluctant, somehow to support a family amidst the rush and turmoil, the dingy air, the irreverent and boisterous streets of Brownsville.

Fresh off the boat, the greenest of greenhorns, Jacob went to work for his brother-in-law Asa Kalisher in the restaurant on Pitkin Avenue, and Sophie moved in with the children—Sam, Deborah, Hymie, Molly: the Old World spawn—to the apartment upstairs. They had for the six of them two small bedrooms and a kitchen with an icebox and a coal-burning stove. The smells and tumult and grease from the restaurant used to rise up through the air shaft (later they would remember how Sophie always seemed to be scrubbing the children or the walls), and on winter mornings, going out to the toilet, they found strange derelict men asleep on the steps. America! The ceilings leaked; the furniture, which had come secondhand and disinfected from the "agency," seemed to hold the impress of ghosts; and the warped glass in the windows bent and blurred their view of the hectic world outside: the fire escapes, the flapping laundry, the crowds and traffic, the pushcart vendors with their hoarse and immemorial cries. It was, in short, a dismal sort of place, and though the children would later recall it through a fine haze of nostalgia, make of it the immigrant's fond cliché—*this was our first home! here it all began!*—it must have been for poor Jacob Lieber the bleak and clamorous arena of his gloom.

Everything about the new life troubled him. He hated the apartment with its dark corners and looming walls. He hated the restaurant, where the rich, clammy smells of the kitchen made his head spin and the running back and forth put blisters on his feet. He hated the local synagogue; the accents, the chants, the commentaries of the rabbi all sounded alien to his ears. He hated the shops, the clothes, the food, the darkness of brick buildings—everything, even the color of the sky itself, was strange and vaguely sinister. At least in the old country, on a *Shabbos* afternoon, he could go out walking in the fields or woods, and for an hour or two his soul might be at peace; but here the traffic made him nervous, hooligans mocked him, and in the unfamiliar maze of city streets he was afraid of getting lost.

In fact, it was America itself, with all its machinery and sunshine and temptations and flux, that troubled Jacob Lieber. He sensed its implications, foresaw the rough and heathenish sprawl of his seed across the alien landscape. He was by nature a melancholy man, and now, confused and lonely, he became morose. The most famous emblem of the New World, glimpsed from steerage, came to seem to him a gigantic figure of evil, Lilith or one of her daughters, all green and horned and belligerent. He would think of his father, of the smells of parchment and ink and glue that had filled the house of his childhood, and of all the old ritual that once had charted the course of every moment of every day, and mourn for what he—and worse, his children—had left behind.

"Here even the Almighty is a stranger," he used to say.

It frightened him, his drastic and unwilling plunge into this unfamiliar world, and so, like a drowning man, he clung furiously to the wrack and refuse of the old beliefs.

Jacob's father—old Moshe Lieber, the mystery atop the family tree —should probably be imagined as a fierce, fanatical, solitudinous man, a widower, raising his four moody children with the aid of a senile and obese old aunt. He was the follower of some famous rabbi, of whom it was said that his face shed light and his feet never touched the ground, and he would have impressed upon his sons, long before they could have had notions of their own, that the words of holy books were the shadows God cast upon the earth, and that only in those shadows was reality to be found: all the rest was vanity and illusion. And though he was four thousand miles away, a backward journey of months by ship and rail and trudging horsecart, Jacob no doubt lived, as sons do, with the inward and berating ghost of his presence.

Sophie, anyway, blamed most of her troubles on him. She had

never liked the old man, had feared him, in fact, and one of her motives for coming to America must have been to put some unbridgeable space between him and her children. Later she told them such bitter stories about "the *tzadik*, the pious one," as she scornfully called him, that he entered the realm of family legend. When, for example, Hymie took to sitting in closets, they said that "grandpa Moish" was haunting him—thus they would account for the taint of strangeness that ran in their blood.

Sophie was often reticent with her children—it was typical of the Liebers, for all their loud talk, to leave many things unspoken—but never about her father-in-law. She told them how, after she was married, the man never took a meal in her house because he couldn't trust the purity of her kitchen; how he raised a ruckus in the marketplace by accusing her father of selling tainted meat; how, when she was in labor with Sam, he arrived with the village crones and papered the walls with amulets and dragged her up out of bed to march her three times across the threshold to ward off the "evil eye"; and how afterward he quarreled with her family about the naming and refused to come to the *briss*. She told them how he used to spit sideways when he entered a room, how he once went barefoot in the snow to atone for a misspoken prayer, how he claimed to have conversed with angels. They heard about the scene he made when Jacob told him he was going to America, how he called him a fool and a renegade, a creature of the devil, and chased him into the street with a walking stick. They even heard how, soon after Jacob's wedding— "Why he accepted me," Sophie would shrug, "I'll never know!"—he dragged home with him from the synagogue one night a ragged and orphaned hunchback, practically a cripple, and announced to his daughter Hannah that here, this scholar, this saint, was her husband-to-be, and how a few weeks later they dragged Hannah's body out of the icy river. She told it plainly, as though it were merely part of the family history they ought to know, but even then they realized that the simplicity of the telling masked a burden of miseries escaped and crises endured.

Anyway, if Sophie could be believed, this medieval old goblin chaser was their father's father, living within Jacob like a murmur in his blood, whispering to him the demands of the ancient creed, telling him that life in the new land was a kind of sickness, not of the body, of course—for the body is just a prison, doomed to rot and crumble—but of the soul; and that he and his children, seed of the seed of Abraham and Isaac, were already infected.

16

But actually it was mostly Jacob's body that seemed to be suffering. He began to develop "symptoms." He lost his appetite, complained of headaches and backaches, took to sitting up half the night in an armchair, unable to sleep. Though Sophie wanted more children, he no longer was capable of being a husband to her. Sometimes spots of fire would dance in front of his eyes; at other times, no matter how cold he was, he would begin to sweat. He grew short-tempered with the children and went running from the house to get away from their noise, saying it made his ears ring. Sophie had her hands full.

In the restaurant things were even worse. The sight of a woman's teeth tearing into a bit of bread would fill his throat with bile. His fingers failed him and he began to have accidents; his mere presence could send plates and utensils crashing to the floor. Soon he was blaming these accidents—the shattered tumbler, the fumbled bowl —on the imps and demons he said infested the place. The restaurant, he claimed, was the den of Asmodeus and Beelzebub, and Asa Kalisher was in league with them. He said he could hear them at night singing their filthy songs and carrying out their blasphemous rituals.

Asa Kalisher was patient with him. He tried him as a waiter, an assistant cook, a cashier, a busboy, a dishwasher, until finally Jacob was spending most of his time sitting on a stool in the kitchen, grumbling prayers and imprecations to himself and annoying the help. Still, Asa kept paying him.

"Blood is blood," he said, "and if your sister marries a *shnorrer*, what else is there to do?"

But a calamity of some sort was inevitable, and eventually it occurred. One night Jacob came home with his arm in a sling, his clothes soiled, his hat lost, his pale face stained with the bitterness of tears and anguish. Asa Kalisher came in behind him, shrugging his shoulders and raising his palms. There had been an accident in the restaurant. Somehow Jacob had managed to burn his hand so badly that they had to take him to the hospital to have him bandaged up.

Sam would always remember how his mother just stood there— Molly clinging to her skirt—with her lips pressed tight together and little spots of red glowing in her cheeks, looking first at her brother and then at her husband, as if to say, "What sort of *tsurris* will you make for me next?" He would remember how Deborah started to cry, whimpering softly deep in her throat the way she always did, and how Hymie went off to hide in the closet, and how for a moment his heart bulged in his chest, pounding so loudly he was afraid they would hear it. He would also remember how, after his uncle was gone and the children had been packed off to bed, he could hear his parents talking in the kitchen, how his father was saying it wasn't an accident at all, that something, some creature or demon with red eyes and filthy green matted fur and a horn jutting from its forehead, had teased him and taunted him, calling him by name, and then shoved him against the stove. Sam lay in the dark listening to his father who was not crying exactly, not sobbing, but making some low, awful, wrenching noise, and then, with his heart pounding again, he put on his clothes and went down the fire escape because he didn't want to hear any more, and perhaps also because he wanted to see this demon for himself. He was almost disappointed to find everything in the restaurant just as it always was, the waiters polishing the silverware, the fans spinning calmly overhead, his uncle and his uncle's cronies at the corner table dipping egg biscuits into their coffee and laughing at some inexplicable joke. And though he was just eight or nine years old at the time, he would never quite forget that he now possessed the inarticulate inkling of some pertinent and difficult truth: that the most familiar things in life, looked at again, may become at any moment all strange and terrible and new.

In the weeks that followed, when Jacob wasn't at the synagogue, he sat in the house with his arm in a sling and Sophie had to clean around him. He said almost nothing to her after that first night, was drawn up into silence as if the incident had drained him of words and he had to wait for some new well of language to gather again within him.

Once, long ago, on one of his *Shabbos* rambles, he had seen a dying bird, a formerly glorious thing—though he wouldn't have been able to name the species—with blue feathers that shimmered into violet and a dab of scarlet still pulsating faintly at its throat. Now it lay in the mud of a road rutted with cartwheels, its feathers broken and soiled, blotches of blood encrusting its wings, insects gathering to reduce it back to those elementary particles out of which, through God's grace, it had sprung. In his despair and self-pity it came to seem to Jacob an image of himself and his brood.

He never should have come to America; there was nothing for him here; he had fallen into the grip of death and corruption—those were his thoughts when he looked at Sophie, allowing her to read the reproach in his eyes.

Sophie, of course, was troubled by his gloom, but perhaps not nearly so much as she wanted to believe she was. She grieved for him, but she could never quite bring herself, despite her own best inclinations and her exquisite sense of duty, to grieve with him. Even before he burned his hand, some soft space of sympathy had closed up within her. She didn't scorn his sufferings—she was, after all, a wife in the old style—but romantic notions of love were simply not part of her world (though there seems to have glimmered faintly in her background some adolescent flame, snuffed out by her family, or anyway a name, Stanislaus, that her children would hear many years later in the mutterings of her senility), and so she was always able to keep some crucial part of herself cool and aloof. Besides, she sensed something thin and insubstantial about Jacob's miseries, understood that all of it, the symptoms, the accidents, the demons, even the angry red blisters of the burn itself, which she had to help him bathe and rebandage, had about them an air of concoction, as if the poor man, without realizing it, were straining himself to make them up.

In any case, what did it matter? Her brother was still giving her money, she could continue to feed and clothe her children, life went on, better days were bound to come; and in the letters she wrote home to her father she kept on insisting that despite everything, America seemed like paradise to her.

Sophie was the daughter of a butcher, one Yussel Kalisher, who was just fifty years old, still in his prime, when his "treasure" left for America. He was a large loud red-haired man, another widower, with a knife in his hand and blood on his apron, joking and flirting with his customers, while they, all those good pious and kerchiefed housewives of the village, stood trembling like plump birds in front of his chopping block. Sophie adored him, and dreamed of bringing him to New York. After all, didn't butchers quickly become wealthy here? Furthermore, as she put it in those lost letters of hers, sooner or later in the old country the *goyim* were going to murder all the Jews, while on Pitkin Avenue, when you put your head down on the pillow at night, you could sleep without dread. She was also eager to demonstrate her own sagacity, to prove that her gumption or restlessness, call it what you will, was being rewarded, that in America the trains did indeed fly over the buildings and even the poor could hope to live like kings. Remember: the journey had been her doing; she had pushed and nagged and prodded; Jacob alone never would have wanted to go. This by itself would have led her to paint the new life in jewel tones, all gilt and glory.

So she had motives. But she was also the sort of woman—still girlish, of course; still russet-haired and green-eyed and pretty despite her four pregnancies—who had an eye for the future. She possessed the marvelous capacity of enjoying today the sweetness she believed would come to her tomorrow. She loved, for example, to go browsing through the local shops, carrying off in her fancy all the luxurious goods and gadgets she knew she or her children would someday be able to afford. Always the good immigrant, she mastered a few fragments of English, practiced them with Asa and Sam, and then, blushing, proud, produced them like family heirlooms in conversations with storekeepers or strangers. She even started classes at night to prepare herself for citizenship, and though Jacob grumbled at the sight of a woman studying profane books, he couldn't stop her. Snatches of ragtime began to infiltrate the repertoire of tunes she hummed; she went with Sam to the nickelodeon and wept quietly through melodramas she couldn't possibly follow; on election day she stood for hours by the polling place just to watch the proceedings. And what *nachis*, what joy, when first Sam, then Deborah, and later Hymie and Molly went off to the big red-brick public school on Sutter Avenue, and came running home through the afternoon dusk with ink on their fingers and chalk dust in their hair and wondrous American secrets twinkling like gems in the mysterious depths of their eyes.

She loved America. She loved trolley cars and automobiles and the awesome clatter and racket of the subways. She loved to go into the post office and see the picture of the genial and stupendously fat American President. She loved candy stores: their ice creams, their rainbow display of syrups, their piles of newspapers in three or four different languages. Most of all she loved to ride the train to Prospect Park on a warm Sunday afternoon and go gallivanting through the gardens and down to the lake.

What a sight it must have been in those days to see the Liebers taking the air. First would come Sam, a rowdy, lanky, red-haired, and thoroughly Americanized little roughneck, running on ahead of the others and shooting with both index fingers—pow! pow!—the wild Indians presumably lurking in opposing groves of trees. Then Jacob, black coat, black derby hat, hands clasped behind his back, walking alone and aloof, the good European paterfamilias, in an attitude of almost comical abstraction. Then Sophie, in frills and bustles, a flush upon her high and haughty cheekbones—they were taking their meals in the restaurant now, so she was eating well, growing ruddy and stout—pushing a big rattan baby stroller, stopping every so often to bend over and pluck Molly's fat probing fingers from Hymie's vulnerable face. And finally Deborah, as awkward as a baby giraffe, pale, thin, dreamy Deborah, who always lagged behind, her solemn gaze fixed not so much on the grass and flowers (she had plucked a few dandelions and fixed them in her hair) as on her own secretive and lonely thoughts. A delicious parade of Liebers they were, moving across the meadow toward the lake, where Sam was never allowed, no matter how much he pestered, to go out rowing in one of those intriguing boats. Sun, grass, flowers, squirrels, the emblazoned carousel, the kiosk at the lakefront where you could buy bags of peanuts and sweets, the sight of Jewish people at leisure, mingling carelessly with the Gentiles, many of them wearing expensive clothes: Sophie had never seen anything like it, this truly was the promised land; and while the sun cast diamonds on the rippling water and the mild breeze blew murmurous music in the treetops, she would clutch her babies to her, feel her heart brimming over, and—"Look, my darlings," she would say in Yiddish, "Oh, look, just look, at those beautiful ducks!"

For Sophie such moments redeemed all. Besides, what for Jacob seemed ordained and permanent, his misery a punishment inflicted upon him by powers he would never comprehend, was for Sophie merely a temporary and regrettable and commonplace inconvenience. Her optimism was boundless. She handled Jacob as she handled her children, fussed over him, ached for him, worried about him, but saw his agony as simply another problem to be solved, another difficult bump and bruise to be dealt with.

"It's homesickness," Asa Kalisher had assured her. "They all suffer from it, the greenhorns. But time heals everything, just wait and see."

So she waited and hoped to see him rouse himself to the pleasures and opportunities of the new life. She waited through the months in the restaurant, tolerating his complaints and visions, and through the weeks when he sat in the house with his arm in a sling, staring alternately at her and the walls in an agony of reproach. She waited when he refused to return to the restaurant and tried, haplessly, to earn a living giving Hebrew lessons to local *bar mitzvah* boys for pennies an hour. She waited while he drifted into the garment business, first trudging bundles of cloth and patterns through the streets, later trying to learn the craft of a tailor—which was mostly, for him, a jabbing of needles into his awkward thumbs. She waited through the terrible days when he sold herring from a rented pushcart, and the even worse days when he did nothing at all and the family had to live wholly on the generosity of her brother.

She waited. What else could she do? Return to the old country? Divorce him? Go to work herself? There may have been times—there *must* have been times—when her optimism failed her, when she would lie alongside him in the tepid, trembling, impotent darkness and feel the heft of his misery like a weight upon her heart; times when the failed and brooding sight of him would fray her nerves and start a flutter of panic inside her. But she had her children, and her brother to help her, and the old patience of her kind; and besides, as she told Asa Kalisher, whatever else he might be, Jacob was a "good" man, kindly, well intentioned, honest, far better than most. Wasn't that enough?

Expectations: the tricks the imps of desire play upon the mortal limits of our lives. What the mind grasps in its craving, what desire can merely imagine, the simple heart hurries to devour. There, perhaps, one can glimpse a provisional path into the terra incognita of the family, a landmark in a wilderness all vast and dim. They were, they are, hungry people, the Liebers and Kalishers, and sometimes only heaven and earth mixed and gobbled together could begin to sate them. One day, all by herself, Sophie rode the subway into Manhattan and spent an adventurous afternoon browsing among the skyscrapers and department stores, and then walking up along Park Avenue because she wanted to see for herself those granite temples which someone had told her were the homes of rich Jews. It was early spring; a nip was in the air; she began to shiver and pulled her shawl close around her shoulders. A black woman in a nurse's uniform was pushing a blond child in a gleaming pram; a beer wagon went by, the hooves of the matched horses clopping on the cobblestones; a fellow wearing white gloves tipped his top hat to her; the sun, momentarily eclipsed by a small cloud, burst out again; and then, somehow—she would tell her children about it years later, but the details were vague, and one must suppose that she never really understood it herself—she knew she was tired of waiting. She was trembling now not from the chill but from a sudden surge of feeling that was released within her, a rushing sense of her own strength and will and expectations. Once again (for this was no doubt the same sort of mood that had led her to America) she was aware of her power to move her husband, to shape and form her own life by inserting herself with force into the dank and hopeless miasma of his. It wasn't pleasant, it was some fierce instinctive boldness all her upbringing had taught her to control, and she came back to Pitkin Avenue that evening flustered and red-cheeked, with a throbbing in her head and a flame of ambition searing her heart. But really, it was so simple. She should have thought of it months ago. Vivid, bustling, she marched into the tumult of the restaurant, through the rich smells and tinkling confusion of the dinnertime crowd, found Asa Kalisher at the cash register and told him in just so many words, as he led her, gruff and courtly, to a table in the corner, that she had come to a decision. They were going to put Jacob into a business of his own.

ASA KALISHER, BY THE TIME the Lieber children were old enough to absorb the image of him they would pass on to the grandchildren, was a huge and boisterous man with the belly of a glutton, high blood pressure, green eyes, and a shock of brilliant red hair, which Sophie used to say was a sign of Kalisher blood. He had only four fingers on his left hand. When he was seventeen years old and still lean—or so the story was told years later—hearing that officers of the czar's army were recruiting in the village, Asa ran down to the marketplace, put his hand on his father's chopping block, and severed his pinkie with a cleaver. Later he kept the finger carefully preserved in a small chased-silver box he had acquired somewhere in his travels between Siberia and San Francisco, and which he carried in his pocket to combat nostalgia. Whenever his cronies started reminiscing about the old country, out would come the box and there would be the finger.

"Never forget," he would roar at them, "we left behind nothing but *tsurris* there!"

The family would remember how he used to say he wanted the finger to be buried with him because a Jew needs two good hands on Judgment Day so that he can dig his way through the earth to Jerusalem, and though he must have been joking—he was, after all, a socialist and an atheist, notorious for his blasphemies—with Asa Kal-

23

isher you were never quite sure. His tone, as time passed, became ever more elaborately ironical; there was often some imponderable discrepancy between his words and his intent, and perhaps in the end he managed to baffle even himself in the labyrinthine intricacies of his disillusion.

In the early days Sam adored Asa Kalisher. He would never forget those Friday nights on Pitkin Avenue when, after the restaurant had closed for the *Shabbos* and his father had gone off to *shul*, Uncle Asa would come upstairs with a bottle or two of kosher wine, plop himself into the armchair by the stove, fill a tumbler to the brim, and abolish a few hours by telling Sophie stories about his life in America. There in the warmth of the kitchen, while Molly sucked her thumb and Deborah daydreamed and Hymie played his own shy and solitary games behind the icebox, Sam learned his first English listening to his uncle talk. And what a talker he was! He told about theaters and music halls, about the uproar of a boxing match and the harsh sour smells and brawls of an Irish saloon. He told about unions and strikes, the garment district, the Catskills, about Communists and Zionists and Wobblies, about anarchist rallies where men from many nations, Jews and *goyim* alike, linked their arms like brothers and fought with the police. He recalled how, new in America, stranded on what he took to be the wrong coast, he zigzagged eastward from San Francisco, peddling pots and pans across the vast and hopeful continent. He talked about seeing outlaws and Indians, sandstorms and blizzards and floods, about huge mountains and immeasurable forests and deserts so hot and barren that only snakes and demons could live in them. He told of trainloads of women arriving to seek husbands in a Colorado mining town and of certain dark and treacherous streets right there in New York where poor immigrant girls were bundled into hackney cabs and shipped off to be "slaves" in Buenos Aires. Sometimes he would break off in the middle of a sentence, slapping his knee and laughing and winking ponderously at Sophie, who, because little children are all ears, would already be saying, *"Sha! Sha!"*—and what Sam had to suppose was the best part of the story would be left unspoken. Perhaps it was those hints of obliquity that most of all stirred Sam's bowels and inflamed his imagination. He was led at such moments to believe that American life—this strange, new, unexpected tumult they had dragged him to—was burrowed through with dark and forbidden places, and that his uncle had somehow penetrated them all.

This notion thrilled and tormented him. Often at night, overstimulated, he would lie awake in the compelling darkness, with Hymie dreaming and gnashing his teeth alongside him, and feel stricken with the awe and longing his uncle had aroused in him. Through the haze of boyish fancy he saw Asa Kalisher moving like some vigorous and cheerful giant through a world far richer than his own—a world from which his own father, for all his prayers and moods and homilies, had been excluded. He spent restless hours struggling with an inarticulate anguish that was mixed up somehow with the journey to this new home and the night they had slept in a forest. Years later, when he was working for Asa Kalisher, and still later, when they were partners together in the factory on Bergen Street, and quarreling, the shadowy memories of those early days made him feel vaguely ashamed and deflated. Asa Kalisher, he would learn, was also a braggart. But by then he would have already forgotten what he may, in any case, never really have known, that for a time Asa Kalisher was for him a kind of second or alternate—or why not just say American? —father; and though he could never express it, or even know there was something to express, there was in this unwilled shift in his allegiance a hint, a tone, of a hidden and squeamish betrayal.

Anyway, it was Asa Kalisher who brought the family to America. His letters home (so matter-of-fact in mood, so hyperbolic in detail) supplied kindling and fuel for the fire of Sophie's ambitions; his money paid for the passage; his brisk, knowing presence, as he helped them through the random cruelties of the immigration halls, his red hair bobbing like a beacon above the huddled crowd, was the first note struck of the new world's possibilities. It was Asa who settled them into that initial apartment above the restaurant; it was Asa who gave Jacob his first job, and found through his cronies and connections most of Jacob's other jobs, and fed and clad them when Jacob wasn't working at all; and so, of course, it was Asa to whom Sophie ran with her feverish scheme. She probably never even bothered to question his generosity. Blood is blood, she would have told herself, and besides, the poor man had no wife or children, no real family of his own.

So when she marched into the restaurant that day, she assumed that merely to ask was already to be given. A business for Jacob? The shrewd and caustic Asa Kalisher would have smiled at first, one imagines, would perhaps even have laughed out loud were he not subdued by his pretty little sister's sincerity and the simple protective love he felt for her and her brood. But even while smiling, even while hearing the submerged rumble of his own suppressed laughter, he would have been reminding himself that he supported them anyway; that for a few hundred dollars in capital you could, in fact, open a small shop somewhere, stock the shelves with dry goods or groceries, and dream of profits; that he also once upon a time had run errands through the streets of Brownsville; that, all things considered, it wasn't such a bad idea. And so, still smiling, still withholding his laughter—while Sophie stood there with her flushed and eager face, her hands clasped in front of her in a gesture of fervent supplication—he was already contemplating what sort of business a man like Jacob could possibly be fit for.

Eventually he found one.

There was, he learned, a bookstore for sale on Livonia Avenue, the previous owner having died or perhaps just conveniently vanished. It was little more than a hole in the wall squeezed between two tenements, darkened by the shadow of the elevated train and crammed with old books. There were tables of books and shelves of books and boxes of books. There were bundles of books tied with string in the corners and more books in the subsidiary hole that served as a storeroom, and still more books—some with lovely marbled endpapers and tooled bindings—spilling out into the sweltering and gloomy and periodically clattering street. Books sacred and profane; books in a Babel of languages: English, Yiddish, Russian, Polish, Hebrew, French; books of vellum and leather meant to last forever, and books of cloth and cheap paper already crumbling, merging with the omnipresent dust. If heaven is, as some say, a timeless democracy of souls, then that bookstore was an image of it. Here crude recent American regionalists rubbed shoulders with subtle old Jewish mystics, Charles Darwin and Moses Maimonides had a nodding acquaintance, and rare and beautiful antique volumes of Talmud might at any moment be unearthed from beneath a clutter of Victorian moralists. There were also magazines, stacks of penny dreadfuls and pulp westerns with garish yellow covers (*The Further Adventures of Buffalo Bill Among the Cherokees*), and some picture postcards, and even some boxes of stereopticon cards, which the mystified Jacob brought home for the children to play with since he was sure no one would want to pay good money for two identical sepia-toned views of, say, the Grand Canyon, the Statue of Liberty, or the sun-speckled giant sequoias of California.

It wasn't much then, that bookstore, just a sort of addendum or afterthought to a jammed and impoverished neighborhood, but, as Asa Kalisher said, it had potential. When he took Jacob and Sophie to look the place over, he stood there in his pearly-gray suit snorting dust through his big nostrils and waving his arms, conjuring up for them a pleasant image of the neat and friendly and profitable little shop it could become, with the books all sorted and sized, and electricity installed to replace the gaslights, and maybe a shelf or two of candies and gums set up near the cash register to bring in those few extra pennies that could make all the difference.

"Don't look at what is," he told them, "imagine instead what can be!"

Sophie needed no convincing, though initially she must have had something grander in mind, but Jacob, as one might expect, was reluctant. He had no head for business, he told them, and was already too much in his brother-in-law's debt. He put on quite a show that morning, picking up books at random, blowing at the dust, scratching his neck below his beard, blowing his nose, walking across the street at one point as if he could take the measure of the place only from a distance, then coming back with his face all screwed up in a parody of serious concentration. But beneath this display a subtle slide of emotion was taking place within him. He was readying himself, after months of rage and confusion, to arrive at some sort of truce with America. Books? Well, why not books? He was opening himself at last to the realm of possibility. There would be lots of conversation before the deal was closed, lots of planning and cajoling and accounting; but a course had been set for him, and with all the baffled hesitation of a weak and stubborn man, he was preparing himself to accept it. After all, if God had troubled Himself to bring Jacob Lieber to America, He must have had some purpose in Mind.

How pleasant it was for Jacob the morning he went with Asa Kalisher to the bank, and there, amid cool marble and gleaming brass, put his hand to a sheaf of documents in a language he couldn't read and received in return the substantial and satisfying heft of a set of keys. Pleasant because for the first time in years—probably since those bewildering months after his marriage when Yussel Kalisher tried to make a butcher out of him—he could turn his thoughts to the future and find himself a niche in it.

So Jacob was settled at last, and the worst days of his "homesickness" began to slip backwards into the softening haze of troubles remembered, troubles survived.

During those initial weeks as an entrepreneur he was almost lighthearted as he busied himself with the necessary cleaning and sorting and rearranging, trying to bring some order to the mess. Sometimes, while Sam and Deborah were at school, Sophie would come down to the store with Hymie and Molly to help out. For a while they made some progress. Jacob noticed, for example, that though the stock came in many languages, he had only three different alphabets to contend with, and so he and Sophie spent hours dividing the store into areas of Semitic, Cyrillic, and Latin type. Next they arranged the books according to size and condition, and worked out a kind of basic pricing guide, though when you were dealing with secondhand merchandise, haggling had to be expected. The problem was that Jacob had acquired along with the store a number of contracts from wholesalers and auctioneers; more books kept arriving, and he could never really catch up. But it didn't matter. His regular customers— those poor students and neighborhood scholars whose company and conversation he was learning to enjoy—seemed to relish the random challenge of the place. Anyway, books materialized and disappeared again. Jacob didn't know that to help things along, Asa Kalisher was sending his cronies over to buy books by the armload, never mind the titles; later they would be donated anonymously to some local hospital or workmen's club. But he did know that Asa had arranged for him to serve as a middleman selling texts and prayer books to a large yeshiva, and during the early years that was the primary source of his profits.

The business prospered, then, in a modest sort of way, and life for Jacob began slowly to improve. It suited him to sit there all day amidst the dust and clutter, more like a custodian than a merchant, reading away the hours or chatting with the customers. Somehow, to breathe daily the atmosphere of books, to spend his hours amidst the substantial and yielding order of paper and ink, made him feel at home. On occasion he could even sense his soul brimming with a sly and muted exaltation, a thrill of property: this is mine; this, all of it, belongs to me. Gradually his headaches, his insomnia, the spots of fire that danced in front of his eyes faded into memory. Oh, he was still troubled; a vague exhaustion had settled into his bones; when he climbed into bed at night, he still felt no swell of passion for the woman who lay alongside him; and when he closed his eyes, his head would spin and he would have to mutter prayers to calm his beating thoughts. Then it would be morning and he would come awake with cramped legs and shoulders, as though his dreams had been all struggle and flight, with a sensation of grime and filth on his fingers and under his nails so that he now understood clearly the wisdom of the injunction to wash one's hands upon arising. In fact, he became ever more scrupulous about his prayers and devotions. But for the first time in his life he was earning a living on his own, and he found that it was good. There was even a kind of unexpected joy in coming home to Pitkin Avenue on a Friday afternoon and slowly flattening a few dollar bills on the kitchen table and recording his net gains in a notebook while Sophie and the children watched. That weekly accounting could be added to the stock of forms and rituals by which he lived.

"So you see," he would say to Sophie, teasing her, "I'm becoming, in the end, a real American."

Nonetheless, soon after he settled into the bookstore, he joined a new *shul*. It was a memorable event. He had summoned his courage and gone off exploring strange neighborhoods, seeking a congregation that would suit him. The one he found occupied the bottom two stories and basement of a row house on Sterling Place, two miles from Pitkin Avenue. The rabbi was a bent and rheumy-eyed man named Trauerlicht, and most of the men who gathered on the *Shabbos* came from the same dim region in Poland or Russia that the Liebers had once called home.

As soon as he walked into the place one Saturday morning, having heard about it from one of his customers, he knew he had discovered what he was looking for. He recognized the melodies of the chants, the ordering of the prayers, the pronunciation of the holy words. He even seemed to recognize the little children, with their shaved heads and curled sidelocks, playing in the vestibule; and the shape of the memorial candles; and the way the light of the morning filtered through the dirty windows and glowed behind the dingy yellowish curtain of the women's section. A bitter taste, he told Sophie, had been washed from his tongue. He melted into the service, and when the ark was opened and the Torah removed and held aloft, among the shouts of jubilation his voice was the loudest. Afterward, as he lingered at the *kiddush* to drink a glass of *shnapps* and nibble on egg cookies and introduce himself to the rabbi—who was, he immediately decided, a saint—what he felt was the rapture of an apostate returning to the fold.

To Sophie it was never clear why a man like Rabbi Trauerlicht had bothered to come to America. He seemed to her, as she talked over this latest complication with her brother, to have carried with him all the fanaticism, the stringency, the impossible limits of the old country intact to that miserable, hot, rancid-smelling, and flea-ridden hovel where, on the holidays, she would now feel obliged to go. Sterling Place itself was ramshackle and muddy as if the Old World were a contagion that had infiltrated the neighborhood. It was all too easy to envision how on weekday mornings the local women would come with their slaughtered and unplucked hens to ask the *rebbe* questions about the laws of purity, and how, blushing, they would add a few questions about the laws that governed their unclean days. She could see the rabbi—"a *tzadik*, like my father-in-law"—seated on his carved wooden throne, examining the pips and gullets of the dead chickens with all the absurd dignity of a Solomon pondering a crisis in his kingdom. She could see—it was stored in her blood; she didn't have to witness these things for herself; she could evoke it all before her eyes the way some unknown grandchild of hers many decades later might summon up an old movie on a videotape machine—the rabbi with his humped back and his silk coat and his great round fur hat entering the little side room which served as a *cheder* to teach Talmud to a dozen or so boys, some of them already with the beginnings of beards fuzzing their cheeks and chins, hot-eyed and servile and weak-chested *yeshiva buchers* with their musty gabardines, and their droning voices, and their sidelocks, which they would tuck behind their ears when they walked the profane streets, dangling down to their restless and ruminating jaws.

She had heard about the *cheder* from Jacob. It didn't take him long to decide that Sam ought to go there. They even made of it the occasion for one of their quarrels, which arose sporadically from the constant and irresolvable tensions between them, and which usually revolved glumly around the raising of the children. There was little else worth quarreling about—little else, that is, worth the risk of exposing the mute chasm that constantly widened between them. In most things they agreed implicitly to go their own way, but they quarreled about the *cheder*. To an outsider it might have appeared that they were just talking it over, that Jacob was talking and Sophie was listening, such was their reliance on restraint. Only a member of the family would have detected the harsh urgency in Jacob's voice, or the look on Sophie's face of proud and stubborn indifference—an indifference which nothing Jacob said could penetrate. Because she was already forearmed with an irrefutable answer. "We're in America now," was all she had to say to silence him. So they quarreled, and when it was over, Sam stayed in the public school and took Hebrew lessons four afternoons a week in a desultory and uproarious Talmud Torah on Blake Avenue, and was exposed to the denser religion of Sterling Place only on Saturday mornings and holidays.

Sophie, let it be said, had a religion all her own. It was concocted of those traditions her rather open-minded mother had thought were important—lighting candles on the Sabbath, praying for the dead, fasting on Yom Kippur, and so on—adjusted to what Sophie took to be the requirements and conventions of America and held together by a reliance on her own good common sense and her conviction that whatever she did, since her heart was honest, was precisely what God wanted her to do. She had no metaphysical qualms whatsoever. She rummaged at random through the vast store of Jewish laws and traditions, kept those that seemed reasonable to her, and discarded the rest. Anything more than her own observances she called fanaticism; anything less, on the other hand, smacked of irreverence. She was capable of practicing a dozen different superstitious habits for warding off an "evil eye" which she taught her children did not exist. And while she kept a kosher home, she was not overly scrupulous, when Jacob was not around, about separating the milk dishes from the meat. God, after all, had her welfare in mind; He certainly did not intend for her to be inconvenienced.

Don't misunderstand. So long as Jacob was alive, the Lieber children grew up in a home that was far more bound by the rituals and conventions of the old way of life than the homes that they themselves would later establish. Every Friday night the candles were lit, the prayers said, the wine poured, the *challah* sliced, the songs sung. Every Saturday morning, as soon as they were old enough, Sam and later Hymie accompanied Jacob to *shul*. The holidays were observed, the quotidian prayers for food and drink and ablutions uttered. At the *seder*, when the door was opened for Elijah, there was every expectation that the prophet might actually come in. Sophie was liberal or lax in her religion only in contrast to Jacob; from another point of view, Asa Kalisher's for example, she was conventionally, stubbornly devout.

When Sam was ten, eleven, twelve years old, he immersed himself for a while in the clammy world of his father's beliefs and was distressed by what he took to be his mother's lapses and carelessness. He would later remember—with a strange, bittersweet mingling of fondness and regret—how on *Shabbos* mornings in winter he would accompany his father to the *shul* on Sterling Place, walking himself warm and awake in the gray, cold light through streets that seemed already burdened and sanctified with the prayers and devotions to come. He would remember learning to *daven* with conviction in a language he did not understand, when to bend the knees and bob the head, when to shout the prayers and when to be silent; and how he would sit squeezed in among the men on the crowded bench, amidst the rich, rough smells of fabric and breath and beard; and how his head would sometimes swim and blur with the endless drone of the chants. But he would also remember that even then he was afraid of the damp glistening of devotion he saw in his father's eyes; that as he watched his father kiss and bless his *tallis* and wrap it around his head and shoulders, he was inevitably reminded of the time his father came home with his arm in a sling; and that there was always some part of himself, some small, mocking skeptic within him, holding him aloof from the noise and passion and overheated air.

He did not understand it then, and perhaps never would, but he knew that there was between his parents in matters of religion a kind of space or emptiness over which he felt suspended, into which, after a while, his own beliefs eventually slipped and vanished.

None of Jacob Lieber's children turned out to be religious in any sense that their father would have recognized. For Sam, as for the others, there would be in the end only the simple fact of Jewishness itself, a kind of odd family relic to be kept and treasured. In later years Sam Lieber, the successful businessman, would go on the High Holidays to a Reformed service in a bright modern temple which a chunk of his own money had helped to build. There would be a couple of stained glass windows with the names and memorial dates of his parents on brass plates below them, and organ music drifting down from the choir, and lots of irreverent children running through the vestibule. Sam would shake hands with everyone, he would mutter the benedictions, he would be called up for honors— which always embarrassed him—he would doze off during the sermons, or "scoldings" as he called them, of the clever young rabbi who had graduated from Cornell, and he could derive from it all a thin, dry satisfaction. But every so often the intonation of a blessing, or a glint of light on the silver crown of the Torah, or his own reflexive bending of his knees and bobbing of his head would bring the ghosts of Sterling Place swarming around him. He would never quite learn how to shrug them off, and as he got older, he was less and less sure that he wanted to.

HOME FOR JACOB LIEBER was now the *shul* on Sterling Place or the bookstore on Livonia Avenue or the occasionally exultant and arcane recesses of his own immortal soul, which he lived with secretly and gloatingly the way a miser lives with his gold; but it was not, and never could be, the apartment above the restaurant on Pitkin Avenue, the very walls of which seemed stained and scarred by the memory of his earlier torments. Passing the restaurant, entering the doorway, climbing the dark staircase to the noise of the children above, he would feel the old, bitter weight of his troubles bending his back and filling his head. Evenings were all the same. The children—those polyglot strangers who grew larger and louder and more alien each day—would prattle on about their lessons and toys and explorations and quarrels until Sophie managed to bundle them off to sleep. Then they would sit, the two of them, Jacob in the armchair, Sophie at the kitchen table, sewing or reading one of her American books, not talking, not really being together, but merely defining a space for a time, while below them the nightly din of the restaurant slowly faded to a mere rattling of dishes and eventual silence and the tumult of Jacob's thoughts rose complementarily toward the roar and tension of their going to bed.

He had come to dread it. As he lay next to Sophie in the expectant darkness, he would hear beyond the roaring in his ears the sounds of the children—all of them, now that Molly had outgrown the cradle, sleeping together in one room, separated only by the papery thinness of a wall from the beating of his brain. Hymie would be gnashing his teeth, and Molly would be snoring—for already at the age of four or five, so pretty that people stared at her on the street, she snuffled and wheezed incongruously through the night—and every so often Deborah would cry out, a small, soft, heartbreaking whimper that emerged from her difficult dreams. Only Sam slept quietly, having exhausted his quotient of noise in the rough-and-tumble of his boisterous day. Jacob would listen to them, and some tendril of his heart would creep out toward them and gently caress their cheeks and lips and shining eyelids with all the pent-up and proper affection he seemed unable to express in their actual awake and vivid and threatening presence. Silently, mournfully, feeling his own best hopes embodied in them, he would bless them, wishing for them a world of righteousness and plenty. Then he would become aware—this was the moment he dreaded—of Sophie's warm and still-young body breathing and yearning alongside him. The room itself seemed to fill with breathing and yearning, whispering to him the first law of Creation: *Be fruitful and multiply!*—and he would be stricken, night after night, with a terrible sense of shrinkage and softness, as though his manhood were nothing but some failed fruit rotting and aching in his groin.

Impotence is what his grandchildren would have called it in their more clinical age, but Jacob didn't have the word or even the notion; for him it was a blight that had fallen upon their marriage, as mysterious and implacable as a plague. He could only mutter to himself, "I am no more a husband to her," and feel the frustration of his seed as a sin against the generations of Israel that he, in this time, in this place, represented. They probably never even discussed it. Neither of them would have known what to say. She couldn't say to him, "I want more babies," because he already knew that—to utter it would have been superfluous. At first, during the days of the restaurant and the pushcart, she would have thought that he was merely waiting, that babies would come after they had settled into America, that they couldn't afford any more hungry mouths to feed. Later, when he was in the bookstore, she would have thought not that he was unable but that he was unwilling, that their marriage itself had shattered on the edge of his earlier troubles. "It's the place," he might have told her. "It's the proximity of the demons of the restaurant that has done this to me." But he said nothing, and night after night the condition, or rather what they took to be the absence of a condition, festered between them.

Eventually she began to seek remedies. She made up little cakes filled with dates and sesame seeds and fed them to him in the evening. She brought home bottles of tonic from the pharmacy and made him drink them, claiming that they were meant to strengthen his lungs. She hid carrots and cloves of garlic in the bedclothes, and sprinkled the room with perfume to hide the odor. She intoned prayers against the "evil eye" and prayers that were meant to bring fertility. On occasion she even tried to arouse him, touching her leg to his, resting her breasts against him on the pretext of keeping warm, running her fingers up and down his body as no one had ever taught her to do, stroking his back and arms and chest and belly until he made her stop—because such advances were forbidden; because the threshold of such an arousal would have seemed to him, and probably to her as well, the gateway to evil.

And then for a while she simply gave up. When bedtime approached, she would find some reason to stay up late, a book to finish, a floor to wash while the children were out of her way, a dessert for tomorrow that had to be put together tonight and placed in the icebox to set. It was easier for her that way, waiting until he was asleep, climbing into bed without the strain of hope or expectation. "I have four children," she told herself, "and that will be enough." But really they weren't enough to absorb her brimming energy. She was now spending more and more of her time fussing over them, insisting that Sam have a clean handkerchief in his pocket and that Deborah have her hair properly braided before they went off to school, passing the long daytime hours with Hymie and Molly, telling them stories, feeding them treats of cakes and cookies that spilled from the oven like an overflow of her love, singing lullabies to them and petting them as she held them in her arms. She also spent more money on them since she had more money to spend. She bought them clothes and toys, and pampered their never-ending hunger for sweets by taking them, when Sam and Deborah came home from school, down to the candy store for an ice cream or a bag of candies. Inevitably, as her life increasingly revolved about them, she also began to worry about them more, babied them, particularly Hymie, who at four and five was shy and awkward and big-eyed and made Sophie pick him up and hold him in the presence of strangers. When they caught cold or became feverish, she put them to bed and hovered over them, gave them alcohol rubs, piled blankets on top of them if they seemed chilled. She fussed about their appetites, their digestive systems, their bowel movements so that later in life they would remember with a pang the maternal administration of laxatives and enemas—that sudden warm violation and flood.

She might have gone on babying them forever if the public school system hadn't plucked them out of her arms. Eventually Hymie and then Molly had to be registered for kindergarten, and the apartment was empty and Sophie had to find some new way to fill up her hours and desires. That's when she decided they should move. The morning she walked Molly to school for the first time and watched her vanish, chubby and red-haired, into the crowd of children—without any of the tears and clinging and looking back that there had been with Hymie the year before—she returned alone to the apartment above the restaurant, to the heaped-up bedclothes and dingy windows and stained walls, and felt all its cramped and soiled emptiness as a violation of her hopes and schemes. Now that it was void of children she could finally focus her attention on it, as though she had never really bothered to look at it before. The secondhand furniture, the coating of smoke and grease that made everything tacky to the touch, the low cracked and mildewed ceilings beneath which rusty pots waited gaping for the next rain, the way the floor around the icebox was rotted by leaks and spills, the lines of laundry in the courtyard and the *yentehs* with their big mouths yelling a crude mishmash of two broken languages across to each other—all of it she had tolerated in the beginning because it didn't matter, because it was the idea and not the actuality of America that enthralled her; and tolerated later on because she had no choice, because they couldn't afford anything better; and tolerated finally, she realized, only because toleration itself had become a habit. Well, she didn't have to tolerate it anymore. Didn't they have over a hundred dollars sitting doing nothing in the bank? Weren't new buildings going up all over Brooklyn? Possibly she discussed it with Jacob that very night, or maybe she waited a week or two, waiting for her will to gather itself and give shape to the arguments she believed she would have to use, thinking that she would have to talk him into moving as she had talked him into everything else, thinking: he is a man who does nothing unless he is pushed.

She was surprised when he not only accepted the idea but claimed it as his own. He said that for months he had been trying to get her to move, and probably he thought he had. That is, for months the notion of moving had been on his mind. There had been odd hours, which she knew nothing about, when he had wandered the neighborhood around Sterling Place, looking at apartments and inquiring about rents. He had also muttered and grumbled about how far he had to walk to *shul*, about how hot and airless the apartment had been all summer, about how dangerous Pitkin Avenue was for the children with its traffic and transients and noise; and perhaps he believed that his mutterings and grumblings amounted to a statement that Sophie had chosen to ignore. He may even have told himself that he was working to overcome her resistance, hinting and suggesting, letting the notion of moving infiltrate her thoughts. Anyway, when she finally said she wanted to move, he was able to feel an unfamiliar surge of triumph. For once, he believed, he had set his mind on something and gotten his own way.

That feeling, so pleasant and unexpected, set him up for the quarrel to come, a quarrel which sometimes diverted itself into absurd

36

bickering about how much rent they could afford or how many rooms they would need or how close to the ground the new apartment should be, but which had as its impetus and substance the touchy question of what neighborhood they should explore. Sophie wanted to move to one of the new buildings that were going up near Highland Park on the border of Queens—Asa Kalisher had recently moved out there, and the area in those days was still practically the country, close to fields and hills and trees and the Ridgewood Reservoir, which Sophie kept calling "the lake"—but Jacob had set his heart on living in the vicinity of Sterling Place. There among his *landsleit*, close to the throne of his rabbi, he thought he could feel at home.

They never raised their voices. They merely talked it over night after night, week after week, talking around it and through it with flushed faces and tight throats, saying the same things over and over again, waiting not for agreement but surrender. They sat at the kitchen table, putting numbers down on scraps of paper and tracing trolley and subway routes on a map of Brooklyn that Jacob had brought home from the store, discussing schools and shopping areas and electric lighting and steps to climb, pretending that reason and sense and convenience had some part to play in their decision; but all the while they were struggling with each other, measuring and testing and maneuvering as they had never quite done before. You would have thought they were deciding whether to stay in America or go back to the old country, so fierce, so exhausting did their quarrel become.

For Jacob the struggle went on even when they weren't together. Sitting in the store, half dozing, his eyes closed against the pressure that throbbed in his cheeks, he would imagine himself back at the kitchen table, hear himself saying those bitter and negligent and definitive words he never in reality quite dared to utter, as though some part of her had gotten inside of him, a specter that went on grappling with him, trying to wear him down. At times it would all slip away from him, sliding down beneath his thoughts into some region of darkness where, though they continued to grapple, his mind could no longer see or hear them, as if the struggle were at bottom too vast and naked to endure. Then a shrill ringing would start up in his ears and a shimmer of heat would unfold through his body and he would be wide awake again, trembling and aching and damp, with a sense of disorientation, of having passed through some sort of opening—a portal in time—and everything, everything was new.

At first some part of him, some old soft cluster of habits, was ready to acquiesce to her, but as the quarrel continued, he discovered that he had within himself a source of will or pride or just plain stubbornness. As they sat at the kitchen table, night after night, he became increasingly aware of that other part of himself, which was calm and hard and already victorious. Maybe it had always been there; but because he was so used to giving in quickly to her, he had never been able to locate it before. In short, he was learning how to say no, and he was delighted to learn that the more he said it, the easier it became to say. There was no climactic moment; there was only, near the end of their quarrel—it was November already, bright and crisp—the sense that the issue had been decided, that there had taken place, invisibly, inexorably, some vague readjustment of power between them. Now Sophie was doing most of the talking; she had to talk herself out before she could capitulate, but he could already hear the tone of surrender in her voice; so he just sat there and listened to her, enjoying his newfound sense of calm indulgence, knowing that soon there would be nothing more to say and thinking, fondly, that his victory somehow would please her.

"Sterling Place, Highland Park, what difference does it make?" she said at last. "So long as there is room enough, and big windows, and fresh paper on the walls."

There was no rancor in her tone, no implicit threat, only a kind of soft yielding, a relief that it was finally settled.

They moved in time to celebrate Hanukkah in the new apartment. It was a third-story railroad flat on the corner of Park and Kingston, five blocks—"Far enough!" Sophie told her brother—from the *shul* on Sterling Place. There were four bedrooms off the hallway, a kitchen with a gas stove, a dining room, and a front room. The ceiling was freshly plastered and painted, and there was new wallpaper on the walls. At first it felt big and empty and burdened with echoes, but they hung drapes and put down rugs and bought some new furniture—a table and chairs for the dining room, a love seat, a new bed —with money they borrowed from Asa Kalisher, and it began to fill up. Across the street was a little park with a playground for the children and a small fountain and a cluster of trees and bushes, barren now, but charged with the promise of springtime greenery. The lights were electric, the gas stove burned with a celestial blue flame, the woodwork shone rich and dark when Sophie polished it, and the children loved to run and tumble through the long hallway. By Passover they had settled in and were beginning to feel at home, and at the *seder,* between the feast and the songs of jubilation, Sophie informed the family that she was pregnant again.

TWO

LATER IN LIFE SOPHIE WOULD THINK BACK over all her pregnancies and all her deliveries, and the details would blur in her mind so that it sometimes seemed she had been in labor only twice, once in Europe and once in America, and that in two prolonged agonies she had somehow managed to spawn all nine of her children; but mostly it was Sam's birth and Walter's she remembered. She would never forget how, with Sam, her father-in-law and the village crones had opened the drawers and doors and closets, and marched her across the threshold, and made her recite the seventeen names of Lilith and the protective psalms, and even brought in the *shamus* to blow the *shofar*; and how the long wailing cry of the thing had terrified her until her father came up from the marketplace, wearing his bloody apron, and chased them all away. And she would always remember how, when it was her time for Walter, Jacob wanted to bring in a midwife and perhaps had even prepared the amulets and candles, but Asa Kalisher insisted that she go to a hospital and hired a motorcar to take her there, so that Walter and all the rest of the American brood were delivered among doctors and nurses, with everyone's face masked in gauze, and everything clean and white and crisp, and electric light bulbs shining overhead, and her thoughts clouded by a sort of sweet cotton wool from some vapors they made her breathe.

"Here," she would say, "they make even labor a luxury."

Walter came into the world with a head of black hair, big open eyes, and long translucent fingers that curled themselves around Sophie's thumb and wouldn't let go. His birth marked the end of a phase; the early days were over, and the family entered an enchanted and fertile zone of routine and habit in which every year or two or three Sophie would swell up around the middle, slowing her pace as she burgeoned until she was doing nothing much at all; then she would disappear for a week or a fortnight, to be replaced temporarily by one of the aunts or cousins or wives of cousins who kept arriving from Europe in those days (and often lived for a time in the Lieber apartment while they searched for houses and jobs of their own); then she would be home again, shrunken and pale and tired, with a few new wrinkles in her face and a few more streaks of gray in her hair, and there would be a new baby to occupy the small crib, and last year's baby—first Walter, then Rose, then Ruthie, then Evelyn —would be rotated in turn to the larger crib and then to the bed in the back room. In the years between Molly's birth and Walter's, Sophie had almost forgotten what it was like, the caring for infants. She was plummeted, so to speak, into a second phase of motherhood, an exhausting round of milk stains and soiled diapers and wrecked sleep, from which she would finally emerge—after Moe, the last of that generation of Liebers, was weaned and yoked and talking—already a widow, into the cool gray light of her middle age. But that was years later. Now, nursing Walter and already quickened with Rose, crooning lullabies to Rose and feeling the one they would call Ruthie kick and poke within her, she sensed her life flowing steadily and naturally. Seeing her with her brood in those days, you might have thought, as Asa Kalisher put it, that her purpose in this world was to populate America.

She was content, or at least she told herself she was, by which she meant that her hours were occupied and her body fulfilled, and she no longer felt so restless or expectant. Each new child she bore enlarged the possibilities of her life since whatever they might accomplish or acquire later would be hers as well. She could see their lives as threads unwinding and crisscrossing into some blurred but radiant future to which, with each new baby, the plain drab thread of her own life was more securely affixed. She loved to imagine them grown and married, with fine clothes and good jobs and homes filled with luxury, real Americans, with lots of babies of their own. Wasn't that, after all, the reason she had struggled across an ocean, so that they could have what she could only dream of? In the inevitable moments of drudgery or crisis, those were the thoughts that soothed her.

She was helped by the fact that Jacob during those years, at least until his illness, was less of a headache for her. His newfound potency had not utterly transformed him; he was still, the poor man, haunted and heckled by the same old ghosts; but though he went twice a day to the *shul* on Sterling Place, and told stories at the supper table of Rabbi Trauerlicht's sanctity and wisdom—tedious and homiletic anecdotes which Sam would repeat mockingly and shamelessly to Asa Kalisher—the moody fanaticism of his religion was tempered and subdued by the presence of infants in the house. There was no more talk about demons, and he no longer raged or brooded so much about his family's lapses and indifference.

He also responded to his new obligations by demonstrating in small ways an unexpected knack for business. He traveled all over Brooklyn, visiting synagogues and yeshivas, securing contracts to sell them books. He added to the store a line of religious articles—menorahs, mezuzahs, prayer shawls, embroidered velvet bags—and learned how to deal more efficiently with the wholesalers and importers on the Lower East Side. He made some contacts with congregations in places like Ohio and Wisconsin, and started a modest shipping service to supply their needs. What a *mitzvah* it was, after all, to send prayer books and memorial candles into the wilderness.

Eventually he even hired a contractor to knock down some walls and install some new shelving and put up a new front for the store, with a big glass window upon which his name appeared, in gleaming gold, in both Hebrew and English letters. There seemed to be no way to rid the place of dust, which settled permanently into his clothes and hair and nostrils; but at last he had enough space to bring an order of sorts to the chaos of his merchandise, and he could hold his head up when Asa Kalisher dropped by for a visit—he could talk to his brother-in-law now in the American way, one man of business to another.

Best of all, as far as Sophie was concerned, he was showing more interest in the children. On Sundays he would take the younger ones across the street to the park and sit and watch them play on the swings and slides and seesaws, rewarding them when they were good with a trip to the candy store and punishing their fights and squabbles and miscellaneous naughtiness by pulling on their ears, the punishment he had suffered so often himself back in the village *cheder*. He frequently quarreled with Sam, and he was baffled by Hymie's moods and withdrawals; but he was always kind to his daughters—perhaps because he expected so little of them—and he doted shamelessly on Walter.

One of Sophie's sweetest pleasures, when Walter was two and three and four, was to watch him climb up onto Jacob's lap and tug at his beard and poke his long fingers into his mouth, while Jacob bounced him and made cooing noises and screwed up his face to get the child to giggle.

"I have a wicked son and a simple son," he once told Sophie, "and now God has blessed me with a wise one."

He loved to bring Walter down to the store and feed him chocolates from the wire rack on the counter and get him to recite the blessings and invocations for the wispy, gaping yeshiva students who came in. He would tease them, saying, "Four years old and he knows more *Mishnah* than you do."

It was only later, when Rose and Ruthie and Evelyn began to fill the house with their noisy squabbles and girlish catastrophes, that Jacob began to spend less and less of his time at home; but that was after his illness, when the pieties of his old age had come upon him, and by then, as far as the younger children were concerned, Sam had already displaced his father.

Sam in those days, lean and red-haired, gap-toothed and rebellious, was an ambitious and self-confident boy, smoldering in the embers of his puberty. Of his life in the old country he had only meager and dreamlike recollections: a whiff of boiled groats; a sensation of mud clinging thickly to his shoes; a glimpse of a horsecart driven by a white-bearded peasant whose feet were wrapped in rags against the cold; a vision of chickens flopping headless and bloody-feathered in the courtyard of his grandfather's butcher shop; a vague, painful sense of the family's long journey to America, and not much more. All the rest had been submerged by the current and vivid reality of Brooklyn and his own natural inclination to live in the future, which he imagined as a vast, sprawling, hostile territory that could be taken only by storm. He had been quick to learn the language of the New World—even his thoughts now manifested themselves in a flawed street English, which flowed above and was often enriched by the old latent substream of his imperfect Yiddish—as well as the schoolyard varieties of baseball and brawling, and the crucial arithmetic of dollars and cents. His teachers in elementary school (a sequence of powdery women merging years later into a single blurred image of a scrubbed, shrill, intolerant old maid named O'Hearne or McIlvaney) doted on him because he was quick and bright and possessed, in embryo form, all the sense and amiability and simple aggressiveness that would carry him through his life. He was friends with the rowdiest boys in the class, but he was seldom rowdy himself, and often appeared to have a calming effect on the others. It was as though, there in the classroom, before *goyishe* eyes, his dignity kept his boisterousness in check.

For Sam in those days there were three distinct codes of behavior: one for school; one for home; one for the streets. His teachers would have been amazed (as his parents were occasionally appalled) had they seen their "darling child" out of doors. He spent his free hours running with a pack of "hooligans," who inhabited a kind of intermediate zone of belligerence and self-defense between the hapless, Orthodox *"faygelehs"* and the rock-throwing, brutish, anti-Semitic "micks." Sam and his friends stood around under lampposts, smoked butts they picked up from the gutter, and swaggered down Kingston Avenue with their hands jammed into the back pockets of their knickers. They were forever punching each other and swearing and spitting gobs of phlegm, all of it in obeisance to some crucial and obvious notion of toughness. They also gambled, and discussed the local teenage girls with a sort of facile pseudoprecociousness, and talked endlessly about what they would do when they were rich.

In that crowd of future merchants and racketeers and comedians they never doubted that someday, somehow, money would eventually be theirs.

Money delighted Sam Lieber. He loved to have it and he loved to give it away. He was always "finding" pennies and nickels and taking his sisters to the candy store for a treat. When he was nine years old, he started a "bank" by filling up a cigar box with cut rectangles of paper on which he printed in green crayon the various denominations. He would sit for hours cutting and counting and cutting some more, and keeping track in a school notebook of the loans he forced upon Hymie and Molly. One day he even announced to Sophie that he had become a millionaire. He said it so plainly, so solemnly, that she didn't dare laugh. He kept the "bank" going right up until he went to work in the afternoons and evenings for Asa Kalisher and started bringing home five authentic dollars a week. At the end of the first week he slapped four of those dollars down on the kitchen table for Sophie and gave the "bank" to Molly, who cherished it for a couple of days, wrapping it in gaudy ribbons and flaunting it in front of Deborah, then stuck it in a drawer and forgot all about it. That was typical Molly, but Sam didn't care; he never even asked her about it. He had already acquired the useful capacity of leaving things behind.

In much the same way, over the next couple of years, coolly, item by item, he jettisoned the burdens of his boyhood.

He went to work for Asa Kalisher the year that Walter was born, so he must have been twelve at the time. He stacked dishes, helped the cooks, bussed tables, ran errands. Jacob was unhappy about it. He said that if Sam wanted to work, there was plenty he could do at the store, but he couldn't argue against the obvious logic of more money coming into the house.

Sam would later remember how soft and small and ashamed he used to feel, at first, after his work was done, as he sat with his uncle and his uncle's cronies at the table in the corner and drank coffee with them and listened to them argue in deep, loud voices about their politics or their women or their business deals. He would remember how their hands were big and thick-skinned and blunt when they pounded the table to emphasize a point, how the hair in their ears and nostrils was copious and dark, how the smoke of their cigars made his eyes water, and how secret and threatening was the substance of their jokes. Sitting there with them, unaccountably shy and nervous, he felt himself peering into a bold and energetic world, the blurred contours of which he could still only dimly perceive, and for a while his whole life focused on his desire to attach himself to it.

Then there came a moment in the kitchen, as he stood mixing batter in a huge copper bowl, breathing the dryness of the flour and half hypnotizing himself by trying to count the swirling beats of the wooden spoon, when he felt himself crossing a threshold of sorts and knew it was his destiny to be just like them. He sensed the binds of his life coming loose for a moment and reknotting themselves in a new way. That night he came home through the dark streets swaggering, swollen, incipient, almost hoping for a fight; only some quick flailing violence, received and inflicted, could discharge his mood. A couple of boys, obviously Irish, were lounging on a stoop, and he moved past them, bouncing on his heels and staring, brimming with the nerve of his obvious affront; but they just pretended to ignore him—perhaps they realized the powers he had absorbed into himself —and then he turned a corner and was back on Park Place, breathing again, hearing the thin dry rustle of the trees above him and the soft impatient gallop of his burgeoning heart.

It was then that his struggle with his father began. There had always been quarrels between them, but now they merely punctuated the single long conflict in which they were engaged. They argued about his clothes and his friends, his comings and his goings, his language and his religion. What didn't they argue about? At his *bar mitzvah* Sam stood up in front of the congregation on Sterling Place, wearing long pants, with his hair slicked flat and a new *tallis*, which Yussel Kalisher had mailed from Europe, spread stiff and glistening on his narrow shoulders, and his smooth face pink and shining in the dense liquid heat of that jammed prayerhouse on a humid summer morning, and delivered his *haftorah* flawlessly, but with a strange, cynical smile on his face—because he had already lost in the tumult of the restaurant the habit of belief.

A few weeks later he calmly told Jacob he was no longer going to *shul*.

Jacob raged and sulked and brooded, but there was nothing much he could do about it. Finally he got Sam to agree to talk it over with the rabbi. Oddly distanced and calm, Sam sat there in the rabbi's office with his arms crossed in front of him, so bored and restless that his shoulders ached, while the rabbi, enthroned and pompous and smelling vaguely of a morning breakfast of fish, lectured him on the rights and obligations of a Jewish man. Afterward there lingered on Sam's fingers the final sticky dampness of the rabbi's hand.

There was, Sam believed, a choice to be made between *shul* and restaurant, and so he had chosen. He loved the restaurant. He loved the proximity of the patrons, the politicians, the theater people, the businessmen, the criminals, all of whom he had come to believe were the movers and shapers of the world. He felt he could absorb their powers through the pores of his skin, along with the cigar smoke, the food smells, and the perfumes of their women. There in the restaurant the possibilities of life were spread out in front of him, and his only problem was what to sample first.

One day he witnessed a murder. The victim was a man named Lefkowitz, who owned a laundry on Blake Avenue and who walked around with a wad of bills in his pocket fatter than any laundry could produce. Every night Lefkowitz would come into the restaurant alone and study the sports pages of a newspaper while he was eating his meal. He was a bulky man with huge hands and a wart on the side of his flattened nose, and he used to tease Sam, calling him a "pretty *boychik*" and blowing him kisses. That night Lefkowitz was eating stuffed cabbage when a man Sam recognized from the neighborhood as a horseplayer, though he didn't know his name, came up behind Lefkowitz and put the muzzle of a gun to his neck. Sam saw it happen. He saw Lefkowitz, his mouth full of cabbage and meat, becoming aware of the gun and trying to say something, lowering his head to spit the food back onto his plate. He saw him put his hands on the table, trying to push himself up, saw how the flesh swelled around the big rubied ring that Lefkowitz wore. He heard the explosion. He saw bits of Lefkowitz's face splattering on the tablecloth and heard another explosion and saw Lefkowitz's body rising and falling simultaneously, and the horseplayer daintily sidestepping to avoid the chair that Lefkowitz's legs, in spasm, had thrust at him. Then it was all confusion and noise, with people running and the horseplayer looking around, apparently astonished by the commotion he had caused, and then Sam was in the kitchen, sitting on a chair with his head between his knees, swallowing and swallowing until he knew for sure that he wasn't going to vomit.

Weeks later he was still seeing it happen, still swallowing back the bitter acid that had crept up into his throat, but in time he told the story so often, with so many embellishments, that the reality was cloaked and mastered.

"That was the time they shot Lefkowitz," he would say, "and the funny part of it was, the guy just sat down and put the gun on the table and waited for the cops."

Eventually he was pleased to have been there, as though to have witnessed a murder were some sort of privilege or had assured his own vitality. He practically swaggered with the memory of it: tested and proved durable, he felt ready for anything life had to offer.

He was fourteen when he started to shave. He never discussed it with anyone; he never even considered the possibility that there was anything to discuss; he merely arrived home one night carrying a paper sack and practically gleaming with the light of his expectations. The sack held a shaving mug with his initials on it, a brush, a round white cake of soap, a bottle of lilac water—which later he gave to Molly, who loved to dab it behind her ears and into her chubby armpits, though it was impossible to say, since Sophie used no perfumes, just what notion of what woman she was trying to mimic—and a straight razor that shone brightly when he brandished it.

Sophie was in the front room, nursing Rose, sitting in the big rocking chair, which she had filled with embroidered pillows, dozing together with the usually colicky and cranky infant in a rare sweet moment of bliss, when she heard a commotion from the bathroom. Rousing herself, carrying Rose, she went down the long hallway to see what it was and found Molly, her face smeared with lather, bawling because some of it had gotten into her mouth, and Sam trying to stanch with one of her best towels the flow of blood from a decapitated pimple on his chin.

For a moment Sophie was back in the old country, in her father's house, watching Asa Kalisher shave himself in a basin of cold water; then she began to feel old.

"*Meshugganeh*," she said to Sam, "what will you tell your father?"

What *could* he tell his father? Their struggle seemed infinite and pointless because they talked in different languages about different things. He would remember his pain and bewilderment when he saw the neighborhood brats mocking his father's slow bent progress—head down, hands clasped behind his back—along the street. Or the times he tried to explain things to his father, and his father turned away, shrugging, ignorant, condemning a whole world without knowing anything about it. They no longer talked to each other; they no longer even saw much of each other; and when they were together, a kind of sullen something bristled between them, rousing itself every so often into another of their fights.

The last of their fights was also their worst. Sam later forgot the occasion of it—perhaps it was about the shaving, but it might just as well have been about any ritual neglected, any talmudic crime. He would remember only that they were in the kitchen and that they had been shouting at each other, and his father was struggling to control himself, pacing around the kitchen, his face red and blotched, muttering to himself like a man deranged. He would remember how he tried to dissipate the tension of the moment by saying something, wanting to be pleasant, and how that only set his father off again, shouting in Yiddish some choked incoherence about the laws of God and the ingratitude of children, and how finally his father had gotten hold of his ear, yanking at it—the old punishment—and how the pain had brought tears, involuntary, hot, stupid, humiliating tears, as he lurched sideways to relieve the pressure.

There was a moment of clarity during which Sam felt his ear burning and saw his mother standing by the stove with her hands pressed flat to her cheeks and what seemed to him a peculiar gleam of encouragement in her eyes—and all the while his father was shouting at her to look at him, her treasure, her darling, her prince. He cursed his father, vilely. His father reached for him again, and he ducked his head down and grabbed hold of his father's wrist. Some part of himself, some old respect and caution, saw his hand restraining his father's and was simply amazed. He almost burst out laughing, such was the weird primordial tension of the moment, as his father's hapless weight pushed against him and his own fingers tightened on his father's bone-taut and hairy wrist. He knew that he was stronger than

48

his father, not merely in muscle but in will; and the knowledge they shared while they struggled—silently, absurdly, miserably, their faces close, their breaths intermingled—was dreadful. There was a moment when anything might have happened, anything at all, and then it, the moment, the pressure in Sam's hand, the secret surrender that had tingled from nerve to nerve between them, was gone.

Sam turned away, almost sick with guilt and pride and victory and shame, and found nothing in the blurred and narrow space of the kitchen on which his eyes could settle—not his father, who was rubbing his wrist and muttering words he couldn't hear; nor his mother, who was rocking back and forth in a meaningless display of agony; nor his sisters and brothers, who had been there all the time, looking on with that strange, bleak curiosity children always bring to a family quarrel—so he hurried out of the dense air of the apartment, down the steps and into the street.

He walked through the night, breathing heavily, self-absorbed, trying to walk himself cool and steady again. His ear still burned; his astonished fingers still held the sad and yielding pressure of his father's wrist; the random stars above the rooftops might have been created just a moment ago, as though they along with all the rest of the world had emerged full-grown and new from the confusion of his thoughts. It occurred to him that though his mind was tumultuous, the street was calm. People weren't throwing open their windows to look at him and curse him for what he had done. He would never forget how monstrous that seemed, how he wanted to call up to the old curtained and blinded windows, invoking their wrath.

He must have walked five, six, seven blocks into the night, walking quickly at first and then more slowly, as if bound somehow to the apartment on Park Place by an elastic string. Finally, having entered the nervous fringe of an alien neighborhood, he stopped. He sensed dimly that to go any farther would be to pass beyond the familiar circumference of his life, to enter fully and irrevocably into that more tumultuous world he had so often desired—a world in which, he realized, he might be utterly lost. So he stopped, trembling slightly, roiled inside, feeling the dampness of the night's mist on his face and the last dying embers of pain in his ear. He probably never quite realized how very frightened he was. The moment came and went, slipping away from him like a dream that is remembered just long enough to be forgotten, so bizarre, so foreign to one's senses, that the mind cannot hold onto it. He merely told himself that it was just another fight, that they'd manage to patch it up, that, anyway, he had to go home.

Tired, exhausted even, he walked back to Park Place, wondering what he was going to say, groping for some words that would soothe his father without undermining his own independence. He never found any, but it didn't matter. By the time he got upstairs his father had gone to bed. He sat with his mother in the kitchen and drank a glass of tea, not talking about anything, scarcely talking at all, just sitting and drinking tea with her, the dutiful son, and by the next morning the fight and the surrender had started slipping back into the healing haze of time. When he finally saw his father again at dinner, the ferocity of the moment was spent and diminished and there was no reason to say anything. They both knew that though the old quarrel wasn't resolved, there would be no more fights.

Years later, standing in front of his father's coffin, gazing down at the gray, diminished thing that had been his father, Sam tried to murmur some sort of apology; but he still couldn't find the appropriate words, and it still didn't seem to matter. Their struggle had been, after all, the sort of thing that happened to everyone.

IN THOSE DAYS there were always extra mouths to feed. Every steamer docking in New York seemed to bring in its bowels relatives, *landsleit*, from the old country. Most of them were Sophie's aunts and cousins from her mother's side of the family—the matchmakers, Asa Kalisher called them—but Jacob's sister Bea also came, and then, a few months after Moshe Lieber "entered paradise," while Jacob was recuperating from his illness, his brother Chaim arrived. That was in 1917, and everyone always wondered how Uncle Chaim had managed to travel in the midst of the war.

"I walked and I walked," he would tell them, shrugging, and that's all he would ever say.

This was the Uncle Chaim of whom Walter once remarked: "He's my father writ small."

There were nights during the years of Sophie's pregnancies when more than a dozen people took their meals and slept in the apartment on Park Place, sometimes two and three to a bed. Occasionally there might even be some bearded young stranger, one of Rabbi Trauerlicht's followers, on the sofa in the front room. Later Molly would say that they had to draw numbers just to go to the toilet. But Sophie didn't mind. She believed in family and she loved to feed people and she was pleased to be able to demonstrate through her generosity that she was "doing well." As for Jacob, it must have occurred to him, as the relatives arrived, that the old country was reconstructing itself bit by bit in America, bringing along with it all the customs and accents and faces that he missed.

He especially doted on Bea and loved to spend time with her. She was a short, stunned, asthmatic woman, always wheezing, always with a handkerchief balled up in her palm, always *kvetching* about her health. She was married, comically so far as the Lieber girls were concerned, to a huge slab of a fellow named Yonkel, a six-footer, which in those days made him practically a giant. Whenever they came to visit, Molly would rush down the hallway, shouting, "Big and Little are here! Big and Little are here!" which would send Hymie scuttling for the closet. Yonkel was a quiet, gentle soul, a tailor by trade and a Zionist by heart; on those sporadic occasions when he was moved to speech he talked only of going to Palestine, *Eretz Yisroel*, where the agèd were rejuvenated and the sick made well; but he would spend the rest of his life in Brooklyn, and somehow he frightened poor Hymie. The boy wouldn't enter a room if Yonkel was in it.

"Come," Jacob would scold him, "he won't eat you up!"

But he never coaxed him any closer than the doorway, where he would stand with his shoulders hunched and his legs tensed and twitching, ready to run.

Anyway, they managed. There was always food on the table and clean shirts in the drawers, and after Sam quit school and started working full time in the restaurant, they could even afford a few luxuries. He worked hard; he would be there at six-thirty in the morning to lug the crates of eggs and milk from the alley into the kitchen, and often he was still there at midnight, kibitzing with the cronies. Sometimes he would take a few hours off in the afternoon to help his father in the store. But at least business in both places was good. With the war going on in Europe, people in America had more money to spend. Prices were rising, but the family income was rising even faster. In the front room there now stood a big mahogany gramophone, its horn hidden in the cabinet behind a piece of cloth woven with what the children took to be real gold, and a new sofa with claw feet and handmade antimacassars pinned to the arms, and a pair of Delft china lamps, and a genuine oil painting, purchased on Broome Street, of cows watering themselves in a murky pond.

Sophie had also indulged a whim by purchasing an artificial fire to put in the sealed-up fireplace. When you plugged it in, the red light of the bulb, diffracted by a little tin spinner hidden beneath the plaster logs, leaped and vanished and reappeared just like real flame, and somehow, on cold evenings, the device was a comfort.

Hymie, especially, was fascinated by the thing. He must have been eleven or twelve at that time, a fat boy with pale skin, small, dark, hurt eyes, and big ears that jutted out all the more when Sophie started cropping his black hair because he was always getting candy or grease or glue into it. He still had no friends outside the family, and they had put him into a "special" class at school—the teachers claimed he was "slow." Of course, he wasn't slow at all. If anything, he was too quick, too alert, too frightened by too many things. Dogs, knives, neighbors, the iceman, the sound of coal rumbling down the chute—the world at large flashed painfully through his nerves. He wouldn't go out to play on the street unless Molly or Deborah was with him. Big as he was, he would wake up in the middle of the night, spooked by a dream, and come crawling into his parents' bed. What could they do but indulge him?

"He's a shy one," Sophie would say, "so let him be shy. Someday, God willing, he'll outgrow it."

He loved to sit in front of the fireplace, watching the glimmering light, staring at it and smiling, as if life finally had offered him some pleasure. He used to try to get the other children to join him, but though they wanted to humor him, Deborah never had the time, or Molly the patience, to sit there with him, and even little Walter felt too grown-up for such nonsense. Only Rose—four years old and already wearing the pathetic wire-rimmed glasses with the blacked-out lens that was supposed to correct her weak and wayward eye—would sit with him, silent and patient, not so much interested in the artificial fire as in making her brother happy. Sometimes she would drag a blanket off her bed and wrap it around them, and Sophie would find them there, Hymie staring and Rose fast asleep, curled up beneath the blanket on Hymie's lap. She couldn't help worrying, seeing them like that, what on earth would become of them.

She worried. It was in her nature to worry. She worried about

Hymie and she worried about Rose and she worried about Deborah, who spent so much of her time reading and brooding, and more and more, she found herself worrying about Sam. She couldn't say exactly what she was worried about. He brought money into the house, he was good to the younger children, he even had arrived at some sort of tenuous truce with his father; but he was always so restless, so quiet, as if his heart were in one place and his thoughts in another. Maybe it was that he had begun to talk like Asa Kalisher and his cronies, and to dress like them, spending the money he didn't hand over to the family on fancy suits and silk ties and expensive shoes which he stored in a closet in the restaurant kitchen while he was working. He sported a mustache. He slicked his red hair down and parted it in the middle. He dreamed of buying a car. He was always telling Molly about the hoodlums and politicians he met in the restaurant. He would tap the end of a cigarette on his thumbnail before lighting it, and then dangle it from his lips, letting the smoke drift up in front of his eyes, squinting out as though through a mask. He had girl friends—names were mentioned—but Sophie was never allowed to meet any of them. He ran to shows in Manhattan and to baseball games at Ebbets Field, and on Fridays he would stay out all night playing pinochle with his friends.

"What," Sophie would say to him, "you think you're Mr. Edison? You don't need sleep?"

He would just laugh and tell her he would sleep when he was tired, but thank God, he wasn't tired yet.

So she worried. He was thin and pale, and there were dark purplish circles around his eyes, and she knew he wasn't at peace with himself, that behind the cigarette and the fancy clothes he was still an astonished and perplexed little boy, groping for who or what he was. All she could do for him—her firstborn, her favorite, for whom she would have laid down her life—was to watch and worry.

Then came the chilly autumn when Jacob got sick and Sophie had something more immediate, more urgent, to worry about.

At first it was just a cold and no one thought much about it. Jacob was always catching colds in bad weather and would walk around hacking and wheezing, with moisture gathering itself into a pendulous drop at the end of his big chafed nose. But this time the cold settled into his chest, and he came home one night burning with fever. As it happened, this was only a few weeks after the letter arrived from his brother Chaim telling him that his father had died—that old rock-hard lump in his abdomen finally spreading and killing him —and Jacob was still wearing on his lapel a piece of torn black cloth and still saying *Kaddish* every night at the *shul*. But that night he came straight home. He walked into the house with his face wet and blotchy, his eyes tinged with pink. A bluish haze seemed to emanate from his pale forehead. When Sophie helped him off with his coat and jacket, she found that his shirt was soaked through. She got him to bed and sponged him down with alcohol and sent Deborah to bring the doctor.

For three days he hung between life and death. The family went around talking in whispers and looking desolated as though they were already in the presence of a corpse. The doctor, a big, gruff man named Lipsky, who was just beginning his practice in those days— and who would go on ministering to the Liebers and being in love with Sophie for the next thirty years—would come to the apartment twice a day to take Jacob's temperature and listen to his faint heart and clogged lungs and give him aspirin and sit in the kitchen sipping tea. There was really nothing more he could do. He suspected that Jacob was going to die and tried to prepare the family "for the worst" by taking Sam aside and asking him if he knew how to make "arrangements." Sam said he did—that was typical of him—then went to Asa Kalisher, who draped a heavy arm around Sam's shoulder and told him not to worry, he would take care of everything.

Lost in the maze of his fever, Jacob became delirious. It lasted all day, though for the patient the earthly rules of time and space were suspended. One moment he was in bed, in Brooklyn, with the faces of his family hovering around him; the next moment he was in his father's house with demons of every kind coming out at him from the drawers and closets. Some had blistered red skin; some had scales; others had thick fur matted with filth. They chattered about him, laughing and blaspheming, saying he had forsaken God and was lost. He knew there were words that could scatter them and drive them back down into the pit from which they had come; but he couldn't remember the words, and even if he could, his tongue felt as dry and hard as a piece of rope and he wouldn't have been able to utter them. They crowded around him, jabbering in a language he couldn't understand, talking about him and putting their clammy hands all over his body. One of them urinated on his legs; another poked at him from behind, entering and violating him. His father came running from his workshop with his walking stick, his hair mussed, his hat thrown off, and tried to chase them away; but they tripped him and held him down, and while one of them sat on his head, another pulled off his trousers. Jacob wanted to close his eyes, remembering that to gaze upon his father's nakedness would be a sin, but his eyelids had become transparent, like shimmering glass, so he wrapped his head in his arms and looked away. Then he saw the holy words written in gold on the parchment of a scroll, but though each of the letters was distinct, he couldn't make any sense of them, as if he had forgotten how to read. One of the creatures took up the scroll and lifted it above his head, as the Torah is lifted on the *Shabbos*, and more words appeared, this time in black ink. He couldn't read those either. He knew them as he knew his own name, Yakob ben Moshe, Jacob the son of Moses, and yet they were utterly strange. He moved closer to the scroll; now he could see that the words weren't written; rather, they were cut through the parchment, each letter opening into the darkness that lay beyond. The letter *daled* became a door through which he entered, the demons plunging in behind him, catching him in their arms and carrying him down and down through circles of darkness to a mountain island where Lilith was waiting for him. She, the temptress, had made herself appear kindly and beautiful, but he knew that his eyes were deceiving him, that beneath her pious kerchief her hair was a nest of snakes, and that her flesh, which looked so milky and fair, was actually green with rot and corruption. His nostrils filled with her smell, a sweet smell which, like a perfume, masked some familiar foulness he could not name. She held out her arms to embrace him, and he knew that he was dying, that the cosmic powers were battling for his soul, and that her touch would plunge him forever into the abyss. He squirmed against the demons that were pushing him forward, but he had no strength in his arms and legs. Red smoke arose from the fires they had prepared for him, choking him, hurting his lungs. His head began to throb, but at last he remembered, or perhaps was given from out of the blue, the ancient words that could save him, and he began to chant them—*Sh'me yisroel adonoi elohainu adonoi echod!*—as Lilith took him in her arms and flung him across the void, tumbling down and down through his delirium, through circles of darkness, back into life. . . .

Sophie was in the bedroom, preparing a cold compress to put on Jacob's brow, when she heard him mumbling the *Sh'ma* and decided he must be dying. Something like a jolt of electricity went through

55

her as she imagined herself widowed, bereft, alone with her children. For a moment she rocked back and forth, stunned and wailing; then a kind of anger came.

"Jacob!" she cried out, taking his frail shoulders in her hands and shaking him roughly. "Jacob! You mustn't leave me, Jacob! You hear me, Jacob, you mustn't leave!"

The next thing she remembered—never mind the cliché, that's how the family would tell the story later on—she was in the front room, sprawled on the sofa, with Deborah kneeling in front of her, slapping her wrists and pinching her cheeks, with a cold compress, probably the one she had prepared for Jacob, cooling her head.

What went on there that day!

Deborah, who usually came through in a crisis, necessity driving her out of her usual abstraction, immediately upon hearing her mother's screams gave Molly a nickel and sent her around the corner to telephone Sam at the restaurant. Sam took the call in the kitchen, listened to Molly breathing and crying at the other end, and suddenly felt as though he were riding an elevator rising rapidly upward: blood, organs, strength—everything was rushing down into his legs. He closed his eyes, letting the swell of his feelings precipitate a thought.

Damn it to hell, he told himself, *now I've got to take care of them!*

Later the family would repeat the story of how Sam hurried home that day, running coatless and hatless through a blizzard, believing his father was dead; how, when he finally got there, he walked into the bedroom and found his father, the fever broken, the miracle complete, sitting up and eating chicken soup; and how for weeks afterward he was so mad at Molly that he wouldn't talk to her.

But, as always, the truth wasn't quite that simple.

To begin with, there was no blizzard, though there would be one later on: there were just a few dingy flakes of snow drifting through the gray afternoon like bits of ash, and you could still make out the pale, cold, useless disk of the sun floating through the gathering clouds. And Sam didn't run, he walked—walked slowly and contemplatively, in no hurry at all, believing that when he got back to the apartment, his new obligations would steal his freedom forever. And while it is true that he found Jacob propped up on a pillow with a bowl of chicken broth cooling on the dresser, Sam had already forgiven Molly for the false alarm because Dr. Lipsky was in the kitchen with Sophie, trying to convince her that she hadn't summoned Jacob back from the dead, and as Sam came through the door, braced for a household filled with hysterical women, he learned everything at once from the tone of the conversation.

"Miracle or not," Dr. Lipsky was saying, "what he needs now is bed rest, no noise, and plenty of liquids."

So Jacob lived; but he was never the same man again, and the next morning—"just temporarily"—Sam took over the store.

How he hated it! He would sit there, watching the sporadic and shabby customers grazing among the shelves of books or fingering some silver-plated menorah they couldn't afford to buy, and feel himself trapped in a drab and alien world. He tried to convince Sophie that it would make more sense to close up the store and let him go on working in the restaurant, where he was making good money and thought he had a future. Didn't Asa Kalisher keep hinting at the possibility of some future partnership between them? But Sophie told him that words were cheap, especially her brother's—he was, after all, the sort of man who promised the moon and delivered a cheese sandwich—and besides, if they didn't keep the store going, they would lose it. Did the bank care if a man lay sick in bed? Did he want maybe she should run the store, trying to make change and keep an eye on the *gonifs* with a baby in each arm? There was no use talking to her about it. Something had stiffened within her: you could read it in her eyes and in the small tight vertical creases that gathered in her upper lip. It was as though, having summoned Jacob back from the dead, she had discovered within herself a reservoir of new pride and strength and stubbornness. Certainly Sam's own pleasures and desires were as nothing against the necessities of the family and the weight of her expectations.

He told himself that sooner or later his father would be healthy again and he would be allowed to return to the restaurant, where life gathered and swelled and brimmed with possibility and the tumult he believed he loved—where he would be able to shape himself to the forms of power and wealth and ambition he waited upon—but a week went by, and then a month, and his father's recovery was measured by no more than the slow traipse he made each day from his sickbed to the chair in the kitchen where he took his solitary and meager meals. There had been permanent damage to his lungs. He wheezed and coughed and spat blood into the handkerchief he kept balled in his hand. His beard had turned white and wispy, and the skin on his forehead was so pale and transparent you could trace the blue lines of his veins through it. The fever also seemed to have damaged his mind. The few words of English he had acquired over the years vanished from his vocabulary; you would be talking to him and realize he wasn't understanding you; he would stare off into space with a worried expression as though he were anticipating a slap. Three times a day he would pull himself up and lean against a wall, facing eastward, softly muttering his prayers. The flesh hung flaccid from his arms and gathered itself in loose wrinkles around his elbows, and his eyes were bloodshot and bleary with fluids.

Seeing him like that, Sam told himself it was impossible that his father would ever resume the burdens of the store, and while the thought initially increased his sense of entrapment, it also, as time passed, set him free.

It was simple enough. During the first few weeks of winter Sam had tried to adapt himself to the store, running it the way he thought his father would have run it, keeping it intact for him, so to speak, until he returned to take it over again. Seen thus, everything, the books, the religious articles, the letters from the customers out West, appeared permanent and oppressive, the very walls of the place rigid and implacable and formed to his father's dimensions. He cramped himself trying to fit. But then he began to sense—there was no great moment of insight, of course; just the usual slow process of time filtering through his thoughts and altering his way of looking—that the store had been handed down to him, and since it was his, it was malleable. That damned showcase of mezuzahs against which he was forever banging his shin could be moved; that crate of books which he deemed unsellable could be returned to the shipper; the cash register with its missing numbers and jammed keys could be sold off, another bought and put in its place. Nothing was ordained; he could change everything.

For example, he noticed with amusement at first and later with interest how often the customers who came into the store would browse among the books for a while, weighing their desires against the limits of what they could afford, and then buy nothing but a couple of pieces of penny chocolate from the little wire shelf on the counter, as though they sought to console their poverty with a taste of sweetness in their mouths. He also noticed that often enough people would come in just for the chocolates, since they were labeled kosher and were of a better quality than the usual *chazerei* available in the local candy stores. By the end of a day those pennies from the chocolates actually amounted to a substantial portion of the gross receipts. Curious, Sam dragged out of the storeroom one day the jumbled boxes of bills and papers his father had saved and spent a dizzy afternoon sorting them and adding numbers until he had located a significant pattern. With books and religious articles, he discovered, the markup was small, the turnover slow, and the costs for shipping and handling and insurance excessive. Furthermore, the book business had actually dwindled as the neighborhood changed and the yeshivas and synagogues learned to deal directly with the publishers themselves. In a sense the whole weight of the store's profitability—a word he had learned from Asa Kalisher—rested more and more upon those chocolates.

He decided to experiment. He installed a second wire shelf next to the first one and stocked it with some chocolate-covered mints, which the salesman from the chocolate factory had called a "terrific item." They sold. A few weeks later—it was February now—the store sprouted hearts in the window, and the wall where the foreign-language books had been was emblazoned with boxed and beribboned sweets. In March he borrowed some money from Asa Kalisher and purchased a machine that could be filled with fancy nuts, cashews and almonds and pecans, which were kept warm by the heat of a bulb as they revolved behind glass on a little carousel driven by an electric motor. In April he put out a sign, lettered by Deborah in her neat, exquisite hand, saying: "Chocolates and Holiday Confections/Certified Kosher for Passover."

Like magic, the stuff converted itself into money.

During that time Jacob was scarcely interested in the store. The only questions he asked were about the out-of-state customers, to whom he felt a special obligation, since he believed that he alone connected the "pioneers," as he called them, to the necessities of their religion. He would listen to Sam explain what he was doing, for Sam was scrupulous about pretending to seek his advice, but Sam's words never registered for him an image of change. His mind was in another world. He had recovered some of his strength by then: he was going to *shul*, taking short walks, and spending a few hours in the afternoon, now that spring had come, sitting in the park across the street and watching the children play; but he was still thin and pale, and he tired easily, and he had to stop to catch his breath, coughing and choking and spitting into his handkerchief, as he tediously climbed the stairs back to the apartment. He was old and spent and quiescent; the fever had burned out the last remnants of his vitality and his rage, though in just a few months Sophie would astonish everybody by announcing another pregnancy; it seemed unlikely that he would ever return to the store.

Thus Sam felt increasingly free to follow his inclinations.

By May of that year, when according to his immigration papers he was supposed to be celebrating his eighteenth birthday—the actual date still lay a few weeks in the future, obscured in the murk of the Hebrew calendar—Sam was handing over to his mother more money than he and Jacob had previously brought home between the two of them. He had purchased a huge ledger with pale green numbered pages to supplant the little dog-eared notebooks in which Jacob kept his accounts, and had set Deborah to work in the storeroom, filling up boxes with liquid-center cordials, hand-dipped marshmallows, fruit gums, and marmalade slices. Profits increased, he realized, when you packaged the merchandise yourself. Imagine the money to be made if you could manufacture the stuff! Occasionally, when he managed to get away for a few hours, leaving Deborah to mind the store, he would walk through the fanciest streets of Manhattan, studying the wares and displays in the bonbon shoppes that catered to the wealthy.

"Know what Park Avenue is buying today," he would explain, "and you already know what Pitkin Avenue will buy tomorrow."

He was learning. He taught himself bookkeeping, sitting up all hours over some volumes from the library, absorbing the dank mysteries of advanced billing and accounts receivable. He knew where to get ribbons and boxes and little brown paper cups at a good price and how to finagle the manufacturers and suppliers, playing one off against the other. He could open a sack of salted peanuts and tell you with just a glance and a sniff what grade they were. He brought home hunks of chocolate and bottles of flavoring and conducted candymaking experiments on Sophie's stove. He had a head for these things, and when he didn't know something, he would go to Asa Kalisher and his cronies for advice.

Years later, when he was running the factory on Bergen Street and the nine retail outlets in all the best shopping districts of Brooklyn, and giving jobs to everyone in the family, Sam would recall with nostalgia those early days in the store and tell himself he had been content. But in fact, for all that early flush of prosperity, he believed in those days that his life had jammed and turned back upon itself, that he had lost the trail to the future, that Jacob's illness had shunted him onto a track that led away from the dark and hidden places, the vivid realms of grief and ecstasy he hoped to explore. Even while he was planning the next expansion of the candy shelves, even while he dreamed of pushing out the books and religious articles altogether and devoting the business wholly to sweets and nuts, he would tell himself this was only temporary, that sooner or later he would move on to something else.

His chance came when America entered the war.

There is in one of the family albums a picture of Sam in uniform leaning on a flagpole at an army camp in New Jersey. You can just make out through the artificial smile the expression of boredom on his face.

"Go, *shmuck*, fight for the millionaires, get yourself killed," Asa Kalisher said to him the day he walked into the restaurant and announced that he was going to enlist, but the closest he ever came to the muddy battlefields of the war was that camp in the New Jersey swamplands, where he worked as an aide to a brigadier general named Sharpe, and learned how to eat pork, and was fascinated by the habits of the Yankees and southerners who surrounded him.

Once a week Sophie would receive, along with a portion of his poker winnings, a letter in English detailing the events of the previous seven days. Once a month Sam would come home for the weekend and all the relatives would be invited over to spend an afternoon with the hero. Sophie would prepare *kreplach* soup and *gefilte* fish and raisin-and-noodle puddings, and Molly would run around wearing Sam's army cap, and Ruthie would pout and carry on until she had replaced Rose or Evelyn on her brother's lap. Somehow the color of khaki in the house excited everyone, even Jacob, who would rouse himself from his torpor and ask a lot of questions about the food and the hardships and the proximity of *shuls*. They would listen to Sam tell about the parades and the paper work and the baseball games and the firing range practice as if those were the activities that made up the substance of the war. Sam, of course, knew better. He knew lots of boys who had gone overseas and a few who weren't coming back. Whenever he watched a batch of recruits shipping out and a new batch of recruits arriving, he felt cheated of the chance to measure himself in combat, to taste for himself the unimaginable muck and murder of the trenches; at such times he would even think about asking for a transfer, but some inbred caution, some stubborn sense of limits, always forestalled him.

So he served his time and thought about the store, which the family somehow kept going, and built up a small bank account out of his poker winnings—winning because he was shrewd and careful and played against reckless boys who expected to be shipped overseas—and when it was over, he came back to Brooklyn and the family and the candy business. By then it seemed to him that the candy business was all he had ever wanted, and that the nations of the world, in their insane and tragic conspiracy, had only postponed for a while the pursuit of his original ambitions.

DURING THE WAR YEARS MOLLY ENTERED her plump and passionate pubescence. It happened all at once: she went skipping off to school one vernal morning an ordinary, chubby little girl with inky fingers and carroty braids and metamorphosed by afternoon into a full-bloomed redhead, stunning and vulnerable. It got to the point where Sophie was afraid of letting her out of the house alone; the honey of her scent and the dazzling promise of her smile sent signals through the neighborhood. Lean and hungry boys of several national origins would camp on the stoop in the early hours of morning, waiting to walk her to school, and then returned in the evening to fight among themselves in the park across the street to determine who would be there tomorrow. Sometimes one of the more venturesome among them even scaled the fire escape, hoping to catch a glimpse of her preparing herself for bed. It became a nightly ritual for Sophie to remind Molly to pull down the shade—and she usually needed the reminder. She had the body of a woman, the heart of a sensualist, and the habits of a child. She seemed to have been created without a sense of shame or guilt or sin or limits, and nothing that Sophie said instilled it in her. She just couldn't understand the aching dreams her ripening flesh aroused. Her innocence bordered on depravity. She traipsed around the house in the flimsiest of undergarments—upsetting Hymie and causing Jacob to avert his eyes—or went gallivanting down the hallway, naked and dripping and pink from a bath, in a casual search for a towel. Careless about buttons and pins and ties, she offered up to the world, as summer came on, a heartbreaking show of calf or gleaming shoulder. Grizzled candy store operators with fancy cravings gave her free ice cream cones and taffies, and even the pious old men, Jacob's acquaintances, who followed the sun from bench to bench in the park, caught themselves staring at the playground, ashamed and helpless, as Molly kicked her legs skyward on the swing or bounced up and down with Hymie on the seesaw.

No one bothered to explain to Molly—perhaps no one in those days could have adequately explained to her—the curious chemical changes that had reshaped her body, and brought on her periodic discomfort, and set wild urges and passions flaring in her soul. In practical terms, she knew nothing about sex. She had derived some crude notions concerning the origins of babies from watching Sophie's belly swell and diminish, but it never occurred to her that the mysterious exertions through which grown-ups populate the world had anything much to do with the way her shoulders tightened and her breath came hot and dry when men stared at her. She only knew, this child of a large and preoccupied family, that she liked the attention.

Her new flesh, with its hills and vales, its plains and russet forests, its slippery spots and sensitivities, was for her a kind of gift, a vast deed of territory, a rich and promising wilderness she was delighted to explore. She loved to tickle herself, rubbing the tips of her fingers ever so lightly along her arms and legs, ruffling and smoothing again the faint downy hairs that grew along her skin, until everything tingled and itched. She loved to sit for an hour in the bathtub, half dreaming amidst the tepid suds, licking her lips and enjoying the touch of the water as it lapped gently against her armpits, her nipples, her backside, her thighs, knowing only, as she touched her own most sensitive spots, curiously, guiltlessly, that it relieved a certain pressure.

She was already a *nosher* in those days. She devoured cakes and raisins and candies and sweets of every kind and was forever at the icebox, despite Sophie's scoldings, poking her fingers into the leftovers. Sophie didn't know what to do with her. She remembered how even as a baby Molly was always famished and went on sucking greedily long after the breast was sore and dry. But her appetites weren't putting fat on her then, as they would later on. Instead, everything she ate merely fueled the fires of her vitality. She was restless and fidgety and couldn't sit still for a second. She had no patience for the quiet womanly skills, the sewing and knitting and mending, which Sophie tried to teach her. Even while she slept, some part of her was always in motion. She kicked and snored and turned and stretched and rasped and moaned, caught on the rack of some perpetual and vivid dream. It got so bad that Deborah demanded and had to be given her own bed. And what a temper! You never knew when the least inconvenience or frustration, a lost shoe, a wrinkled blouse, a stubbed toe might set Molly off on a tantrum. She would go raging through the house, Molly on the war path, weeping and furious, sending the younger children scurrying for a corner where they settled like little rabbits watching a summer thunderstorm.

"She should only live and be well," Sophie used to say, "but I pity the man who falls for her."

Among those who fell for her in those days was a *luftmensh* named Levitch—no one, not even Molly, ever recalled his first name. He was twenty years old at the time, a student at City College, which in those days, in that neighborhood, made him something of a rarity. Recently orphaned (it had been one of those old-fashioned cases of a doting wife quickly following her cancerous husband to the grave), Levitch lived alone in a second-story apartment down the block. His father had owned a fish store in Greenpoint and had left a few dollars, which, thriftily managed, would support Levitch through school. God only knew what the poor boy would do after that! A touch of asthma kept him out of the army. His clothes were shabby and his dark hair grew in uncombed heaps and he sported a patchy mustache, which he seldom waxed or trimmed. He was a dreamer, an idealist, a man with his head in the air; and since he kept to himself and hid his shyness behind an expression of contempt, the children in the neighborhood were a little afraid of him.

Through the long, slow afternoons and pale evenings of summer he would sit by his window with a book in his lap, glancing down at the street, averting his eyes if you happened to glance back at him. The fact of the matter was that he was looking for Molly. He had forgotten the first time he noticed her; he only knew that he had fallen into the squeamish habit of hoping to see her, was addicted to the damp, dull, throbbing pain the sight of her aroused in him. He couldn't call it love, and he didn't dare call it lust—he kept reminding himself that she was only a child—so he didn't bother to give any name to the miserable nervous longing he felt. He just lurked, guilty and half-deranged, there at the window, waiting for another glimpse of her.

Deborah was the first to divine his secret.

Deborah, at the age of sixteen, was a tall, plain, awkward girl with a high, pale brow and a fine, aristocratic nose of the sort that would emerge every so often in the generations of the family, exciting a lot of foolish speculation about the intermingling of Polish counts and dukes in the family bloodline. Pensive, serious-minded, her head a bit fogged by the romances and gothics she loved to read, she had quit school when Sam went into the army to help out in the store, but she dreamed about finishing her education, and she was always running to the library and returning home with her bagful of books.

"She has books instead of boys," Sophie would complain, sensing something sad and solitary and stubborn in her, and worrying that she was the sort of girl who ended up unmarried.

But Deborah was just biding her time. She believed—this most "European" of the Lieber brood—that somewhere, somehow, a man had already been chosen for her by Heaven or Fate or call it what you will and that sooner or later he would waltz into her life, carry her out of the squalor and boredom of Brooklyn to a nobler and more passionate level of existence, to the heights sublime. He would be handsome and gentle, spiritual and kind, utterly worthy of her sacred love and the pain of her waiting. In the meantime, while she saved herself for him, she was perfecting and purifying her soul. Those thoughts lurked behind the annoying smile she wore whenever Sophie pestered her.

Anyway, it was Deborah, with her touch of clairvoyance and her rage for truth, who pointed out to Molly that Levitch was looking at her.

Poor Levitch. He hadn't expected Molly to notice him. He probably suppose that even if she did, she wouldn't understand that he was spying on her, or wouldn't think it was important. He never realized that as the summer went by, she kept passing his window more often, slowing down her pace a bit in front of the building, and dropping things on the sidewalk because she knew he was watching her bend down to pick them up. He thought it was just an illusion, that he only seemed to be seeing her more often as his loathsome desires grew and his lunatic dreams blotted out the hours between her appearances, and he was amazed and appalled when she began, tease that she was, looking up at his window and smiling at him, showing her perfect teeth. He didn't know whether to smile back or ignore her, and the compromise between his soul and his sense dragged his face into a tortured grin. As he sat there, all blood and heart and terror, it occurred to him that at any moment he might go insane. It happened to others, and it could happen to him; one read about such things in Mr. Hearst's newspapers—the mind surrenders to its own wild urgings, and the next thing you know you have been locked away to contemplate the sweet gore of your deeds. He became afraid to go out of the house lest he meet her face-to-face on the street and, in the proximity of that pouting mouth, that blaze of red hair, lose the last remnants of his self-control.

Sulky, obsessed, he would take to his reeking bed and stroke away the swell of his grotesque passion, but he could never quite accomplish, whatever his fantasies, a spasm of authentic and permanent release.

Then it happened.

She strolled out of the playground one empty summer afternoon and walked directly to his window and said: "Hey, you up there, how come you're all the time looking at me?"

She stood with her hands on her hips, an image of amused and lovely exasperation, wearing that pretty frock of hers in which there mingled the colors of roses and blueberries and cream, smiling at him, showing him her teeth and the pink damp tip of her tongue, and he couldn't help himself—his eager heart knotted and heaved.

"Because you're the best-looking girl in America," he told her, astonished at how easily and boldly the words slipped out.

"So why not at least come on down here where you can see me better?"

"Come on up," he said.

They sat in the murderous heat of the kitchen—he had immediately, absurdly, offered her a glass of milk—and he contemplated the floor, the ceiling, the doorway, his own damp and clutched hands, the smeared window, the icebox, the milk bottle, the oilcloth-covered no-man's-land of the table between them, telling himself that as soon as she finished the milk, he would send her home, thinking that time flies and maybe in a few years—

"So why did I bother?" she said. "You're not even looking at me."

Her tongue jabbed at the milky mustache on her upper lip; her shoulders moved gently up and down as she breathed. He finally managed to rest his eyes upon the pink and freckled skin beneath her neck. Maybe he would kiss her, just once; he knew she would let him; he would kiss her on the forehead or on the cheek, a brotherly sort of kiss, tender and modest and chaste, a kind of salute to her vigorous bloom and beauty, and then he would send her home. Maybe a kiss would break the spell. That thought calmed him. She is lovely and precious and warm, he reminded himself, but she is only a child.

He began to talk to her, teasing her, saying whatever nonsense came into his head, asking her where she got such a cute nose, and why her eyes were that marvelous shade of green, and whether she was always faithful to her boyfriends—"Don't have no boyfriends yet," she said—and whether she went under the stairs to kiss them or kissed them out on the street where all the *yentehs* could see.

The words he spoke were camouflage: behind them, beneath them, within them, he was calculating effects and distances, struggling with his deceptive heart, rising from the chair, circling the table toward her, trying not to frighten her away, holding her there, mesmerized, with nothing more than the modulations of his voice.

He could smell the faint, acrid, sunny aroma of her skin as the shimmering space between them diminished. He braced himself for the moment they would touch, and the moment came. She lifted her face to his, and the way she rose up and pressed herself against him, pressing her bosom against his chest and her legs against his buckling knee, opening the sweet, wet flower of her mouth for him, was beyond all his expectations. He felt himself drifting into a new and uncanny realm of existence where anything was possible, anything at all, and he gave himself over to it—yes, he told himself, this feeling, this miracle, is love—and the years between them, as far as Levitch was concerned, melted into a single wet, throbbing point and vanished.

That sweltering night Levitch arrived at the Lieber apartment and stood in the doorway like a little lost pup, asking to speak to Mr. Lieber. He was shaved for the occasion, and his thick hair was still damp from a recent combing, and the suit he wore was too small for him and so old-fashioned that it must have been his father's. Streams of sweat poured down his shiny cheeks into his stiff collar. For nearly an hour he sat in the front room with Jacob, the sliding door closed, Sophie stationed at the dining room table to mend some clothes and keep guard over their privacy. It must have been a difficult conversation. Levitch's Yiddish was meager and Jacob in those days, white-bearded and wheezing, was still refusing to comprehend English. Nonetheless, something must have been communicated between them because the sliding doors eventually opened, and Jacob whispered a few words to Sophie, and Sophie smiled to herself and went down the hallway.

In the first bedroom she passed, Hymie was squatting on the floor, whispering to himself, his arms wrapped around his knees; in the second bedroom Molly sat in front of a mirror admiring herself as she combed out her brilliant red hair; in the back bedroom Sophie found Deborah telling a bedtime story to the younger children.

"Wash your face and come," said Sophie. "That nice young man is asking to marry you."

"Don't be ridiculous," snapped Deborah, who understood everything and wasn't amused. "I'm not the daughter he wants."

The family would always remember how Sophie chased Levitch from their house that night, shouting threats and curses at him in Yiddish as he ran down the stairs, and how a few days later Levitch moved out of Park Place, and out of the neighborhood, and—for all they ever heard of him again—possibly even out of this world. They would also remember how Molly refused to understand what all the fuss was about and how Sophie tried and tried but couldn't drag out of her any sort of explanation. But then what was there to explain? For Molly it was just a simple adventure on a dull summer afternoon, and years later, recalling it for her nieces and nephews, she would laugh at how it led to her first proposal.

"Imagine," she would say, a coarse, fat woman laughing at her own beautiful lost girlhood, "I let the *shmegehgeh* give me a smooch and he decides he has to marry me!"

Of course, there was more to it than that, quite a bit more, even though when she left Levitch's apartment that day, she was still essentially intact. She had manipulated his passion with a groping and childish curiosity, as if it were merely some new kind of toy or gadget, but its explosion had seeded nothing more than Levitch's cramped and overeager heart.

" 'Marry you?' your grandmother said to him. 'Marry you? How can she marry you—you *momzer!*—when she doesn't even know you?' "

Laughing, uproarious, her face red, her chins aquiver, her fat arms pink and mottled with hypertension, her head rolling from side to side with the mirth of her memory; that was Molly all over.

A FEW MONTHS AFTER THE BIRTH OF MOE—that ruddy and mild baby who rounded out the brood and, at least in Sophie's mind, gave purpose to those last, miraculous years of Jacob's life—the war in

Europe came to an end. People were hugging and kissing each other on the streets. In front of Asa Kalisher's restaurant a huge bonfire burned through the night, sending showers of orange sparks roaring skyward to mingle momentarily with the benevolent stars. For a while the Liebers felt themselves caught up in the joy and hope and pandemonium of the times. They flew a flag outside the front-room window—all along Park Place flags fluttered and snapped in the brisk November wind—and Deborah hung patriotic bunting in front of the store; Molly walked around for weeks wearing a pinafore that was all stars and bars; and when home-based soldiers, surrogates for the victorious troopers, paraded in their helmets and leggings along Eastern Parkway, the whole clan, even Jacob, mingled with the giddy, poppy-speckled crowd.

For Sophie, of course, the armistice was most worth celebrating because it meant that Sam would soon be home, and when she received the letter from him saying he wouldn't be "out" until the following spring, her mood quickly darkened.

"What do they need him there for?" she complained. "To shine the general's shoes? They can't find a *shvartzer* for that? They need my Sam?"

It was as though, her hopes dashed, she had finally begun to comprehend the misery and injustice of war.

That winter was dismal, perhaps the worst Sophie had known since they were living above the restaurant and Jacob was *meshuggeh* with his goblins and ghosts. The weather turned wet and foul, and contagions of all sorts flourished in the crammed corridors and classrooms of the public schools. Only Molly seemed spared by her immense vitality from the plague of colds and fevers. Sophie's existence became a tedious, nerve-racking routine of wiping noses and taking temperatures, administering on schedule the patent medicines that Dr. Lipsky prescribed, and preparing for her brood those well-remembered gargles of honey and aspirin dissolved in warm salt water. Jacob went around wheezing and shuffling (he had started using a walking stick), looking, as Deborah said, like death warmed over; and Molly, now that the weather kept the crowd of boys away from the front stoop, was crabby and impossible. She disappeared for hours on end and carried on long secret correspondences with unknown "beaus," who were forever breaking her heart. At the smallest provocation she would start hollering or burst into tears. She would tease Walter—the two of them never got along—and then complain when Walter, eight years old and bright as a button, teased her right back. If she wasn't quarreling with Sophie about some mess of undergarments shoved into a corner or a dish of leftovers that had vanished from the icebox, she was arguing with Deborah about whose stockings were dangling from the string above the bathtub. When she went to help out at the store, they would find her in the storeroom, nibbling away the profits.

In January, to add to Sophie's *tsurris,* Walter came down with chicken pox and the illness spread through the family. Even the baby caught it. Hymie had it worst of all. He had sores all over his body and more sores in his mouth and nostrils, and Sophie ate her heart out, watching him scratch and pick at them. For weeks the poor baffled boy oozed and bled. At last gruff Dr. Lipsky threatened to tie Hymie's hands to a bedpost, which so frightened Hymie that for the first time in months he went and sat in the closet. Sophie had her hands full with him. He was fifteen years old and had added four inches to his height in the last year; the first pale shadow of manhood was beginning to fuzz his chin and cheeks; but he was still "shy"— still, that is, had failed to grow over the raw flesh of his sensibility the calluses one needs to survive. He hated loud noises and bright lights. The everyday odors of onions or floor wax or fresh paint made him dizzy or nauseated. If you put a knife alongside his plate, he would refuse to sit down. One morning he walked into the bathroom when Molly, with typical carelessness, had neglected to hook the door, and the glimpse he caught of her on the toilet seat, coping with her monthly flow, became an obsession with him.

For weeks afterward he would point at her lap and say in a voice that was all startled and mystified outrage: "She's bleeding! I saw her! She's bleeding!"

Finally Dr. Lipsky sat him down for a "talk," but whatever he said, he failed to exorcise that troublesome image from Hymie's mind.

There were moments when Hymie seemed to improve, when Sophie could convince herself that he was outgrowing his problem. Occasionally, as the family jammed around the table for one of those dense soup-and-meat-and-potato-and-*kugel* suppers that Sophie believed a body needed in wintertime, Hymie would take over the conversation. He would start talking quietly about the food they were eating or some incident at school or some new toy he had set his heart on, and then the words would start coming faster and faster, louder and louder, until they were tumbling out of him so rapidly that they collided with one another and transformed what he was saying into gibberish. It was as though he had been saving up his thoughts during his periods of silence and had to get them all out in a hurry. Pathetic, really, how those monologues of his rose in pitch and intensity, pushed by some secret desperation no one understood, then subsided again to murmuring and moody silence, with that look of disappointment on his round and damply shining face, as though despite his enormous effort, the words had failed to relieve the relentless pressure of his anxiety.

In February Brooklyn was hit by an ice storm.

All night rain came down while the temperature hovered near freezing, and in the morning a thick gray glaze of ice covered the streets and the lampposts and the occasional parked car, and sealed up the windows on the north sides of buildings. Schools and factories and stores were closed, and everyone sat home waiting for the stuff to melt. For days the streets were too slippery for walking. Sophie sent Molly around the corner for some groceries and she returned an hour later, empty-handed, saying she had to crawl home on her hands and knees. That evening a horse fell down on Kingston Avenue and they couldn't get the poor beast back on its feet. Its heartrending cries as it lay there freezing to death infiltrated the neighborhood and made everyone edgy until they sent an officer around from the police station to put the creature out of its misery.

Every night a thin layer of snow would fall, covering the ice like a blanket, and in the afternoon the wind would come up and blow the stuff away, leaving the slick surface of the ice fresh again for the new snow that would fall in the night. It was a gloomy kind of fun to sit at the front window watching some rash pedestrian trying to get to Kingston Avenue, but through most of it, cooped up in the apartment, everyone got on everyone else's nerves. Walter would turn up daubed with Molly's perfume and Molly would scream at him and start chasing him down the hallway and Evelyn and Ruthie would laugh and the baby would start howling and everything would turn into chaos. Sophie became a disciplinarian by necessity, borrowing one of Jacob's belts and for the first time in her life hitting her children with something other than her hands. Mostly it was Walter and Ruthie who got hit; they were the mischievous ones, the wild ones, though she never hit them hard enough to put an end to their shenanigans. She knew only a father could do that.

Then the ice was gone and the children went back to school, but still the winter continued.

In Washington the attorney general of the United States began a postwar crusade against communists and anarchists, and on Pitkin Avenue tired and dreamy men clustered in small gray groups to lament the situation. A fellow from some government bureau came to the restaurant and asked Asa Kalisher a lot of questions, and on the following Friday night Asa showed up on Park Place with a bottle of wine, just like in the old days—only this time it was Walter eavesdropping on the conversation—to tell Sophie about the interrogation and to laugh at the evasive answers he had given.

"It's the same old story," he told her. "They're *meshuggeh* on the subject of Jews. They're afraid we're taking over their country."

"So what will they do?"

"They'll put a stop to the immigration is what they'll do. They'll punish the ones waiting to come in."

That conversation renewed Sophie's old desire to bring her father to America. Her letters to Yussel Kalisher became ever more burdened with urgency and optimism and expectation. She tantalized him by singing the praises of the grandchildren he had never seen. But the butcher was stubborn. He wrote back that with the war over, life in the village would improve; besides, he still had plenty of family there, Sophie's younger brother Saul, and Saul's wife, and Saul's seven children.

"To have a piece of meat on the table and the sun in the sky, I don't have to come to America," he wrote.

Sophie was disappointed. To make matters worse, she wasn't sleeping well. She would lie there listening to the small night noises that filled the apartment, dozing and coming awake again, and in the morning she would be stiff and exhausted. She walked around yawning and dreaming on her feet, the life of the family flowing thickly, sludgelike about her, her attention shifting slowly from one problem to the next as the need appeared.

One day Rose pulled a pot of boiling noodles down off the stove, scalding her left hand and wrist so badly that she wore a bandage for weeks and was marked for the rest of her life with a rippled patch of scar tissue. Rose was the most luckless of the Lieber sisters. She always ended up battered and bruised. At school the other children were nasty to her; they teased her, pulled her hair, hid her books, spattered her with ink, sent her home in tears. A lunatic once molested her in a local alleyway. For years she had to wear, on doctor's orders, those glasses with the blacked-out lens that never quite managed to straighten or strengthen her weak and wayward eye. But she had learned—necessity had taught her—to endure with quiet stoicism the calamities that came her way. She had, as the family would say, the temperament of a saint. Sophie would never forget how she sat there, stiff and silent, while Dr. Lipsky peeled back the dressing from the raw and blistered skin and painted the wound with some agonizing yellow ointment, never crying throughout this ordeal.

Sophie marveled at her self-sufficiency and her patience, and so tried to be patient herself as she nursed her baby, tended to her children, counted her pennies, and waited for spring to roll around again. Sam's presence, she was sure, would solve all her problems. At least, she told herself, she would again be able to sleep.

Demobilized at last, Sam came home to a houseful of children he hardly knew and a meager store still groping for its identity between candy and books. At first he seemed changed. He was high-spirited. He tossed and tumbled the little ones until they squealed and giggled with the pleasure of his return. He bought his father a new coat for the holidays and dragged him off to a photographer to have his picture taken. He kept talking about how he was going to expand the store and make a lot of money and give the family all the luxuries they desired. He had emerged from the long marking of time that was the war for him with an inarticulate sense of his own energy and the remarkable possibilities that might grow from it. He had seen for himself, as he ministered like a manservant to the brusque whims and habits of General Sharpe, that things didn't just happen in this world, that they were made to happen by the few men who were bold and willful enough to take a hand—the whole tribe of General Sharpes who sat in their offices and played with the destinies of lesser men.

But in a few weeks Sam found himself caught up in all the old dreary routines, and for a while his ambition faltered.

He could extend the shelves of candy, he could watch the sum of his profits slowly inflate, he could buy new clothes and run to theaters and movies and ball games, and win a few dollars playing poker or pinochle, and sit up all hours in the restaurant trading brags with Asa Kalisher and his cronies; but nothing satisfied his blind and restless expectations. He suspected that though he was just twenty years old, he had already lived the portion of life that was assigned to him, and all that remained was work and repetition. His mood curdled. The months and years ahead became for him a kind of murk or fog through which he groped, seeking some balm for his disorderly and overstimulated heart. At two or three in the morning, when he climbed into bed for those few hours of sleep that were all his tough young body required, his brain would flicker with the pent-up charge of his fears and desires. Phantasmagorical visions, as gaudy and brilliant as the new electrical advertisements they had begun to install in Times Square, would blaze out at him, startling him as he neared the threshold of sleep. Each night he added to the pattern of his fancies until drowsiness closed down upon some vivid scene with an oblivious embrace. Each morning he awoke with aching jaws as though he had been gritting his teeth through the night. In the gray, harsh, limited environs of workaday Brooklyn there was, aside from crime or art or religion, just one possible focus for such a blaze of emotion. It was inevitable, then, that Sam would find himself in love.

Her name was Essie Schonwald. She was the daughter of Isaac Schonwald, who was one of Asa Kalisher's cronies, and Sam probably never suspected that uncle and father had conspired to bring the "two nice young people" together. He thought it was fate or destiny or some other trite notion of a manipulating hand. He even said it was love at first sight, though sitting that day in the restaurant, staring at her across a table burdened with food, he actually felt little more than a sort of amazed fascination with her pale and perfect complexion—the product of a cosmetic art, of time and money and training, he had encountered only once before, in the exhalant personage, all-blond-sighing-southern belle, of General Sharpe's wife.

Essie was heart-achingly pretty and almost totally empty-headed, and Sam was enthralled by the combination. She burdened her mind with just one firm conviction, that she would be "pure" when she entered her nuptial bed, but she conceived of that purity in such strictly mechanical terms, and was, the dear girl, so "modern" and eager to please, that Sam soon discovered there would be throughout their long engagement plenty of alternative pleasures available to him. She had a lovely painted mouth, and the same dark Hebrew eyes that had allured Holofernes, and the slimmest waistline and the whitest and softest hands that Sam had ever seen. Her voice was filled with a thin, voluptuous music, and the essence of unknown flowers wafted up from her warm powdered skin. Next to her even Molly seemed dank and coarse and heavy. She was an adorable, doting, and apparently rich little *babachka,* and Sam decided almost immediately that he would marry her. She was molded to the shape of his dreams;

he could place her easily among the rich rugs and summer-colored furniture of his imagined future. It never occurred to him that his desires might produce difficulties he could not overcome.

When he brought her to the house for dinner (the first time he had ever allowed the family to meet one of his dates), she perched herself on the edge of a chair, and nibbled at her food, and batted her eyes, and tried out on Jacob and Sophie her odd Germanized brand of Yiddish, and everyone kept staring at her—even Hymie was entranced—as though a fairy or a butterfly had fluttered down into their midst.

Isaac Schonwald was a Viennese Jew, a kind of cartoon of a man, short, round, dapper, and perfectly bald except for a cottony white puff around each of his small, shiny ears. He owned a clothing factory on Seventh Avenue and some apartment buildings in East New York, and everyone thought he was a millionaire. He loved to dress his wife and daughter in silks and pearls and send them off on lavish holidays to the Catskills or Atlantic City, even though, as it sometimes turned out, he scarcely had a nickel for himself to ride the subway to Coney Island and was stuffing pieces of cardboard into his worn-out, freshly polished shoes. In the Schonwald family appearance was everything. They lived in a brownstone near Prospect Park with a crystal chandelier in the dining room and a Venetian credenza in the living room, and a pair of huge ornate silver candlesticks, a family heirloom, which Mrs. Schonwald would light on Friday nights as a token of her ancestral religion. She was quite the "lady," that Hilda Schonwald. Molly said that when she died, God would have to refurnish heaven to make it posh enough for her. She was a skinny, shrill, attenuated woman with glossy black hair and idiotic pretensions. She believed in her heart that her daughter, her treasure, her only child, ought really to be married off to a Belmont, perhaps, or a Guggenheim, but for some obscure reason she appeared to take a liking to Sam. Perhaps she was captivated by the courtly southern mannerisms he had borrowed from General Sharpe and donned on occasion like a cloak over his rude Brooklyn habits. There in the soft immaculate sheen of the Schonwald living room, while he waited for Essie to "put on her face," he would sit with his legs neatly crossed and his head politely tilted, and Mrs. Schonwald would tell him all about some item she had plucked from the society pages of the *Times* or some famous hotel she had just "come away from," and he was clever enough to realize that all she expected from him was a nod and a smile. He never minded the nodding and smiling. He knew that Isaac Schonwald kept a Gentile woman in an apartment on Liberty Avenue and that helped him tolerate Hilda Schonwald's condescension. He didn't dislike the woman, he merely despised her; and he was too young to foresee how precisely in time daughters tend to replicate their mothers.

He courted Essie in the new up-to-date American way, escorting her to shows and "socials" and restaurants and ice cream parlors, and walking her home through Prospect Park beneath the gleam of an indulgent moon, stopping every so often to kiss and pet and fondle. On Sundays, in good weather, he liked to take her out rowing. They would glide round and round the glittering and caparisoned lake, and she would rest her pretty head in his flanneled lap, and he would toy with her silky, stylishly bobbed hair and spin for her the enticing web of his dreams and plans.

In those days he had their future all figured out. They would have lots of money and half a dozen children, and they would live together in a big old house somewhere near a beach—one of those gaudy Long Island castles is what he imagined, with turrets and towers and huge sun-speckled windows blinking out across gardens and blue lawns and clusters of shade trees—and they would lavishly entertain all their relatives and friends. In the evenings he would drive home to her in a big powder blue car and spend the last soft pink hours of the day romping with the children, who would have all the advantages he never had: fine clothes, expensive toys, a room for each of them, a college education, plenty of leisure time, and a loving, proud, sympathetic father to whom they could come crying with their nightmares and bruises. There was also somewhere in the picture a huge bed, a four-poster draped with acres of some glossy fabric the color of robin's eggs, and every night, between lovemaking and sleep, she would cuddle in his arms and he would recount for her the events of his day, which he foresaw mostly as a series of favors to his family and philanthropic services to the world at large. How wisely, how generously, he planned to use the power and leverage his envisaged wealth would bring him.

Those, anyway, were his dreams—the fictions of his heart—and he spun them for her because they excited her and made her breath quicken and her slender bosom heave, and because they usually ended in some sort of perfumed and intoxicating embrace; but one may suppose that in her presence, there on the lake, he half believed them himself. Wasn't the future an essentially vulnerable place, a kind of rickety treasure-house ready to swing open its fabulous doors to anyone who was strong and clever and energetic, to a man who was willful and basically good-hearted—and wasn't he all of these? Wasn't his success assured?

He never formally proposed to her. He contemplated and rejected as undignified the rotogravure image of the sappy suitor down on one knee thrusting a diamond ring toward his blushing girlfriend while the prospective in-laws peeked out from behind the curtain with happy smiles and glistening eyes. Besides, he couldn't afford the ring. He merely presumed they would be married, and brought her small presents—flowers, candy, lockets, trinkets, that sort of thing— and kept his pocket filled with nickels so that he could call her up on the telephone which the gadget-minded Schonwalds had recently installed. He hoped that if he took their marriage for granted, so might everyone else. Then one night an utterly dry-eyed Mrs. Schonwald said to him, as she concluded a long-winded anecdote about some cousin who had recently gone bankrupt:

"I suppose Essie will need a rich husband; we've spoiled her terribly, you know."

Sam touched the mustache he was still wearing in those days and felt the blood begin to throb above his ears.

"Oh, don't worry," he told her, as calmly as he could, "I plan to support Essie in style."

"My dear boy," smiled Mrs. Schonwald. "I'm certainly not going to worry. After all, you're both so young."

Love, or some approximation of love, or some inexplicable yearning that could be mistaken for love—whatever his feelings for Essie were, Sam took her mother's comment as a warning and a challenge and, freshly motivated, set to work with a kind of feverish intensity, expanding the shelves of chocolate, adorning the store window with fresh signs and ribbons, badgering salesmen for new items and extra discounts, experimenting with creams and fondants and nuts and fruits on the stove in Sophie's kitchen, seeking some magical concoction that would precipitate success.

But the numbers he set down onto the pale green pages of his ledger were never large enough to cover his obligations. There was a limit to how much business a small store in a shabby neighborhood could generate. His profits had risen satisfactorily during the months following his return, but now they were leveling off, while the demands of the family kept increasing. There were simply too many mouths to feed and bodies to clothe, too many eager hands held out for the pennies and nickels he dispensed so freely. He had become "the man of the house" (later Evelyn would say he was the only father she ever had), and there were times when he felt trapped and sullen and resentful. But it never occurred to him—it just wasn't in him—to escape that burden. If anything, he grew ever more devoted to the "babies," as he called them. He was charmed by Ruthie and Evelyn, who were noisy and cute and vivacious and, in their hand-me-down dresses, their hair done up by Sophie in identical clusterings of curls, looked almost like twins. He felt nothing but fond sympathy for Rose, with her glasses, her stuffed nose, her scraped knees and elbows. He even took a liking to Walter—the "brat"—who at the age of nine and ten was all ears and nose and precocious chatter.

In short, he lived in the family as a fish lives in water; the circle of them enclosed and defined and nourished his life; it was not for him, or his generation, to go beyond it.

If only he could open a larger store in a better neighborhood, he told himself, slide out from under the shabby nickel-and-dime remains of the old book business, and start selling his own brand of chocolates, first-class merchandise, luxuriously boxed. His obligations had outgrown the limits of the old store. He never doubted that he could take care of everything. Essie and the family all at once, if only he had room to expand. What he required was money and time, and money, after all, was merely a convenience he lacked. Money would come to him eventually, he was certain of that. It was time—time alone—that had become his enemy.

You see, in practical terms, his marriage to Essie had receded into the hopeful future; her mother had seen to that. Meanwhile, the damn snob kept dragging Essie off for a week or a weekend to those fancy hotels in the Catskills or Atlantic City, where college boys in boaters and blazers, the privileged sons of the wealthy, were waiting to steal her away from him. He was sure that Essie loved him, that so long as he was with her his hold on her was complete. But she was so easily confused and distracted, so eager to please, that if her mother told her to change her dress, Essie rushed to change her dress, and if her mother told her to smile at young So-and-so, Essie would no doubt smile and be nice. There had been incidents. Sam wouldn't talk about them at home, but the family could perceive in hazy outline the shadowy rivals who darkened the luminous world of Sam's romance. For weeks on end he would be moody and indrawn, all his furious attention focused on some vague and far-off struggle.

"Listen, there are plenty of pretty faces in America," Sophie once said to him, and he turned upon her with a rage he had never shown her before and told her to mind her own business.

First Molly, now Sam. In America, Sophie decided, this business of courtship and marriage was badly managed since it embittered the young people and turned them against their families. Love! What was this love they were always talking about? Wasn't love something that came, if you were lucky, after years of living together? She was frustrated. She wanted to help Sam, but she didn't know how. His problem existed beyond the periphery of her experience. When it came to dealing with people like the Schonwalds, she was ignorant of the rules. She knew only that they were hurting her Sam and making him unhappy, and she hated them for it. She had never even met them. When she tried to imagine them, she conjured up the caricatures of bloated, top-hatted capitalists she had seen in the socialist newspapers. Who were these people, after all, for whom her Sam wasn't "good enough"?

"A boy like Sam," she said to Asa Kalisher, "what more could they want?"

"Money," Asa Kalisher told her.

That renewed her old grudge against Jacob. Her bitterness and outrage had nowhere else to focus. Over the years, whatever the provocation, she had scrupulously avoided complaining about him to the children, but now, all of a sudden, she began to harp on the opportunities he had missed. It was during this time that the younger children heard about his days in the restaurant, and the pushcarts, and those weeks in the old country when Yussel Kalisher had tried to make a butcher out of him.

"He just didn't have the stomach for it," Sophie would say.

Sam believed that he understood his mother's mood, that voicing of her thwarted expectations. She seemed to be warning him, to be warning them all, about the traits of dreaminess and passivity and inaction they had inherited from their father, the old suffering and defeat that ran in their blood. His brooding, his sense that Essie was slipping beyond his control, his dull anger and hapless outrage— these were the legacies of his father, she seemed to say, and he was going to have to struggle against them.

Thus motivated, eager to assert his will, he concocted a scheme and went running with it to Asa Kalisher, the two of them—with the same red hair, the same green eyes—sitting and talking it over at the usual table one night while they drank coffee and nibbled at a platter of cheese Danish, which in those days was one of the restaurant's specialties.

It turned out to be a touchy conversation.

Asa Kalisher had conspired with Isaac Schonwald to bring Sam and Essie together, but he had not expected Sam to lose himself to the girl so thoroughly. He was probably disappointed that Sam had lost himself at all. As far as Asa Kalisher was concerned, women were essentially unreliable and frivolous creatures whose occasional company was necessary, alas, for hygienic reasons—he himself courted a sequence of blowsy widows and abandoned wives with all the bluff practicality of a man traipsing to a wholesaler to buy a suit of clothes —but with whom only a fool or a child would become permanently entangled. To be sure, he also had moments of sentiment; he cried at weddings, and ran to movies starring Lillian Gish, and made a great display of quartering the checks of obvious newlyweds who wandered into his restaurant; but though his misogyny had its limits, it was also ingrained and instinctive. Only Sophie, who reminded him of his mother, was wholly exempt from it.

So he might have turned Sam away that night after one of his patented little lectures on the stupidities of the heart, rejecting not the scheme but the desire for marriage that lay behind it, had Sophie not previously been working on him. It was her agony, not Sam's, that moved him. It was her image he saw when he finally held up his hand and said:

"Okay, I'll help you out. But it will be up to you to help all the others."

The scheme was to find a large store in a good neighborhood, with room in the back to set up machinery so that Sam could start producing his own brand of confections. Part of the money would come through selling off the store on Livonia Avenue, along with its slow-moving line of books and religious articles; Asa Kalisher would raise the rest by putting up the restaurant as collateral. It would be a partnership. Sam had already chosen a location, a site on Fulton Street, a former dry goods store, from which he would eventually build up the business—"Out of nothing, with his own two hands!"—until it occupied the factory on Bergen Street and the nine retail outlets in all the best shopping districts of Brooklyn. But that was years later. Now, to close the deal, he needed Jacob's signature, and as Sam should have anticipated, Jacob was reluctant.

In fact, he was practically impervious.

He was spending more and more of his time in the *shul* on Sterling Place, sometimes taking Walter along with him but usually going alone. They had even set up a cot for him in the basement storeroom so that he wouldn't have to walk all the way back to Park Place on Friday nights. There, beneath the sanctuary, feeling at home in the cold and the dark, he would sleep in his clothes amidst barrels of torn prayer books and the upturned legs of broken chairs.

The sickness in his lungs had left Jacob shrunken and almost senile. His eyes watered constantly; his back was bent; his nose and ears had grown gigantic. His hair lay in thin white patches on his scalp, as though a lifetime of wearing skullcaps and hats had rubbed him practically bald. The flesh of his face was sprinkled with bluish liver spots. Worst of all, as far as the family was concerned, his breath was foul. He seemed to exhale the stench of his lungs as they rotted in his chest. Three times a day, along with his ritual ablutions, he would gargle with salt and baking soda, as Dr. Lipsky had advised, which left his beard and lips flecked with white, though it scarcely alleviated the problem. He would shuffle around the house in an old, torn pair of slippers, with his ritual fringes hanging loose from his shirt, gasping and hacking and spitting into a handkerchief gobs of bloody mucus. On those occasions when he felt strong enough to "give a hand" at the store, he would just sit behind the counter on a stool or go peering down one of the few remaining bookshelves, seeking a volume for one of the old customers with all the irritating slowness of a man for whom time was no longer significant.

The younger children would remember him as "gentle" and "good-natured" and "old-fashioned"—a sort of pathetic and ruined old grandfather, smiling at them sweetly and sadly across a hazy space of years. He never scolded them or expected much from them; he was scarcely interested at all in their everyday bruises and squabbles and tears and triumphs. When he spoke to them in his hoarse Yiddish, which would trail off into a whisper as his meager breath ran out, they had trouble understanding him, and when he roused himself to give a command, they would glance at Sam or Sophie or Deborah for the surreptitious nod that meant they should obey. Most of the time they simply acted as though he weren't there. They probably thought his silence with Sam was a result of his illness, and they but dimly understood the agony and turmoil that Molly's carelessness and shenanigans were causing him.

Poor Jacob, poor displaced feverish man! He would sit for hours on a straight-backed chair at the front room window, staring out at the street and the park, and then, *kvetching*, would prop himself onto his feet with his cane and make his way ponderously to the toilet to relieve his bladder. During the last year of his life his teeth fell out and his mouth collapsed in upon itself. Sophie tried to get him to go to a dentist—false teeth, for her, were one of the emblems of America—but he wouldn't listen. He was as stubborn as ever. She had to prepare special foods for him, mashed vegetables, soups, bits of ground beef, tapioca puddings. He appeared to have outlived the need for sleep and spent whole nights sitting up in a chair, chomping his gums and muttering to himself. When he closed his eyes for a moment, he would tumble into a dream and start muttering to himself, holding long, indecipherable conversations with the creatures and ghosts that appeared to him. His hold on reality grew increasingly dim and unstable. He would alternate moody silence with outbursts of pointless chatter and then for an hour or two emerge from the bleak confusion of his thoughts and talk quite lucidly to Deborah and Walter, telling them stories about the old country, his childhood, his saintly mother, who had died during an influenza epidemic when Jacob was ten.

"Life is bitter," he would lecture them, "but the Law of Israel is forever sweet."

There was a time toward the end when Jacob seemed to improve. His appetite returned and a flush of color appeared in his cheeks. He experienced a sensation of peace and well-being unlike anything he had ever known before. His eyes cleared and the world became bright and fresh as if it had been newly created just for him. A kind of mist, which he had lived with so long he had forgotten it was there, finally dissipated. Colors were vivid, sounds were clear, his food tasted better, and he started eating with the appetite of a younger, more vigorous man. Even the voices that nagged him fell silent for a while. He told himself he had been tested, had struggled, and had won. When Dr. Lipsky came to call, Jacob said he was feeling fine, and the good doctor didn't have the heart to inform the family that euphoria was anticipated, that it was a sign of the progress of the patient's disease.

It was during this period that Sam had to convince his father to sell the store.

"What about the books?" Jacob kept saying. "What about the pioneers?"

There was no reasoning with him. Perhaps in the midst of his euphoria he believed he was going to regain his health and return to his merchandise; but most of all, he seemed to comprehend in his own slow, dim way that the wheel of authority between father and son had turned again, that finally—*finally!*—he had been given a sort of temporary leverage with Sam and he was stubbornly making the most of it. If nothing else, he could now make Sam listen.

So for weeks they haggled and bargained and talked it over. Patiently, knowing that only patience could get him what he desired, Sam would try to soothe his father and hold back the pressure of the rage that burgeoned within him. He knew that each passing day meant profits unearned, marriage money that he wasn't accumulating, Essie being sweet-talked by still another college boy in some wretched hotel garden beneath a seductive moon. Quietly, willfully. Sam mustered his arguments, the invincible logic of his case, but his father kept putting him off. He had a thousand quibbles and questions. Those chocolates Sam would make, would they be perfectly kosher, he would ask, no *trayf*, no filth mixed in? And on Fridays in winter would Sam close down early, not violate the *Shabbos*? What assurances could he offer, what guarantees? Especially when one is asked to sign papers with a man like Asa Kalisher, for whom there is no God, and thus no honor. Is such a man ever to be trusted? Is this the sort of man to whom one signs over a store, a life's work, the fruit of one's exertions and labors? Is this what the Almighty desires of us, that we should give up everything for a taste of chocolate in the mouth, a momentary pleasure? What was this but vanity and illusion?

"Don't rush headlong," he would say, stomping his walking stick. closing the conversation. "We have to think it over."

He knew—he must have known—that eventually he would sign those papers, that he had no choice, that he could put Sam off but he couldn't thwart him. "Let them be Americans," Sophie would say to him. "Isn't that why we came here?" He wasn't strong enough to hold out against them. But what did it mean to be an American? To throw off one's skullcap? To cut one's beard? To eat tainted food? The old world of righteousness was truly a narrow place. To step outside it, to break a single one of God's laws, was to enter into the confusion and torment of sin. Why, just that morning (this was a Friday, and he was on his way to *shul*) Molly, the wild one, had come to breakfast with a look about her, an air of frenzy and dissipation, that had torn at his heart. What had she been up to? What crimes had she already committed? What foulness lay in her future? And if his own children could come to this, what of their children, and their children after them? What new world of madness would they make?

As Jacob Lieber moved along Sterling Place, a dull dry wind blew sideways, scattering a trace of dusty snow into the gutters and around the edges of stoops, and cellarways. It was the sort of wintry day when both pavement and sky are equally gray and dark and ragged, and there is no obvious distinction between them. Each step Jacob took, jabbing with his walking stick, was little more than the length of his shoe. His derby was slanted down in front of his eyes, and the fur collar of his coat was raised to keep the chill off his neck. A drop of water clung trembling to his nose as he coughed up from inside himself a sickly-sweet mess and swallowed it down again. Each time he coughed a little spark of pain flared in his chest. He was not feeling fine anymore. He was feeling old and tired and sick and near to death. Tediously, with a kind of hectic slowness, he approached the *shul*. In the doorway he stopped and kissed his fingertips and touched them to the mezuzah before going inside.

"*Gut Shabbos! Gut Shabbos! Gut Shabbos!*"

He knew all the names and woes of the men whose hands he shook in the vestibule; he even considered some of them his friends; but he never participated in their small talk and gossip. Something about entering a synagogue, some sense of awe and longing, made him self-sufficient and alone. So he turned toward the sanctuary where a few men had already begun to *daven*, bobbing their heads and swaying their shoulders to the old mournful rhythms of Hebrew chant. As always, Rabbi Trauerlicht had taken up his position near the eastern wall, alongside the holy ark. In solitude and silence, completely hidden beneath his enormous *tallis*, isolated from this world, the rabbi bobbed and prayed.

Recently a terrible grief had come into the rabbi's life. Anshele, the eldest son, the heir, had initiated a quarrel with his father over some minor interpretations, a matter of the timing and wording of certain secondary prayers, and then had used their quarrel as an excuse to set up a rival congregation of his own. The *shul* had split along generational lines, the younger ones following the apostate to a new synagogue on St. Marks Place, a few blocks away, leaving the rabbi to minister to a congregation of old men. Jacob had never liked this Anshele. He was a tall, weedy fellow with a sparse blond beard and a glaze of pride and dishonesty in his eyes. Now this had to happen. But it was predictable. Ambition, the American sickness: they can't wait for their fathers to die. To make matters worse, Walter had used the incident as an excuse to withdraw himself from the *cheder*. He was still three years away from his *bar mitzvah,* but already a skeptic. Jacob sighed, feeling the pain thicken in his chest. The rabbi, too, was old and sickly. On *Shabbos* mornings, when he rose up out of his meditations to speak to them about the "portion," lecturing them in the harsh, eloquent, uncontaminated Yiddish of the old country, his hands trembled and his face was gouged with sorrow and weariness.

Jacob shuffled into his usual spot on a bench near the back of the sanctuary, found his *tallis* waiting for him, and put it on. He prayed, losing himself in the familiar words, ignoring the pain in his chest, mouthing the words automatically, and allowing his thoughts to wander. He remembered how when he was just five or six years old his father had brought him for the first time to the *cheder*, and how the *melamed* had dipped a spoon into a jar of honey and touched it to his tongue, blessing him and telling him never to forget that this sweetness was as nothing compared to the perfect sweetness of the Torah. The scene came back to him with wondrous clarity, the young teacher, lean and sharp as a stick—Halbfinger, that was it, he could even recall his name!—and the smoke of the wood stove, and the whitewashed walls, and the greasy smoldering smell of the lamps, and the sticky spoon, and his father lurking vaguely in the background, smiling over him. How safe and warm he used to feel there in the *cheder* on winter afternoons, while outside, snow fell silently over the village rooftops, softening and finally blurring out altogether the sad and hostile and inconsequential world. Now it was snowing here, too; he could see the heavy flakes drifting down past a window from which a pane was missing. The long years, time itself, had become nothing more than a momentary interlude between one snowfall and another.

When the service was over, Jacob lingered on the bench, waiting until the others had a chance to shake the rabbi's hand and wish him a good Sabbath. He wanted to talk to the rabbi, but he didn't have anything in particular to say. He closed his eyes trying to think of some question of Law that might initiate a conversation. Perhaps the rabbi might invite him into his study for a glass of *shnapps*. Then he could ask him about Sam and the store. But when he opened his eyes again, the rabbi was gone and the sanctuary was empty and dark. The only light came from the memorial candles near the back wall and the red glow of the perpetual flame that hung in front of the holy ark. He must have dozed off. How long had he slept? He tried to stand up; but his legs had gone numb, and he fell back against the hard bench, waiting for his toes to tingle with life. Suddenly he felt dizzy and broke into a sweat. He coughed, and the smoldering in his chest seemed on the verge of conflagration. He slid across the bench and looked out the window, letting the cold outside air blow across his face. Large cakes of snow were swirling through the night: a thick layer of snow lay upon the refuse in the alleyway; a distant streetlamp threw a sullen glow over the scene. He wouldn't be able to go home in such a blizzard; he would have to spend the night on the cot in the basement.

He felt damp and exhausted, and the pain was getting worse. He struggled to get himself up on his feet and moved through the sanctuary, poking in the darkness with his stick. Slowly, putting both feet together on each step, his chest vivid with agony, he moved down the staircase toward the basement. He was no more than halfway down when he thought he heard someone moving about in the sanctuary. Perhaps the rabbi had returned, as he sometimes did, to continue his meditations, or to sit at the long table studying a passage of Midrash. If only he could talk to him! He would know what he should do.

He turned and climbed back up the half a dozen steps, slowly, leaning heavily on his stick, gasping for breath. Inside the sanctuary he saw no one, but he was certain that someone was in there with him—he could sense it—so he waited, smelling the foulness of his breath as it caught in his beard and mustache. The memorial candles threw dull shadows all around him. His fingers were like ice when he touched them to his hot forehead. He heard a sound, and it seemed to him that a voice was calling his name.

"Here I am," he said.

The thick wheeze of his own voice startled him. For a moment he thought that a demon was teasing him, but he told himself that the evil ones wouldn't enter the sanctuary. Then perhaps it was a ghost. It was said—long ago his father had told him—that the souls of the unburied and unmourned came to *shul* at night to pray for eternal rest.

For some reason he remembered how, after his marriage, Sophie's family had tried to make a butcher out of him, and how the first time he had watched Yussel Kalisher slit open a cow's belly and pull from the carcass the long, shiny, bleeding ropes of the intestines, his heart had sickened and a shrill fierce ringing had started up in his ears. His ears rang now, too, echoing the anxiety of his memory—for a moment he felt slimy with blood and gore—and then the ringing stopped. He was stirred up, confused, frightened. The pain in his chest was getting worse, but that didn't matter so much now; it was far away from him, distanced by the murk of his fear. It was as though his soul had begun to come loose from his flesh, and he could contemplate with a kind of dispassion his body's aches and torments. He moved down the aisle toward the holy ark and the red glow of the perpetual flame, poking with his walking stick, sliding his feet carefully along the floor. Then he stumbled—or rather something seemed to catch his ankle, and he fell sideways, pulled down into the darkness, slamming the center of his chest hard against the corner of a bench. He couldn't breathe. He gasped, panicking, struggling for air. His nose filled with the dusty dead wood smell of the floor, and also something else, something old and coarse and masculine. Whatever it was, the thing that had called him, devil or demon or angel or ghost, it had hold of him. He still couldn't see it; there in the darkness he couldn't see anything, but he felt it tugging at him, sensed the roughness of its beard, the heaviness of its limbs as they pressed against him. Something within him, a kind of heavy sleepiness, wanted to relent and give in to it, let it have its way with him, but some other part of him continued to struggle, pulling and wrestling there on the floor, gasping for breath. He felt his loins begin to stir and swell, embarrassing him, as he kicked and shoved, pulled free of the thing that was crushing his chest, gasped, kicked and shoved and gasped some more.

He was sitting on the floor with his back pressed up against the edge of a bench. He had lost his hat and his stick in the darkness, and he touched the top of his head, feeling for his skullcap, but that was gone, too. Gasping, he took his clotted handkerchief from his pocket, spread it out on his lap and knotted the corners, fashioning a covering of sorts for his head, fumbling with the thing until he had it right. Then he realized that his chest no longer hurt; it was as though the pain had exploded, diffusing itself into the rest of his body, which felt numb and exhausted. He gasped, each breath a triumph now. His mind wandered in and out of dreams as he dozed and woke, dozed and woke again. The red glow of the perpetual flame swelled to fill the space around him. Somehow he was standing in front of the holy ark, wondering how he had gotten himself there, pushing aside the velvet curtains, touching with his fingertips the thick gold threads of the embroidered lions. He opened the doors of the ark. The silver crowns and breastplates of the Torahs blazed with a brilliant bluish light. He kissed his fingers and touched one of the breastplates, making the tiny silver bells tinkle. Vague shadows loomed around him, but he ignored them, intent on what he knew he had to do. He removed one of the Torahs from the ark—it was remarkably heavy—and lifted off the crown and breastplate, the velvet covering, and untied the silken cord that bound the two halves of the scroll. While he worked, he chanted prayers, his voice growing stronger and louder, filling the sanctuary, staving off whatever was lurking, waiting for him, there in the darkness. When he held the scroll aloft, spreading it, the words blazed out at him. Here, this was the world in which a Jew must live. Outside this world of holy words was nothing but torment and desolation and madness and eternal pain. Exultant, triumphant, he held the scroll high above his head. He could see the demons that had taunted and tortured him shrinking back into the shadows, avoiding the radiance the scroll cast. Eternity glared in the sanctuary. He took a step forward, his arms wavering under the weight of the thing, and then his legs dissolved from under him and he tumbled, falling and falling and falling, and he was not afraid even though he knew there was nothing under him to interrupt the endlessness of his fall.

THEY WOULD REMEMBER RABBI TRAUERLICHT praising their father at the funeral, embarrassing them with his extravagance, calling him a wise man, a *tzadik,* a world-preserving saint. They would remember tramping through snowdrifts at the cemetery to get to the grave site, where Molly became hysterical and would have thrown herself onto the coffin if Asa Kalisher hadn't caught her 'round the waist and dragged her away; and sitting for a week on hard wooden *shivah* benches to mourn their loss in the Orthodox manner, the household mirrors draped with sheets and towels, a memorial candle flickering in a glass above the fireplace; and Sophie's cousins taking over the kitchen to prepare platters of bagels and hard-boiled eggs for the neighbors and relatives who came by to pay their respects. They would remember how Sophie frightened them by keening and wailing and carrying on generally in the fashion of grief she had learned in the old country, her face ashen and her lips pale, refusing to eat anything until finally Dr. Lipsky warned her she was ruining her health; and how she kept telling everyone that she had been just half as old as Jacob Lieber when she married him, and now, having buried him, she was just twice as old as her firstborn son, as though the chance symmetry of the arithmetic were a measure of her loss.

All these things they remembered, and later their memories became anecdotes to tell.

They would tell about Hymie disappearing, and Sam going out to look for him, finding him hours later on Livonia Avenue, chilled to the bone; about Rose sitting in the dark with Ruthie and Evelyn and Moe, patiently describing for the little ones the glorious heaven to which their father had gone; about Deborah thinking she saw her father's ghost emerge from the bathroom and rushing to embrace him—proud, aloof, melancholy Deborah—and how it turned out to be Uncle Chaim, who with his beard and his derby and his long black coat looked remarkably like the Jacob Lieber of the early days.

They would laugh later on when they retold these stories, adding them to the stock of legend the Lieber grandchildren would absorb.

Of course, once the *shivah* benches were returned, the mirrors uncovered, the formidable cousins routed from the house, the family discovered that no matter how much the shock and sorrow of their loss might shadow their memories, it scarcely altered the daily routines. Even Sophie, once her initial grief was spent, found herself preoccupied just as before with the familiar hungers and crises and tantrums of her brood. And though she was reluctant to admit it, she knew—she must have known—that Jacob's death had relieved her of her greatest burden.

Nonetheless, she missed him. She missed him far more than she ever thought she would back in the days of his illness, when she couldn't help wondering what her life was going to be like after he was gone. She missed the aura of sanctity he brought into the house, the provocation of his complaints, and the restless weight of him shifting alongside her as she sought some never-to-be-found comfort in the bed they shared. She understood that his absence made her less patient with the noise and squabbles of her children—before he died, her dull, inexplicable, constantly simmering anger could somehow be blamed on him. She missed the sympathy he aroused in her, the occasional moments of fondness, and—why not say it?—the love. She was just forty-two years old, still plump and healthy, still vigorous despite her swollen legs and the softened and stretched flesh nine pregnancies had produced, but she had already sensed a whiff of her own mortality arising like an odor from Jacob's grave. They had ordered a double headstone; the plot of earth in which she would spend eternity was purchased and prepared; if there was an afterlife, Jacob was waiting for her to join him there, to be his eternal bride, his footstool in Paradise: these thoughts led her to rearrange her memories until she located in her tangled feelings a sort of glowing retrospective affection. She persuaded herself that their souls had indeed been bound together through the substantial ties of miseries shared and sufferings endured, that despite everything, their marriage had been a good one, that between them there was love.

"Two heads on the same pillow soon become the same head," she told her children.

She conjured up out of grief and fear and nostalgia and loneliness a new image of Jacob Lieber and convinced herself in the end that he had been all gentleness and patience and hard work and piety, a man who was worthy of the fullness of her mourning. The children tended to accept and absorb that image in inverse proportion to their age; Sam and Deborah and Molly knew better—they had their own clear memories against which they could measure Sophie's claims— but the younger ones grew up loving and honoring and commemorating Sophie's sentimental creation. She even reassessed for them the motives that had brought the family to America. She told them, and maybe even believed, that it had been Jacob's decision to uproot the family from the muddy limits of the old village in order to pursue his expectations; that it was Jacob who imagined America as a land of freedom and opportunity and safety and wealth; that it was Jacob who had struggled to make a new and better life for them all.

In this way the memory of Jacob Lieber became a mask for Sophie's will. She could stifle practically any argument with Evelyn or Ruthie or Moe by invoking the ghost of their father. "It would have pleased Papa," was all she had to say. It became the primary implement through which she manipulated her brood, and even Sam and Molly were not wholly immune to it. But you had to give her credit. She was a widow for twenty-five years, and though she was courted and had opportunities, she never remarried. Right to the end she was loyal to the myth she had concocted, to her own crude, sentimental, and necessary illusion.

THREE

DIE VILDEKEH, THE WILD ONE, that was Molly. Molly more than any of the others in those days brought chaos into the Lieber household. She was loud and she was brazen, and she knew all the new songs:

> My sister sells snow to the snowbirds
> My brother sells bootlegger gin
> My mother she takes in the washing
> My God! How the money rolls in.

She dressed like a flapper and did the Hucklebuck for the little ones, swinging them round and round the front room until they were breathless and dizzy. There was no living with her. The family couldn't decide which was worse, her ecstasies or her tears. Even before Jacob died, she was being courted by a man named Davey Furst, and though she was just fifteen years old—"Still a *pisher*," said Sophie—she had decided she was going to marry him.

This Davey Furst was a short, thick, bullish man who appeared to have been carved out of a chunk of knotty wood. He looked like a prizefighter and claimed he was an actor, but in those days he was making his living as a traveling salesman, selling camera equipment and darkroom supplies to small-town professional photographers up and down the eastern seaboard. To hear Molly tell it, he was always on the road, so you had to wonder how he found time to woo her, but woo her he did, with all the blunt and energetic and single-minded intensity of his nature. It was breathtaking to watch the man walk along a street; he would put his bull head down and swing his fists out in front of him and send opposing pedestrians scattering in every direction. He wouldn't step aside for anything or anyone, not even women; in fact, Molly's first sight of him came as she was sitting on the sidewalk of Kingston Avenue, a sack of groceries scattered around her, and he loomed over her, flexing his hard muscles, helping her to her feet.

"Sorry," he murmured in that strange soft voice he had, "I didn't see you."

She must have appeared to him, as she sat there, like some plump, overripe fruit waiting to be plucked. She had passed the initial brilliant bloom of her girlhood, and everything about her, skin, figure, tone, had subtly coarsened. For two years, ever since that thwarted afternoon in Levitch's apartment, she had been more or less making herself available to boys and men of several varieties, and she couldn't understand why none of them had been able to satisfy what she still thought of as her "curiosity." She had been kissed and stroked, pinched and handled, fondled and fumbled with, but always —always!—some compunction or fear or inexplicable shrinkage on the part of her would-be seducer had left her intact. It was as though some gauzy specter hovered between her and men, lending her a safety she didn't need, a protection she didn't want. She brooded in particular about a fellow named Blomberg, who confessed to her, as she lay supine and anticipant beneath the damp, haplessly heaving bulk of him, that something about her, some perfection of her innocence, terrified and unmanned him.

Naturally she had no theories about sex. The word itself was not even part of her vocabulary. What could she know, after all, this sheltered and scarcely educated child of greenhorns, about the newfangled cult of Freud or the passionate experiments the children of a different social class were conducting in Greenwich Village and Greenwich, Connecticut? One must suppose that she was merely a healthy and vigorous child with an intuitive sense of life's primary processes, and a sensual and slippery soul upon which the smirch of guilt simply wouldn't stick. It would be years before she felt any need to justify herself; in those days she had simply decided, without giving it much thought, that she was ready for anything, she wouldn't resist, and probably that readiness more than anything else had saved her, until she met Davey Furst, from the experience she believed she desired.

The family never liked Davey Furst. There was something sullen and congested and hostile in the way he sat in the front room, poised on the sofa, "dressed to kill," tapping his blunt fingers against his thick thigh. The way he abruptly grabbed Molly's elbow as he ushered her out of the apartment and down the stairs made it seem that he was stealing her away. His single-mindedness made him rude; his strength made him threatening. He gave off heat. You would not have been surprised to learn—though, in fact, he was an honest and diligent soul—that he consorted with gangsters and thugs. He immediately surpassed Uncle Yonkel on Hymie's list of people to avoid. Sam, who was closest to Molly, tried to warn her, telling her he wasn't the sort of man you could depend on or trust, but you couldn't talk sense to Molly—she did exactly as she pleased. At that time she had quit school and was working for Sam in the new store on Fulton Street, so she had her own money to spend. She made weekly trips to the beauty parlor, she painted her face, she decked herself out in beads and bangles and those outlandish dresses that had become all the rage, she took up smoking, and no matter what you said to her, she would tell you she was in love.

In retrospect it would occur to Molly that she loved Davey Furst more simply, more lucidly, than she would love any of her other husbands, with the possible exception of Max Gold. She loved Davey's toughness, his edge of belligerence, the way the flesh bunched up in reddish pockets beneath his hard eyes. She loved the pet names he whispered to her—"My sugar, my honey, my sweet"—when they were together in his apartment. Right from the start it was a joke between them that he couldn't remember her name. As far as he was concerned, she was "Milly," and after a while she no longer bothered to correct him. She was Milly on their first date and Milly on the night that he satisfied her curiosity and Milly all through the year after Jacob's death, as they waited for the period of mourning to end so their wedding could take place. She went on being Milly during the sixteen months when they lived in two rooms on Blake Avenue and Molly spent most of her evenings waiting for him to come home, and he even addressed her as Milly in that hasty letter which informed her he was going to Hollywood and would send her money to join him later. She waited nine months for the money to arrive, or even for another letter, and then sued for divorce on the grounds of abandonment. Later, when she finally stopped crying, she realized how very obscure the situation had been. Would he have sent her money if he had any? There was no way to know. She only knew that he would have been ashamed of his failure, and that it was years before he managed to find work as the villain's chief henchman in a series of cheap cowboy movies, in which (sound had come in by then) he never got to say very much more than "Yup" and "Nope," probably because to the end of his life his gentle tongue would be gnarled with overtones of Yiddish and Brooklyn. Years later she would point him out to her nieces and nephews as he went sprawling across a barroom table or rode away in a murk of dust down the inevitable wagon trail with the hero or the posse close behind.

"That son of a bitch never even knew my name," she would say, "and to tell you the truth, it didn't really matter."

All that mattered was that she loved him. The night that he satisfied her curiosity, as she squirmed and fluttered beneath him, punctured at last, impaled like an insect on a great rubied pin, she felt her mood, her childish solitude, opening up like a door. Behind that door there seemed to shimmer another, less lonely, more vivid kind of life, and though she wasn't prepared for it—her upbringing had taught her the rudimentary pride of self-sufficiency—she stepped on through, or perhaps the abandoned heaving of their shared flesh drove her through, and in a few moments her innocence, her solitude, that girlish perfection which a dozen different suitors had failed to damage had exploded, so to speak, and was gone forever.

The next day, by appalling coincidence, her father died. Her lips were swollen, and her cheek glared where Davey's rough chin had scraped against it, and she still felt all torn and damp inside; and it seemed to her that she had discovered the loss implicit in what she had gained. Her initial mourning was driven by the ferocity of a guilty conscience. She could see Hymie staring at her and read in his wide, dark, startled eyes the reproach of the entire family. Sitting through the funeral service and, later, walking along a path of trampled snow to the gruesomeness of the grave, she felt that her grief would be endless. There came upon her an eerie, hysterical moment when she believed that the only thing that could save her was to tear open her father's coffin and somehow with her tears and her regrets and the heat of her body bring him back to life. The next thing she knew they were dragging her back along the path of trampled snow, and she was struggling with them, and crying as if she would never stop. ("Some actress," Deborah later said.) But of course, she proved to be more resilient than she knew. She was no longer crying by the time they got home. She wasn't even feeling guilty anymore. She was merely ravenous, and stuffed herself with the eggs and bagels the cousins had prepared; but it turned out to be an emptiness which only Davey Furst could adequately fill.

During the year while she waited for her wedding, she worked for Sam in the new store, helping out behind the counter or operating the machinery that was set up in the back room, nibbling at the merchandise and putting on weight. Evenings she would spend with

94

Davey Furst—or at least those evenings when he wasn't on the road. They would go out dancing at one of the social clubs that were popular in Brooklyn in those days and then back to his apartment, or if they hadn't seen each other for a while, they would go directly to his apartment, and there, like the innocents they were, they would "play." That's what they called it. They played on the bed, on the floor, on the spring-jammed and tattered couch, on tables and chairs, in the bathtub, leaning against walls, or moving in strange muscular configurations around the room. They were very good at it, so good that Molly would be disappointed by all her subsequent lovers and husbands, even Max Gold. Davey Furst's sensual imagination seemed as inexhaustible as his substantial tool. Their only regret was that she possessed such a limited number of orifices and receptacles. A later generation, for all its treatises and theoretical manipulations, would fail to find the locks and keys of pleasure that Molly and Davey discovered on their own, and each spurt and spasm added to a reservoir of remembered bliss which, later in her agonized life, Molly could draw upon for comfort and release. So charmed, so magical, was their lovemaking that it scarcely occurred to either of them to wonder, as the months went by, why she didn't become pregnant.

There were, however, other complications. He would deliver her to the doorstep at all hours and she would enter the apartment, reeking and sore and satiated, to find Sophie waiting up for her.

"What time is it?" Sophie would call from the bedroom, as if she didn't have the old alarm clock in front of her.

"Late," Molly would say.

Thus the rebuke was delivered and acknowledged, each of them pretending that Molly's transgression was merely chronological.

Sophie, nonetheless, ate her heart out. She knew—her maternal sense told her with precision—what was going on; but she cautioned herself that it was better to feign ignorance than expose a scandal in the house. In a sense, only the sheer blatancy of the fact, the way Molly seemed to fling her lewdness before the eyes of the world, her crucial lack of shame, made that year bearable for Sophie. She consoled herself with the odd notion that maybe here in America such carryings-on were expected. How could she know, after all, with only Deborah to judge by (poor, plain, pensive Deborah, whose response to Jacob's death was a quiet melancholy that lingered for months), that all lively modern American girls weren't doing the same? New customs for a new land. The promise of heaven made manifest in flesh. And perhaps she also understood that of all her children, Molly was in some ways most like herself. Maybe—who can pretend to understand such things?—maybe she even derived from Molly's freedom a mute vicarious satisfaction. Anyway, she said nothing, not to Molly, and not even to Sam, to whom she now confided almost everything else. So long as it should end in a wedding, she reasoned, then God would forgive them. Thus, though she was forced to disapprove in public of Molly's marriage, wailing to her cousins that the girl was still so young, complaining that it was only proper that Deborah should marry first, though she was cool and distant through the ceremony and the feast, saying to Uncle Chaim, "Thank God my Jacob didn't live to see this!" privately she felt relieved, even a little elated. The mess had finally been deposited into a suitable container. To have consorted like that and then not to have married would have been much worse.

So in Sophie's eyes, and thus in the eyes of the family, Molly's marriage redeemed and canceled her egregious past. She had been wild, she had been sluttish, she had tormented Jacob and overstimulated Hymie and embarrassed Sam and tore at Sophie's heart, but she was a married woman now—she had entered the Promised Land—and thus was removed from the harsher realm of maidenly expectations. Her shenanigans would continue to amaze them, but somehow they no longer belonged to quite the same category of shame and grief. From now on, whatever her antics, Molly would be tolerable.

"Molly, Molly," Sophie used to say, "Molly should be the worst of my heartaches."

HYMIE WAS GOING from bad to worse. Jacob's death had given a shock to his fragile system, and now, inexorably, it started shaking itself to pieces. He put on weight. He complained of stomach cramps and ringing in his ears. His skin erupted violently, and sores on his face oozed and bled. For days on end you couldn't get a word out of him, and then he would burst out in a babble of pointless chatter. He had stopped going to school—they had called Sophie in and told her they couldn't "do anything more" for him—but when Sam suggested that he come to the store to help out, he ran and sat in the closet. He spent most of his time in the house sitting by a window or hunched in front of the artificial fire or dogging after Sophie like a three-year old as she went about her daily chores. To keep him occupied, she gave him simple tasks to perform in the kitchen, peeling potatoes or slicing apples for a pie, but he lost track of what he was supposed to be doing, and she would find him staring at the knife or scrubbing the same apple over and over again at the kitchen sink. Occasionally she made him go downstairs ("Go, Hymeleh, get a *bissel* fresh air!") and he would obediently shamble across the street to the park and sit himself down on a bench among the old men. Sophie probably didn't know that Sam had told him to keep out of the playground. Though he liked the swings and slides, he frightened the little children, and the neighbors had complained.

He passed through phases of self-torment, each stranger than the last. He became obsessed with what he called "blood and filth" and cried if he cut his finger. He would take all his clothes out of his dresser and dump them into the laundry basket so that "Mama can make them clean again." He thought that people were putting dirt into his food and would sit at the dinner table refusing to eat, or eat nothing but bread, or examine and reexamine every morsel on his plate before putting it into his mouth. He began washing his penis every time he urinated. He was forever constipated, and Sophie had to give him prune juice and laxatives. He took endless baths.

"Hymie," Sam would shout through the bathroom door, "I've got to shave. What's taking so long?"

"I'm cleaning my business," he would say.

He was also fascinated by keys. He roamed around the house with a strange, serious expression on his face, his tongue working in his cheek as it did when he was busy, locking and unlocking doors and closets. His old oak dresser had keys for its drawers, and he spent hours playing with them. He would hide something in the top drawer, lock it, hide the key from the top drawer in the second drawer and then lock it, hide that key in the third drawer and so on, until he was left with the final key, which he would sit holding in his fist, staring, befuddled, as though he couldn't quite imagine what it was for.

Sometimes he disappeared. They never knew where he went—he had his own secret hiding places in the neighborhood's cellars and alleyways—and he might be gone for hours before showing up again with a shy, half-guilty smile spreading slowly across his round moon face.

There was the time that he ran out to the street without any clothes on. There was the time he threw a stone at Davey Furst and broke Mr. Neuman's window. There was the time he jabbed a knife into the socket (because he wanted to "kill the electricity") and plunged the whole building into darkness. There was his imaginary enemy, "McKee," who, he said, was always teasing him. He got worse and worse, and the family just didn't know how to handle him. They pretended to each other that he was merely "strange" and "shy" and that someday he would outgrow his problems, but the only one who still believed that was Rose. She could talk to him. When something spooked him and he ran to the closet, she was the one who could coax him out. How pathetic it was to watch them play "house" together: she was the mama and he was the baby and she would put her arms around him and rock him gently as he lay there—sixteen years old, nearly two hundred pounds—with his head on her lap, pretending to sleep.

Nonetheless, Sophie refused to give up hope. "Spend a little time with the boy," she would say to Sam. "He needs someone to look up to."

Sam tried. He would later say he did everything he could for Hymie, had been better than a father to him. He took him to ball games; he bought him new clothes; he made it a point when he came into the house to tousle Hymie's hair and slap him on the arm and say, "How's the kid?" He gave him a wristwatch, a pocket compass, a fountain pen, and an old pinkie ring. He even let him tag along on Sunday afternoons when he took Essie to the park. But it was an aggravating business trying to deal with the boy. One day he decided to take Hymie to Manhattan. He thought they could see a movie, grab a bite to eat at a restaurant, and just talk things over, brother to brother, man to man; but the ride on the subway, with Hymie tense and pale and picking at his scabs, unnerved them both, and when they came up out of the station into the bustle and dazzle of Times Square, the boy panicked. Terrified, whimpering, attracting all sorts of attention, he clutched and clawed at Sam's arm, his eyes rolling around at the looming and emblazoned buildings as though he were sure that at any moment they were going to topple down and crush him.

"I'm through with him," Sam told Sophie when he got home that night, "I just don't have the time or the patience to deal with his *mishegoss.*"

In those days Dr. Lipsky was spending more and more of his late-afternoon hours in the Lieber kitchen. After he had closed up his office, he would come upstairs and sit there with Sophie drinking tea from a glass and nibbling egg cookies. His excuse was that he was checking up on the children; there was always someone down with a cold or a sore throat or some mysterious childhood fever, and in an era without antibiotics, when the heartbreaking sight of small coffins was a commonplace, one couldn't be too careful. Nonetheless, those visits became a family joke.

"Moe's nose is running," Walter would announce at the supper table, "better call the doctor," and everyone would laugh and giggle until the blushing Sophie said: "Sha! Sha!"

The fact was, she had taken a liking to the man. He was big and loud and exuberant—he reminded her of Asa Kalisher—and something about him, the booming of his voice, his easy air of authority, made her feel girlish again. How her cheeks would burn and her heart flutter as they sat there in the kitchen, not daring to look at each other, talking about everything but what was really on their minds. At night she would go to bed feeling taut and restless, and in the morning she would wake up aching, exhausted, having spent the hours of darkness in the embrace of a hectic dream. But it was too soon for wooing, too close to Jacob's death, and since they were old-fashioned people, they had to keep on pretending that the visits were professional. It was Hymie who gave substance to the pretense. They found themselves talking about him more and more until he finally became Dr. Lipsky's "special case."

That good, gruff doctor, who at the age of forty was as stout and dignified and antiquated as a cathedral, had been trained in the old school of medicine. He believed in enemas and gargles, darkened rooms and lots of blankets. Words like "will" and "character" and "dignity" came easily to his lips, and it was typical of him to administer, along with the usual aspirin and laxatives, a stiff dose of homily. He carried in his bag of tricks a fierce bedside manner ("He scared us into getting better," Moe would later say of him), but he also prided himself on being "up-to-date" and "modern." He dabbled in Freud. He had acquired over his old core of propriety a veneer of H. L. Mencken. He was convinced that most of the world's miseries were caused by the "damn Puritans," and he had carried his bachelorhood and his migraine headaches into the best whorehouses in Brooklyn. American-born himself, he clucked his tongue over the superstitions of the immigrant rabble around him. Behind Hymie's symptoms he saw the ghost of Jacob Lieber and all that fool man's unearthly morality. Thus, as far as he was concerned, the case was not only scientifically interesting, but also culturally significant: the cure, when it came, would be a triumph for the new.

But it was a frustrating business. Two or three times a week he would take Hymie into the front room and close the sliding doors and sit the boy down to talk things over, but he couldn't coax out of him anything much about his dreams or desires or fears. Even when the boy was in the mood for conversation, which wasn't often, he would insist on telling the doctor how he had broken his wristwatch, or how he loved to eat candy, or how many pennies he kept in a jar, or how filthy were some monkeys he had seen at the zoo.

"Hymie, Hymie, Hymie," the exasperated doctor would scold him, "you're seventeen years old. It's time to put away these childish things and become a man."

Eventually Hymie took to lurking by the front door and running to the closet when he heard Dr. Lipsky's heavy footsteps coming up the stairs. It might have been comical if it weren't so sad, the doctor pulling up a chair and settling by the closet door, Hymie muttering to himself, and Rose peeking in at them with eyes that were all hurt and worry behind her thick glasses.

Dr. Lipsky had read and reread a couple of textbooks on psychological abnormalities and disorders and had learned from his reading that adolescent boys were peculiarly susceptible to the illness known as schizophrenia. Why this should be so apparently confused the serious practitioners in the field, but it didn't confuse Dr. Lipsky. He recalled his own furtive and guilty adolescence, his stern father, the hot misery of self-inflicted spasms, and the sense of release he had felt in the bed of his first prostitute. It was so simple, really. In adolescent boys the primitive drum of sexual desire beats haplessly against some imposed moral shame. Hymie's symptoms—the sitting in closets, the obsession with filth, the listlessness, the bouts of babble, the inverted silences, the fright that filled the boy's dark eyes—were the result of the thwarting of his natural energies. Thus the cure would have to come in the form of a catharsis, a kind of psychic purge, gently and carefully administered. There was a jam-up in the boy's psychic plumbing, and Dr. Lipsky took it upon himself to unplug it. He decided to show the boy that there was nothing to be feared in that simple and slightly ridiculous act that had created the world.

He waited until spring. That was the year Molly was living with Davey Furst in the apartment on Blake Avenue, and Deborah was being courted by Buster Stern, and Sam was enjoying his first real taste of success in the store on Fulton Street. It was a glorious season. The park across the street had exploded with greenery in March and by April was flushed with flowers and birdsong. In the evenings it rained and then the morning sun would burn away the dampness, leaving the streets of Brooklyn fresh and clean. On Easter Sunday Sam took the whole family up to Fifth Avenue to watch the *goyim* parade their finery, and something about that day—some gorgeous interplay of breeze and sunshine, of people and clothes and sparkling cars—stirred up expectations. For weeks the simple hopefulness of the occasion lingered in their memories. It flickered in the candles and gleamed in the goblets of wine that Sophie set out upon the *seder* table. It encouraged Sam to start talking about setting a new wedding date. Even Hymie seemed to respond to it. His sores and pimples began to heal, and he let Deborah take him down to the store where he asked Sam some intelligent questions about the machinery. He also stopped running to the closet when Dr. Lipsky showed up. Once more they sat together in the front room, talking things over, and Dr. Lipsky thought he was making some progress. In fact, he told Sophie, they were making so much progress that he wanted to take Hymie out and spend an evening with him.

"I'll show him a good time," he told Sophie. "We'll paint the town red."

He winked and he leered, he grimaced and guffawed, but he couldn't quite bring himself to tell her his plan. He was sure that if he told her, she would feel compelled to oppose him—her old-world morality would get in the way. But he probably believed that she had already guessed, and anyway, punctilious about seeking some sort of permission for the adventure, he had earlier talked it over with Sam.

"Why not?" Sam shrugged. "What do we have to lose?"

Years later the grandchildren would hear that Dr. Lipsky tried to cure Hymie by taking him to a whorehouse. That was all they would hear because that's all the family knew. No one ever asked the doctor for details, and the doctor never volunteered any. The grandchildren would imagine some hackneyed smoke-filled parlor and half-naked girls and a honky-tonk pianist flashing lewd white teeth. They would imagine this uncle that they never met, still a boy, with all the Lieber attributes—nose and fat and strangeness—carried to an extreme, abuzz with anxiety and excitement as he entered the place, panicking (did he cry, run, hit?) as some hard-faced girl settled back upon the bed and revealed her damp secret for him. But all they would know for sure was that the experiment was not a success. They had no way of knowing that the place was one of Dr. Lipsky's favorite haunts; that more than anything else it resembled a nice, quiet, old-fashioned hotel with lace curtains on the windows and pretty lamps and young girls sitting around in a foyer that was vaguely clinical; that the three of them, Hymie, the doctor, and the girl the doctor had picked out, sat for a long time, talking things over, making the boy feel comfortable; that when the girl finally took Hymie's hand and led him toward the staircase, Hymie's face lit up like a light bulb; that right to the end of his life the doctor would believe he had done the correct thing, that it could have worked—but how was he to know that before Hymie got halfway up the stairs, he would bump into that damn brother-in-law of his, Davey Furst, still tugging at his zipper as he galumphed down?

Hymie returned to the closet. They could look through the half-open door and see him sitting there with his arms wrapped around his knees, his knees pulled up to his chin, his eyes staring off into the mystery of the comfort he sought. Some trick of light made it seem that a faint violet halo had gathered around his big pocked and pitted moon face. It was as though he had wandered thoughtlessly over some unmarked border and now, in a space all his own, was irrevocably lost. He sat like that for three days, sitting in his own wet and filth and stench, and not even Rose could get a word out of him. Every few hours Dr. Lipsky would come up to the apartment and talk to him, trying to coax him out, but there was nothing he could do. Finally, exasperated, all his hopes dashed, he grabbed hold of his arm and tried to pull him out of there by force.

"Hymie," he shouted, his voice booming through the hushed and stricken household, "enough of this monkey business! Don't you realize how you're hurting your mother!"

In the end the doctor talked it over with Sam, and Sam had to take upon himself the miserable chore of convincing Sophie that something had to be "done." He would never forget how he got the papers from Dr. Lipsky and made his mother sign them, how she printed her name in the blockish and childish letters that were all the English writing she ever learned, too gloomy and exhausted to cry, and how the next morning, after a brutal and sleepless night, Dr. Lipsky showed up with two Irishmen, who entered the house like a couple of burglars with political connections, boisterously talking to each other about the job at hand.

"We'll get him under the arms," they kept saying, "but if he starts to kick we'll have to jacket him."

Sophie had ushered the smaller children into the front room and left them there with the sliding doors closed and Deborah to watch over them. She didn't want them to see—bad enough that she and Sam would have to—their brother being carried from the house. Bad enough that the two of them would have to live with the pain and disgrace of it—Hymie hoisted between those *shkutzim* like a piece of furniture. Had he struggled, had he glanced at her, had there been just a single moment when he looked at her with a glimmer of reproach, she would have tried to stop them, would have grabbed her baby out of their arms. But there was no such moment. They carried him out, and he let himself be carried, as bewildered and trusting as a child roused from sleep.

"Now don't imagine anything horrible," Dr. Lipsky said. "It's really modern and nice out there. They have grass and trees—why, there's even a little lake. And if the treatment succeeds, he can be home in a month or two."

She wanted to believe him. Certainly she tried hard not to disbelieve him. He was their doctor, and she trusted him, worshiped him even, as doctors are always worshiped by the uneducated. But as she watched him following Hymie down the stairs, as she stood at the front window—the children now having been shooed to the back of the house—and watched them lift Hymie in and close the ambulance door, as she felt Sam's arm tighten around her and let herself cry a little bit on Sam's shoulder so that at least he could have the relief of being able to comfort her, she knew that her loss was twofold: she had lost the boy and she had lost Dr. Lipsky, too. Not as a doctor—he would go on treating the family; he might even go on visiting her and sharing a pot of tea—but never, now, never, never, could she allow herself the luxury of thinking she could marry him.

BETWEEN DEBORAH AND MOLLY there was always a quarrel going on. They needled and tormented each other as only two sisters of opposite temperaments can. Deborah couldn't forgive Molly for the noise and mess and crudeness she brought into the house, and Molly wouldn't forgive Deborah for refusing to come to her wedding. It was, Deborah insisted, not just a matter of the tradition that the oldest sister should marry first; it was that she had "sensed"—don't ask how—that this union with Davey Furst was doomed to a bad end, and she intended to have no part in it. Besides she was still peeved at the way Molly had carried on at their father's funeral, at the hysteria, the scene-stealing, the sheer tumult of it. Deborah herself had been subdued and mild in her grief, and for months afterward had drifted around the house like a sibyl in a black dress, with a strange, satisfied look on her face as though she had been waiting all her life to go into mourning.

Tall and lean, with beautiful long dark hair and more of the Old World accent than any of the other Lieber children, Deborah was a bit of a mystery as far as the family was concerned, and also a bit of a problem. She lived in a world all her own, rich in lore and poor in experience. In business she had proved herself practical and reliable —almost single-handedly she had kept the old store going while Sam was in the army—but as soon as she stepped out from behind the counter or the cash register, she floated off into the clouds. Her favorite hangout was the library. She spent most of her girlhood reading her way along shelves of popular romantic fictions and then ascended to more exotic stuff: gothics, ghost stories, manuals of magic, alchemies, Oriental esoterica, tattered old mythologies of every kind. She received in the mail the publications of half a dozen mystical and spiritual societies. She rambled on about matters the rest of the family couldn't begin to comprehend, using words like "divine" and "rood" and "anima." So when she announced one day that she had met a man, the whole family became taut with expectation.

His name was Ruben Stern, but for obscure reasons—perhaps it was some sort of joke—the family always called him Buster. He came to the house wearing a straw boater, a striped jacket, flannel pants, and spats, and when he smiled, his teeth were white and straight and perfect. He had a high forehead and a nose like Ramon Novarro's, and he spoke in a crisp flat English that sounded affected, at least to Lieber ears. Sophie took one look at him and decided he couldn't be Jewish. She went to the kitchen and grumbled to herself while Deborah entertained him in the coolness of the front room.

"A Jewish boy doesn't look like that," she told Sam later, "with the hair slicked down flat and such a pretty face."

"Well, he looks like he stepped out of a storybook," Sam reassured her, "but he's Jewish all right. I asked him."

Anyway, he was good for Deborah. He courted her chastely, modestly, taking her to museums and concerts and "literary" coffeehouses, where gentle poets with doomed eyes provided local color. Then they would come back to Park Place and sit on the stoop in the cool of a summer evening beneath the generous silver pepper of the stars, holding hands and whispering and looking at each other so fiercely you would have thought they were trying to peer into each other's souls. They talked about the books they had read, the dreams they had dreamed, and the oddly coincident premonitions they had experienced as children. They were, they believed, created for each other. Their minds were attuned to the same gentle delirium. They both believed in the magic of numbers, the benevolence of the universe, and the immortality of love. They both had been born under the sign of the water carrier. They both relished the sensation of some unknown and lovely snatch of melody lingering in their thoughts. It was more than love even: there in his presence Deborah's spirit, so long contained, seemed to brim full and tip itself over. Night after night, as she lay in bed thinking about him, her face would be wet with sweet, happy, luxurious tears.

He introduced her to the opera. They sat in the balcony of the Met, in "obstructed seats," which were all he could afford, and she was mesmerized by the music, the lights, the gigantic chandeliers, the gilt, the gowns, the reflected brilliance of the wealthy patrons below. Here she felt relieved of the burden of having to protect herself from the grimy coarseness of her everyday life. The strains of an aria would soar to a climax and the pressure of his fingers on hers would tighten gently and she would turn her head to him, their eyes catching in shared enjoyment. They didn't have to say anything. Their thoughts moved freely, perhaps even telepathically, along the ties that bound them. It was the same in museums. They would stand together in front of some picture they both admired—Watteau's moonstruck "Mezzetin," for example, or Cot's "Storm"—and their swooning souls would merge together, melting, as it were, in the transcendent glow of some Old Master's achievement.

There was something so harmonious, so airy in their romance that they seemed only tenuously tied to the demands and limits of earth and their own imperative flesh. Deborah would keep forever the sweet memory of their parting kisses, in which their lips barely touched and she could sense the subtlest, most velvety hint of his breath and tongue. A droplet of moisture, all sacred honey, would be deposited, and then he would walk around the corner to catch the bus on Kingston Avenue, leaving behind a shadow of himself, an essence she had absorbed.

Love changed her, at least in superficial ways. She took more trouble with her appearance because she thought that would please him. She became more stylish, though not in Molly's garish way. She affected a cloche hat and painted her mouth into the bright red heart shape that was fashionable in those days and rubbed circles of rouge into the hollows of her powdered cheeks. She bought new dresses in subtle shades of mauve and lavender, with matching shoes, and wore constantly around her neck the pretty gold chain with the sapphire pendant he had given her. Her bliss, her glow of contentment, spread through the household. All she had to do was walk into the room and she invoked serenity; in her presence even Ruthie and Evelyn momentarily ceased their squabbles. During the gloomy days and weeks after Hymie was "sent away," Deborah brought a measure of happiness into the Lieber household.

Then one night she didn't come home. They had gone to the opera to see a performance of *The Magic Flute,* and then for a "bite" in a restaurant near Central Park. As fate would have it (to borrow an expression Deborah might have used), the moon was in eclipse that night, and when they left the restaurant, they wandered into the park, away from the glare of the streetlamps, to get a good look at it. It rode above the treetops huge and rubied like the great clear eye of some benevolent and philosophical deity. Buster spread a handkerchief for her, and they sat down upon the grass amidst small blue wild flowers and murmurous insects. Deborah felt that if she reached out her hand, she might touch the shadowed moon and that the feel of it on her fingertips would be soft and warm and yielding, like the feel of her lover's lips; so she touched his lips instead, and when they opened in a smile, the moment was complete. He took her, or rather they took each other, gently, quietly, without haste or violence, and afterward there was no sense of shame or sin: they felt married. The living universe itself had witnessed and blessed their union, and it was only for the sake of the family that they agreed to go through with the more meager ceremony of a Brooklyn wedding.

The family was delighted indeed to turn its thoughts and its conversation toward that joyous event. What a stir of sewing and fitting there was in the house, what plans they made! They foresaw Rose and Ruthie and Evelyn coming down the aisle, spreading flower petals from baskets, and Moe carrying the wedding ring on a velvet pillow. Buster didn't have much family, just an old ailing mother, to whom he was devoted, and a couple of old-maid aunts, but the Liebers could provide a crowd of their own. The hall was hired, the music arranged, the flowers ordered, the wedding gown bought.

And then he died.

The cause of his death didn't matter. Years later, recalling it for the inquisitive Lieber grandchildren, the family would even argue about it.

"Influenza," Ruthie would say.

"No, no," Evelyn would tell her, "it was scarlet fever."

"A lot you know," Molly would shout at them. "You were both babies then. It happened to have been his heart. The man had a weak constitution."

In the memory of the family Buster Stern died a dozen different deaths, each more improbable, more pathetic than the next.

But it didn't matter. All that mattered was that a couple of weeks before the wedding Buster Stern was dead and Deborah was desolated.

Her mourning was brief and terrible. She acquired a *shivah* bench and put it in the back bedroom and for seven days she sat there alone, the vanity mirror cloaked in a towel, her hair in disarray and her black dress—the one she had worn to her father's funeral—ripped down the sleeve. She didn't cry. For seven days she just sat, staring at nothing, making occasional small whimpering noises down deep in her throat, her eyes fixed on some point in time or space that had no dimensions whatsoever. She never left the room except to go to the toilet. She shook her head pathetically when anyone tried to offer words of condolence. Sophie brought meals into her on a tray, and she let them stand until they were cold, then nibbled a bite or two, sighing to herself as she swallowed. There was no comforting her. She wouldn't talk about it. She was transfixed, caught in the dreadful fullness of her mourning.

On the eighth day she was still sitting. Sam went in to tell her that the *shivah* week was over, that she had to get up and go on with her life, but he came out shrugging his shoulders and lifting his palms. Sophie fretted. Deborah's silence, her isolation, her rigidity were too vivid a reminder of Hymie sitting in the closet or of Jacob that time when he burned his hand and sat for days, doing nothing, with his arm in a sling. The taint of Lieber strangeness, the legacy of her mad father-in-law, seemed about to appear again. In the bleakness of her fantasies she could see her children succumbing, one by one, to the darkness of their most secret desires. She envisioned Dr. Lipsky's men, with their loud voices and their muscular arms, appearing again to carry them off, one by one, to that awful hospital with its skimpy fringe of trees and its muddy little pond—that place which in her own personal geography, the map of her mind, existed (though Sam took her out there every other weekend) in a separate, remote, disconnected world.

That evening she went into the bedroom and took the towel off the mirror. She was frightened when Deborah did not look at her and even more frightened when she looked at Deborah's reflection in the beveled and patchy glass and thought she saw a pale blue glow of light like a halo around Deborah's forehead. She turned to her daughter.

"Deborah," she said. "Now you must get up."

Deborah made no response.

Sophie took three steps across the room, peered for a moment into the emptiness of her daughter's eyes, muttered to herself, "God in heaven, not again!"

Then she hit Deborah on the jaw with a closed fist, the way a man might hit another man.

The blow knocked Deborah off the *shivah* bench onto the floor. There was a moment, a single terrible moment, when Deborah contracted into a little lost fetal bundle, a moment that Walter, who was standing in the doorway (twelve years old at the time, sharp as a tack, always putting his two cents in), would never forget. Deborah lay there while a kind of shimmering series of muscular contractions swept through her body, and then life and shame and fury raged back into her.

She rose up, her face red and contorted, and started yelling so loud the neighbors could hear her.

"Don't you ever put a hand on me! Don't you ever touch me again!"

And then she began to cry, a storm of hot tears; Sophie put her arms around her, and she cried and cried, released from the final madness of her expectations.

"We learned right then and there," Walter said later, "that no matter what happened, whatever the circumstances, *we* weren't going to be allowed to go crazy."

* * *

SAM'S FIRST SUCCESS was a chocolate-covered cherry clad in gold foil with the sugared stem of the fruit sticking out at the top. Lots of candymakers were producing chocolate-covered cherries in those days, but Sam was the only one who had developed a technique for leaving on the stem. It was an expensive touch of verisimilitude, but it was worth it. That stem, rising out of the gold foil, held between the thumb and forefinger as you unwrapped the thing, gave you the impression that you were enjoying a cherry that happened to be covered with chocolate rather than a mere shell of chocolate that happened to hold a cherry inside. You could almost imagine that cherries grew that way on the trees of paradise.

Next he came up with an idea for "chocolate *matzoh*." Or maybe Solly Poverman came up with the idea—later they would argue about whose idea it was. Anyway, Solly Poverman had just gone to work for Sam in those days and Sam was already selling a thin, flat slab of bittersweet chocolate with chopped almonds and pistachio nuts rolled into it. All he had to do to produce "chocolate *matzoh*" was to stamp the stuff with Jewish stars and merchandise it in the weeks before Passover. It was a great success, especially during those early years before the other chocolate companies began to imitate it. It would have brought in more money than the chocolate-covered cherries except that the appeal of it was seasonal; still, it kept the machinery running during those late winter months when cherries were rare.

The rest, the slow broken rhythm and accumulation of success, the fancy nut clusters, the candied fruits, the lemon slices, the marvelous butter crunch, is familiar enough. Imagine an old-fashioned montage in an old-fashioned movie: cash registers jingling and clattering; Sam and Molly and Deborah in white aprons and white paper hats; a succession of storefronts, each larger and gaudier than the last; some complicated machinery tumbling sweets and candies into boxes made out of shiny apple-green paper; a close-up of the gold-embossed lettering proclaiming in fancy script: "Lieber's Confections and Novelties/Our Chocolate Is Divine"; Sam and Asa Kalisher haggling over a set of books; Sam and Solly Poverman making a trip to the bank; and a long, lingering view of the factory on Bergen Street in early morning with a couple of old-fashioned trucks rolling up to the delivery gate to unload their crates and barrels and sacks. Imagine Sam handing out paychecks, imagine spools of gold ribbon, imagine great vats of warm rich nougat, and everybody growing up, while the pages of a calendar blow and riffle and fly away in some magical Hollywood wind.

In retrospect it would sometimes seem just that way—and not only to the nieces and nephews, who were nurtured on the established fact that Sam was the "rich uncle" of the family, nor to the Lieber brothers and sisters, who were old enough to watch the process of building the business unfold itself day by day in the nervous tedium of real time, but even to Sam himself. Looking back, he could believe that success had come to him more or less instantaneously, that one moment he was running to the synagogue to say *Kaddish* for his father and selling off the store on Livonia Avenue and setting up the new store on Fulton Street and trying to scrape together enough money to support Essie Schonwald "in style," and the next moment (for in memory time coils back upon itself, creating an illusion of proximity for moments that in life were often separated by months or years) he was a husband and a father and a "boss," running the factory on Bergen Street and the nine retail outlets in all the best shopping districts of Brooklyn, and giving everybody jobs like some troubled and benign potentate enthroned at the center of a rowdy kingdom, most of the residents of which were related to him by marriage or blood. At least it seemed that way when he wasn't really thinking about it. It lay that way in his mind, neatly coiled, waiting to be uncoiled by a focusing of his attention, with the slow ache and burden and labor of it, cumbersome detail, exposed.

He could remember, when he wanted to, how his father's death deepened his dilemma, how even during the *shivah* week, as he shepherded Walter and Hymie to the *shul* on Sterling Place to utter the prayer for the dead—rising up, flushed and proud, in that glum sanctuary, where some vague presence of his father seemed to linger—he knew that now more than ever he would be the man of the house, the one they would count on, and that his marriage to Essie, which had once glimmered like a light so close he could reach out and grab it, had receded into the darkness of the unknown and exhausting future.

He could remember how, in the weeks and months that followed, despite the long days of hard and ceaseless work, the insomnia that was to plague him throughout his life became almost absolute. Night after night he waited until he was drowsy and heavy-limbed before entering the small white wilderness of his bed, but the moment his hot face touched the cold pillow he felt wide awake, as though the approach to sleep were a treacherous journey he was afraid to undertake. And his mind no longer conjured up for him, to compensate for his restlessness, those phantasmagorical visions his desire had provoked a year or two before. Now he thought only of the store and the machinery and the boxes of chocolate stacked up in the storeroom, of his engagement and the treacheries of Hilda Schonwald and the drab pressure of current, daily necessity.

No, that's not quite right. There was something else, too, some old childhood dream or memory, he wasn't sure which, lurking there behind his thoughts, lingering on the verge of his consciousness like an old wound, too raw to be remembered. If he managed to catch a few hours of sleep, it would be there when he woke up again, tantalizing, elusive, slipping away from him as his first morning thoughts —a bit of business to conduct that day, or a snatch of song, or the urge to urinate—barged in and elbowed it aside. He knew it was something that had happened long ago when the family (as it was then) was journeying to America, some small incident along the way. He thought that if only he could grab hold of it, his restlessness might come to an end, so he tried to re-create the events and circumstances of their travels bit by bit, the way one might assemble a jigsaw puzzle; but he had been just six years old at the time, key pieces were missing, and the fragments memory yielded up were incompatible and scattered. He could remember leaving the village in a horsecart, Molly nursing under Sophie's shawl, a train and a drift of cloud, and a night when for reasons that were hopelessly obscure they had been forced to sleep in a forest—or did he remember that? Maybe all he really remembered was how his mother would sometimes allude to the night they slept in the forest as if it had contained for her all the elements of struggle and hardship and triumph she wanted to believe had accompanied their journey to America. Occasionally he would ask her about it, try to drag out of her a piece of the puzzle; but somehow his questions lacked force, and she would end up telling him it wasn't important to think about such things, that one should better think about the here and now. What pain could produce such reticence? he wondered. Was there some awful climax to the thing? Or was it, after all, merely a dream? His mother was right. He had become of necessity a practical man, and it just wasn't in him anymore to speculate about the obscurities of the past. Seeing no profit in it, he let it go. Better to pass the slow hours of insomnia thinking about his store and his engagement and the discomfort of his immediate surroundings—the crumpled sheet, the hammered pillow, the stab of his heartburn, the random fury of some late-night trolley car clattering down Kingston Avenue.

He would toss all night and be exhausted all day. He went around stretching and yawning and dozing off for a minute or two, with a cigarette still dangling from his lips, only to snap awake again with a kind of tingle shooting through his nerves. This went on for months until the yawns and the stretching began to affect the whole family. For a time a contagion of lassitude fell over the household. The children were drowsy and preferred curling up for a nap after school rather than playing outside with their friends. During their naps they would stir and murmur, caught up in vivid dreams and nightmares they were later unable to recall. Dr. Lipsky prescribed tonics and mineral waters, but these did no good. At school the teachers complained that Walter and Rose and Evelyn and Ruthie were dozing off at their desks. Even Sophie succumbed to it. The household routines fell apart. Laundry was scattered everywhere and dishes piled up in the sink. It was as though in those months they lacked motive and desire. Perhaps some delayed reaction to Jacob's death, grief manifesting itself as exhaustion, had taken hold of them. They would sit at the supper table picking at their food, listless and nodding. There was a rash of little accidents, spilled glasses, broken dishes, tumbled lamps. All night long children would be groping their way through the dim hallway to go to the bathroom, and in the morning they had to prod each other and slap cold water on their faces to wake themselves up. Molly alone was immune to it, and it was only when they began to prepare for her wedding that they snapped out of it. Her excitement, her noise and tumult and energy, was what finally roused them.

Sam in those days felt himself bound by the family. They were a magic circle drawn around him with chalk and incantations, and he, the subdued demon, was not even trying to burst out. He didn't know, and wouldn't know for a long time, how much he resented it. All he knew was that he and Essie would set a wedding date, and then postpone it for one reason or another, set it again, and postpone it, and this went on for years. First they couldn't get married because Sam was short of cash; then they couldn't get married because Hymie had been hospitalized and the family was upset; then they couldn't get married because Buster Stern had died and they didn't want to appear to be mocking Deborah. They couldn't get married on half a dozen different occasions, and each time Hilda Schonwald would start up again with her hotels and her conniving. Yet somehow they held onto each other. In the end the holding on itself was what they were clinging to. By the time Sam finally stood beneath the *chuppah*, listening to the rabbi intone the blessings (not Rabbi Trauerlicht, who had died, but a young, shaved rabbi from the bright new Reformed temple that had sprung up on the other side of Kingston Avenue) and watching Hilda Schonwald dab with a lace handkerchief at her cool, dry eyes, the event seemed to him absurdly anticlimactic. Later the family kidded him about how he smiled and smiled and smiled all through the ceremony and all through the rowdy and extravagant reception in Asa Kalisher's restaurant, smiling as though he were the happiest man in the world; but he had learned long ago that a smile was a convenient mask to wear against the expectations of his relatives. Behind that smile he was tormented by doubt and dreariness and acute indigestion. He felt that he was going through with the rigmarole of the ritual, joining his life to Essie's, just to prove his tenacity or maybe to spite Hilda Schonwald. He had grown accustomed over the years to confusing his love for Essie with his fear of losing her. Whatever he once felt for her, whatever he chose to call that old innocent dead passion, had long since resolved itself into mere stubbornness and familiarity. He had gotten so used to hanging onto her through all those trips to hotels and naïve flirtations by fabricating a semblance of the old passion that he coudn't—it just wouldn't be *nice* to—let her go. Anyway, he reassured himself, a wife was wanted to complete the ambitious image he still held of his future, an image that was beginning to fill with detail now that he had opened the factory on Bergen Street, and Essie was certainly decorative and convenient. Besides, he was too busy with the business—too busy haggling with Asa Kalisher and pampering Solly Poverman—to go seeking an alternative. But he had no illusions. As he danced with Essie within the boisterous, clapping, overheated circle of the family, as he cut through the rich wedding cake and fed her the first creamy sliver from the knife, as he smiled at the coarse wedding-day jokes of the men and gave himself over to the damp hugging and kissing of the women, as he went through all this madness with his stomach churning warm and queasy within him and his jaw aching with the effort of his smile, he couldn't help thinking he was a victim of circumstances, that, in a sense, he had long ago been *doomed* to this marriage.

For a while they lived in the apartment on Park Place, occupying the double bed, shy of love noise—Sophie was sleeping in Deborah's room on the other side of the wall. It was supposed to be for just a few weeks ("until we can find a place of our own"), but it dragged into months because Sam had his cash tied up in the business and the factory on Bergen Street was just beginning to hum and throb. Anyway, when it came to house hunting, as with everything else, Essie was difficult to please. She saw no good reason why her own home shouldn't be immediately as lavish and elaborate as her mother's, and she spent most of her time traipsing through department stores and "wholesale houses," choosing furniture and fabrics and lamps and adornments to be held in readiness for the day they would move. Meanwhile, she lived among the Liebers like an elf among apes, shuddering through every minute of it, but telling herself, probably, that patience had already proved to be the means to what she wanted. She never complained out loud; she didn't have to. The way she pursed her lips at suppertime told you what she thought of Sophie's robust cooking, and the way her brow furrowed as she probed her temples with her fingertips was all the comment she had to make about the children's noise. She just couldn't get along with Ruthie and Evelyn and Rose. They laughed at her behind her back, called her the princess, and imitated for each other her shrill voice and airy affectations. Some princess. Beneath the twenty mattresses that Sophie piled up for her, so to speak—she was Sam's *wife*, after all; nothing was too good for her—there lurked not just a pea, but a whole nest of thorns and pebbles. She was special, she was fragile, no one ever asked her to iron the sheets or wash the dishes or scrub the floors: the younger Lieber daughters, *balabustehs* all, resented this, and to the end they would never forgive her.

She also had problems with Deborah. Deborah was "strange," and Essie, of course, was wholly conventional. In those days Deborah had taken to going to séances, using a Ouija board, laying out tarot cards, getting up out of bed in the middle of the night to practice automatic writing. It was a tedious and frustrating business, this communicating with the dead, but she had already derived from it a few spectral glimmerings—taps on the séance table, arcane messages assembling themselves on the Ouija board, a couple of tortured but palpable sentences with a certain air of authority about them blinking at her like a beacon through the murky garble of her automatic writing—which were enough to convince her that the soul of Buster

Stern was struggling to come down to her or to help her ascend to him.

"We live in a world of the dead," she said. "There are ghosts all around us, and if we wait long enough, we're bound to join them."

She was thinner and paler than ever, and her face shone with the illumination of her beliefs. She was still wearing the same hats and dresses she had worn during her engagement, still painting her lips into a heart shape, still rubbing bright circles of rouge into her cheeks, as though by clinging to those fashions, she could cling to that time. She was so haughty and disdainful of the everyday world of desires and cash and furnishings that she made even Sam nervous. He set her up in her own store on Kings Highway and put Molly to work in her place at the factory office. He didn't know what else to do with her. One night she upset the whole house when she came home from a séance with a message from their father.

"Hymie is the blessèd one," she said he had told her.

Deborah terrified poor Essie, who never quite got over the night she went for a glass of seltzer (Sophie's *gefilte* fish had given her heartburn) and saw Deborah in the front room, dressed in a long white nightgown, muttering to herself—or, no, there seemed to be something there with her in the darkness, not a person, not even a figure, but just a kind of glow. The glimpse of it, the note of intimacy in Deborah's voice, the darkness, the whole mood of the moment frightened Essie so much that she forgot about her heartburn and ran back to bed where her trembling and sobs roused Sam. "Now what?" he asked her, in that tone of impatience he had used since their marriage, and she realized there was no way she could tell him what had happened. All she could do was avoid Deborah as much as possible, but how can you avoid your own sister-in-law when you're living in her house? They sat down together for meals, they bumped into each other in the hallway, and it seemed that whenever Essie had to use the bathroom, Deborah was in it. All of this made Essie a nervous wreck.

"Deborah was haunted by ghosts, and Essie was haunted by Deborah." Thus Walter later summed up the situation.

The only Lieber sister that Essie got along with, oddly enough, was Molly. They had long ago become good friends. In the days of Molly's first marriage it was Essie she went running to with her loneliness and complaints, and now, on the verge of her second marriage, it was Essie to whom she confided. They would go "uptown" together on a Saturday afternoon for lunch and shopping and return home loaded down with bundles, exhilarated by the crowds and the subway ride and their own company. What a sight they made, plump, brassy Molly with her red hair and bright dresses, slim, dark Essie all propriety and good taste, clicking and wobbling down the street together in the high heels that neither of them were used to, both of them talking at once—a garbled duet: Essie soprano, Molly alto—so that you had to wonder how they communicated anything at all. Maybe they never did. Maybe they just enjoyed the warm hubbub they made, and all that held them together was their devotion to Sam.

Anyway, it was while he was still living with Essie on Park Place that Sam bought the first of his automobiles. It was a big royal blue Oldsmobile loaded with chrome and gadgets and polished to a mirrory sheen so that driving in it on a bright day, you felt that you were seated amidst a burst of sunshine. He drove it to the factory every morning, parking it behind the gate near the loading dock; and he drove it in the evening, taking Essie and Molly and Solly Poverman to Coney Island for a ride; and he drove it every other Sunday, with Sophie and Deborah and Rose jammed into the back seat, out to the "home" to visit Hymie. He never "went up" with them; he would deliver them to the entranceway and help them gather their shopping bags full of magazines and homemade cookies and little presents, and then he would cruise around for an hour or so before returning to pick them up. When Hymie was in Greenpoint, he would go along Atlantic Avenue to the Brooklyn Bridge and over the river into lower Manhattan, deserted on a Sunday, enjoying the way the sound of the engine and the whisper of the tires echoed off the empty buildings on Wall Street. Later, when they transferred Hymie to the place in Bay Ridge, he would head down through the southern part of Brooklyn, which in those days was still mostly swamp and farmland, with a couple of leftover windmills looming up, their arms spread like lost giants, over the flats of Canarsie. He loved those solitary rides, loved being able to step hard on the gas pedal and watch the needle creep up and around the dial of the speedometer, and feel the wind and dust and emptiness rush in at him through the open windows. He would close his eyes for a moment, tantalized by danger, and then open them to see the road hurrying up to meet him. In summer miragelike heat shimmers lay across the road like little lakes, and he would go faster and faster, half believing that if he went fast enough, he might splash right through them. He loved driving an open road in those days the way he loved nothing else in the world. If only he could drive and drive and never turn back! But his return was always punctual. When Sophie and Deborah and Rose came down from their visit, he would be parked in the usual spot, the smoke of his cigarette rising up to meet the brim of his hat, which was pulled down low to mask his eyes.

"How is he?" he would say.

"He was better today," they would tell him.

But they were usually so glum that he had to cheer them up on the way home by stopping off for some ice cream.

Like many another man, he imparted to his car a fervor and devotion that had nowhere else to focus. The family used to laugh about how he was always plucking a handkerchief from his pocket to wipe away a dab of grease or a spot of dust from a gleaming fender. When he finally ran it into a telephone pole in 1929—having already acquired the dangerous habit of falling asleep at the wheel—he consoled himself by buying the first of his Packards, a yellow one, bigger, brighter, and brasher than the Olds. But it wasn't the same. He didn't have to struggle to possess the Packard. When he bought the Olds, Essie said they didn't have a home of their own yet, so why did they need a car? Sam had actually added to his debts to purchase it. But that was Sam. He insisted that success came to those who lived in the eyes of the world as though they were already successful. Anyway, those were the good times and the business was beginning to prosper. A couple of weeks after Molly went away for a weekend and came home married to Solly Poverman, Sam and Essie moved to a sunny apartment on Ocean Parkway. In retrospect it would seem that no time at all elapsed before Rich was born and they were moving again, to the big house in Manhattan Beach with eight rooms and pale carpeting and a huge picture window looking out on the grass and the rose bushes, and all of it just a block and a half from the beach. By then, of course, money was no longer a problem.

For the next thirty years all that was good for the Liebers seemed to emanate from the chocolate factory. In the family's imagination it sat there on Bergen Street like a great jovial machine spewing out candies and coins. In actuality, it was a grimy red-brick building with small windows meshed against the rocks of street urchins and an inconspicuous entranceway tucked into its modest façade. (Eventually Sam installed on the roof a red neon sign blinking "Lieber, Lieber, Lieber" for all the world to see, and he used to love to take Carrie and Rich out on the Staten Island ferry and show them how, if they looked carefully, they could spot the family name flashing between two power company smokestacks.) The place exhaled, to a jumbled neighborhood of row houses, cheap furniture stores, railroad tracks, and a busy police station, a rich, sweet odor that was mildly stifling, like the smell of a bread factory, only subtler, sweeter, more deliciously rare. In the morning trucks would grumble up to the loading dock to deliver sacks of sugar, barrels of milk, crates of fruits and flavorings, and huge slabs of semifinished chocolate that were shipped in from a supplier in Pennsylvania; in the candy business one never has to see a raw cocoa bean. Sam would melt the chocolate down, add some extra cocoa butter, and run the mix through a "conch" for seventy-two-hours until it took on that texture of creamy satin that distinguished the Lieber line from the chocolate of its competitors. In those days—even during the Depression—Sam had a superior brand of merchandise to peddle.

Of course, quality in chocolate is mostly a matter of taste. Some people actually prefer their chocolate sweet and grainy, crumbling in the mouth, and Lieber chocolate was not for them. Right up until the war Lieber chocolate was made to melt at precisely 97.5 degrees Fahrenheit so that it coated the palate and left a faint blush of chocolate on the tips of your fingers. It was "bitter" more than "mild," "floral" more than "nutty," to adopt the terminology of the trade. Three times a week Sam and Molly and Solly Poverman and a few of the others would gather in the office for a tasting session. These were grave occasions. On Sam's desk would be a pitcher of ice water and a stack of little paper cups, and perhaps a few samples of the competition's latest concoction, for comparison; and when you had cleared your palate with the ice water, one of the "boys" from downstairs would bring up on a slab of marble a thin smear of chocolate, fresh from the "conch." Sam would cut the stuff into wedges with a silver knife that was used for no other purpose, and you would put a sample on your tongue, not chewing it, just letting it melt there like a lozenge, breathing openmouthed so that the air would enliven your taste buds, and maybe closing your eyes, as Sam always did, against any possible distraction from this delicate communion. Sometimes you sampled the fillings, too, the creams and fruits and nougats and mints and marshmallows and caramels, but it was primarily the chocolate, the famous Lieber chocolate, that you were supposed to worry about.

"Anyone can make sugar sweet," Sam used to say. "It's chocolate that we sell."

Over the years he sold a lot of chocolate. If he never became a millionaire, there were times when he was close enough so that a few dollars on one side or the other of that fine round number really didn't matter. All day long the green panel trucks with the Lieber name and motto painted in dark brown on their sides would crisscross the city, delivering the factory's product to the retail shops the business owned outright and the other outlets it had franchised. You could buy the Lieber brand of chocolate in all the best department stores. It was shipped in bulk to the retail shops and in wrapped, beribboned packages to the franchised outlets, but whichever way you bought it, you always received in the box, between the lid and the protective quilt of white paper, a small booklet, printed in green and brown, with a little gold ribbon looped through a hole in the upper left-hand corner. It was called *The Romance of Chocolate*. Sam liked to take credit for it, but Solly Poverman wrote the thing, which was, in its way, a fascinating document. Sam was interested to learn, for example, that chocolate was first used by the Aztecs, who drank it in the form of a spiced and fermented liquor—a sublime intoxicant!— and fed it to the slaves and prisoners who were about to be sacrificed on the gory altars. They believed it converted to chocolate the human hearts they offered up to their idols, for which reason scientists would later name the cocoa tree *Theobroma cacoa*, "the food of the gods." Sam was even more interested to learn that in the seventeenth century chocolate was believed to be an aphrodisiac, that the famous Casanova used to feed the stuff to his girl friends, and that chocolate does contain, in fact, along with a dose of caffeine, a stimulant called theobromine—to which Essie was apparently immune, for no matter how much of the day's run Sam brought home for her to nibble, their lovemaking remained a kind of sporadic drudgery, especially compared to the cloaked and partial pleasures of their long engagement.

"Chocolate," wrote Solly Poverman, "is the joy, the sweetness, the very essence of life!"

To which Sam might well have appended "Amen!"

* * *

SOLLY POVERMAN WAS THE JUNIOR PARTNER, the "outside man." Sam had known him ever since the days back on Pitkin Avenue when he used to hang around the fringes of the schoolyard crowd, a quiet boy with a scrubbed handsome face, clean clothes, and the kind of blood red cheeks that reminded Sam of rare roast beef. Sam could remember old Mrs. Poverman, the loudmouth, the *yenteh,* leaning out the window to call the poor boy home for supper.

"Solly," she would bellow through the neighborhood, "Solly-boy, come up now, I make you eat!"

The gang used to tease Sol about her ("Mama's callin' ya, Solly-boy!") and send him running home in tears, but these boyish hurts pass, or get put away, or become grafted over with a tougher sort of skin. Eventually Sol went into the army and got shipped overseas. By the time he came home with his medal his mother was dead, and something in that experience, the discovery of his own courage, perhaps, or the subtle flattery of French whores, made him glib and bold and exuberant. The Solly Poverman who walked into the shop on Fulton Street one day looking for a job had acquired force and smoothness; he was a real backslapper, eager to please. Sam recognized right away the gift of the salesman in him. His jokes could make you laugh not so much because they were funny but because you felt it necessary to pay a tribute of some sort to his energy and his enthusiasm. He could make you believe when he fixed you with those big gray eyes of his that his interest in you, his line of patter, his friendly smile came straight from his open and innocent heart.

Later the family would argue about how important Solly Poverman was to the business, but it wasn't the sort of argument that could be satisfactorily resolved. All they knew was that he went to work for Sam running the store on Nostrand Avenue and the business prospered. By the time he married Molly he owned twenty-four percent of the company (Asa Kalisher owned twenty-five percent, Sam the rest) and worked on the "outside," peddling the Lieber brand to department stores and fancy food shops and exploring locations for new retail outlets. He was tall, he slicked his sandy hair straight back on his head, he kept his fingernails manicured, he wore a bold pale mustache above his white smile, and when he came to the house to call for Molly, Ruthie and Evelyn would giggle and blush. The only one who didn't like him in those days was Deborah.

"That man is all flavor and no substance," she used to say.

He was also a fine dancer. It was probably the dancing that first attracted Molly to him. Going out with him was "fun"—by which she meant that he had money to spend and didn't mind spending it in nightclubs and fancy restaurants where "hot" jazz bands propelled exquisitely dressed couples around a polished dance floor. As far as Molly was concerned, that was enough. Compared to the sequence of hard-faced men she had dated since her divorce, Solly was "fine." She never bothered to pretend to herself that she was passionately in love with him.

"Last time I had love, and a lot of good it did me," she told Essie. "This time I'll be practical."

"Sure," said Essie. "He makes a good living, don't he?"

Practical. That's how she justified herself, as though the word itself in those months after her divorce gave form and purpose to her immense vitality. She had thrown herself so thoroughly into the business and had located within herself such a reserve of toughness and common sense that she quickly supplanted Deborah—dreamy Deborah with her spirits and her moods—as the one Sam could count on. He had always adored her; now he came to respect her, too.

"Molly," he told people, "is worth half a dozen men."

When he opened the factory, he took her out of the shop on Fulton Street and put her in charge of the "floor." She had the sanction of his authority, and it didn't take her long to learn how to use it. She would put on a smock and go downstairs, and soon, it seemed, the machinery was humming in time to her own beating pulse. It was Molly who collected the time cards; Molly who doled out raises and bonuses, curbing, when necessary, the natural flow of Sam's generosity; Molly you went to when a machine broke down or you found a dead rat in a sack of sugar; Molly the cops and health inspectors came to see for their *shmears* and Christmas presents. But she was still Molly. She had put on twenty pounds, and she ran to the beauty parlor every week and let them add a rinse of red to her hair —"Just to tone it up, darling!"—but she still breathed a vivid, hot sensuality through every pore and orifice, and she could still stir up wild urges in the loins of ambitious men. And Solly Poverman was ambitious. He would breeze into the office in those pale flannel suits he used to wear, all spiff and humor and long legs, plunk himself down on the desk, and whisper off-color stories to her, trying to get her to blush. Of course, there was very little in the world that could make Molly blush, and that gave Sol fancy notions. Thus the dinners and the dancing. He probably had no idea at first what sort of exquisite trap he was falling into. He fancied himself a man of experience, but nothing the French whores had taught him could have prepared him for Molly. Poor Sol. He was like a man stretching for one sweet apple without ever realizing that the whole tree was planning to tumble down on him. Through the warm haze of his own vanity he saw a promise invoked of easy delight, and was amazed when their dates ended in a bafflement of late-night kisses abruptly broken off.

"Why not?" he would beg her, his throat thick and clogged with the desire she had roused in him.

"I'm saving it," she would say.

Practical. Calculating. Smiling at him with a smudge of lipstick on her teeth. Oh, all she wanted was to get out of that household full of crabby and squabbling children, and she loathed the idea of living alone. She was not cold-blooded enough to have thought it through; in her own eyes she was never a tease; but the bulge of her flesh against those bright patterned dresses she wore, the faint acrid scent that rose up off the grapefruit skin of her neck—all she had to do was *exist* and say *No!* and Solly Poverman's pent-up passion brimmed full and overflowed into confusion.

He called that confusion love. He began to have about him the harried, hectic flush that the family had seen before in Levitch and the schoolboys who had fought among themselves in the park. He would come home from a date and climb into bed and feel himself taut and tingling with an imbibed image of her. He was "with Molly" the way a woman is "with child." He became obsessed with her, with the thought that in her arms, limbs entwined, there would be the possibility of pleasures he had never before experienced. If the price of that possibility was a wedding ring, then a wedding ring she would have. Afterward it may have occurred to him that he had never formally proposed to her, or even surrendered; he had merely flown blind and reckless into that marriage like a moth to a flame, all compunction or fear or hesitation shoved out of mind like the throb of an old awkward wound.

Some marriages are doomed from the start; others have to play themselves out along a daisy chain of circumstances and quarrels and opportunities snatched or missed before their end is determined. Molly's marriages, alas, tended to be of the former sort. Even on their wedding night—there in that Catskills hotel room with the ugly lamps, the clunking radiator, the cold wind blowing through the flimsy walls, and his hands clammy and chilled with nervousness as he fumbled with her—she understood that when she married Davey Furst, she had merely been stupid, but this time, with this fellow, she had made a serious mistake.

"How was I to know," she later told Essie, "that the man had a problem?"

It was such a little thing to begin with, a crude wedding-night joke about a hasty, bumbling bridegroom and spilled champagne. She told him to go to sleep, it wasn't important, they would make up for it in the morning; but he insisted on talking about it, and talked and talked and talked until the talking made it awful. He apologized, he explained, he groped, he fumbled with her, trying again, and failing, until Molly was afraid the morning would never come. It was as though he had to sell himself to her—the glib, frantic salesman hoping to peddle what had turned out to be upon demonstration a defective product—as if he thought that words alone could fill up that clammy emptiness which, as the night dragged slowly along toward the cold meagerness of the dawn, seemed to be all there was between them. It wasn't the failure; she was used to that: it was the words. They spattered her, soiling her hopes, making of her bright practicality something dirty and void. Later she would understand that there was a moment during that night when she began to hate him; only she didn't recognize it then because it was, for her, such a new sort of feeling. She had never hated anyone before.

They moved to an apartment in a brand-new building in Crown Heights and bought a lot of overstuffed furniture and hung some pictures of boats and mountains on the walls and pretended to everyone that they were happy. They even tried to pretend to each other that they were happy. He would come into the office and make a great display of pecking and nuzzling at her, and Sam would yell at them: "This is a place of business, save that stuff for home!" They went out dining and dancing, and he brought home fancy presents—pieces of jewelry, bottles of perfume, frilly nightgowns—as if by throwing enough money into the marriage, he could fill that emptiness between them and make everything all right.

He was hopeful. He carried his "little problem" to a doctor, who had a name for it but not a cure; he went to a second doctor, who smiled and said he should think of baseball, say, or the stock market when he felt the moment coming on; he went to a third doctor, who gave him an ointment, said it would work wonders, but Molly complained that it left her numb inside. Anyway, as far as she was concerned, the problem wasn't the lovemaking, the feeble jab and spill and shrinkage, the way he seemed to be deliberately stealing away her pleasure. She could do something about *that*, after all, in the warm private luxury of a bubble bath. It was the afterwards, the remorse and self-pity, the way he would torment her by tormenting himself.

She had no one to talk to. It wasn't the sort of thing you could discuss with the family, and outside the family, though she knew a lot of people, she had no friends. Finally she confided the situation to Essie, but that was a mistake.

"Listen," Essie told her, flapping her hands, "I sometimes wish my Sam would have such a problem. Believe me, you're not missing much."

It troubled Molly, that privileged glimpse into Sam's moods and silences. It made even more obscure what once upon a time had been so clear, the plain, turbulent ecstasies of flesh on flesh. She had always assumed that what she had with Davey Furst, the pleasure of their playing, was natural and inevitable, and that the rest of the world, one way or another, was having it too. Now she had to wonder. There was in Essie's bold denial a simplicity that frightened her, and made her thoughts whirl.

One day in the bargain basement of A&S, of all places, some chance cojoining of crowd and heat and noise, and the relentless pressure of her failed marriage, produced in Molly a moment of revelatory panic. A buzz started up fiercely in her ears and she burst into sweat and for a few seconds she stood in a kind of swoon, swept by waves of revulsion. The moment passed, or rather she passed through it and came out into what seemed another world. A minute ago she had been surrounded by a commonplace scene of shoppers and salesgirls and heaped-up merchandise: clothes, linens, housewares, crockery; now she was seeing suffering objectified, the tokens of pain. She could sense behind all the gabble, the grabbing, the smeared makeup and the averted eyes, the heaped-up dishes and goblets and knives, flaring out like a light coming on in a darkened window, the hurt and madness of naked animals, two at a time, pawing and groping and licking at each other in the dire bitterness and disappointment of bed. Because you can never have enough, she told herself. Because there is always more and more and more. And that's why they're so afraid of it, that's why they're all like him. She packed this bitter insight into her shopping bag and carried it home on the subway,

124

knowing that with Davey she had often been lonely, but with Sol, for the first time in her life, she was alone.

That's when she knew that she hated him. She hated the way he would stand in front of the bathroom mirror for half an hour, plucking hairs from his ears and nostrils, humming to himself—God how she hated his humming! She hated the way he was always picking at his fingernails with a penknife, and the way he would shower twice, sometimes three times a day, scrubbing his body over and over again as if he could scrub away his misery and his failure. She hated him when they went to Park Place on a Friday night for dinner and he would flirt with Ruthie and Evelyn, using his salesman's lines on them. She hated him for making her tell him about the men she had known, about her first marriage and what sort of performer Davey Furst had been, hated him because she ended up telling him so much —reluctantly, to begin with, but later on with a kind of furious spite and vengeance—that it seemed Davey Furst was in the bedroom with them, laughing, mocking her, flexing his hard muscles. Most of all, she hated the way he touched her, as if for him there were in the softness and heat and partings of her body a taint, a terror, he could not avoid. She could feel his dread, and she hated the rebuke and punishment implicit in it.

She didn't leave him. Later she would wonder what wild perversity had held her, mesmerized, locked into her mistake. Maybe she didn't leave him because it never occurred to her that she could—leaving, after all, was something that men did to *her*. Or maybe it was, though she wouldn't admit it, the pressure of the family, that gravity in the faces of Sophie and Sam which kept this marriage from flying apart. In any case she was no longer trying to be practical. A kind of madness had grown up between them, a madness that was not *of* or *in* either of them, but which—nature abhorring vacuum—occupied the space, the emptiness, the insufficient fit of their marriage. She took to taunting him.

"Are you finished?" she would say to him. "Can I go to sleep?"

It astonished her, the terrible scenes they played out, the little cuts and threats and tears. Oh, there were tears all right, *his* tears: she had become by then as dry and hard and mean as a stone. That, too, was his fault. It seemed to her that he was putting into her mouth the vile words she was uttering, that some terrible thing inside him, his need to hurt and ruin himself, was using her as an instrument of its purpose. She was appalled by how his madness compelled her. One miserable day she allowed a man, a *goy,* an Irish laborer with sour breath and filthy jagged fingernails, to follow her home from the subway and make love to her in their bed; she knew it was part of the madness because even as he jabbed and thrust at her, leering, hurrying toward the blind zigzag of his spending, she was thinking of Sol, invoking his face in front of her, thinking of how he would look when she told him about it.

The family knew nothing of this. The family only knew that "things weren't working out," that Molly was getting fat and that Solly was deteriorating. That high professional sheen of slicked hair and snappy clothes was becoming pitted and tarnished like an image in an old mirror. Suddenly he was capable of being rude to customers and of losing track of appointments he was supposed to keep. His eyes were bleary and red-rimmed and there was a sag to his shoulders, as if his clothes had grown too big for him, and a kind of blotched puffiness in his ruddy, handsome face. If you asked him what was wrong, he would tell you his stomach had "gone bad" on him. All day long he went around swigging Pepto-Bismol and exhaling a bitter mixture of acid and mint. He would nick himself shaving and show up at the office with a piece of toilet paper clotted to his chin. His trousers were rumpled, his collar frayed, his shoes unshined.

"For cryin' out loud," Sam scolded Molly, "can't you take better care of the guy?"

"Sure, take care of him," she would answer. "Can I help it if he won't take care of himself?"

Maybe Sam knew; maybe Essie had spilled Molly's secret to him; but even if he knew, he wouldn't have understood it and couldn't intervene. All he could do was observe the outward manifestations of the struggle and make his own glum estimations of the effect it would have on the business. Sol would come into the office and you could tell by the flush of red on the back of his neck that he had been drinking. When the family got together on weekends, Sol no longer told jokes or flirted with his sisters-in-law. He just sat, withdrawn and quiet, softly tapping his feet like a nervous schoolboy, shying away from the intimacy the family offered.

"What's the matter with that man?" Sophie would ask Sam.

"His confidence is shot," Sam told her, but that was just a phrase he had picked up in the dime detective novels he loved to read, and he knew that it didn't explain the problem. It was more than confidence Sol Poverman had lost. It was as though a quality that had once emerged brilliantly to face the world—his energy, his eagerness, his desire to be liked—had swung around and focused inward again, revealing a dark tangled underside, some old wound that had been there all along.

There are no stories in life. There is only the slow accretion of choices and disappointments, small victories and abrupt endings, an accumulation of time and experience pushing toward change. Stories are only in the telling, in the shaping of expectations, in the awe and hush of a child dawdled on some old relative's reminiscent knee. One seldom pays to life that sort of attention. The family looked at Molly's fouled marriage and worried that the mess and bitterness would damage the business, and then glanced away. What else could they do? Solly kept complaining about his bad stomach and Molly kept putting on weight, and it went on and on and on. It went on for five excruciating years—for what remained, that is, of Molly's youth —while the family watched and wondered and felt sorry for them and said nothing, holding its breath, as it were, at the pathetic spectacle.

Until one night Sam's telephone rang and there was Molly hysterical on the other end of the line. Sam threw his clothes on over his pajamas and sped clear across Brooklyn in the small hours of the morning with his windshield wiper beating against fog and rain; but by the time he got to the hospital it was all over, Solly Poverman was dead on the operating table. Peritonitis, the doctor called it; his gut had ruptured and spilled the poisons of digestion into his fragile system. Sam would remember how he sat with Molly in the hospital, waiting for the shock to sink in, waiting for her to cry. But she didn't cry. She just sat there, struggling with her face as though she couldn't find an appropriate expression, as though she had decided for once in her life not to be hysterical and yet whatever other feelings she had were wrong for the occasion. So they sat—he would remember lighting cigarettes for her to keep her from chewing her nails—and while they sat, the hospital stirred itself, coming awake for the morning chores, and the wet, dreary windows slowly turned pale blue, and in that new light Sam felt himself looking right through some old image he had of Molly and seeing for the first time how fat and coarse and florid she had become. She's not pretty anymore, he told himself, staring at her, and she must have misread his eyes. She smiled at him, a brave and heartrending smile that boasted to him that she would get over it—get over, that is, not the shock of the death but the ravages of the marriage—and he wanted to do something, say something, to release the old thick warm emotions that were aflow within him; but he was afraid to touch her, and all he could find to say was what he always said when one of them needed him.

"Don't worry," he told her. "I'll take care of everything."

WALTER BAFFLED THEM. He wasn't the only one of his generation of Liebers to manifest symptoms of the old family strangeness—there was Hymie, of course, and Deborah, with her ghosts and her tarot cards and her out-of-date clothes—but Deborah at least was predictable, and Hymie they didn't want to discuss, whereas with Walter you never knew what to expect next. Walter, the dreamer, Walter the *brilyant,* Walter the scholar with his hands in his pockets and his head in the clouds. He had inherited, along with his black hair, his long nose, his moist eyes, his slumped shoulders, his little potbelly, a dose of that unworldly abstraction the family believed had killed their father. He had the unnerving ability to be aroused by ideas. The plain gray stuff of books and newspapers was vivid and palpable to him. Even as a child he was curious and methodical, and went poking into all the drawers and closets and cupboards, or sat in the kitchen watching Sophie make supper with the wide eyes and suspended smile of someone about to have revealed to him clues to an ancient mystery. He loved to accompany Deborah to the library and would come home, at the age of seven, eight, nine, with his skinny arms wrapped around a clumsy stack of books. But while Deborah's tastes ran to romance and magic, Walter was primarily charmed by obscure facts. He had a passion for the random cruelties of history and could spout all sorts of information about wars and calamities, crimes and persecutions. He was fascinated by the Crusades, the Spanish Inquisition, the Thirty Years' War. He took pleasure in recounting for the other children the details of, for example, an auto-da-fé, and more than once he gave Rose or Evelyn nightmares with his vivid, breathless descriptions of medieval pogroms or the symptoms of the Black Death. In those days he was still going to Rabbi Trauerlicht's *cheder,* and he was especially curious about the age-old torments inflicted upon the Jews. He kept pestering Sophie with questions about the old country, and she would try to please him—she was fond of talking about her father's butcher shop and the way they used to celebrate the holidays and festivals—but he found her gentle recollections disappointing.

"Were you ever attacked?" he would want to know. "Did they ever burn down the *shul*? Was anyone ever murdered?"

"*Sha!*" she would say to him. "Don't even mention such things!"

What a nuisance he was with his impossible questions! Why, he wanted to know, were some people rich, others poor? Why was money so important? Why did God allow children to die? Why? Why? Why? With that edge of belligerence in his voice, that glint of some unfathomable fury in his eyes—as though he believed that by probing the world, he could somehow master the mysterious ache of it.

He got into everything. Sophie couldn't bring a bag of groceries into the house without Walter rummaging through it. One day he took apart Sophie's gramophone because he wanted to examine the mechanism, and left on the floor a mess of gears and pulleys and screws, which Sam had to sweep up and lug to a repairman. He had no talent for tinkering; like his father, he was clumsy with his hands. What talent he had was for struggle and thought and outrage. Somehow he had acquired a stubborn sense of justice and honor that nothing could beat out of him. He was always getting into fights with other boys. Sophie would glance out the window and there was Walter, in knickers and knee socks, scrawny and pale, kicking and flailing wildly at two or three hefty opponents. Afraid he might get hurt, she would yell for him to come upstairs, and he would arrive with a bleeding lip and scraped elbows, furious at her for interfering.

"But I had to fight them," he would tell her. "They were calling Molly names."

That was Walter. He couldn't let anything pass. He simmered with a relentless anger which blazed out here and there as the occasion required. He fought with Sophie, he fought with Sam, he fought with his teachers—whom didn't he fight with? Before Jacob died, Walter even had a fight of some sort with Rabbi Trauerlicht and left the *cheder* and that strange other world of the Talmud in which he had been immersed, and which, later on, he would mock and mimic:

"Now then, we ask, do we eat the egg that is laid on the Sabbath? We eat the egg, says Rabbi Akiba, so long as it is collected after the sun is coming down. But, asks Rabbi Ben Ezra, has the chicken not

129

itself sinned in the act of laying that egg? To which Rabbi Boreh appends: the sin is not in the chicken but in the lust for the egg."

Two weeks before his *bar mitzvah,* with his *haftorah* memorized and all the arrangements made, he announced that it was a "stupid" ritual, and he wouldn't go through with it. He might have broken Sophie's heart if Sam hadn't sat him down and talked some sense into him, and anyway, at the dinner in Asa Kalisher's restaurant, in front of all the aunts and uncles and cousins and neighbors, he got up and made a speech attacking the "hypocrisy of fat Jews." He was impossible, and the coming of his adolescence, with its pimples and its moods, made him worse. He walked around the house grimacing at everything anyone said to him. He stopped asking questions and arguing but there was a perpetual smirk on his face. He would buy the afternoon newspapers on his way home from school and carry them into the bedroom, and there he would be, the genius, sprawled out, clucking his tongue and shaking his head at the latest horror or absurdity, blackening with newsprint ink his pale awkward hands, which were all joint and knuckle. He knew everything there was to know about what Molly called "Scopes and Vanzetti." Every murder, every strike, every lynching, every scandal, every child burned to death in a tenement fire seared his imagination. Beyond the immediate horizon, just around the corner, there lay for Walter a dark landscape of suffering and conflagration that it was up to him to do something about. He spent hours daydreaming of all the good that could be accomplished if only someone like himself, with a superior mind and an honest heart, could be made president or king or emperor of the world.

In the evenings he would sit at the dining room table with the noise of the family all around him, pretending to do his homework, abstracted, isolated in his own thoughts, fabricating with a heat and urgency he didn't understand another world, the world as it ought to be, with crime and hunger and greed and ignorance abolished by his own decrees and wisdom, and everything—people, houses, clothes, stores, streetlamps, signs, the sky itself—clean and fresh and new, drenched, as it were, in the brilliance of primary colors. It was so vivid to him that his heart would start pounding and his breath would quicken with the bright vision of it, the polychrome future that would abolish the smudged gray of the oppressive now. He believed then that everyone everywhere must be in essence as good-natured and well meaning as himself, and that therefore, all human misery was founded on nothing more than mistakes, miscalculations, errors, like the botched algebra to which he would soon return. Let x equal the series n_1, n_2, n_3 . . . Let Walter equal the whole human race. Then there might be equality, brotherhood, love in the world. Then he might be freed from his rage.

In those days he told himself he hated the family, hated them not because his thoughts were not their thoughts but because, as far as he was concerned, they didn't think at all. Sam, for example. Sam would come to the house with his smiles and his money and that smell of chocolate which lingered about him, and Walter would feel himself drawing away, becoming sulky and sullen. He no longer bothered to argue with Sam; there was no point to it. Sam didn't care about Walter's visions and hopes; all he cared about was what Walter planned to "do for a living," as though "doing" and "being," "work" and "life," were all the same. He couldn't make Sam see, he couldn't make any of them see, what was so simple and obvious to him: that dreaming makes reality. They lived inside a kind of bubble painted with the emblems of their meager expectations, dollar signs, furniture, automobiles, the next meal, and mistook that small sphere for all there was. But there was more to the world, there had to be.

Sometimes he felt so cramped and oppressed by the environs of home and school and family that he would go down to the subway and ride and ride, switching trains at random, enjoying the lurching throb and racket, emerging in strange neighborhoods, blinking and wide-eyed like some naïve explorer. But he soon tired of that, or perhaps was frightened off by his inevitable encounters with hostile gangs of boys, and he started spending more and more of those restless hours either in the big new library at Grand Army Plaza or way uptown at the Museum of Natural History. For a time, when he was fourteen, fifteen, sixteen, he loved the museum most of all.

He had been introduced to the place by his eighth-grade teacher, a dedicated old pedagogue named Stowe, for whom civilization consisted of Christianity, taxonomy, and the novels of Charles Dickens, and who bestowed these privileges as a matter of duty upon upstart immigrant children, whom he secretly despised. Walter was fascinated by the dinosaur bones, the reconstructed whales, and the encased souvenirs and relics of the late President Roosevelt. But more than that, there was something about the building itself that enthralled him. The huge stairways, the outcroppings of marble, the bronze tablets inscribed with the names of benefactors—the place seemed to him a kind of dynamo; he could almost feel through his shoes the secret hum of power and wealth and authority it embodied.

As he roamed the big encrusted halls, the richness of it all made his teeth ache, as though he had eaten too much candy; but the sensation was pleasant, and he returned again and again to ride the elevator up to the Hall of Precious Gems and warm himself in front of that subtle blaze of rubies, diamonds, sapphires; or to study the endless variety, tray after tray, of beetles and moths and butterflies in the insect collection; or to wander with the crowd through the dark theatrical halls of dioramas with those glass ponds and inert trees and subtly painted skies, and all the beavers and grizzly bears so cleverly posed that they seemed just once removed—and the distance no more than an eyeblink—from life. Once he stood for over an hour counting the annual rings in the giant cross section of an old redwood tree, seeing the thing as a porthole to the past, amazed that little more than his own gangling length could measure the vast interval between the fall of a sequoia seedling in some ancient forest and his own birth date, marked out, as it were, at the edge of the ragged circumference.

Then there was the Hall of Primates with its diagrammatic depictions of the descent of apes and humans, its skeletons and skulls, and its plaster reproductions of the staring, brutish faces of Neanderthal Man, Piltdown Man, Peking Man. Eventually these became for him as familiar as the faces of his own family. In fact, one day he realized that they actually were, in a sense, the faces of his family. He had known this theoretically, of course, but that day, for no apparent reason, mood and thought and moment combined to overwhelm him with the brutal truth of his ancestry. His mind seemed to open; his imagination was released and driven back to that dawn of human time when the first ape-genius—his great-grandfather, as it were—stood upright and lifted his face and stared at the suddenly mysterious sky, howling all the wounded rage and astonishment that must have accomplished his initial awareness of his new condition. Walter would never forget it. Later he would say that the scales had fallen from his eyes, but that was just a phrase he had learned from old Stowe, a banal articulation of a moment that was profound. What he saw that day—so keenly and passionately that his scalp tingled and his ears buzzed and his mouth went dry with the sensation of it—was his own brute connection backwards through the generations of his ancestors, men, cavemen, apes, whatever, his blood their blood, his rage their rage; what he understood (though the image itself wouldn't come to him until later) was that human life at any given moment is a kind of subterranean thing, a worm or a mole, moving here and there, blindly, through the endless maze of tunnels burrowed out by a multitude of predecessors. And so he himself was nothing but what *they* had accomplished—because life isn't merely a moment here, a moment there, every moment significant and complete unto itself. That's just an illusion that memory provides. Life, rather, is process, ancient and interminable, a thousand centuries of slow, stupid struggle, an invisible and ruthless flow of growth and mutation.

Of course, those weren't his thoughts then; those were the thoughts he would come to later as he unraveled the experience, trying to master the unexpected passion of the moment by rendering it for himself into a sequence of words and ideas. But as he rode home on the subway that day, he went on feeling within himself the thrust and spasm of the single ancestor who had fathered them all, apes and men, Gentiles and Jews, Liebers and Kalishers, and he realized that he couldn't hate anyone anymore. In a moment the fire of his old rage had transformed itself into something warm and fluid and cleansing, love and pity, pity and love, for himself, for his family, for all mankind. Because their life was his life, and for all those things he had raged against, they weren't to blame. Even a torrential river must settle now and then, come to rest in stagnant pools. Ignorance and selfishness and hunger were merely the consequences of their condition. Things—things that perhaps were not beyond control—had stunted and thwarted them. And so there was nothing to do but love them. As he walked from the station on Eastern Parkway up the long hill to Park Place, his head kept echoing the sensations of the museum and his feet seemed to skip lightly somewhere above the sidewalk in tune with the rapid, optimistic patter of his heart. Because if ape can become man, man can become anything. All that was needed was an agent of change. It was as though his mind had been upturned and watered, and now lay fallow, waiting for seed.

Walter went off to City College in September of 1929, the first of the Liebers to have a chance at an education—and how proud the family was of him! How fine and studious he looked in the blue worsted suit that Sam had paid for, with a silver fountain pen in his pocket and a new briefcase in his hand, and his lank black hair slicked down flat and shiny with Glossola oil—and the next thing they knew he was courting a girl named Sarah and preaching revolution. He joined the party officially in the bitter springtime of 1931, and there was simply no living with him. He brought into the house all sorts of cheaply printed newspapers and pamphlets and tried to get Rose and Ruthie and Moe to read them. He was forever arguing with Sam, who told him to forget all that nonsense, study hard, learn a profession, make a *mensh* of himself; but every other word out of Walter's mouth was "Labor" or "Injustice" or "Freedom" or "Exploitation." Strangers would call him up on the telephone and refuse to leave a name. He went to rallies and demonstrations, carried picket signs in front of factories in the garment district, and fought with "company hooligans" on the docks. Once he disappeared for a week and came home with his arm in a sling, his clothes torn, stubble all over his face, and a big purple bruise on his forehead—he had been, he explained, to Ohio. That was Walter. Walter the Communist, Walter the Red. He was as fervent and impractical as ever, signing petitions, conspiring with thugs and lunatics, condemning the New Deal, dreaming always of a new and better world—a world in which what he called the innate potential of mankind would be free to express itself.

For a while the family blamed Sarah. They wanted to believe that she had seduced Walter into the wildness of her own politics. After all, she came from a family of old Warsaw radicals and was herself a "real freethinker." She smoked, she swore, she talked politics like a man, she wore gray, dowdy clothes, and she refused to use makeup on her face. If she was in a room with Molly or Sam, the sparks would fly. But it wasn't Sarah. If anything, after their marriage, after they had settled into that grim basement apartment on St. Marks Place, Sarah proved to be the more practical of the two. It was Walter himself. Something in his blood and his upbringing, something stubborn and proud and inevitable, drove him to his follies. He was bound to seek in the black and white of some ideal system a vision of the future that would coincide, if only for a while, with the old extravagant rainbow confusion of his hopes, his dreams.

FRIDAY NIGHTS IN THOSE YEARS the whole family came together for dinner. Sophie would light the *Shabbos* candles—chanting the prayers quickly to herself as though she had grown ashamed of them —and then they would all gather 'round the table and gorge themselves on Sophie's home cooking, the tang and flavor of which memory would later improve. There would be *gefilte* fish or chopped liver, with eggs and *gribeniss* mashed into it, *kreplach* soup with the fat floating on top like little gold coins, the invariable main course of pot roast and roasted chicken, a potato *kugel*, a green vegetable, and slabs of that rich braided and poppy-seeded *challah* which Sam used to pick up from the bakery in Brownsville, with fruits and cakes and chocolates for dessert—and for the rest of the night there would be a great running back and forth to the kitchen for glasses of seltzer water to damp down the digestive fire. The conversation when the family got together was loud and chaotic, a kind of chain reaction of jokes and taunts and complaints and broken anecdotes, with shouts and whoops of laughter booming brassy and shrill above the general hubbub. The women generally dominated the table talk. Even Ruthie and Evelyn, by the time they reached their adolescence, had learned to chatter and scold like a couple of little *yentehs*. Sam would sit there, silent and benign, his eyes hooded, dreaming perhaps of the card game he was going to escape to later that night, smiling at the noise and heat and tumult that surrounded him, and at the pleasure of knowing that his efforts had put all that food on the table, and the lace and crystal and silver as well. In that circle of flushed faces and hot gabble he was a model of genial restraint and final authority. Should the conversation ever turn serious, should there be a real problem to solve, it was taken for granted that the family would turn to him.

He took care of everything. He arrived at the house with a great roll of bills and left with his pockets emptied. From his little sisters all he ever heard was: "Sam I need this" and "Sam I need that." He didn't mind. "Indulge yourself," he would say, slipping them a five or a ten. He especially doted on Ruthie and Evelyn, liked to see them in new clothes, and scolded Sophie when he caught them wearing hand-me-downs. The only one who wouldn't accept money from him was Walter. The rest simply took it for granted that Sam would provide for them. When Deborah decided she needed an apartment of her own, Sam helped her find a place near Brighton Beach, lent her money for the deposit, and arrived one morning in the Oldsmobile to lug her books and clothes across Brooklyn. When Moe caught scarlet fever and they had to rush him to the hospital, Sam not only paid the bills, but showed up with a bag full of toys, and promised ball games and movies, as if he were bribing the kid to get well. That's the way he was.

He loved them then, loved them with a clarity and simplicity and sweetness he would lose later on when they were growing up and marrying people he didn't approve of and starting families of their own. He had the pleasure of providing for them, of feeling their dependence on him, without the *tsurris* of having to live with them —with their mess and crises and noise. He liked to stop off at the apartment on his way home from work, climbing softly up the stairs and letting himself in with his key to catch them unawares. He would wink at Sophie, who was pot-wrestling in the kitchen, and creep down the hallway, and there would be Walter sprawled out on his bed contemplating his stamp collection, and Ruthie and Evelyn giggling at each other in the bathroom as they tried out new styles on each other's hair. He wished he could be silent and invisible so that he could go on watching them without their realizing he was there. With Deborah and Molly it was different; they were born where he was born, and so belonged to his world, but the others, the American-born, existed, as far as Sam was concerned, in a kind of magical and enchanted space of their own, the very enticement of which for him was his exclusion from it. He seemed to be watching them on a screen or a stage—there was just that sort of pleasure in it, just that tinge of unreality.

No Old World memories, no night in the forest, no stained and haunted walk-up on Pitkin Avenue fouled *their* dreams and ambitions. They took for granted the things that Sophie and Sam himself had struggled to attain: the apartment, the furniture, the pictures on the wall, the clothes, the schooling, even the shape of the words they shouted, whispered, sang. It occurred to Sam that they moved through the world, *their* world, with a hectic grace and comfort that he, despite his posing, could never achieve. For him America was a kind of garment, a disguise; for them it was flesh and blood and bone itself. There were times when he felt himself to be merely the instrument through which they would accomplish their ends. Oh, he was successful all right; he had looked around, drawn his conclusions, and acted accordingly; he had stolen a chunk of the future and made it his own. But he also sensed the limits of his world, the boundaries of Brooklyn and Manhattan beyond which he was afraid to go. When Asa Kalisher came back from Florida and told him he had discovered Paradise, and that there was money to be made there, Sam shied away from the investment. He ended up looking shrewd, since Asa Kalisher dropped a bundle when the speculative bubble burst, but he knew it wasn't shrewdness alone that had held him aloof from the temptation of palms and oranges and endless sunshine. It was also fear. Fear that beyond the circle of familiarity he had drawn around himself the world—the great incomprehensible expanse of the continent—was alien and hostile, that *out there,* where the American-born Liebers might feel at home, his own life and fortune would be exposed to ferocious and unpredictable elements. As with Asa Kalisher's extravagant subdivision on the Gold Coast, a hurricane might come along and blow it all away. So he smiled, and hid his thoughts, and turned his back on certain opportunities. He had settled, he had blazed a trail, and it was up to the others, if they could, to break through, to go beyond, to inhabit what remained of the wilderness.

You have to see Sam as he was in the prime of his life, shortish, ruddy, red-haired, brusque, efficient, casual, as compact and purposeful as an alley cat, with a hint of the racketeer in his accent, his swagger, and his expensive clothes. He favored pale suits and dark shirts and bright silk ties, with a perpetual cigarette, a Lucky Strike, dangling from his lower lip, the smoke drifting up to his squinting eyes, and the inevitable broad-brimmed fedora pulled down low over his face, shadowing it, assuring the privacy of his moods. From beneath the hat, from behind the blue-gray smoke, he beamed out at the world—at responsibilities accepted and expectations fulfilled, at the simple pleasure of being the prosperous center that held together a household full of shrill women and impractical boys. You have to see him, for example, entering the chaos of Asa Kalisher's restaurant at lunchtime for a bowl of barley soup, a corned beef sandwich, a side of *kishka,* a celery tonic, sitting at the table with his pals and cronies, some of them the sons of Asa Kalisher's cronies, with his hat still on, laughing and lighthearted as though for him the general misery of the time—this would be 1930, 1931, 1932—was a kind of joke.

"Well, boys," he would kid them, "who went under today? Anyone I know?"

For even in those bad times, and even after the loss of Solly Poverman, the chocolate business not only survived, but in a small sufficient way continued to prosper. When you can't afford luxuries, you can solace yourself with a piece of chocolate, a bite of butter crunch, a moment of sweetness in the mouth. So what if the business never grew as large as Sam once hoped it would? So what if he trimmed his dreams to the stark pattern of the times? Even in the worst days of the Depression he was able to give the family what they needed, and wasn't that enough?

Of course, he also had a household of his own. Rich had come along in 1929, and then, a few years later, after Essie went through the trauma of a stillbirth, she produced Carrie. But the soiled diapers and mess of caring for babies didn't interest Sam very much. He liked to come home and dawdle Rich on his knee and slip silver half dollars into his gigantic piggy bank, and to throw Carrie up over his head to get her to smile; but the squawls and smells and sleeplessness of raising babies were Essie's domain. Not until the children were old enough to go to Coney Island and Ebbets Field and the factory —when they were old enough, that is, to appreciate what Sam and Same alone could do for them—did he begin to be interested in them. He believed he was a good father; he loved them, he indulged them —spoiled them, his sisters complained—but until they were eight or nine or ten, they didn't have real substance for him. When he was away from them, they almost didn't exist.

He had set Essie up in that big house in Manhattan Beach where everything was light and airy and comfortable, but he wasn't home very much. His habits refused to yield to Essie's schedules and desires. He still liked to stay out playing pinochle or bridge till all hours of the morning, and to spend his weekend afternoons at the ball park with his cronies. He had joined a social club, which was housed in an old building on Second Avenue and was made up mostly of "show" people—comedians, songwriters, vaudevillians, with a sprinkling of businessmen to pay the bills—and he went there to play cards or to sit in one of the red leather chairs swapping jokes and brags with the "boys." He liked the atmosphere. He liked the rowdiness, the caricatures on the walls, the show-business lingo, the way the smoke and leather and wood and hair oil mingled to create an aroma, an atmosphere, that can be achieved only in rooms from which women are purposefully excluded. In an unusual flight of imagery he once described the place as having about it the smell of new dollar bills.

The factory, the club, Asa Kalisher's restaurant, Ebbets Field and Yankee Stadium, the house in Manhattan Beach, the apartment on Park Place—this was his world, and only later did he realize how very narrow and circumscribed it was. The family would tell the Lieber grandchildren that Sam had been on the verge of a huge success when the Depression started. They believed, because he had told them, that he had once upon a time planned to expand the business, set up factories in Boston, Chicago, Miami, California; that he could have been as big as Barton's or Fannie Farmer or Barricini. They even believed that he once had the idea of selling candy at stores that would be attached to gas stations on highways all over the country.

"It could have been Lieber's instead of Stuckey's," they would say.

But the fact was that Sam had early on reached some sort of limit. There had come not a moment but a phase in his life when he took stock of what he had accomplished and said to himself: this is enough. He would go so far and no farther. There was in him some strange, unrelenting sense of boundaries that checked his ambitions. He was bold up to a point, and then his boldness dissipated and some old stubborn caution—which he took to be the heritage of the family—intervened. He loved to gamble, but never for the highest stakes. The Depression was just a convenient excuse.

Anyway, within that small world he had acquired the pleasures of expertise. He could taste in the bitterness of raw chocolate the smooth, mellow sweetness of the finished candy just as he could read in the neat columns of numbers set out on the apple green pages of the ledger the sum of the favors he could bestow upon the family. To be with them on a Friday night, to share their warmth—why ask for more?

It was always warm in the Lieber apartment. In winter the radiators thumped and hissed and sputtered at the connections, and the oven poured out its own fragrant warmth to mingle with the heat of flesh and breath and conversation. When the family got together for a meal, Sam would take off his jacket and loosen his tie, and Molly would sit there dabbing at her pink damp face with the lace handkerchief she kept balled in her sleeve. The windows would fog and the cold dark street outside, with some pedestrian hurrying by huddled in a shabby overcoat, would seem as distant and irrelevant as the moon.

Nonetheless, in her sixth decade of life, with her bones grown brittle and her blood thin, Sophie felt constantly chilled. She walked around with two or three sweaters over her housecoat, and a pair of Sam's old socks on her feet, rubbing her hands together, hunching her shoulders, pressing her elbows tight against her sides. Dr. Lipsky said she was anemic, gave her iron tonics and told her to eat liver, but that didn't help. On the coldest nights she stayed up all hours in the kitchen, preparing breads and cakes and cookies that she would give away to the neighbors, just to keep the oven going and to stave off that mournful moment when she would have to thrust herself into the icy emptiness of her bed. All winter long she couldn't wait for summer to come, but as the years went by, the bright liquid days of July and August hurried away ever more quickly until it seemed to her that the seasons had failed and the world was perpetually in winter. Her children teased her about it. Moe promised that when he grew up and made a lot of money he would buy her a house in Florida. She laughed and let herself be kidded, but she didn't think it was funny. More and more the coldness reminded her of the snow-covered and frozen earth, there alongside Jacob, where she was destined to lie. Every time she shivered, every time she blew her own warm breath upon her chilled fingers, the dreadfulness of it touched her.

There were odd moments while she was cooking or cleaning or mending clothes when she would stop and turn inward, listening to the basic processes of life within her, the beat of her heart, the whisper of breath as it entered her throat, the vague hum of blood in her ears, all that hushed and complicated mechanism that we usually ignore, and she would worry not about her health, for she was healthy enough, but about—about—oh! she didn't have words for it, for that simple sensation of being, and the fear that it might cease. At such moments, though she had experienced little of death—except for Jacob and her mother she had lost none of the people who were closest to her—the force of life seemed especially puny and insignificant, like the brave wisp of a candle flame so easy to snuff out. She thought it was a miracle that all her nine children were still alive (her cousin Rachel, for example, had lost three of her four), and her fear, deflected from the insupportable notion of her own death, would shape itself into a premonition that one of her brood would die before she did. This grew and grew. One night she dreamed of a funeral; she hurried to the open coffin to see which of her children lay within it, saw the corpse vividly, but couldn't identify it when she woke up.

Her imagination grew morbid. More and more she was aware of diseases, dangerous machines, violent criminals, any one of which might snatch her children from her. If a day or two went by and she didn't hear from Sam or Deborah or Molly, she would fret and worry.

"What?" she would say to them when they finally called or dropped by for a visit. "You forgot you had a mother?"

The force of her anxiety fell most heavily on Evelyn and Ruthie and Moe. She never fell asleep until she knew they were safely in the house. She picked out almost at random neighborhoods they weren't supposed to enter ("Who knows what sort of *meshugganehs* live over there?"); she scrutinized the school mates they brought home until she assured herself they weren't some sort of menace. She forbade them to play on the roof with their friends, and even when they were teenagers, she would lean out the window to watch them cross the street. She also made them wrap scarves around their mouths on chilly days—"So you shouldn't, God forbid, like your father, catch cold in your lungs." Moe especially she babied and cuddled. She believed that because he was the youngest, he was also the most vulnerable. She must have realized that when he was grown, the mothering that had occupied her life would be over, and so she kept thinking of him as younger than he was. Sam used to complain that between his mother and his sisters, who were always fussing over Moe—combing his hair, scrubbing his ears, dressing him up in sailor suits, feeding him candies—they would turn the kid into a sissy. But what could he do? The family doted on Moe not just because he was the youngest but because he was handsome and intelligent and soon learned to be charming. In school, though he never worked as hard as Walter—he had a lazy streak, and liked to indulge and pamper himself—he came home with 100's anyway. (And years later, silver-templed and successful, with the degrees of his education framed on his office walls along with the portraits of the five daughters he himself had fathered, Moe Lieber would still be the baby of the family, and sometimes, despite years of psychotherapy and his own good sense, he would want it all over again, the fussing and petting and cooing of all those solicitous women.)

There were times during those years when Sophie came awake in the blue hours of dawn so taut and enflamed with her fears and premonitions that she would hurry down the hallway, listening from room to room, as though they were infants again, to make sure her children were still breathing. Her anxiety came in spells, like the moods and hot flashes of her menopause. There were terrible mornings when she was certain the day would bring the catastrophe she feared. Sometimes she caught herself almost wishing it would come, so that whatever it was, that unknown shadow of death which haunted her, would be over and done with—but those days, like all the others, flowed on smoothly and steadily into weeks and months. Despite her premonitions, the children grew and flourished, surviving illnesses and wounds and the hazards of traffic, and occasionally, when her fears receded for a while, Sophie would realize how very foolish she was, know that it was mostly time that troubled her. She had fretted away her years and gotten old.

She felt particularly old when Ruthie and Evelyn started bringing boys into the house. All she ever heard from those two was boys, boys, boys, until she was sure that they thought about nothing else. There was a ceaseless parade of boys up and down the staircase, boys with slicked pompadours and boys with pimply faces, boys who talked about going to college and boys who had quit school to look for work in the garment district, boys who were broke and boys who managed despite the harshness of the times to have a few dollars in their pockets. There hadn't been anything like it in the house since the days before Molly's second marriage when she was being courted by that sequence of hard-faced young men, and it pleased Sophie, despite her nervousness, to see her "babies" so pretty and popular. On the other hand, she felt ever more sorry for Rose. Poor Rose seemed to have skipped right from her childhood into a lumpish and dowdy middle age. She was still wearing those thick glasses—she was now practically blind in one eye—still breathing through her mouth and, at the age of eighteen, nineteen, twenty, working for Sam in one of the retail shops, still waiting for some man to notice her. Sophie was afraid she would end up like Deborah, who lived with her ghosts in that bizarre and gloomy apartment near Brighton Beach and planned never to marry. But at least Deborah was bright and clever and kept herself occupied with her books and her séances, whereas Rose was dull-witted and slow and spent her free hours plodding around the apartment, helping with the housework. In the evenings, while Ruthie and Evelyn entertained their company in the front room, Rose sat drinking tea with Sophie in the kitchen, uncomplaining, always pleasant and dutifully cheerful, getting along with her younger sisters as though she thoroughly lacked within her nature the capacity for malice and envy.

Ruthie and Evelyn were the "real Americans" of the family, or so it appeared to Sophie. She could find no trace of the Old World in them. Their religion was nothing but foods and holidays and Friday night candles, and their conversation, when it wasn't about boys, was all clothes and hairdos and music. They sang popular songs that never made any sense to Sophie no matter how hard she tried to penetrate the lyrics. (What could it mean, this *yes we have no bananas today*?) They were a year apart in age and "ran" with the same group of friends, and Sophie had trouble telling one friend from another. There were always the same polite smiles, the same giggles, the same uproar, the same "serious problems" to be talked over in the privacy of the back bedroom. On Friday nights Ruthie and Evelyn went to "socials" and on Saturday nights, if a boy happened not to be calling for them, they were mopey and irritable and sat in front of the radio claiming to have nothing to do. They studied popular magazines to learn the sweet-smelling arts of makeup and fashion, were constantly raising or lowering their hemlines, and made fun of the styles of their older sisters. They were smart enough, but they ignored their schoolwork and filled their heads with dreams of marriages to men who would provide them with fur coats and diamond rings and all the rest of the rigmarole of teenage expectations.

There were also differences between them. Ruthie was "wilder" than Evelyn, louder, bolder, more audacious. She was, in some ways, a little hectic edition of Molly, the same moods, the same freckles, the same hot look in her eyes—but she was also far more conventional, far more home-conscious, far more reined in than Molly would ever be. Evelyn was quieter, more social, more basically conventional. It took Sophie awhile to figure it out, but eventually she realized that the girls who came to the house were Evelyn's friends, with whom Ruthie just tagged along, while the boys were mostly attracted to Ruthie—she got Evelyn her dates. They revolved around each other that way.

They married young. Out of the bewildering array of young men they "kept company" with, out of that ever-changing kaleidoscope of faces, a couple of particular ones emerged. Evelyn had her Milton and Ruthie had her Lou and they planned a double wedding. That didn't quite work out—nothing in their lives ever quite worked out —but despite the problems that Lou's parents caused, both couples got married and settled down around the corner from each other near Utica Avenue, and Sam gave his new brothers-in-law jobs in the factory, and everyone knew it was just a matter of time before they started having babies.

"I can't understand them," Deborah used to say. "They're in such a hurry to get married that they grab the first *shtarkers* who come along. Don't they want more out of life than to be just like everyone else?"

Anyway, the family was scattering across the borough of Brooklyn, and with just Rose and Moe to feed and care for on a daily basis,

Sophie rattled around in the big old apartment on Park Place, which echoed for her in its very silence the tears and tumult of the early days. She still had premonitions, but as the years went by, they troubled her less and less. Mostly she complained now that her feet hurt, that she couldn't see well enough to read anymore, and that her children were neglecting her. Friday nights the family still gathered together for dinner, and on Sundays Sam lent his car to Milton or Lou so that Sophie and Rose and any of the other sisters who wanted to go along could be driven out to visit Hymie in the new state hospital, which had risen like a series of giant upended bricks way out on the bucolic fringe of Queens. It was a long ride up along the convoluted and dangerous Interboro Parkway past the cemetery where Jacob was buried. When Lou was driving—the man was harsh and reckless and in love with speed—it was like taking your life in your hands. Sophie would sit in the back seat, her lips pressed together, her hands moving nervously in her lap, looking straight ahead over Lou's shoulder as though it might help if she could be the first to spot the potential accident. At the end of the long day, when she climbed out of the car and stood once again on the relatively secure pavement of Park Place, she would glare momentarily at Lou—she had never much liked him anyway—and in her steady green eyes there would be an exquisite mingling of relief and reproach.

So the round of life went on.

Ruthie had her first boy, and Uncle Chaim, the moyel, performed the circumcision, and everyone waited to hear from Evelyn. Sure enough, a month or two later she announced that she was expecting.

Molly in those days was going around with a man named David Greenberg—Davey Second the family took to calling him—and all in the space of a year they were engaged, married, quarreling, separated, and divorced. It happened so fast that in retrospect the family would remember the man as no more than a name, his marriage to Molly no more than a number, and even for Molly herself he was merely a misjudgment, an interlude, hardly worth thinking about, between Solly Poverman and Max Gold.

Then, miracle of miracles, Rose met a fellow. Everyone was excited about it. The Lieber sisters spent hours on the telephone talking it over, clucking their tongues, passing their judgments. They were so used to feeling sorry for Rose that they couldn't quite bring themselves to feel happy for her.

His name was Irving Malish, and he lived with his mother, though he was nearly thirty years old, in a shabby tenement building on Dumont Avenue, not far from that glum and impoverished street where Jacob had run the bookstore. All Sam had to do, the first time he met the man, was take hold of his limp, damp hand and glance once at his frayed and food-stained clothing to murmur *shnorrer* to himself and to wonder what work in the factory he could possibly perform. But Rose claimed that she loved him—a kind of eager, flushed brightness had come over her—and that was enough. Whatever they might have said behind her back, they never whispered a word of discouragement in front of her. So what if Mrs. Malish turned out to be a fat, crude, ignorant old *yenteh* who called everybody darling and dearie and had the nerve to sit there, when she was invited to the house for dinner, and tell them what a wonderful smart boy her Irving was and how fortunate was their "Roisele" to have caught him. The families Ruthie and Evelyn married into were no bargains either. If Sophie could endure the Grossmans and the Himmelfarbs—not to mention the snobbishness of the Schonwalds—she could tolerate Mrs. Malish as well.

So the family started planning another wedding.

It turned out to be a joyless, grim event. Rose was as unlucky in her nuptials as she was in everything else. She had to walk down the aisle with Sam on one side of her and Deborah on the other, the tears streaming down her cheeks behind her bridal veil and her eyeglasses, so that the faces and flowers were all a blur; she had to go through with the ceremony and the feast, because it didn't make sense not to, with her hateful mother-in-law smirking at her and her own mother not there at all; and though her brothers and sisters did their best to be cheerful for her sake, she could tell that their hearts weren't in it. Sophie lay in the hospital, paralyzed and speechless, with tubes in her arms and her nose. The week before, she had gone to bed early, complaining of a headache and dizziness; in the middle of the night Rose heard a noise and went to investigate and found her mother lying on the floor, her arms sprawled out, her legs tucked up under her, like a big rag doll some careless child had flung there, with a look on her face of mild and witless astonishment. Rose woke up Moe, and together they hoisted her back onto the bed and made the appropriate phone calls. All the rest of that night and through the next day Dr. Lipsky prepared the family for the worst, and though Sophie survived the crisis—the force of her vitality pulling her through—she would never be the same. The bubble of blood that had burst in her brain, and the second stroke which followed a few weeks later, put her to bed for the rest of her life. She regained her voice and her memory in time; but she never walked again, and for the next ten years her younger daughters had to take turns playing mother to her. And though the irony of it was commonplace, that foretaste of their own eventual diminution was, nonetheless, inexpressibly real.

How but in custom and in ceremony
Are innocence and beauty born?

—WILLIAM BUTLER YEATS,
"A Prayer for My Daughter"

FOUR

THE FAMILY LIVED ALL OVER BROOKLYN in those years. They lived on Carroll Street and Montgomery Street and East Fifty-first Street and Blake Avenue and Ocean Avenue and Ocean Parkway and Union Road and St. Mark's Place. They lived in Brighton Beach and Sheepshead Bay and Manhattan Beach and Crown Heights and Brownsville and East New York, under the elevated trains. They lived in loud apartment houses where the hallways were jammed with baby carriages and tricycles and the courtyards were crisscrossed with clotheslines, and in rowhouses with a butcher shop or a grocery store beneath them, and in two-family houses with a nosy landlady right downstairs, and in little "studio" apartments that were chiseled out during the Depression by the owners of brownstones, and even in private houses with a bit of grass and trees. They moved around a lot because they were having babies and they kept needing more room. Each time they moved, they noticed that they had accumulated more furniture and adornments and clutter, and sometimes they would take a moment out of their packing and unpacking to wonder at the acquisitiveness of their lives.

Among their possessions, embedded like fond memories in the routines of the everyday, there was always some familiar old chair, or a lamp with a Delft china base, or a lacy tablecloth, because they had closed the apartment on Park Place after Sophie's stroke and distributed the old furnishings among themselves, with the usual round of quarreling and hard feelings. They had also distributed among themselves the burden of caring for Sophie. At a meeting in Sam's house, while Lou Grossman grumbled to himself and Essie kept cleaning the ashtrays, they agreed that Sophie would live six months at a time with her youngest daughters, with Rose and Ruthie and Evelyn, since they would best be able to tend to her. To help them out, Sam hired through an agency that Dr. Lipsky had recommended a private nurse, Mrs. Gillicutty, who became a kind of adjunct to the family. She was a sweet old soul, this Mrs. Gillicutty, as devoted, efficient, and well scrubbed as a nun, and the Lieber grandchildren would later recall how every December their parents used to *shlep* them on the subway all the way out to Bay Ridge so they could have the pleasure and instruction of viewing the traditional blaze of Mrs. Gillicutty's Christmas tree.

They liked to live close to transportation, the Liebers, close to subway stops and trolley lines and busy intersections where in a pinch you could grab a cab. They liked to live near "shopping," so that they could walk to Nostrand Avenue or Fulton Street or Kings Highway and find right in the neighborhood a good Jewish bakery, a kosher delicatessen, and a vegetable man whose produce was fresh. They also favored—as part of their upbringing—living near parks. They lived near Prospect Park or Highland Park or Fort Greene Park or Seaside Park, and when the shopping and cooking and cleaning were finished, they bundled their babies into carriages and strollers to get some fresh air. They were great believers in fresh air, that generation of Liebers, and even on the coldest nights they would prop open their windows a couple of inches.

Wherever they lived, they lived among Jews. There were always a few synagogues in the neighborhood whether they frequented them or not, and those they did go to for the holidays they chose as a matter of convenience: not for the Liebers the subtle shades of doctrine that separated Reformed from Conservative, or Conservative from Orthodox. All that mattered to them was that they avoided settling into those alien and hostile regions where the Gentiles were a majority, though it was in the nature of the borough of Brooklyn that one couldn't avoid having around the corner or down the block or sometimes even on the other side of the building a small bristling enclave of Irish or Italians or Slavs or even "coloreds," with whose rowdy offspring they prayed their own children wouldn't mix. Another prerequisite was a local candy store so they could stop by for an egg cream or an ice cream cone and pick up a magazine or a newspaper. The family read the *News* in the morning and the *Post* in the afternoon, and on Sundays they would also buy the *Mirror* so that they could keep up with Joe Palooka and Li'l Abner. A few of them—Walter and Moe and Milton—also read the *Times,* and so escaped, to some extent, the Liebers' tabloid view of the increasingly grim and precarious world. But none of them ever read, say, the *Journal-American* or the *World-Telegraph* or the *Sun.* They believed that these publications were *goyish*, though they couldn't say why. They also never bought the *Brooklyn Eagle* unless they were looking for new apartments in the classified ads.

There were in those days family habits and patterns and customs that were so engrained that they became remarkable only in retrospect. For example, the Lieber women always put a hot supper on the table, except on Saturdays, when they would "run out" to the appetizing store and bring home herring and whitefish and sturgeon and lox and cream cheese and Swiss cheese and bialies for the evening meal. This was called eating dairy. Sunday mornings the men would throw on some old clothes and go, unshaven, for newspapers and fresh hot onion rolls and bagels from the bakery while the women, still in their housecoats though their faces were "done," would fry up a batch of eggs and set out on the table the leftovers from Saturday's supper.

When company dropped in on any of the Liebers, the women would hurry to the kitchen to "put up" water for coffee and tea and to look for something to eat. If the company was unexpected, the women would fuss and apologize because there was "nothing in the house," but they would manage anyway to serve along with the coffee and tea a platter heaped high with cookies and cakes and crackers and bread and cheese and butter and jams. It was "not done," incidentally, to offer a visitor alcohol. Except for Lou Grossman, who was fond of his beer—and thus in the eyes of the family practically a drunkard—the men were seen drinking only at "occasions," and, as they poured a second shot of *shnapps*, their wives would start to look nervous. As for the women, every one of them, even Molly, believed that she was especially vulnerable to the loosening effects of strong drink, and would claim to feel hot and giddy after just a sip or two of the *seder* wine. Nonetheless, in some high kitchen cabinet in every family household there would be a few bottles of scotch or rye or cherry liqueur saved up for some future celebration, and these would vanish inch by inch on chilly winter mornings when the man of the house claimed he was coming down with a cold. Somehow that did not count as drinking.

The family did a lot of visiting back and forth in those days, and when they couldn't visit with each other, the women would spend hours chatting on the phone. How they loved the telephone! It was their primary means of being connected to each other and to the rest of the world. It smacked of magic. The system of wires and cables stretched along the telephone poles or buried deep beneath the streets was connected securely and permanently to their eager and hungry hearts. Sundays, if you tried to call one of the sisters, you usually got a busy signal. Milton and Irving and Walter made sure to carry plenty of nickels in their pockets so on the way home from work—before descending into the push and jostle and filth of the subway—they could stop off at a telephone booth to ask if they should get a bottle of milk or a loaf of bread on the way home. They were in that way good husbands, the family men, all except Lou Grossman, who had turned out to be a son of a bitch.

The Liebers would later associate with those days—along with their nostalgic memories of President Roosevelt, and a few snatches of theme music and commercial jingles from their favorite radio programs, and their exaggerated recollections of the economic hardships they had endured—a certain seasonal sequence of odors; the wintertime smell of simmering soups and damp wool and rubber galoshes drying under a hissing radiator; the springtime air that was all sunshine and mothballs; the aromas of summer, of seawater and suntan lotions and men sweating in thick humid air that still held a whiff of ozone from a morning thunderstorm; and the sharp tang of autumn, holiday time, with its new clothes and its crowded synagogues. They would also remember the inevitable smells of babies, a compound of talc and cod-liver oil and milky formulas and mashed peas and scented disinfectants and soiled diapers soaking in a bucket; and the heady perfumes the Lieber women wore, dabbing their stuff behind their ears and along their arms as Molly had taught them to do; and lingering within all those other smells, in every season, so basic to them that, like the very smell of life itself, they hardly ever noticed it anymore, was that aroma of chocolate which Sam and Milton and Lou and Deborah and Molly and Irving and Walter brought home with them from the factory or the retail outlets or the warehouse in Canarsie that Sam had added to the business. This, most of all, was the Lieber odor.

At one time or another they all worked for Sam. Even Moe was put to work in the factory during the summers while he was in college. Later Sam would say that if he had invested in the business as much time and energy and money as he gave to the family, he could have been a millionaire ten times over—which was not a complaint, at least not then; it was an assessment of the facts. Because doing for the family was Sam's greatest pleasure. He made it his habit on his way home from work to stop off at their houses to see how they were getting along. When they had babies, he showered them with cribs and bassinets and crisp new hundred-dollar bills that were supposed to go into the bank "for the kid's education," but somehow never did. He paid for Mrs. Gillicutty, and he paid for Sophie's medicines and doctor bills, and he paid for the ambulance they had to hire every six months to move Sophie to her next resting place. He also paid for a semiprivate room for Hymie so that he wouldn't have to sleep with the lunatics on the ward. When it came time for Moe to go to college, and City wasn't good enough for the prima donna, Sam agreed to supplement the small scholarship the boy had won and let him go to Columbia—"Columbia University!" the family would exclaim, "Imagine!"—and took him up to a wholesale house owned by one of his cronies and let him pick out three or four expensive suits "so he shouldn't, God forbid, feel embarrassed by his clothes among all those rich kids." He was more than generous, and inevitably they took advantage of him. In the days when Lou Grossman was running the warehouse in Canarsie, for example, everyone knew he was selling merchandise out the back door, but Sam ignored it. And Evelyn: all of a sudden, after she was married, she developed fancy tastes. She bought expensive furniture, and had a *shvartzeh* woman come in to clean her house, and decked herself out with charm bracelets and fur coats, and then complained that she was broke. So Sam gave Milton a raise.

"Family is family," he used to say. "You can fight like wild animals one day, but you're still family the next."

Anyway, it didn't matter. There was enough to go around. They should live and be well and maybe someday show a little appreciation, that was all he asked of them. It tickled him to see them—"the babies"—marrying and settling down and raising families of their own. It was like watching some fine old flowering tree, laboriously transplanted to new soil, take root and flourish. As far as Sam was concerned, his sisters' happiness gave retrospective meaning to Sophie's troubled and now bedridden life. And wasn't that enough? That she should live to have the pleasure of her grandchildren at play around her. He was glad—he was more than glad; he was proud —to be the instrument through which she fulfilled her dreams. He loved to sit by her bedside, holding her hand and bending his ear close to her mouth to try to make sense of her mutterings, to see in her faded eyes the *nachis* that he, and he alone, could give her. They shared between them, along with their memories of the early days, the implicit and inexpressible belief that it was upon the younger Liebers that the future of the family in America would depend. There were moments when Sam's pride in them was so intense that he could imagine that he and his mother had conspired to produce them, and that through them, he himself would be the father of some glorious world that was still unborn.

For his own children, of course, nothing was quite good enough. The backyard of the house in Manhattan Beach was cluttered with swings and slides and fancy toys. Carrie, once she outgrew her crib, slept like a princess in a big four-poster with a lilac-colored canopy—in fact, the whole room, said Evelyn, was like something out of a magazine. She had expensive dolls with a whole wardrobe of clothes for them, and a handmade dollhouse with exquisite miniature furniture, and a doll carriage that sported chrome and springs and a little lacy pillow, and probably cost more than the sturdy full-size carriages in which Evelyn's and Ruthie's kids were wheeled to the park for their daily airings. As for Rich, even at the age of eight and nine and ten his mother dressed him up in white linen suits, and Sam gave him a little replica of an automobile with a real gasoline motor in it, and you would have thought to look at him that he was being groomed to inherit a throne. Sam used to bring him to the factory, and he would sit himself down behind Sam's desk and start pushing buttons and ordering people around. Sure, he was a good-natured kid at heart, quick with a joke and a smile, rushing dutifully to give his aunts a hug and a kiss, but Sam was letting him run wild. At school he was always in trouble and didn't pay attention to his work; at home he drove Essie wild. He just couldn't get along with her—years later he would complain that all she ever cared about was whether his ears and fingernails were clean—and consequently he was only happy when he was gallivanting with Sam. Sam used to take him to ball games and movies and to Asa Kalisher's restaurant, where he would sit like a regular little *mensh,* swapping jokes with Sam's cronies. He loved the attention of adults, and knew how to get it; but he had no friends his own age, and the family worried.

"Just wait a couple of years," said Ruthie, "and Sam will have his hands full with that one."

But there was no use talking to Sam. Not when it came to his children. They were his darlings, they were his joy, they were the glitter of perfection in a tawdry and damaged world, and he believed that

154

not even Essie with her migraine headaches and her incandescent silliness would manage to mar them.

Sam had observed by then that whatever you are, time makes you more so. Time exaggerates; time produces caricature; time takes your minor quirks and *kvetches* and enlarges them into a parody of the self you are doomed to become. How odd it was, to mark in the full-blown flesh and mannerisms of his brothers and sisters the old family habits and tendencies, as though growing up were merely a fulfillment of the children they had been. And so it was with Essie. The years had magnified her shrill and compulsive faults. She went around the house like some quick, nervous little bird, peeping and scolding and darting about her those dark button eyes. She was oblivious to his moods. She was oblivious, in fact, to the simple human realities of anyone but herself. If something was on her mind —a new dress, a fault in the plumbing, a child's scraped knee, a nightmare about Adolf Hitler—she expected it must be on Sam's mind, too. Her chatter was free-form, her logic bizarre. She was capable of picking up a conversation in the middle of an anecdote she had failed to finish the day before, or of racing ahead of what you were saying to arrive at some erroneous conclusion of her own. Since she had a woman coming in every day to cook and clean and care for the children, she had nothing to do with herself. She passed her time by moving around the furniture and talking on the phone and traipsing through department stores and worrying about her weight. She must have weighed ninety pounds, but she was always on a diet. She seemed to believe that if she relented for a moment from her lettuce and tuna fish and toast and coffee, she would be transformed at once into some fat, coarse country housewife, the image, one supposed, of some old-world ancestor still lurking in her blood.

Her home was impeccable. It was a family joke that all you had to do was flick your cigarette once at Essie's house and a fresh clean ashtray would instantly appear. When her babies were born, she made the relatives wear surgical masks when they came to visit. She boiled the silverware. She had a phobia about insects: a spider in the bathroom could send her to bed with a headache. An endless sequence of rattled cleaning women were taught to iron Sam's underwear and socks. Should Sam neglect to shower before climbing into bed, Essie would turn her back to him. She would also turn her back to him if she decided that his beard was too rough or his feet too cold or his embrace too muscular, and then Sam would be alone in the darkness with his moods and his dreams. She positively loathed the out-of-doors. It was too hot or too cold, too wet or too dry, too windy or too still.

"Look," she would complain, rubbing her fingers together, "the air is full of soot!"

She lived a block and a half from Brooklyn's best beach but she hadn't set foot in the ocean since she was married, and she was ever vigilant lest her carpets be invaded by sand. That deep, lovely tan she displayed in the summer came from a jar and a sun lamp. She complained that the proximity of sweat made her "physically ill," and though she had married into a family that expressed itself damply with hugs and kisses, she always managed to evade the lips and arms of Milton and Irving and Lou. If Rich came in hot and red-cheeked from an hour of play, she would scold him for getting "overheated" and make him sit down for a rest. One day he fell from a slide in a playground and broke a bone in his wrist; the way Essie carried on with her hysteria and her phone calls, you would have thought the kid was dead. And through all this, Sam indulged her. What else could he do? Quarrel with her? There was nothing to quarrel about. Her main obligation, after all, was to complete some image he had once concocted for himself, and that she did, and that was enough. As for the rest, he merely circumscribed and gave over to her that portion of his time and money and attention she required, placed her, so to speak, in a small, impermeable sphere of household and children which she was free to polish, to fret over, to adorn.

There were times—oh, in every life there are such times—when his pace would slow and his routines fail him, and in the midst of his daily rounds he would suffer glimmerings of unreality. For a night or two or three his dreams would unsettle him with their masked longings and hectic strife, and he would awaken with a headache or in a mood of despair. He would be aware at such times, through the static of the everyday, of the murmur of his innermost self; he would feel himself driven back toward his old schemes and hopes and restlessness, and wonder why they still gnawed at him. Somehow, somewhere, there was something he had missed or ignored or avoided, like an unintended insult or a moment of cowardice hidden now, forgotten, in the mists of time. Occasionally there would linger at the fringe of his memory the night he had slept in the forest and the mystery it contained. There seemed to be at the core of him a small, per-

156

manent residue of bitterness that nothing—not the business or the family or the card games at the club or the warm, slow summer afternoons at Ebbets Field or Yankee Stadium—could diminish. He tried not to show it. He hid behind his smile and his hat brim and the blue-gray smoke of his cigarettes; but at such times the family could usually sense that Sam was in one of his "moods."

Briefly, inexorably, as that gray decade with its somber headlines unfolded itself toward the next war, Sam started "running around" with another woman. The family never knew her name or what she looked like; they knew only the simple, blunt, astonishing fact of it, the way they also knew about Lou's "chippies" or Deborah's ghost. They knew about it because Sam apparently wanted them to know. In some vague way he teased them with it, dropping hints, leaving his tracks uncovered, as though for him the purpose of the affair was not in the dull heat and froth enacted in a tawdry bedroom, but in the grief and worry it caused them. The mysterious phone calls that made him wave everyone out of the office, the blank hours he never tried to account for, the vague air of guilt and odor and stain with which he returned from "lunch," that hysterical night when he neglected to come home and Essie called everyone up, looking for him: it was as though he meant for them to read into it all some lurking and obscure declaration of his freedom, or his misery, or his need for a space he could inhabit, secretly, all by himself.

Her name was Elana. Never mind how he met her—the city had thrown her randomly into his path, and they had collided like a couple of atoms. She was a *poilisheh,* an abandoned wife, and she lived over on Pacific Street with a six-year-old daughter, who was all freckles and hurt, and an old ash-colored cat which used to leap onto the bed in the midst of their heaves and exertions. For a while he thought he loved her, this warm, somber woman with her massive breasts and her sad past and her crucifix on the wall. He found in the ample folds of her flesh a heat and a response that Essie couldn't provide. But it wasn't love, no matter how much he believed at the time the endearments he felt compelled to whisper to her, the promises that he made. It wasn't love; it wasn't even lust; it was just a kind of little mess he had willed into the pattern of his life the way an artist might for the heck of it blotch or smear a canvas that is otherwise too orderly, too precise; and even then he was disappointed with the effect he had created. Because when Essie found out about it (after he had done everything but draw her a map and exhibit a photograph), she simply didn't care. And why should she? Hadn't she known for years about the *shiksa* her father had kept in an apartment on Liberty Avenue, and believed—because the sly, proper Hilda Schonwald had led her to believe—that such monkey business was inevitable, and maybe even desirable, given the nature of marriage and men? She looked at it because Sam for his own reasons wanted her to look at it; looked at it, saw at once that it wasn't going to disturb her routines, shrugged her thin shoulders, suffered an extra night or two of headaches, and didn't bother to look at it again.

"Let him run around where he wants," she told Molly, "so long as he remembers to come home to me."

That was Essie. She was exquisite; she was invulnerable. They would be married for more than forty years, and not once in that time did Sam ever feel he was capable of damaging her. She had on her side the advantage of clear and limited expectations. She required nothing of him but form. And meanwhile he had on his hands, like a memory you can't shake off, this other woman, this Elana, with her demands and her raptures and her tears, with all her lively *goyische* sense of sin and hellfire and the obligations he owed her. In the end Elana, not Essie, was the problem, and it took him months and months before he was able finally, guiltily, to disentangle himself.

MILTON HIMMELFARB WAS A MAGICIAN—or, as he preferred to say, an illusionist. If you asked him, and sometimes even if you hadn't asked him, he would tell you in his slow and ponderous way all about his twelfth birthday, when his parents took him to see the great Houdini perform. He had never gotten over it. Something about that day had left a mark on his blood and given a shape to the musings of his innocent, lumpish soul. Even now, in his thirties, married, working for his brother-in-law in the chocolate factory on Bergen Street and riding home on the subway every night to a wife he believed he still loved and a baby boy he knew he adored, Milton could close his eyes and the sway and clatter of the train would evoke that special memory: again he would be dressed in his holiday clothes riding uptown, squeezed between his parents, with the hot air blowing out

158

from the ventilator between his legs; again he would be in the theater with its velvet seats and gilded moldings, and the big crystal chandelier which slowly dimmed against the rising glitter of his excitement; again he would be caught up in that astonishing performance which seemed to suspend the rules of time, rushing to the awe of its ending when he thought it had hardly begun; and again he would be riding home, half dozing, his belly plump and warm with a restaurant meal, his mother's arm wrapped soft and heavy around him, his sleepy, bedazzled brain charged with wonder, with joy, with ambition, all of which, alas, would soon be dissipated by the arrival of his stop.

From that moment he had set his heart on being a conjurer, and by the time Evelyn met him he was really quite good. He could break an egg into a hat and show you the hat was empty. He could make a cigarette dance in the air. He could pluck a rainbow of colored handkerchiefs from the palm of his hand. He could perform marvelous stunts with a simple deck of cards. If craft makes a magician, Milton was one. He had read all the manuals; he kept a drawer filled with the latest catalogues from magic stores and stunt suppliers; he belonged to the union; he had studied carefully and with a kind of mute shrewdness the masters of his art. He had even analyzed for himself the nine categories of illusion—Escapes, Multiplications, Transferences, Materializations, Mesmerizations, Disappearances, Levitations, Mind Readings, and Restorations—and he incorporated each of these categories into his act.

The problem was that though his skill was substantial, his stage presence was ordinary. He had dandruff beneath his magician's top hat. His complexion bore faint scars of his boyhood acne. No matter how much tailoring he submitted himself to, his clothes looked ill-fitting and rumpled—he seemed to bulge with secret pockets—and he couldn't manage to develop, no matter how brilliant his stunts, an adequate line of patter. His fingers flew, but his thick tongue limped and stumbled. In the big time, in that bright world of success, the audience wanted more than magic; it wanted romance, and that was a commodity that poor, methodical Milton, with his hesitations and his solemnity, was unable to provide.

So he inhabited the hopeful and pathetic fringe of show business, like so many others, awaiting a breakthrough that would never come. Occasionally there might be a weekend job at some family hotel in the Catskills, a half hour routine shuffled in between the bow-tied comedian and the pederastic baritone, with the audience drowsy and fogged with food. More often nowadays he merely picked up a few extra dollars on Saturday afternoons, performing in a rented hall for the congregated children of Odd Fellows or Knights of Pythias, and even then the kids were likely to fidget and tease, despising his air of nervousness, his flubbed jokes, his brusque, sullen manner. He was best in a living room, an inspired amateur, entertaining a handful of relatives or friends. There it didn't matter if he stuttered and coughed: the cards still levitated; the furry white rabbit still wonderfully reappeared.

Sometimes he would amaze even himself with the tricks he could accomplish. It was a matter of little things. In a series of knotted handkerchiefs there might appear a magenta one he couldn't remember putting there between the red and the blue; a coin that he "vanished" into a secret pocket would be gone when he went to look for it; a mind-reading gimmick might produce for him behind the blindfold a scary moment of apparently authentic telepathy. This was happening more and more lately, and he didn't know what to make of it. It was as though the illusions of his trade conjured up a reality of their own. There would be moments when he felt himself possessed of certain strange and willful powers. Occasionally, in a bold mood, he would work at mastering them. He discovered, for example, that he could move small objects—a button, a spoon, a key—by tenaciously foreseeing their motion. Riding home on the subway, he would fix his attention upon a fellow passenger—that stout woman, for example, with her swollen legs and her feathered hat—and feel himself suddenly drenched, as it were, with the clammy contents of her thoughts. There was a time when he tried to incorporate these powers into his performance, but he quickly learned that his audiences, even the children, preferred the illusions. Real magic, even when it worked—and it was all so haphazard and momentary that he could hardly believe it himself—looked clumsy and forced compared to the skilled manipulations of sleight of hand. Besides, the effort was exhausting, and accompanied always by a spine tingle, a dry mouth, a sense of dread, as though some interior door had opened and he was about to tumble through. Maybe he was only playing tricks on himself, losing his mind. Best, then, to leave it alone.

He never told anyone about his powers because if he told, he would have to confess that he was afraid, and he had learned quickly, harshly, in the streets of Brooklyn that a man never admits to being afraid. He masked his fear with sullenness. He would come home with his lower lip jutting and his brow creased, and Evelyn could tell by looking at him that they were going to have a fight. They fought often but never meanly. They would pick at each other, then scream at each other, until he stalked out of the house to walk around the block and cool off, coming back sheepish and beaten and ready to make up. It wasn't a happy marriage, but it was a substantial one, and compared, say, to Ruthie and Lou, it was a kind of paradise. Evelyn, after all, was ferociously practical. She understood that Milton lived his life in a dull and ordinary world, to which the magic was merely an appendage, an adornment, and that secretly, deep down, he liked it that way. His greatest desire, never mind what he said, was to be like everyone else, which suited Evelyn just fine. That was the quality she saw in him when he came to the house to court her.

Evelyn, more than any of the others in that generation of Liebers, was bent on adapting herself to what she took to be the American tone and style and mood—that mishmash of hairdos and hemlines and household decorations she diligently culled out of a mess of magazines and newspapers. Sophie's grand desire, that her children should "fit," that they should live their lives unburdened of the sufferings and superstitions of the old country, had rooted itself most firmly into the rich soil of Evelyn's dutiful and unimaginative heart, and had blossomed at last into a pretty tangle of conventionality. The sight of pious Jews, for example, wandering down Pitkin Avenue with their sidelocks and their gabardines, made her feel ashamed. She had fond, illusory memories of her dead father, but she was also secretly glad that he was not around to embarrass her. The past, for Evelyn, was nothing but a furtive graveyard she had been lucky to escape. Her eye was formidably set on the future, and the future was defined in her mind by a powerful and amorphous "they," the real Americans, whose manners and codes and pleasures she was eager to ape. When she was a little girl, she had fantasized in a perfectly commonplace way (believing she was daring and bold) that she was a princess or an heiress, kidnapped in infancy, and sold into the tawdry confines of Lieberdom. Someday, somehow, if she did all the right things, she would be restored to her proper world, the world where "they" lived happily ever after. The problem was that "they" kept changing. "They" wouldn't hold still long enough for her to catch up. No sooner had she applied to herself the "right" shade of lipstick or nail polish, the "fashionable" length of hair or skirt, when "they," as though to spite her, moved on to something else. "They" retreated forever in front of her, eluding her, slipping away from her expectant grasp.

Consequently she was nervous—"high-strung," the family said. With Evelyn it was laughter one minute, the next minute tears. Circumstances kept passing beyond her control. Accidents amazed her, and she would react to them by laughing hysterically, helplessly, her face turning red and water pouring from her eyes, while someone else had to hurry to wipe up the spill or apply the Band-Aid to the kid's scraped elbow. But she was, despite it all, so transparent and vivacious that people liked her, and she had a dozen girlhood friends she would go on seeing, and criticizing, for the rest of her life.

As soon as she was married, she made it clear to Milton that magic was a fine hobby, but that a man's primary obligation was to the job that made him his living. She would tolerate his catalogues, his props, his habit of lighting a cigarette with a flame plucked from thin air; she would be appropriately amused at family get-togethers when he drew a chain of dollar bills from Sam's jacket pocket, or attempted, hilariously, to hypnotize the grumpy and uncooperative Lou; she would let him try to pursue, on evening and weekends, his dreams and his ambitions; but since he wasn't educated, and had no trade, or well-to-do parents who might set him up in business, he would have to go to work for Sam. He turned out to be a good worker. He did what he was told. He was dull, but he was reliable. He never opened a big mouth or took the aftenoon off to join Lou Grossman at the racetrack. He got himself out of bed in the morning and made his own breakfast and went off to work in the white shirt and tie that Evelyn insisted that he wear and came home in the evening, tired and sullen, with a newspaper tucked under his arm, as if he had never wanted anything else. The neighbors thought of him as a nice man, slightly timid, and awfully long-winded when he was well launched on an anecdote, and maybe a little henpecked, and they learned to overlook the occasional shouts and poundings that resounded so clearly through the thin apartment-house walls.

"With Milton, at least, I get my money's worth," Sam used to say. Meaning that Lou Grossman was another story.

Lou and Milton, Milton and Lou: they had almost nothing in common, but they were fused in the family mind because Evelyn and Ruthie were so often together. Where one moved, the other followed. During the years when they were having their babies (Ruthie would end up with four, Evelyn with two), they lived around the corner or across the street from each other in three different neighborhoods before settling down in the pleasant, tree-speckled community of Crown Heights. Milton hated Lou, and Lou despised Milton, but they rode to work together, usually went out to lunch together, on Friday evening got together with Evelyn's friends to play gin rummy, and on Sunday mornings ran into each other, grumpy and unshaven, in the bakery or the candy store. So they learned to suffer each other. What else can brothers-in-law do?

During the summer in those years Ruthie and Evelyn rented adjacent bungalows in Far Rockaway so that their children could be at the beach. Milton and Lou would have to get up at five in the morning and ride the bus and subway to Bergen Street and wouldn't get home, to a late, moody supper of hamburgers and mosquitoes, until eight at night. Molly loved to tease them about the traveling. She told them the reason her sisters liked Far Rockaway so much was that it kept their husbands out of the way.

"Who knows?" she would say. "They probably got themselves a couple of boyfriends out there—the lifeguard, maybe, or the ice cream man."

This sort of kibitzing meant nothing to Milton; he would smile slowly, good-natured, essentially humorless, exposing those long yellow teeth which were all going to be pulled someday; but it used to rile Lou, and the more it riled him, the more Molly teased. She was fatter and brassier than ever, and her voice would fill the office.

"Listen," she would say, "sauce for the goose is sauce for the gander," and you could see Lou's jaw working, a muscle throbbing in his cheek, and his eyes fixing themselves momentarily on some point in space into which he had conjured a sudden and explicit nightmare.

Lou was a big, heavy, blustering sort of man with black greasy hair and swarthy skin and a bent, sneering mouth, from which he dangled a cigarette, dripping ash. When he first came into the family, courting Ruthie, everyone said that he looked like a "wop." Later they would say that he acted like one, too. His parents owned a murky little grocery store in Greenpoint, which was a "tough" neighborhood even in those days, and they lived above it in an apartment as dark and clammy as a cave. Lou used to brag about how his father, now dead, would whack him a few with his belt, not to punish him but just to let him know what the world was like. Once he even took

Milton and Irving into the men's room at the factory to show them the scar on his backside where the belt buckle had opened a gash that later festered. The family never understood what Ruthie saw in him. Deborah declared immediately that he had a bad aura, that his soul was blotched and cramped; Sophie used to be almost rude to him whenever he came to the house. When Ruthie announced that she was going to marry him, Molly was the only one who defended her, probably because Lou reminded her of Davey Furst. He was handsome in a rough sort of way, and his body was lean and hard and strong. Later the Lieber grandchildren would be astonished by old photographs of Lou at the beach—there he was, all wiry muscle, with Ruthie and Evelyn perched like a couple of lovebirds on his shoulders—because as soon as he was married he started putting on weight. It wasn't food weight, that soft accretion of flesh that plagued many of the Liebers; it was liquid weight, which settled in his bloated belly. Over the years his stomach grew enormous while his arms and legs and face stayed thin. Constantly thirsty, he poured into himself vast amounts of beer and sweet sodas, and the carbonation blew him up like a balloon. It became part of the family lore how Milton or Irving or Sam would go out to lunch with Lou and watch amazed as he downed along with his meal half a dozen beers or a couple of quarts of Coke, and no one was terribly surprised when eventually he developed kidney trouble.

The family never understood why Ruthie put up with him. He was a loudmouth, a braggart, a bully. Even when he was with her, he couldn't keep his eyes off other women, so you could imagine what went on with him and his "chippies" when she wasn't around. He liked to gamble—the big shot!—and walked around with a fat wad of bills in his pocket, but God forbid Ruthie should buy herself a new dress or a bit of luxury—then he would grumble that he wasn't made out of money. Their first years together were hell. In those days, while his father lay dying of cancer in a bed upstairs, he ran the grocery store in Greenpoint, and between his work and his women and his gambling, he was never at home. Ruthie would sit in the house alone with her baby—they were married in March and Jeffrey arrived in November, but who's counting?—worrying about him. She had plenty to worry about. Among other things, a couple of hoodlums had jumped him at the bus stop one night, bloodied his nose, and stolen his watch and wallet, and the next day the big stubborn jerk went down to Pitkin Avenue and bought himself a gun.

164

Ruthie would sit there and her mind would conjure up for her, so vivid it made her heart pound and her breath quicken, those same two hoodlums attacking him again, taking the gun from him and shooting him—boom! boom! boom! boom!—right in his bulging belly.

But she wouldn't think of divorcing him. "You make your bed, you sleep in it," Sophie used to say, and so Ruthie slept in it, even on those occasions when she had to sleep alone. Maybe it was the baby, or some concurrent wildness in her, or some strange desire for suffering; or maybe it was just that she quickly learned what to expect of him. Dimly he understood her limits, and while he often pushed right up to them, he never went beyond. For example, though he might threaten her with violence, he never actually hit her; he knew that hitting her would send her packing, and he was, in his own dim, brutish way, afraid of losing her. There was between them just that much of an odd, muted, hungry sort of love. He could even be tender with her; he would show up all of a sudden with a box of candy or a bunch of flowers or a gold-plated chain he had bought from a peddler on the street, with a big guilty leering smile spread across his congested face, and in a hectic flurry of lovemaking many things would be forgiven. He was, at least until his belly began to get in the way (Ruthie would later confide to Molly), awfully good in bed.

Oddly enough, Lou got along with Sam as well as he got along with anybody. There was between them some tangled bond, which slackened or tautened depending on Sam's mood. They shared a passion for pulp detective stories, which they traded back and forth like a couple of kids, and they affected the same hard-boiled way of dressing and smoking and talking about things. In the days when Sam was embroiled with Elana, he would allow Lou to tease him about it.

"Sure," Lou would say, "a man needs a little nookie on the side."

Lou was always taking liberties that way. They would go out together for lunch, or to the racetrack, and then at work Lou would throw his weight around, become the big boss, until with a quiet word or two Sam put him in his place. When it came to Lou, the family believed, Sam had the patience of a saint. They never quite understood that Sam enjoyed Lou the way some old potentate might have enjoyed a pet bear, proud of the brute energy he had tamed and mastered, savoring those moments when they might go down to the pit together to caper and growl. Lou was leashed—Sam had seen to that.

The family wouldn't hear until many years later, after time had softened the story, about a certain Friday night when Sam stopped off at Ruthie's place to see how she and her baby were getting along. This was in the days when Lou was still running his father's grocery store in Greenpoint, and though it was late, almost nine o'clock, Lou wasn't home. There was a plate waiting for him on the kitchen table, and a piece of overcooked liver nested among greasy onions in a pan on the stove. The baby was still up, crying his eyes out, and Ruthie was bouncing him and hugging him and walking him around trying to make him stop.

"Come on now, darling," she kept saying, "stop crying, stop, please stop."

"Maybe the kid's hungry," Sam told her. "Give him a bottle."

She was wearing a housecoat torn under one arm, and a loop of her copper-colored hair had fallen loose over her face, and she had a strange, puzzled glitter in her eyes as if she couldn't decide whether the trouble she was about to cause was any worse than the trouble she was already in. She hemmed and hawed a bit, then confessed that there was no milk in the house. Lou had promised to bring some home, she said, and she hadn't expected him to be so late, and she wasn't able to get out to the store, and anyway—blurting it out almost belligerently, too stubborn to cry—he had left her without any money. When she was finished, Sam walked over and opened the refrigerator, not because he didn't believe her but because the fact, no milk in the house, was so astonishing he had to absorb it through his eyes; and afterward there lingered in his memory that outrageous sight of beer bottles, a piece of bologna, a jar of mustard, a scrap of lettuce rusted brown.

Through a warm spring night that had turned ferocious Sam drove the quiet and familiar streets of Brooklyn to Greenpoint. By the time he got there his anger had cooled and hardened like a lump of steel spat from a furnace, and he already knew what he was going to do. Lou was behind the counter, half dozing, surrounded by breads, cheeses, cans of vegetables, bottles of milk. He came awake when Sam entered, alert and flushed and blustering, as though all along, ever since he married into the family, he had anticipated a struggle, a fight; but Sam didn't speak to him, didn't even bother to look at him; he just went around the store, picking things up and piling them in front of Lou on the counter. Then he said to him, with that quiet, cold dignity he had acquired years ago on Pitkin Avenue:

166

"Go on home, Lou; and take this stuff with you. I'll settle up with you tomorrow."

The next morning Sam showed up at Ruthie's house and told Lou to put a shirt on, he was taking him to the ball game. When Lou climbed into the Packard, Murray Pinsky was in the back seat. This was the same Murray Pinsky who was later shot down by his "business partners" in front of the funeral parlor on Empire Boulevard, right across the street from the police station. Sam knew him from the days when they played handball together in the schoolyard—the time some racketeers tried to get a piece of the chocolate business, it was Murray Pinsky who intervened. Sam didn't bother to introduce him to Lou; he didn't have to; he just said: "This is the brother-in-law I was telling you about," and as Lou turned around, awkward, reaching his arm over the seat to shake hands, Murray Pinsky nodded grimly and glared at him.

Lou never got over that mute, astonishing drive up to the Polo Grounds, riding next to Sam, feeling the gangster's eyes drilling holes into his back, thinking that at any moment they were going to veer off into an empty lot or an alley or an underground garage and that would be the end of him. It was seared into his memory how he sat through the long, slow, hot afternoon behind them in a box seat, in his own sweat and wild fear, with the scar on his backside throbbing and itching, watching them make random bets on whether the next pitch would be a ball or a strike, ignoring him, passing back and forth to each other, as the game went along, bills in denominations larger than he had ever seen before, while the sun scorched his back and his stench rose like steam to enclose him, waiting for—what?—a warning, a threat, a punishment, whatever it was that Sam had in mind to do with him; and how nothing happened, nothing at all. The Giants won and they drove him home, still ignoring him, and when he finally stepped out of the Packard, the sidewalk was like water under his feet. Murray in the back seat nodded at him again, grinning this time, and then Sam called his name, and Lou had to stand there, in sweat and fear and amazement, while Sam leaned toward the window and said to him:

"Don't forget to remind me that I still owe you for those groceries."

And that was the end of it.

But now Lou understood that whatever else in this world he might do, whatever pleasures he was allowed, a rough circle of sorts had been drawn around him, a kind of incantation uttered, and that the part of him which once had raged at liberty through the selfish and brutal streets of Greenpoint would never, never be quite so free again.

SOPHIE WOULD SAY: "WHERE'S MOE? Why don't I ever see him?" And they would tell her in that slow, loud way of talking to her they had in those years that Moe was busy with his studies and his laboratories and whatever other mysteries they kept you busy with up at Columbia, and Sophie would subside momentarily upon the pillows that propped her up, her eyes dimmed, her hands fretting on the blanket, and her lips would start working, as if she had to practice moving them before she could actually speak, and she would say again, in Yiddish:

"Where's Moe? Why don't I ever see him anymore?"

You couldn't tell what she was thinking; her face had congealed into a mask of age and pain and helplessness; but if she hadn't seen him for a week or two, her tone would become urgent as though she believed that something terrible must have happened to him, so terrible they refused to tell her about it. Then Sam would have to call the kid up and remind him, bluntly, of his family obligations. And when he finally showed up at her bedside, you could see her looking him over, her lips working. Of all her children he was the one she most wondered and worried about. He was special; he was the baby of her brood; he was so clever and handsome and "promising" that he carried with him at Columbia the full heft of the family's hopes and expectations. ("With a head like that on his shoulders," everyone said, "there'll be no candy business for him.") For Sophie, his very existence was holy and ordained. After all, she had dragged Jacob back from the grave to produce him. You could see in how eagerly she searched his face for some clue to his condition that he was the one who mattered most to her, the one who would justify her struggles, her sins, her ambitions.

"*Nu*," she would whisper to him, "so tell me a word or two already. What's going on with you?"

He never knew what to say. He would sit there with the smell of

168

the sickroom around him—the medicines, the milky oatmeal and mashed bananas, the dry thin odor of withered flesh itself—resenting the way her feebleness clutched at him, unable to rouse within himself the proper tributory emotion. He loved her, sure he did, or rather loved within her the traces of the vigorous mother she had been, but there were times when he scarcely recognized her, just as there were times lately when he scarcely recognized himself. How could he explain anything to her in terms she could comprehend? He would be glad to escape from her bedside, from Ruthie's house or Evelyn's house or Rose's house, wherever she happened to be, and ride the subway back to Morningside Heights, where among the bookstores and cheap restaurants he had begun—at last!—to feel at home.

Columbia, Morningside! Those words were magic for Moe. They evoked for him a bright new ideal realm and made of Brooklyn an insubstantial landscape of shadows. He remembered how he rode the subway up to campus that first time, wearing one of the pinstriped double-breasted suits Sam had bought for him at a wholesale house on Seventh Avenue, lugging in his damp hand a fat shiny new briefcase, with his hair parted near the middle and slicked down flat with Glossola oil, so that he looked like some gangster's kid brother. Morningside, Columbia! How lost and nervous he felt! A couple of upperclassmen were lounging casually in their rich tweeds and flannels soaking up the sun on the bright steps in front of Low Library, and when he stopped to ask directions—

"Can you tell me, please, where is John Jay Hall?"

"I not only *can,* my boy, I *will.*"

Never in his life had he been so awkward and exposed. There was nothing malicious in the way they looked at him; they were ever-so-nice; but as he walked across the brilliant campus, following their directions, he suspected they were laughing at him; and anyway, his eyes were dazzled and blurred by the bright hard blue of that September morning, and his heart suddenly lunged ahead of him, spilling an unexpected burden. He was stepping through a portal into another world. Here, in unknown rooms behind those glittering rows of windows, was everything he had ever wanted—and how hard it was going to be to return to Brooklyn, to go back down into that subway again.

But he had to.

During his freshman year he lived with Rose and then with Evelyn, and every day he rode the subway between Brooklyn and

Morningside Heights. He carried his briefcase jammed with books and notes, and when he got a seat, he would pull something out and pretend to read, but usually during those hours of transit his thoughts were a tumult. The train would lurch and rock and clatter and jolt, and people would be reading newspapers or staring at the floor, and he would look at them curiously, secretly studying them, imagining all the shame and guilt and fear and yearning there was to hide; and despising them, because he had already acquired at Columbia—it didn't take long!—the notion that riding the subway twice a day was something you were supposed to despise.

To abolish these thoughts, he would look for pretty girls. There was a time when the search became an obsession. He would thrust himself from car to car through the rush-hour crowd, seeking a face and a form that might approximate the perfect, soothing image he had in mind. Usually he was disappointed. The world, after all, did not casually yield up its beauties on the IRT. But every so often he would catch a heart-jamming glimpse of the loveliness he was looking for. There she would stand, clutching a pole, the adorable one, the chosen one, with her pale pretty face and her snubbed nose and that clean smooth line of chin, just as he had imagined her, and for a moment or two, until the door hissed open and the rude crowd swept her away, he would tumble into a trembling hot fantasy of love. Oh, it never amounted to much; he never even worked up the nerve to speak to any of them; but years later he would still be haunted by squeamish memories of the times when he managed by stealth and madness to steal the tingle of a soft, perfect breast against his elbow or shoulder.

The secret erotic bliss he pursued in the subway, however, was merely a sideshow to, a distraction from, the substantial agonies of that first year. He had discovered that he was nowhere at ease. He was troubled in Brooklyn by what he was becoming, and he was stricken at Columbia by what he still was. How he envied the comfortable way the other students, and not just the *goyim*, could talk to the instructors. For him to visit a professor's office was humiliating. He would stumble and stutter and rub his damp palms on his trousers, believing that young Meyers or old Van Dorn could look right through him and see the whole ignorant, sprawling crowd of Liebers —Sophie and Sam and Molly and Hymie and Lou Grossman and Irving Malish—clustered behind. He would flee across the campus, head down, believing that at any moment someone might accuse him of trespassing. He suffered more and more as the months passed from a

170

peculiar sort of snobbism that was directed primarily against himself. Sure, he had classmates that were like him, children of immigrants and common laborers riding the subway from the outer regions of the ignorant boroughs, commuting, as it were, between incompatible worlds, but as far as Moe was concerned, they simply didn't count. He shunned them. He fixed his attention on the others, the ones who were *born* to Morningside, the ones with money and manners and connections, whose roots ran deep into the continental soil. Stubbornly, opaquely, Moe set his foolish heart on becoming one of them.

He worked hard at it. He learned bit by bit to wear the proper clothes and the proper haircut and the proper shoes and even the proper bland, confident smile on his face. He finagled an invitation to join the Jewish fraternity, a real coup, for which he had to humiliate himself by riding out to Manhattan Beach to beg Sam for the initiation money. He labored to shed his accent, that familiar nasal brand of Brooklyn and Yiddish that burdened his speech like a layer of scar tissue, learning to enunciate a more "standard" variety of English as though it were a foreign language, practicing before a mirror until the tip of his tongue showed pink between his teeth when he said "these" and "those," and suppressing the tendency to swallow the double *t* and so make an ugly grunt of words like "bottle" and "glottal." He also worked hard at his books, hoping that a display of sheer industry and intelligence might gain him entry into that other world—Morningside, Columbia!—though he suspected right away that when it came to probing the arcane recesses of academic life, raw intellect wasn't enough. He did fine in the sciences; science was democratic, in science a fact was a fact, a theory was a theory, and everyone was equally a parvenu. But in his other courses, in Contemporary Civilization and Humanities I, he sensed himself entering a maze where style was substance and substance was style, and the floor plan had been given out to the lucky ones at birth. Homer, Aeschylus, Plato, St. Augustine, Thomas Aquinas, Dante, Rabelais, Voltaire: he experienced as he read them a dismal sense of insufficiency and regret; he was exposed through them to a tradition, a civilization, a world that would remain forever foreign to him, as though they embodied a strange spiritual arithmetic based on some biological quirk, like having twelve fingers, and so would forever elude him. Not until the class arrived at Dostoyevsky, Marx, Kafka, did he feel himself, at last, on substantial and familiar ground.

Weekends were hell. Weekends the demands of the family closed around him and he had only the claims of his studies (which they persisted in calling his "homework") to protect him. They wanted him to visit Sophie. They expected him to drive out with them to the Island to pass an anxious and heartbreaking couple of hours sitting and chatting with Hymie—or, more usually, chatting among themselves in Hymie's presence, since the poor sedated soul, summoned out to the sun porch, was usually silent and indrawn. Or there would be one of those awful family get-togethers in someone's garish and overstuffed living room, with all of them sweating and red-faced in the stale heat of their passions, and shouting at everyone else about what amounted to nothing at all. How well he knew that scene. Lou belching and scowling and asking for drinks of water; Milton with his clumsy tricks and his sullen expression; Sam, the bigshot, with his dangling cigarette and his omnipresent fedora, like some parody of a gangland toady; his sisters shoving food at him while they gabbled about money and movie stars and babies. No wonder that among them Moe's insides quivered with astonished and livid oppression. The only ones who had even an inkling of the bold ideas that resounded in his eager brain were Deborah and Walter, but Deborah and Walter were both crazy, each in a special way—Deborah the mystic, Walter the Red, as though intelligence and reading, unmediated by the discipline of real learning, spilled into passionate channels, clogged there, and overflowed into mere idiosyncrasy. Of course, Moe knew that whatever his efforts, however far he wandered into that vivid maze of new manners and new attitudes that surrounded him at Columbia, some part of him was irretrievably bound to them, was forever Lieber, and yet they were, so, so—he plucked a word from a book—so *vulgar!* Oh, sure, "earthy" was a kinder word, and he told himself that he shouldn't blame them for the advantages they never had, the advantages that they were paying to give to him, but look at them, look at them! And all he could do was sit there, not saying much, smiling and being polite, trying to maintain what he took to be the necessary ironic distance, and struggling with his careless and isolated heart lest at any moment he slip back among them, get embroiled in their heat and their noise, and lose everything he believed he had gained.

For a year and a half, like Sophie, he was shunted from sister to sister, depending on who had room for him at the moment, until, in a mood of desperation, he begged, wheedled, demanded from Sam the money that allowed him to move into that cramped apartment on

112th Street, which he shared with two other boys, or rather "men," as Columbia students were taught to call themselves. "If it will make you happy, go," Sam said to him, and he was never able to confess to the family that in those first months of living away from Brooklyn he wasn't happy at all. He fell into a mysterious and persistent mood of despondency. He would come back to the apartment after his classes strangely exhausted and sad, and doze off into a fitful half sleep when he knew he was supposed to be studying. Where had it come from, he wondered, this laziness, this indolence, this penchant for the couch? Homesickness, guilt? Suspended between dreams and reality, he would hear the voices of the family murmuring in his ears, crowding like a mob of ghosts into the confines of what he had expected would be his sanctuary, forcing him to acknowledge over and over again his burden of grief and shame. The family, the family: he was doomed to spin forever in their small orbit, there was nothing he could do to escape them.

Then he met Laura: cool, taut, efficient Laura. She was the sister of one of his fraternity brothers, Joshua Reisch (a sad-eyed and sardonic football player, who would someday receive a posthumous Medal of Honor for throwing himself on a German hand grenade during the Battle of the Bulge), and there was nothing romantic about their first encounter.

"Any of you guys need a date for the party?"

But the second time he saw her, when he spent a week's allowance to take her to hear Duke Ellington in the Rainbow Room, as they danced to the pale horns of "Satin Doll," he believed he was in love. She kept smiling at him with those pretty white teeth of hers, the kind of teeth which only a girlhood of money and milk and a prohibition on sweets could possibly achieve, and there was something about the long, smooth, lovely line of her neck and the firm curve of her jaw that assured you that she could stare at any ugliness, any horror, and never flinch, and he was entranced by a flush of pale pink in the tender hollows behind her small, exquisite ears. Oh! how he longed to kiss her there, as though with a touch of his lips he would possess all the rich world out of which she had come. How perfectly she seemed to fit the configurations of his fantasies and desires. He could imagine strolling hand in hand across College Walk with her, or sitting on the grass in front of the library with a lunch of sandwiches and soda bottles spread out between them—anyone who saw them like that would know at once that they belonged intimately to, somehow completed the picture of the campus that surrounded them.

Boldly, brilliantly, he courted her. He was prepared to make himself over if it would match her expectations. Sometimes, as he talked to her, he scarcely recognized the sound of his own voice, and he would wonder what demon was putting into his mouth those smooth, sophisticated words he was uttering in that gentle, ivied tone. He took her to Broadway shows and quaint little bohemian cafés in Greenwich Village, and rode her around town in taxicabs, and delivered her back to the Barnard dormitory before the lockup hour—lingering for the sweetness of a good-night kiss beneath the shadow of a hospitable tree—and then took the subway home to Brooklyn to beg more money from Sam and his sisters. They began sitting in on each other's classes. They met in the stacks of Butler Library to help each other with term papers. They double-dated with Josh and a sequence of those interchangeable, pretty, brainless girls Josh favored, and learned to compare the magic of their own fidelity with the shallowness of her brother's escapades. They wrote long love letters to each other—"Don't fear the future, my darling, because there is greatness in us, and thus no limit to what we can do"—and even exchanged an occasional love lyric in soggy dactyls and anapaests. He disciplined himself to sit at ease in her parents' luxurious apartment on West End Avenue, exchanging pleasantries with her father about the old tensions between German and Polish Jews, and the effects of the New Deal upon the banking business. He won her mother over by bringing her flowers and boxes of Lieber chocolate cherries, and admiring her antique glass collection, and confessing to her, with clever shyness, his affections and ambitions. During the long cool nights of early spring they would meet in their favorite restaurant on Broadway, and over a cup of coffee and a piece of Nesselrode pie they would tell each other their dreams and fantasies and premonitions—she had, the vulnerable darling, nightmares about rape and mutilation—and if what he felt wasn't love, it was still a close approximation, and the difference didn't matter. What mattered was that by possessing her, he would rise up into her world, and he was terrified of losing her.

There were, he believed, all sorts of ways he might lose her. He might lose her in the excruciating tension of their "petting" sessions, by going too fast or not going fast enough, by touching or failing to touch the squeamish buttons of her pleasure. Or he might lose her to one of his classmates, whose envy was much of the point of his being with her, and who could at any moment offer up to her, more authentically than he ever could, the promise and comfort and sophistication she desired. Or, worst of all, he might lose her to the simple vulgar reality that shadowed him; sooner or later he would have to take her to Brooklyn and introduce her to the family, and one evening of them might send her spinning silently away from him, forever out of reach.

With shame, with self-loathing, he foresaw that scene, the gauzy fabric of his hopes dissolving in Lieber heat and sweat and noise. He kept putting the moment off, thinking in time he could prepare her for it—oh, how he squirmed and hid and lied! If only he might be certain of her love beforehand, attach her life so securely to his that not even the truth of Brooklyn could separate them. But she kept holding some part of herself in reserve, was full of hidden recesses he couldn't touch. One moment they would be chatting happily, the next moment she would fall into the cool silence of her own secret and daunting thoughts. She was visiting his apartment in those days —he would always remember how he had to endure the ribaldry of his roomates when he told them to "vanish" for an hour—and they would struggle together on the bed with their clothes on, kissing and touching and probing until something seemed to give way in her, like ice breaking up, releasing her passion. He would sense her opening up beneath him, even smell the faint acrid scent of her excitement—which reminded him, perversely, of a thin distillation of dead cat—and then she would say something, or touch his hand to stop him, and roll away from him, flushed and gulping and almost crying through a ghastly smile she meant to be reassuring: "Please, I'm not ready, not yet." It was at such moments that she seemed most child-like, as though to have had all her money and freedom and advantages was never to grow up, and she wasn't prepared to spoil it. Kissing him again, telling him she loved him, to be patient with her, while he sat there thinking that he had failed some sort of test.

He took her finally to meet his family on a Sunday early in June. He was moving back to Brooklyn and going to work in the factory for the summer—there was no practical way to avoid it—and he half suspected he was going to lose Laura anyway, believed it was merely the enchantment of Morningside that had held them together. The occasion was a celebration of his mother's birthday, on a date picked more or less at random because the actual date of her birth had been lost when she came to America. The plan was for everyone to gather in Evelyn's house with presents and food and an enormous cake decorated with American flags. For days Moe's usual anxieties were exaggerated by anticipation of the event. He tried to avoid Laura because when he was with her, he heard himself trying to apologize in advance for the scene she was about to enter. Vulgar. The word jabbed against his tender skull as he washed, shaved. dressed, combed and recombed his hair until he approximated the image he was after, and walked up Broadway through a blaze of summer blue to her dormitory. Vulgar, vulgar: it had become the rhythm of his heart as he led her to the subway at 116th Street. They had never ridden the subway together before; he had shied away from it as though it would violate some favorite old dream, but he couldn't justify a taxicab to Brooklyn. He would remember how bright and lovely she looked in a pale green dress with fluffy sleeves and a floppy white sun hat with a scarf of the same green tied around its crown, and how all the way to Brooklyn on the practically empty train he sensed her being soiled and smeared by the soot and filth blown around them by the overhead fans. She kept touching his hand and smiling at him, sensitive to his mood if not the meaning of it, and he kept telling her the names of all the relatives she was going to meet, appending to each a pleasant comment or two—"Now Deborah's quite intelligent, but a bit of a mystic, and then there's Molly, who's never had any luck with the men she marries"—dressing them up so that at least she would foreglimpse them at their best.

But it was a long, grueling, lonely afternoon. The family put on one of its typical displays, and Moe sat there, trying to see it all through Laura's eyes, wondering what she could possibly think of them. Deborah and Molly got into an argument that went on and on until Evelyn shouted at them, "Stop it already, you're scaring the children!" whereupon they both started telling her to mind her own business. Ruthie had her baby there, and everyone oohed and ahed over it, and Rose started to cry. Milton did his famous trick with an egg in his pocket, and Lou Grossman spent most of the afternoon leering at Laura, padding after her, finding reasons to put his arm around her, and exercising his ape fingers by picking imaginary bits of thread and lint off her dress. By the end of the afternoon there were crumbs of food everywhere, and wet glasses, and then men had shed their jackets and pulled their ties loose from their collars, and Sam was dozing in one corner, and children were underfoot, and little Jeffrey, spanked for putting his dirty hands on the baby's face, was howling in the foyer. Laura, escaping Lou Grossman, was arguing politics with Walter and Sarah, and Essie had lost one of her gold earrings and was crawling around on her hands and knees, trying to find it, and Evelyn was sitting on a bridge chair next to the hospital bed, spooning bits of birthday cake into Sophie's toothless mouth. Moe's head ached. Chaos was everywhere. He half expected, as he watched Laura excuse herself and go off in search of the bathroom, that on her way through the foyer she would open a closet door and find Hymie sitting there. And through it all, through his pounding head and gloomy hatred, he kept smiling and smiling until he thought his jaw would break.

Riding back uptown, his brain as stuffed with their noise as his belly was with their food, he didn't know what to say. Laura wasn't saying much either; her face was flushed, and her lips kept moving slightly as though she were talking something out with herself, coming to a decision. He wanted to put his arm around her, but he didn't dare, had lost that privilege. He was as awkward with her now as he had been on their first date. He felt exposed, absurd. Oh, how he hated them! The train lurched and rocked, and he closed his eyes, and a kind of bitter electrical discharge started up somewhere in his brain and swept out along the complicated pattern of his nerves, and he almost enjoyed the pain of it. He opened his eyes and looked at Laura, and for a moment she looked back at him, not smiling, with no expression at all except a kind of bland curiosity, and her features seemed suddenly to rearrange themselves. He was looking at the face of a stranger, so lovely, so perfect, so utterly out of reach. Hopeless, gloomy, he endured the rest of the ride, and led her out of the train at 116th Street, up into the soft twilight of Broadway. Now what?

Maybe it was that for a moment he had set aside his hopes and expectations. Or maybe it was the heady scent of valediction in the warm summer air, the romantic breath of the green and white campus, where folding chairs already lay in stacks awaiting the following week's graduation, or the murmurous music of Morningside itself whispering to them the promise that the worst was behind them, the best was to come. In any case, the mood changed. He started off toward her dormitory, and she overtook him and tugged at his hand and, still not smiling, led him off toward his apartment. He would remember how she clung to his arm and leaned her pretty head against his shoulder as they strolled through the bright astonished evening, and how he said something to her, and how she said:

"Oh, well, that brother-in-law of yours is a real ass, but the rest of them were nice enough, and anyway"—smiling at last—"they gave me you."

She was naked beneath him, holding her breath as she clung to him, believing there would be pain in what she had decided to give him, helping him out with small gracious readjustments of her limbs just as she had helped him remove the pale green dress and the awkward undergarments beneath it to make of them a gorgeous litter glimmering on a chair, so brave and efficient and blushing and lovely —such a good sport—that they had gotten safely past the clumsy, silly, embarrassing stage of the business and were gliding smoothly, kissing and whispering encouragements to each other, toward that moment which would seem to both of them mysterious and profound; and Moe was already trembling with anticipation, fear, longing as she pushed herself up to envelop him and he probed and plunged deep down into what he had to believe was the final warm soft secret part of her; and as he felt the swell of his seed about to spill into the slick yielding container she had become, he knew—or would remember knowing—that he was going to marry her, spend his life with her, raise children with her, merge their worlds together, be, at last, a family man; and then the seed burst out of him in shuddering fragments, and he heard himself uttering the age-old questions and apologies of first-time lovers, and she kissed him to shut him up and reached for the bed sheet, laughing at how unexpectedly wet the process was, and he kept telling himself that life was good and believing, even as drowsiness overtook him, that his troubles were over.

WHEN ROSE FINALLY DELIVERED THE BABY and they called Sam up to tell him the news, he couldn't help himself, he said:

"*Mazel tov*! So what's wrong with the kid?"

That's how it was with Rose: you always expected the worst. For years the poor soul had been as unlucky in her pregnancies as she was in everything else. Her miscarriages had become a kind of family joke.

"Every time she goes to pee," Lou Grossman would say, "she drops a little *bindel* on the floor."

Weak-eyed, and apparently weak-wombed, Rose was forever the most dogged and dreary of the Lieber sisters. She was lumpish and plain. She wore heavy tweed suits in dark grays and browns that matched her dowdy hair, and mannish, orthopedic shoes on her swollen, aching feet. On her chin was a mole, large and black and perfectly round, with a single thick black hair sprouting from the center of it. Through her thick glasses she looked at you with one brown eye; the other, despite the years of patches and blackened lenses, still stared off into a world all its own. Her complexion was pale and humid, and her nose was a smaller replica of Jacob's nose, and when she smiled, she revealed a dead tooth, as thick and gray as a tombstone—she claimed she couldn't afford to get it fixed. The family remembered how shamelessly she had run after Irving Malish because even at the age of nineteen she was afraid—Sophie and her sisters had made her afraid—of being an old maid. Irving was a nice enough fellow, but closemouthed and humorless and slow, and he went around nibbling prunes to ease his chronic constipation. The best Sam had been able to do for him was to establish him in the warehouse, where he stood like a dummy all day with a clipboard and a blunt pencil, taking inventory of the merchandise. It didn't matter. He was good to Rose, and she seemed happy enough with him—at least, unlike her sisters, she never complained. But Irving's mother was a beaut. She was one of those short, fat, ageless widows who seem to arrive at that condition without ever having been married, or even young, at all. She drove the family crazy with her complaints and her woes. It was inevitable that as soon as the baby arrived, and word came that it was alive, she would start a quarrel about the naming. Rose wanted Jack, after her father, whose memory still flickered warm and bright like the memorial candle she never forgot to light on the anniversary of his death; but she discovered right away that there would be no living with her mother-in-law unless she called the kid George. And why George? Whom would the name honor? Some practically mythical ancestor Irving himself had never met.

And if that weren't enough, the "old misery" showed up at the hospital with her limp and her shopping bag and made a scene because the baby had been put in an incubator. She couldn't stand the fact that for a few days she would have to see her only grandchild

—this treasure! this darling little *boychik*!—through a couple of layers of glass. She just couldn't wait to lay her hands on him. She gave a scream that resounded through the corridors:

"But I'm the *bubba*! My germs can't hurt him! What? Is something wrong with him? What are you trying to hide?"

How it must have hurt Rose to see the fresh, freckled Irish nurses smirking and snickering—that bunch of anti-*Semits*! No wonder that behind her thick glasses and her placid smile Rose seemed always to be wincing; the world for her, outside the warm circle of her family, was perpetually discomforting.

Oh, they loved Rose dearly, they really did. She was so easy to love. There was absolutely nothing about her that any of them could find to envy, and it gave them pleasure to repeat to each other the sentimental judgment Deborah had once pronounced: that on the inside, where it mattered, Rose was the most beautiful Lieber of them all. In the years to come they would remember how they had all pitched in to nurse and cajole her through this pregnancy. They cleaned her house for her, brought her meals, kept her off her feet, forced upon her gallons of warm milk and dozens of soft-boiled eggs, which Rose ingested like medicine, holding her nose and spooning the yellow glop down. They sat up with her through the long, nervous, insomniacal nights of those last months, muttering little prayers every time she ran to relieve the pressure on her bladder. They even made Dr. Lipsky call in a specialist to examine her. And now that the kid had arrived, breathing, with all the necessary limbs and appurtenances, it didn't matter to them that they came away from the hospital thinking vaguely to themselves that the poor thing behind all that glimmering glass looked, well, rather distorted and ugly, as though he had been incompletely formed or vaguely unfinished. The way he lay there, staring—it was something you couldn't quite put your finger on—but never mind: they wouldn't even mention it to each other. The kid was alive, and that was enough, and despite old Mrs. Malish, Rose had never looked so happy. My, how she chattered and glowed! They came home telling each other that for Rose's sake, they would make for the baby a particularly memorable *briss*.

It was wartime then, and the Liebers were prospering. Sam had finagled a government contract—it was actually some sort of subcontract, but in those hectic days who worried about details?—and the factory started turning out on its assembly-line military rows of chocolate bars in olive-drab wrappings with a little "US" ("That's *us*," bubbled Molly) stamped into every bite. It wasn't the famous fine Lieber chocolate, of course; the stuff was cooked to War Department specifications, thick and crumbly, with a ridiculously high melting point so that it could survive in the tropics and a faint sour aftertaste that resulted from too little sugar and too many nutritional additives. Sam hated the stuff, remembering with a pang the luxurious chocolate cherries that once had sprouted on the trees of paradise, but this was war, mister, and everyone was making sacrifices. Sam was riding the bus to work. Lou Grossman postponed buying that automobile he had been dreaming about. Essie got out and dug up a patch of the lawn and planted a few rows of vegetables, and Evelyn and Ruthie were learning the dull arithmetic of ration books and black-market beef. Moe was the only one of the family men in uniform; the others had been given deferments because they were over-age or had babies at home or were crucial to the war effort in their jobs at the factory; but Lou and Milton were air-raid wardens, and spent many a night prowling the streets in their helmets and armbands, and Irving was putting his savings into war bonds. As for Moe, the newlywed, the family supposed he was safe enough. His Columbia education was already paying off; he had been able to enlist as an officer, was assigned to military intelligence, and stationed in Washington. It was all hush-hush, of course, and when he came up to New York for a weekend with Laura, he gave the impression that he was some sort of spy or counterspy, running around through the fog with the collar of his trench coat pulled up around his neck, chasing Nazi infiltrators and assorted fifth columnists, winning the war on the home front, when in reality he sat on his ass all day in a drafty Quonset hut, with a view of the sluggish Potomac through a tiny window, reading German newspapers and magazines, which arrived once a week from Zurich in the diplomatic pouch. But he was happy enough. So what if later he would come to feel himself deprived of glory and adventure?

Anyway, even Moe was able to come to the *briss*.

They held it in the living room of Ruthie's house, where Sophie was staying, because they were eager to give her—hoping the excitement wouldn't be too much—a few moments of pleasure. Hard to believe, seeing her in her hospital bed, with her collapsed, toothless face and her thin white hair through which her pink scalp vaguely glowed, that she was barely more than sixty years old. She looked a hundred. A third stroke had devastated her. For several weeks they had been sure she was going to die, but she pulled through, clinging to what remained of her life with all her old stubborn ambition. However, lately she was not only ailing, she was senile as well. Her mind, like Jacob's in his last days, went in and out of focus. Her thoughts wandered; she dozed off in the midst of conversations; she was no longer curious about her children, and, with a kind of pathetic relinquishing, no longer tried to tell them what to do. Sometimes in her confusion she got their names wrong, calling Sam Asa, or Walter Jacob, or Moe Hymie. (And how hard it had been to explain to Hymie why his mother no longer could come to visit him!) She had nothing but her gums to chew with—they couldn't trust her not to choke on her dental plates, those precious false teeth which once had been for her the very emblem of hopeful America— and so Mrs. Gillicutty would have to sit and feed her like a baby, scraping away with a spoon the oatmeal and mashed bananas that dribbled down her chin. Mostly she seemed to be nourished by her pain and her memories. At odd moments she would open her eyes and start mumbling to herself in a hazy jumble of three different languages about the old village, her father's butcher shop, someone named Stanislaus, a fire she had once witnessed, her wedding day, her sister-in-law's suicide, a pet canary, the eternal mud. She remembered things that had been forgotten for years: how it rained and rained in springtime; how her father had come home one night and nailed boards up over the windows, saying the *goyim* were drunk; how she once had dreamed—so long ago, so far away—that she had spoken to an angel who was sitting in a tree. Sometimes she would start singing to herself, wordlessly, harshly, a kind of primitive keening of some unknown ancient song.

Nonetheless, ill as she was, she loved to have her grandchildren around her. This was her joy, she said, and she never minded their noise. She was especially fond of Evelyn's Deanna, who at the age of one and two was dark and gorgeous, and would pull herself up on the bars of the hospital bed, stare at the old woman with those big black eyes of hers, and say, "Baba!" (And years later, during a course of psychotherapy, seeking some definitive thread in the tangle of her life, Deanna would discover that one of her first retrievable memories was a mute vision of her maternal grandmother, bedridden, radiant, and utterly mysterious.)

They would never forget that *briss*. They held it on a Sunday afternoon so that everyone could come: friends, neighbors, distant cousins. For days the Lieber women worked in their kitchens, preparing the food, the egg salads, salmon salads, tuna salads, herring salads, the hot appetizers, the cookies and cakes. Laura turned out a gorgeous mold of chopped liver, which, typical Laura, she called a pâte, and even Molly, who had given up pot-wrestling in those days—"Why should I cook," she would say, "when Max Gold can afford to take me to restaurants?"—chipped in a platter of her famous *gefilte* fish. On Saturday Sarah came and took all the kids to the park so that they would be out of the way, and Deborah showed up to sit with Sophie so Ruthie and Evelyn wouldn't have to worry about her. She was truly amazing, that Deborah. With her long amber cigarette holder, her lips painted into a bright red heart, her cheeks daubed with circles of rouge, her eyebrows plucked and redrawn, in her old silk dresses and gold bangle bracelets and long strands of beads, wearing that sapphire pendant which Buster had given her so many years ago, she created the effect when she entered a room of some old-time and time-stuck silent movie actress, superannuated by the advent of sound. But for once, because of the good news in the family, and even though she claimed to have felt throughout that week the chill of an evil premonition, she was cheerful and useful.

So everything was taken care of. Sam was paying for the drinks, and Dr. Lipsky would be in attendance, and Uncle Chaim, the *moyel,* was readying the implements of the ceremony. When Rose sent Irving over early Sunday morning to lend a hand, because after all, it was their child and their occasion, there was nothing for the man to do but mope around and make a nuisance of himself.

Evelyn, who could open a mouth when she had to, finally sent him home.

"There'll be less fuss," grumbled Lou Grossman, "when they marry the kid off. Though probably with a puss like that no girl'll want him."

"Don't worry," said Evelyn. "Someone wanted you."

By noon that rainy April day the rubbers and galoshes were piled high by Ruthie's front door, and Liebers and Malishes, friends and neighbors, were all congregated, with their heat and their noise, in Ruthie's living room.

It is easy enough to draw the fundamental contours of such a scene. The drinks, mostly rye and ginger ale and sweet kosher wine, were set out on a bridge table covered with one of Evelyn's best linen tablecloths, and in the little alcove that Ruthie insisted on calling the dinette, a great mahogany table with clawed feet was groaning under the burden of food. Everyone was hugging and kissing and saying *"Mazel tov!"* to each other. Soon the air would be thick with cigar smoke and perfume, someone would spill a drink—a mess of dark wine spreading through the intricate figure of Ruthie's fake Oriental rug—and one of the Lieber women, not Rose this time, but Evelyn, would be down on her hands and knees, dabbing hopelessly at the stain with a paper napkin. Sam, in a pearl-colored suit and a chocolate-colored shirt, stood beaming at the mob and patting his breast pocket, which held an envelope into which he had folded a crisp new hundred-dollar bill. Across the room Molly was introducing Max Gold ("my fee-ahn-*say*") to Aunt Bea and Uncle Yonkel; Bea was wheezing and Yonkel offered Max Gold his thick slab of a hand, and suddenly Molly was reminded of the old days when she used to run down the hallway on Park Place, shouting, "Big and Little are here! Big and Little are here!" and Hymie would head for the closet. For some reason that memory made her so sad that she fell silent for the rest of the afternoon, and despite all Max Gold did to comfort her, she cried herself to sleep that night in the warm, strong blond-haired crook of his arm. But never mind, never mind: superficially, at least, family occasions are always the same—a lot of gossip and reminiscence, a quarrel or two, a swelling bubble of suspect hilarity, some rowdy children in the background, soaking up memories for occasions to come, and off in the corner, all by himself, one sullen brother-in-law, Irving in this case, quietly getting drunk.

Odd that no one noticed Irving at the time; he was, after all, the father; but then, somehow Irving didn't count: when you tried to assemble the family in your mind, Irving was the one you might fail to remember.

Uncle Chaim was late, but he arrived at last with his clamps and his knives wrapped in a Yiddish newspaper and tied with string, breathing a hot mix of breakfast herring and his morning dose of *shnapps*. As always, the Liebers felt a certain pang when they saw him. For one thing, the ceremony over which he presided made everyone feel slightly ill. The poor infant would squirm and cry as soon as Uncle Chaim bent over him; then would come the pathetic little wail, drowned in a tumult of congratulations, with Uncle Chaim chanting above the noise an exultant prayer as he smeared an ointment that looked like mustard on the kid's bleeding glans. But there was more to it than that. He smoked too much, Uncle Chaim did. The first two fingers of his right hand were stained yellow with nicotine, and so was his patchy white beard in the region of his mouth; nonetheless, in his black coat and derby hat, with his ancient shabbiness and his shallow chest, he reminded the Lieber children of their father, dead now for twenty years. He had the same jutting Lieber nose, the same drop of water trembling at its tip, the same damp eyes, the same whiff about him of books and prayers, of musty synagogues and shattered nerves, so that seeing him was a little like seeing a ghost. In fact, when he bent over the hospital bed to murmur a greeting to Sophie, she looked startled by the sight of him.

They called Rose down from upstairs, where she had been breast-feeding the baby—much against the advice of her sisters, who preferred for their own children the "modern" and "American" rigmarole of formulas and bottles and rubber nipples and brushes and big cast-iron pots for sterilizing all the stuff—and everyone gathered around so that they could proceed with the ceremony.

Rose had given Sam the honor of being the godfather, so he got to hold the kid. He would remember how when they settled the little bundle into his arms, he was struck by the kid's thin golden hair, which, through some trick of light, appeared tinged with a kind of azure phosphorescence; and how when he looked at the kid's face, seeing him close up for the first time, he registered without quite thinking about it a sense of brooding concern. The strange, mottled complexion, the flattened nose, the little jutting jaw, the way the skin folded down around the eyes, the faint golden hair downing his fore-head and cheeks—he should have seen these as clues, he told himself later on, but he didn't have time to think about it then because Uncle Chaim had already removed the diaper and was applying the clamp. Had Rich's business been so terribly small? he vaguely wondered.

Now the family began to press forward, tightening the little buoyant circle that enclosed the ceremony, and Sam, so that he wouldn't have to watch what Uncle Chaim was doing, looked out at them, smiling. He smiled at Rose, whose face was shiny and damp; at Molly, who was strangely somber; at Asa Kalisher, who was getting old. He smiled at Evelyn, at Deborah, at Lou Grossman. He was enjoying one of those lilting moments when he felt himself to be the strong, proud center of the warm force that drew them together. His ears rang slightly as Uncle Chaim chanted the ancient prayer, and his whoozis shrank in sympathetic response to the operation. He glanced at his mother, who was propped up in the hospital bed, her eyes momentarily bright with ageless and invincible pleasure. The baby shuddered in his arms, cried out just for a moment, subsided, and with a grunt of triumph Uncle Chaim dropped a dismal dollop of flesh into the dish of sand, sprinkled wine over everything, and applied the antiseptic.

"*Mazel tov! Mazel tov! Mazel tov! Mazel tov!*"

The celebration now swelled and swirled around Ruthie's living room.

Sam, with a shot of whiskey warming his belly, was brooding again about the ugliness of infants. Rich, for example, the first time he saw him, had a little red monkey's face with a great blue bruise on his forehead. And Ruthie's Erwin, the second of her three boys, plucked from the womb with the aid of Dr. Lipsky's forceps, had come into the world with two black eyes. Well, give them a few weeks and they all turn out to be adorable.

Across the room Ruthie was repeating to a giddy trio the familiar anecdote about how Evelyn, the time she gave birth to Deanna, was up on a chair stretching to reach a cobweb when her water broke.

"She had to be cleaning!" She laughed and shouted at the same time. "In her condition she had to be cleaning because God forbid in her house there should be a speck of dust!"

Evelyn threw up her hands, Uncle Asa roared, and Uncle Yonkel smiled benevolently.

A few feet away Mrs. Malish in a dumpy black dress was engaged in some sort of solemn conversation with Dr. Lipsky. Suddenly she turned away, her face flushed, her expression somehow ferocious.

Walter was saying to Max Gold: "Limits? What limits? Is there anything a man can't do?"

Lou Grossman was roaring at a total stranger, who must have been one of Irving's cousins: "Sure, sure, he's a marvelous magician. He can make money disappear. Lend him a sawbuck and you never see it again."

While Milton himself, tired of tricks, was telling Moe: "I hate this damn war. You can't even get a decent banana."

Sam was watching Molly, so oddly subdued, bending over the hospital bed to plant a kiss on his mother's pale forehead, when—maybe it was the whiskey, or maybe it was the tumult—suddenly he felt his heart clench as though something terrible were going to happen. He glanced over at Rose, sitting on the couch next to Deborah and Laura, peering down at her baby with a kind of infinitely sad and troubled, yet somehow serene smile on her wet face. Then he turned, looking for Irving. He spotted him over by the dinette, squeezed into

186

a corner, with old Mrs. Malish haranguing him about something. Poor Irving looked as if he wanted to vanish right through the wall. His mother's voice kept getting louder and louder, and Sam felt the urge to shout some sort of warning, but it was already too late.

As though a signal had been sent through the room, the tumult subsided, the bubble of hilarity burst, and everyone became aware of Mrs. Malish, who was practically shrieking at Irving.

"Me? Your own mother? Me you couldn't tell? I didn't have the right to know? I didn't have the right?"

Drunk, pathetic, Irving blubbered: "Please, Mama, please. We were going to tell, we were going to, but afterwards, after the *briss*."

And Mrs. Malish again: "Your own mother and I didn't deserve that much consideration? *Vay ist mir! Vay ist mir!*"

She spun away from him, a dark bundle of agonized energy, wailing.

"Right away I said something is wrong! Right away I said it!"

Then she was shoving through the jammed and astonished living room, limping furiously, lurching toward the couch, where Rose sat clutching the baby tight to her as though forces were conspiring to take it away, blinking behind her thick glasses, raising her face to confront her mother-in-law, who was all vengeance, all despair. Sam's pulse raced, but what could he do? That terrible mouth with its glint of dull gold was already opening again, without thought, without meanness even, but merely blurting out to Rose and everyone else the hot, blind, age-old passion and sorrow and ignorance of her kind.

"You couldn't tell me, Roisele? I wasn't supposed to know?" Clapping her hands in front of her. "You think I don't have eyes in my head? You think I couldn't see?" Clutching her cheeks, her hair, beside herself with misery, she turned to appeal to the whole stricken and amazed mob of Liebers.

"*Vay ist mir!* A mongol yet! A mongol she delivers me! *Vay ist mir! Vay! Vay! Vay!*"

MAX GOLD OWNED AND OPERATED the concession by the lake in Prospect Park. He rented rowboats and swan boats by the hour. He sold hot dogs, peanuts, cold drinks, Cracker Jacks, ice cream, pinwheels, and souvenirs. On warm days people would take their purchases and sit under striped canvas umbrellas at concrete tables and watch the boats gliding round and round the green lake among the little islands and the omnipresent ducks. It didn't seem that there could be much money in such a business, and the family used to wonder how, after the marriage, Max and Molly could afford that fancy apartment in Brooklyn Heights with its splendid view of the Manhattan skyline and the Statue of Liberty, not to mention the weekends at the Catskills, the meals in restaurants, the big diamond ring which Molly sported on her finger, or the mink she kept in cold storage at a French cleaners and wore on special occasions. If he had so much money, they reasoned, why didn't he set himself up in a more respectable and profitable and less seasonal business? Unless it was, as Lou Grossman suggested, that he liked "hanging around in all that fresh air."

He was, anyway, the nicest of men. Certainly compared to Molly's previous husbands and boyfriends, who fizzled and popped in memory like a string of meager firecrackers, he was an angel. He was a huge, blond, bearish sort of man with a lot of finespun gold downing his freckled arms and a big, round, ruddy face that was always ready to laugh. A real *mensh*, said the family, intelligent but down-to-earth, good company despite a streak of shy modesty, a man who exhibited the sort of gentle self-confidence that comes only from great strength. In fact, it turned out, he was capable of physical feats that were amazing. Once he sat Deborah down on a kitchen chair, wrapped his big fist around the chair leg, and lifted her straight up in the air. Another time, to win a bet from Lou Grossman, he hoisted the rear tires of Sam's Packard clear of the pavement. And what a sight it was to see him on the beach at Rockaway, pink and enormous in a bathing suit, with three or four exultant children—Jeff and Erwin and Ben and Deanna—dangling from his arms and shoulders. He loved children, simply and honestly, and they responded by loving him. Even pathetic little Georgie at the age of two or three would relinquish his grasp on Rose for a moment and go scuttling up, with a smile on his flat, round face, into Max's arms.

Molly told everyone she adored him, and why not? He treated her like a queen. He ran to open doors for her, to light her cigarettes, to bring her a pillow to prop up her swollen legs. He often surprised her with flowers or bits of jewelry or vials of expensive perfume, not, like Solly Poverman, to fill up some emptiness between them, but just for the heck of it. In the evening, settled in front of the radio, he would rub her back and arms for an hour at a time, and then make love to her, so attentively, so maturely, so aware of her points of pleasure, that it was like a soothing dream. And in the wake of their lovemaking he did not, like the others, turn his back to her and plunge into selfish sleep; instead, he would massage her some more—oh, how she loved the feel of his strong fingers probing and manipulating her soft layers of flesh!—and tickle her arms and nibble playfully at her neck and blow into her ears and lap at her breast like some mild stupendous baby until their energies were restored and their desires brought them together again. Wrapped in his arms, with the great amiable bulk of him heaving above her, never mind her double chin or the way the fat bunched up in infantile folds around her wrists and elbows and fingers, Molly felt girlish and supple, beautiful and restored. In short, he was everything she had any right to expect in a man, and she told herself that she would have been happy—deliriously, insanely happy—had she not lost over the years, in consequence of three fouled marriages and a dozen pointless affairs, the capacity to be happy at all.

What a crab she had become! In retrospect it would seem to her that she had been born a crab. She remembered herself as a child storming and raging around the apartment on Park Place because she had some chore to do or an article of her clothing had been misplaced. Whatever happiness there had been in her life lay buried now under the years of misery the way her former beauty was buried under all those pounds of frustrated flesh. Especially after her divorce from Davey Second, in the years before she met Max, her life had been nothing but an endless series of self-concocted and bitter crises. She had problems with her bowels. She poured too much salt on her food because she had lost her sense of taste and so had a problem with water retention: her legs and ankles kept swelling up. She was fifty, sixty, seventy pounds overweight, and Dr. Lipsky had to warn her about her blood pressure. It was as though she had set out to make her own body just another reason for howling and tears. Her temper was worse than ever, and she went around picking fights with everyone, even Sam. How many times had she stormed out of the factory, swearing never to return? How often had she promised never again to speak to Deborah or Evelyn or Walter? And how often did she have to swallow her pride and wipe away the bitter tears and patch things up with them—because family is family, after all, and you can fight like wild animals one minute but you're still family the next. Besides, outside the family she had no friends of her own.

And yet there remained something of the old enchanting, exuberant Molly beneath the pink swollen flesh, the hair that was tinted almost orange, the loud dresses and the gaudy costume jewelry, some of that old promise of ecstasy and delight, and that was what Max Gold must have seen in her.

"Never mind how you feel," she admonished herself. "The man is in love with you. Thank your lucky stars!"

When a man is forty and a widower, with a son who would soon be flying missions against the Nazis, and a woman is thirty-six and thrice-married and altogether too experienced in the hard ways of the world, you think about marriage first and worry later if this mild heat is really love. They said their vows in front of a justice of the peace and, as a kind of afterthought, repeated the ceremony with a rabbi at the foot of Sophie's bed. Max had no family of his own aside from his son and—who can understand such things?—maybe part of Molly's attraction for him was the relatives, the *mishpuchah,* he was acquiring. Certainly the way she harped on them, my brother this, my sister that, made him realize right away that they came as part of the package. Anyway, he fit right in. He seemed to have something in common with all of them. He mirrored their moods, their thoughts, their habits. He could sit down with Sam and talk business, and then turn around and reminisce with Walter about how, just a few short years ago though it seemed forever, fellow radicals, they thought they could change the world. With Lou he was gruff and mocking, with Moe he discussed military strategy and jazz music, and with Milton he could go on for hours, a deck of cards between them, absorbing the rudiments of illusion. When it came to other people, he had an open and infinitely curious nature. He put you at ease and he wasn't afraid to ask questions. He soon knew more than all the rest of the family about Rose's agonies and Deborah's ghosts. Even Sophie, when he plumped himself down beside the hospital bed and murmured to her in Yiddish, became animated and coherent. He gave them the feeling that he could share their solitude without insulting their privacy so they let down their guard with him and talked and talked. They never realized, through all their talking, how little they actually learned about him. But what was there to know? That he worried about his son? That he carried in his wallet a snip of his first wife's gorgeous blond hair? That, like everyone else, he could on occasion flash a temper? That he had some money? So maybe he made some shrewd investments years ago. This hardly constituted a mystery. As far as the family was concerned, the man was as clear as glass.

So maybe it wasn't quite love, and maybe Molly would never be happy, but she liked him sincerely—he was so very nice to her—and often during those grim wartime years there were moments when her heart was at peace. For once in her life she could turn her thoughts toward the future and believe that it was good.

Then, one night, something terrible happened. Max Gold, working late at the concession stand, was attacked by a kid with a knife.

The details came out at the inquest. The kid's name was Hendrick Rohm, and he lived in a murky and impoverished Italian neighborhood west of Prospect Park. He was a problem child, a hard case. His father, who had been gassed in World War I, was a school janitor; his mother was a lush. A couple of years earlier, according to police records, she had tried to kill herself by slashing her wrists with a broken milk bottle; they rushed her over to Kings County and patched her up, and now—in the summer of 1945—she was spending most of her time in church. Heinie, as they called him, was not quite sixteen years old, but there were already legends about him. It was said that he once poked a kid's eye out with a pointed stick. He had spent a year in reform school. If there was a burglary in the neighborhood, the police would throw him into a squad car, ride him over to the precinct house, and try to knock some sense into his head; but this did no good. Probably in the dim recesses of his rage and despair he was bothered by the notion that the war was going to end before he could kill someone. You could imagine him—his fingernails bitten down to little half-moons, his neck dirty, his blond hair falling in greasy strands across his pimply forehead—up on a tenement roof, smoking in the dismal heat of the urban sun, dreaming of death and glory. He palled around with a gang called the Lords—his ferocity was no doubt useful to them when they rumbled—but, they later told the police, he was not a member. For one thing, he wasn't Italian; for another, there was something about him that frightened even those swaggering, belligerent young toughs. He was crazy, they said —they expected that someday he was going to kill someone, and they didn't want any part of it.

He had an accomplice, his only friend, a hulking, apish, half-retarded boy named Simmy, who would do practically anything Heinie told him to. You could imagine the pair of them on hot summer afternoons breaking a few windows in the schoolyard and then, as evening came on, wandering over to Prospect Park to look for victims. According to Simmy, they usually picked on Jewish kids because Jewish kids were the most frightened of them. They would move like shadows through the trees, stalking their prey, and Heinie would materialize on the path, demanding money, while Simmy crept up from behind. Sometimes they would just take the coins the victims fumbled out of their pockets; other times Heinie would nod his head and Simmy would curl his heavy arm around the kid's neck and Heinie would start hitting him. They never understood why Jewish kids so seldom fought back; perhaps in their own dim way they tried to puzzle it out, but like much else in the world, it never made any sense to them.

They often stayed in the park long into the night. Probably they found a peculiar sense of freedom in having soil underfoot and trees all around them in the dark—there were no restraints then; it was like inhabiting a little wilderness that belonged to them alone. Along might come some woman walking a dog and they would snatch her purse, or some old man out for a stroll—Simmy would knock him down, Heinie would grab his wallet and wristwatch, and they would run off through the woods, howling, breathless, ecstatic. Sometimes they would wander down to the lake and sit and brood for a while at the edge of the trembling water, feeling dismal and lost, perhaps, between the earth and the stars. To cancel such feelings, they would untie some rowboats and shove them out to drift in the breeze, or slash and tatter a couple of canvas umbrellas. It came out at the inquest that they were the ones who, twice that summer, had broken into the concession stand—not finding any money in the cash register, they had contented themselves with stealing candy bars and exploding bottles of soda all over the place.

So it was on a certain hot, tense August night they climbed a fence into the zoo and lurched around like a couple of sordid characters from a cheap fiction, tingling and leering among the empty cages. They hadn't realized that the animals were all locked inside when the zoo was closed, and this enraged them. The police later ascertained that they tried to pry open the door to the monkey house, but the lock was too strong for them, and the blade of Heinie's knife snapped and stuck in the jamb. At that point he demanded Simmy's knife, which led to a quarrel until Heinie kicked Simmy in the stomach and took the knife away from him—or so Simmy later claimed. Going back over the fence, Heinie ripped his pants, and by the time they got down to the lakefront—encountering no victims along the path—his mood was sullen and foul. He still had the broken knife, and now he took it out of his pocket and flung it far out over the murmuring water, hearing the dull little plash it made, seeing the calm, slow ripples that spread out over the dim-lit surface as a kind of insult to his capacity for violence. One imagines him thinking that if only he had a gun, or even better a hand grenade, then what a roar he could make blowing everything up.

Max Gold heard the splash but thought it was made by a frog or a duck. He had come out of the concession stand to lower the canvas umbrellas, his last chore of the night, and though he was eager to get home to Molly, he stopped for a moment to stare at the stars—more luminous and plentiful in the park than on the lamplit streets of Brooklyn—singing to himself in simple self-delight:

> Toot, toot, tootsie, goodbye!
> Toot, toot, tootsie—

and still singing, moved toward the picnic tables. That's when he saw the kid moving through the shadows of trees to emerge in front of him. A familiar warm, tight feeling started up at the back of Max's skull. The cool, vivid night air slid across his dry tongue, and the chemical flow of his fear and excitement was almost a kind of joy.

"Let's have your money, fucker!" the kid said.

It all started going fast for Max then, faster than thought and maybe faster than feeling, too, so that those final moments were nothing more than a scatter of random impressions: the kid's harsh voice; his own heartbeat; the space between them, which seemed to define and absorb everything else (trees, stars, darkness, breath), closing up and vanishing; the flash of the kid's knife leaping open in his hand; his own harsh voice, cursing; the thin line of blood expanding across his bare slashed arm; his sense of a second, heftier shadow lurking behind him; and his own voice again, amazed and furious and already triumphant.

Maybe there came to Heinie Rohm then, penetrating the murk of his brutish stupidity, a moment of lucid despair in which he knew he had made a mistake, had made many mistakes, because Max Gold was all over him now, huge and sweating and furious, grabbing at him, catching him, lifting him right up off his feet while Simmy slipped back into the shadows. Heinie kicked out, futilely. Like a toy in the hands of an angry child, he was shaken and flung, and maybe he knew then what was happening to him, maybe as he twisted and fell through the heavy night air he tried to pray for redemption, maybe he even heard at the last the awful crunch of his own skull bursting open on the edge of a concrete picnic table and the faint echo of that sound returning across the indifferent lake; but that was all he heard, and all he prayed, and all he would ever know.

You don't forget such a thing. You have to remember it always. In the weeks and months that followed it would recur to Max Gold in visions and dreams, that moment of dreadful struggle, and the afterwards, too, standing there with his handkerchief looped around his aching, bleeding arm while the beam of a cop's flashlight swung through the darkness and illuminated finally the heart-jamming mess of bone and brain and blood at the back of the kid's skull, and the kid's arms and legs all twisted into strange angles the way a cat looks when it's been smashed by a car in the gutter. They told him it was all right, and he wanted to believe them. He had his slashed arm and eventually a row of prickling black stitches and a sling to demonstrate that it was an act of self-defense. But he knew it wasn't all right, and would never be all right again. He knew it through his cold sweat and numbness as he stood in the hospital calling Molly on a pay phone and then couldn't find the words to tell her about it, couldn't say anything in fact, and stood there amazed at himself, choking and sobbing and gasping, with Molly panicking on the other end of the line until the cop came over and pried the receiver away from him. He knew it later that night as he lay in bed, drenched with fear and misery, struggling against sleep as if to fall into a dream might lead him to madness. He knew it at the inquest when he answered their questions truthfully and yet came away with the sense that he had lied, and he knew it through the dim days when he sat in the house, unable to work, and the family traipsed up to Brooklyn Heights to console him as if he were sitting *shivah*. "The accident," they kept calling it, "that terrible accident," until he wanted to rise up and shout at them. Because he had already convinced himself that it was no accident: what he knew, what he couldn't shake from his nerves, was the thrill of rage and triumph that had beat through him when he grabbed hold of the kid, that sense he had as he lifted and shook and flung him—and that lingered on even as the cop shone his flashlight on the gruesome scene he had so easily accomplished—not of guilt or horror or sorrow but of an unexpected and remorseless pleasure.

Unwilling to return to work, enraptured by gloom, he sat in the house with his arm in a sling, brooding, and Molly felt herself reliving a nightmare she could scarcely remember.

"Max," she would say to him, "you have to stop torturing yourself, you'll make yourself sick."

But she couldn't break through to him. He would look at her with frightened eyes full of yearning and hopelessness, and she would curse her foul luck and believe that God was punishing her for her miserable sins.

It is a terrible business to doubt one's own sanity. What tormented Max Gold was the all-too-lucid thought that having killed once, having loosed the lurking potential for murder within him, he couldn't be sure he wouldn't kill again. In calm moments he would tell himself, poignantly, that he was being a fool, but then something would touch off his fear again. He might, for example, look out the window and see an alley cat leap from a garbage can and dash under a parked car, and suddenly, with a surge of heat and horror, he would convince himself that what he wanted—what his instincts commanded—was to dash downstairs and chase after the poor animal, hunt it down, catch it, rip its legs off, and tear its stringy bleeding guts out with his fingers. Gradually the pressure of such thoughts eroded his strength and his will. He developed symptoms. He couldn't sleep; he had headaches; he became impotent. He would wake up in the morning not believing he had slept at all, had merely passed through a kind of oblivion, with the enormous muscles of his neck and shoulders aching as though he had spent the dark hours in struggle and flight. When he sat reading a newspaper, averting his eyes from items of violence, his teeth would throb as if he had bitten into something too sweet. If only he could talk to someone, but whom could he tell? The more he believed he was losing his mind, the more he had to hide it. He remembered vividly the time Molly had dragged him out to the Island to visit her demented brother, and he was terrified by the thought that they would lock him away.

In the afternoon he forced himself to leave the apartment and go for a walk. He thought that if he could exhaust himself, he might find rest. But for Max the shopping streets of Brooklyn were filled with violence. Little children shot each other dead with cap guns or fingers. Wild-eyed, deranged mothers dragged their howling little toddlers in and out of stores. Car horns, sharp as daggers, stabbed furiously in the hot afternoon sun. Cool killers stared icily from behind the glass of movie theater display cases. Everyone seemed to have murder in his eyes and in the tight, angry jut of his jaw. You could hear the cry of blood in every conversation.

"I'll kill ya!"

"Drop dead!"

"I'll bust your head open for ya!"

"I'll break your neck!"

"Do me a favor and die!"

"I'll smash your fucking face in!"

They would all kill, and kill happily, if you gave them the chance. Just to pass a newstand and glance at the headlines was to know that the world was a slaughterhouse. For years his own son had been flinging down bombs on the Nazis. Ashamed, his ears buzzing, Max would hurry along through the streets as though the world were shouting at him: "Madman! Murderer!"

Increasingly for Max in those days the implements of daily existence—kitchen knives, hammers, ice picks, baseball bats—hummed with menace. His own thick strong hands appalled him. He was afraid of driving his car lest in a brief spurt of madness he plunge it into a cluster of pedestrians. He was afraid to make love to Molly because he thought that at the moment of climax, as he abandoned self-control, his darkest impulses would overwhelm him; and he dreaded sleep because he expected to be murderous in his dreams and—who knows?—he might awaken to find that he had strangled the woman who dreamed and snored alongside him. He believed he had lurched by accident across a boundary line, had entered a realm where anything was possible, anything at all, and the feel of violent truth that clung to the thought shook him, this solid and genuine and innocent man, to pieces.

Molly never understood the demons that possessed him. At first she told herself that he was guilt-stricken, naturally enough, but would get over it. As time passed, however, and he grew ever more somber and strange, she lost heart and began feeling sorry for herself. It wasn't fair! Bitterly she would trace her life backwards through the labyrinth of her passions, wondering what she had done or failed to do to deserve such bad luck. By now Max had begun going off at night, leaving her alone—he had taken to prowling the worst neighborhoods of New York, waiting to be attacked, not sure himself whether he wanted to kill or be killed—but Molly knew nothing of this and suspected he was running for comfort to another woman. She couldn't endure it. Her patience was at an end. Night after night she would call up Essie and cry to her on the telephone. Finally, in desperation, she gave him an ultimatum: if he couldn't manage to pull himself together, she was going to leave him.

"Leave," he told her, "it will be better for you."

What choice did she have? She packed a suitcase and went to Manhattan Beach. The saddest thing she had ever seen was the way he stood there watching her pack, staring at her nightgowns and stockings and dresses as though they might contain some message for him, then turning away because whatever message he had received was garbled or irrelevant.

She never saw him again. For days she sat by the phone, waiting for his call, with Essie chirping and fussing around her, but he didn't call, and when she finally decided to call him, either he was out or he refused to answer. She sent Sam to talk to him, but Sam couldn't find him home. Then one day an operator came on the line to tell her that the service had been disconnected. He had vanished. She never found out where he went. She started reading the obituary columns of the newspaper, expecting the worst, but it was three years before she found the item she had anticipated: he had died of an "apparent heart attack" on a street in the Bronx. She would always wonder what he had done with himself in the interim, and she would always remember how for a time her life had been good; for that she was grateful, and never mind the rest, because somtimes in life things happen, and there is nothing, absolutely nothing, you can do.

FOR YEARS WALTER AND SARAH lived on St. Marks Place in a dim and cluttered basement "studio" with low cracked ceilings and linoleum floors. Every morning the walls would hiss and groan as hot water strained up through old pipes to the sinks and bathtubs above; every evening there would descend the awful dissonance of Chopin waltzes played on an untuned piano and the heavy creak of Joe Weinberg, the fat, deaf, grumpy landlord, tromping off to bed. It was dismal.

When you looked out through the small barred windows, you saw a stretch of gray sidewalk, the bottoms of garbage cans, and maybe the trouser cuffs of an occasional passerby. In the old days, when they still belonged to the Party, the place had seemed appropriately proletarian, even a bit romantic; and during the war, since they contributed all their extra time and money to a dozen different antifascist funds and causes, they couldn't consider a move. But this was 1946, times were getting better, and anyway—as the family had been surprised to learn—Sarah was pregnant. She was already exhibiting the first omens of her condition: a thickening of her hips and a faint darkening of the skin on her cheeks and forehead. Everyone was excited. Sam gave Walter a raise, and Evelyn offered to hand on the old crib and bassinet which half a dozen Lieber grandchildren had outgrown. There was no getting around the fact that they would be needing more space and light, and warmer floors, so on Saturdays that spring they explored the better neighborhoods to the south— Crown Heights, Flatbush, Park Slope—seeking at first the ideal apartment they had in mind (spacious, bright, airy, close to a bit of greenery), and later a practical compromise at a rent they could afford.

In those days Walter was still working for Sam in the chocolate factory on Bergen Street, where they had recently added a line of sugared fruits: oranges, apples, berries, bananas. Walter occupied the corner desk in the hectic office. He spent his days cranking long strips of paper from the roll on the adding machine and copying numbers, with a meticulous hand, onto the pale green pages of the ledger. Usually he was so abstracted, so absorbed in the detail of the work, that you had to shout to get his attention. He also handled the occasionally complicated correspondence between the factory and its foreign suppliers. Now that the war was over, things had reverted to normal. Letters, bills, documents, customs forms would arrive from Lebanon or Peru or Ceylon or Zanzibar—places so distant that for Walter the thick manila packets might have materialized from another world—and he would have to spread the stuff out in front of him and pick his way through the usually unreliable calculations and the baffling pseudo-English. He was happy, though, to clip from the envelopes the colorful stamps with their stirring depictions of birds and flowers and the British king. These he would carry home in his pocket to soak in water and dry on a towel and fix into his stamp album with little gummed glassine hinges. Except for some mint-fresh American commemoratives and a small folder of numbered blocks, all of Walter's stamps were canceled. It was a poor man's, or perhaps more accurately a child's sort of collection, and Walter had a child's idealizing fondness for it. Before Sarah became pregnant, he would occupy his idle hours thumbing through the stiff pages, imagining the cocoa plantations, the fruit-filled tropics, the lush and spicy isles, all those spoiled and exploited paradises he would never be able to see. But now, as he readied himself for what he called "the challenge and privilege of fatherhood," he had little time for vicarious pleasures.

He had already immersed himself, wholeheartedly as usual, in a fascinating study of the art of raising a child. What began as a bemusement soon became an obsession. He would send Sarah off to the Grand Army Plaza branch of the library, where she wandered around in her long drab skirts and mannish shoes and white socks, consulting the lists he had drawn up for her and plucking from the shelves books on genetics, nutrition, medicine, psychology, mathematics, music, games and toys, mythology, optics, history, anthropology—his curiosity was labyrinthine and endless—and at night he would settle down beneath a lamp to browse and ponder, make a few notes on a set of color-coded index cards which he kept in a metal file box, and then browse and ponder some more. Methodically, patiently, he was concocting a theory. Typical Walter, the family would later say.

He was still the dreamer, he still had his head in the clouds, and it never mattered that his dreams forever eluded him. The family remembered how years ago all you ever heard from Walter was how he was going to Spain to fight the fascists. He talked and talked, and he was still talking, when that war ended. Later, after Hitler and Stalin signed their infamous pact, Walter marched into Sam's office and burned his Party card in the ashtray and asked for a job; but that didn't stop his dreaming. He became what he called "a small-*c* communist."

"The fact that Stalin is a murderer and a brute," he argued, "doesn't prove anything at all."

For a while the family worried that he might be in danger from his former comrades. They were alarmed by the denunciatory (and redundant) letters he wrote to left-wing periodicals, followed by more letters demanding that the initial ones be printed. But no one ever bothered him. In fact, he rather wished the Party had taken more notice of his apostasy.

"I'm nothing to them," he grumbled, promising someday he would show them "a thing or two."

Anyway, the Depression had been a fine time for a man like Walter, and perhaps he realized that history was leaving him behind. He welcomed the war. He tried to enlist, but the army wouldn't have him—politics, he claimed, though it turned out that the medical examiner had located a mysterious flaw in his heart—and so he busied himself on the home front. He never stopped believing in progress, education, science, human perfectability; and now, preparing for fatherhood, he had conceived a kind of demonstration of his beliefs. It was simple enough; as he explained it to Molly in the office one morning, he was going to raise his child to be a genius.

"She should live and be well," said Molly, "she doesn't have to be a genius."

The world is big and corrupt and ignorant and intractable, burdened with horrors of every kind, but maybe you could create around yourself (there was no way he could make Molly see this, but never mind) a kind of small and perfect bubble in which a family, or a child, or, more particularly, a child's spirit and intelligence could play and grow and flourish. Consider the untapped resources we have within us. Most of our brain cells—some estimates are as high as ninety percent—are unused. Stimulation was the key. Walter fretted about the days the infant would spend in the hospital, where everything was sterile and white and the nurses walked around performing their loveless chores on rubber soles, and where the kid would be exposed through layers of glass to the grotesque masks and inane noises that grown-ups produce for babies. No wonder we're stunted if that's our first impression of life. On a list of absolute taboos he placed baby talk, insipid lullabies, nursery rhymes, and grimaces. He also fretted about the gray monotony of compulsory public schools. The family began to worry: you couldn't reason with the man. True, when you wait so many years to have a child, there is bound to be too much doting, but this was worse. They knew Walter; they knew their own blood; they understood that look in his eyes—the same look they used to glimpse in Jacob Lieber's eyes before he died of pleurisy a quarter century ago.

"He thinks he's spawned the Messiah," Molly said—and that seemed to sum it up.

In June, having borrowed a thousand dollars from Sam and a truck from the Canarsie warehouse, Walter moved Sarah into a second-story apartment in Flatbush, where they had two bedrooms, a long narrow living room, carpeting, and a view, if you stood on the fire escape and craned your neck, of the trees in Prospect Park. Now began the long process of settling in. The family was amused to hear that Walter, so clumsy with his hands, was scrubbing floors and painting walls and installing in the "nursery" a series of built-in shelves. There would be a music shelf, a bookshelf, and a shelf for puzzles. The music—a phonograph, that is, and a pile of records—was mostly Mozart, with a scattering of Haydn and Bach, some political folk songs from the previous decade, and a brand-new boxed set of early English madrigals. The books started off reasonably enough with a few children's classics, such as *Treasure Island* and *Alice in Wonderland*, and then passed, in what Walter called "a ladder of ascending difficulty," through *Great Expectations* and a dog-eared set of the *Encyclopedia Americana* to Freud, Darwin, Marx, Shakespeare, Plato. The puzzle shelf held jigsaws, mazes, twisted and interlocked wires, and a collection of wooden balls and barrels and cones, which fell apart in your hand when you removed a secret key piece. On the walls, which Walter spent a whole week painting a specially selected shade of pale greenish blue (stimulating in daylight, soothing at dusk), he tacked up reproductions of famous paintings he had purchased in the gift shop of the Metropolitan Museum—a Breughel, a Rembrandt, a Goya, a Monet—and he stocked other reproductions in the closet so that periodically he could change the decor. Along one side of the old family crib, from which he scraped the teddy-bear decals, he strung a colored plastic alphabet, and above it he hung a mobile he had concocted himself; in brightly painted wooden cutouts the digits 1 to 9 danced in the mild summer breeze. He built into the ends of the crib a pair of unbreakable mirrors, and filled a toybox he had picked up on sale with a sturdy abacus, a chess set, and some plain functional building blocks. All of this he accomplished long before the baby was born.

In the evenings he would ride home on the humid subway, his starched white collar wilting in the heat and his bony fingers blackening with the ink of the evening's paper, to the joy of finding Sarah waiting for him with her ever-swelling middle. His fondest pleasure was to come up behind her as she stood stirring a pot on the stove, her lower lip jutting out as she tried to blow away stray hairs from her damp face, and put his arms around her stomach, mentally reassuring himself, bit by bit, of the miracle of her growing burden.

Lying in bed—they had, old-fashioned radicals that they were, given up sex after the fourth month—he would rub cold cream into her abdomen to soften the precious skin and minimize the growth of those ugly purple stretch marks that were already beginning to craze her belly. Sometimes on the edge of sleep, as happy as he had ever been in his groping and thwarted life, experiencing for once the pleasures as well as the obvious miseries and injustices of what was, at bottom, a sensual world, he would suspect that he himself was pregnant, and imagine the half-formed child stirring and stretching, precious thing, in his own rumbling bowels.

"Maybe I can't produce perfection," Walter told the family, "but shouldn't I try?"

Through all the talk and preparations, Sarah said nothing. She apparently enjoyed being the quiet and enigmatic center around which everything else revolved. From the moment she arrived in the family, the Liebers had wondered whether she was the cause of Walter's ideas or their victim. They would remember the first time she came to the house on Park Place with no makeup on her face and her hair in a braid and her big, angular body straining against the lines of a severe, gray, man-tailored suit; but by then Walter had been courting her for months and they had no way of knowing if he had found a suitable mate or molded one. Possibly Sarah herself didn't know for sure. In any case, their marriage had turned out to be a good one. They held their dreamy politics in common. In the face of a belligerent world they presented a united front. Their motives were loving and gentle and kind, and that's what really mattered. Now, pregnant, Sarah was happy enough; at times she was even radiant, though as the months passed and her belly grew, she felt sublimely uncomfortable.

Meanwhile, Walter's sisters busily analyzed all the various omens that would foretell the fetus's gender. For Molly and Evelyn the fact that Sarah was "carrying high" indicated that the baby would be a boy, while Ruthie maintained that the darkness of Sarah's "pregnancy mask" and her failure to exhibit any unusual appetites (she had no cravings for strawberries or pickles; she didn't start nibbling bits of plaster) meant that it would turn out to be a girl. How they talked! They dragged Laura and Essie and Deborah into it, and on Sunday mornings the phone lines buzzed with their speculations until Rose got furious.

"Boy or girl," she scolded them, "so long as it's healthy!"

But that didn't stop them. They dropped in on Sarah and placed their hands on her belly to feel the stirrings. They kidded her about her profile and sympathized with her for the patterns of blue veins that were appearing on her legs. They gave her more attention than they had in the previous ten years, as though they were eager, now that she carried the Lieber line in her womb, to drag her into the family.

This went on all through the summer and well into September. Then Sophie's health failed and the family was distracted.

For years Sophie had been slipping away from them, for years they had anticipated what they called "the end of her suffering," and now life was finally eluding her. Her pulse weakened. Her lungs filled with fluid, and her breathing became raspy and painful. Dr. Lipsky arrived and shook his big bearish head over her and said it was no use sending her to the hospital, better she should spend her final hours at home among her loved ones. They could detect in her faint slurred speech, as they sat through the night with her, a new grief and urgency, as though she had nothing more to give them, nothing to leave behind but her imperishable memories of the old country, of that small, nameless, muddy village out of which they had come. "Do you remember?" she would whisper to Sam and Deborah, and they would nod their heads to please her, but she knew they didn't remember, that their earliest memories had been canceled and blotted by the journey to America. Her face upon the pillow burned with a bluish intensity and her feeble mutterings made her appear oblivious to the sorrow and hushed arrangements that surrounded her, but in fact, she perceived everything. There was nothing wrong with her ears, and as she approached the final reverie, she had moments of mute and hopeless clarity. She was troubled by the abruptness and discontinuity of things. In the last hours the creep of death inward toward her vital center focused her life and the life of her brood. It was as though she had been caught up in confusion during the years of her illness as she struggled to keep herself alive long enough to see her grandchildren—those real Americans—at play around her; now, approaching death, relinquishing herself, she saw with new eyes the life of the family and the pressures which had formed them and the shape of the struggles she had willed upon them. Beneath their noise and their joking, their tears and their tumult, her children were unhappy people, all of them, and Sophie was stricken with the thought that perhaps she, not Jacob, was the cause. Somehow in the early years there had opened up at the center of the family a void, a blankness, that announced itself in Deborah's ghost, in Walter's fanaticism, in Molly's coarse, swollen flesh, in Ruthie's bitterness, in Evelyn's pursuit of fashion, in Hymie's madness. Even Sam, her firstborn, her prince, was a lonely and loveless man, who spoiled his children and draped his wife in luxuries because he had so little feeling for them, and who doled out favors to the rest of the family not out of the affection of blood but merely to demonstrate his authority over them. But why? Because she had ripped them out of the past and flung them headlong into an unknown future they didn't want and couldn't choose? Because she had set the flame of her own wild and thwarted expectations to flare in their innocent hearts? Or was it simply that between her and Jacob there had been no love, and thus no example of how to love? Isn't that why she had dragged him to America, hoping to elude what had been there all along, trapped and inexpressible in her own selfish ambitions, the fact that she despised him? Even now she hoped there would be no afterlife: she couldn't bear the thought that she might have to serve as his footstool in Paradise.

Somewhere, distantly, her body fluttered softly; somewhere, in that place where her body was, someone began to cry. For Sophie, it was as though her mother were crying back in their home in the old village, and she was in her girlhood bed, on that aching straw-stuffed mattress, listening, knowing that her mother was crying for her. Because of what had happened with Stanislaus, that silly Polish boy who once had flattered her naïve heart. She wanted to go to her mother and comfort her, say to her:

"Mama, never mind, don't cry, he's not the one I love."

She opened her eyes and saw nothing, and the pressure of her death gathered at the root of her, and how mild and pleasant it was to feel it unfold itself upward until in her last moments, peaceful at last, loving them all, and with no expectations remaining, she slipped away from them, her restless heart heaving one last time before it stopped.

No matter how much you anticipate it, however sickly the patient, death amazes and appalls. Sophie's death wrung unexpected tears out of Walter, and he comforted himself with the thought—bubbling up out of the realm of childhood superstition to subdue momentarily his knowledge and sense—that at the moment his mother died the child in Sarah's womb, *his child*, acquired a soul. He even put his atheism aside and joined the family in Evelyn's house to sit *shivah*, though he made Sarah stay at home, wouldn't even allow her to attend the funeral, because he didn't want the mourning to filter through the subtle membranes and touch the dawning mind of the baby. Why expose it to the way his sisters howled and carried on? He stuck it out all week, immersing himself in the family's ceremonial regrets and recriminations and reminiscences, and arose at the end with the sense that his mother had been dead for years. Anyway, past was past; he had the future to think about.

Toward the end of her pregnancy Sarah's belly grew so large that she appeared about to topple over onto a new center of gravity. Her legs were swollen and her fingers were fidgety because Walter had forbidden her to smoke. Every five minutes she ran to the bathroom, where she would struggle with constipation and relieve her constantly signaling bladder and drink a lot of water—how thirsty she had become!—from a toothpaste-spotted cup. She was nervous. She was thirty-three years old and at that age, she had read, the chances of producing a healthy baby were diminished. Look at what happened to poor Rose. She tried to imagine herself with Rose's *tsurris*, but the effort exhausted her. Sure, Walter was no Irving, but given the hopes he attached to the unseen little demidemon that kicked and roiled so ruthlessly within her, he was bound to be disappointed.

On the other hand, she loved the attention she was receiving. Since she carried his seed and his dreams, Walter doted on her. He refused, after the sixth month, to let her do any housework, reminding her of how Evelyn's water broke the time she was pregnant with Deanna and climbed up on a chair, eight months gone, to reach a dusty cobweb hanging from the ceiling. He took over the cooking and proved himself to be adept at pot roasts and veal cutlets and noodle puddings; he had, after all, spent many hours of his boyhood, wide-eyed and observant tot that he was, in his mother's kitchen.

Again and again they counted the days that had elapsed between the moment of conception—a moment they believed they remembered, for it had ended, as if they had foreseen the result, in a burst of inexplicable and salutary tears—and the due date, so they were a bit alarmed when that day receded into the cloaked and diminished reality of the past. Sarah was officially late, a week, ten days, two weeks late.

"If she doesn't drop that *bindel* soon," Molly remarked, "the poor girl is going to explode."

Walter was insomniacal with his fierce and tender expectancy. Old Dr. Lipsky came by every day to plant the monopod of his stethoscope against Sarah's taut mound, shake his head at whatever private message he received, and drink a cup of coffee with Walter, to whom one day he confessed, in a husky voice, that he used to be in love with Sophie. Walter stopped going to work and passed the agonizing hours with Sarah, playing cribbage and discussing the latest depressing news out of Eastern Europe. He was more than ever the model of husbandly kindness, but in the private and occasionally lurid maze of his most secret thoughts his temper was beginning to flare. He suspected that she was purposely holding the child back from the world, or rather from him, that some old residue of selfishness in her was trying to deprive him—aware more than ever now of the shortness and contingency of life—of those precious days of pleasure and nurture he so keenly anticipated. He believed the problem was connected to Sarah's chronic constipation, and when she headed for the bathroom, a point of pain, symptom of choked rage, would throb in his forehead.

To divert himself, he drew up lists of names. He was a great believer in the magic of names, in their power to create a shape into which the character of their bearer would inevitably flow. He had never much liked his own name, found in it a tone that was both archaic and stodgy, and had earlier in his life—in what he mockingly called his underground days—toyed with aliases: Joshua, Isaac, Eugene, Carlos, Gus. Now the name that invariably bobbed to the top of his lists was Solomon. Let the child have a name it could sport boldly and proudly in the eyes of the world. He could close his eyes and envision the wisdom, the authority, the sunny disposition of his little Sol.

He also discussed with Sarah, for the umpteenth time, the pros and cons of breast feeding. Dr. Lipsky was opposed to it. He argued that mother's milk couldn't possibly provide all the nourishment of a scientifically prepared formula, and besides, there was no practical way to sterilize a mother's breast. Walter was torn. He yearned to be modern and up-to-date. He had seen Ruthie and Evelyn with their cast-iron sterilizers and canned formulas, which reminded him of a laboratory. This appealed. On the other hand, he carried in his head a fond image of Sarah nursing, madonnalike, the child sucking natural nourishment from a beautiful bare white breast. Sarah listened to him talk himself into and out of both positions and finally decided on breast feeding.

"You don't have to pay for mother's milk," she said.

She went into the hospital at last on a cold November night, and there, for twenty-four hours, the poor woman labored. It was awful. For what seemed an eternity Walter sat by her bedside, timing the erratic contractions and mopping her brow and giving her sips of ice water. Every so often a nurse would chase him out of the room so that she could measure the dilation, and come out shaking her head, saying: "Not yet! Not yet!" At times during those cruel hours Walter believed it was all some sort of ghastly joke, that there was no baby inside the straining mound, that it was just a balloon full of air and foulness, about to burst. Every time a contraction came, Sarah grabbed his hand and dug her fingernails into his flesh. She wept, she cursed, she grunted, she strained, she rose up ghastly off the pillow and collapsed again, pale and exhausted, her face and hair pasty with sweat. Walter was appalled. He had anticipated beauty and was finding only pain and ugliness. There were moments during the ordeal when despite himself, despite everything, his rage came and he believed that he hated her. And still it went on. It seemed never to end.

Now in those days Deborah kept having premonitions. She would call up people at all hours to prepare them for things to come. She drove everybody crazy with her warnings and messages, but they were afraid not to listen to her. One day she called up Essie to tell her that Rich was in danger, and an hour later word came that Rich, driving without a license, had rammed Sam's car into a telephone pole on the Belt Parkway. (He walked away from that wreck with a couple of broken ribs, but the girl he had been trying to impress smashed her nose on the windshield and was marked for life.) They remembered how she had phoned Evelyn, crying her eyes out, to say that Sophie's time had come, and even while Evelyn was calming her down, Sophie entered the final crisis of her life. But the trouble was that her predictions were not always so accurate and clear. She pestered Evelyn with warnings about doors and windows, but nothing ever came of them. She walked into the factory one morning and announced that Hymie was going to "pass on" within a month, but the month went, and then another, and Hymie continued to live out the agony of his incarceration. Of course, such inaccuracies did not faze Deborah, or shake her faith in her otherworldly communicants. She had an answer for everything.

"The future isn't rigid," she explained. "Higher forces can intervene."

That was Deborah. How mysterious she loved to be! She dropped in on everyone and never missed a family occasion, but she discouraged them from visiting her in her immaculate, gloomy widow's apartment, with those reproductions of sentimental paintings on the walls, and the tarot cards spread out on the coffee table, and the double bed, and occasionally the singing of dead opera stars issuing thinly from Sophie's old gramophone. The dresses she wore had remained for twenty years oddly fresh and untattered. She still powdered her face white and daubed circles of rouge on her cheeks, and spoke in the same high, haughty whisper, and was as slender and tragic as she had been on the day that Buster Stern died. True, her hands had grown a bit wrinkled, but her fingers were long and exquisite, and gold bangle bracelets tinkled and chimed on her wrists, and every night, every lonely night, she lay in the double bed with the lights off and the pale shadows of distant traffic flowing across her ceiling, and talked to Buster of the life they would lead together when she joined him in the world beyond.

Anyway, that night it was Deborah who called up the family, hours before Sarah went into the delivery room, to spread the news—or so they remembered it—and thus they were prepared for Walter, exhausted and exultant and vaguely punctured, shouting at them across the echoing labyrinth of phone lines the message they already knew.

"It's over," he told them, "and Sarah's fine, and so is my little girl!"

FIVE

IN THE LAST MONTHS OF THE WAR the newspapers were filled with Buchenwald, Auschwitz, Treblinka. When you went to the movies in those days you were compelled to witness in newsreels, sandwiched in between some mundane double feature, gruesome film clips of the liberation of the death camps: the mechanisms of slaughter, the torture chambers, the appalling inventories of glass eyes and gold teeth and human hair, the hopeless survivors staring out from bunk beds and barbed wire with the eyes of relentless ghosts. Along with all the rest of the stunned world, the family grieved and wondered. They could remember how Sophie used to name the aunts and uncles and cousins she had left behind in the old country; now these relatives had vanished into the heaped ash and bone of the millions the Nazis had murdered. And since the particulars were unknown, the family couldn't help conjuring up for those names dozens of different deaths, each more horrible than the next. They were forced to imagine the old-world Liebers and Kalishers marched out into soggy fields and machine-gunned into ditches, or crushed and suffocating in jammed cattle cars, or starving in slave factories, or hanged by their necks in mass reprisals. They imagined them blown up in their synagogues, inoculated with poisons and filth and vile diseases in the Nazi laboratories, whipped and clubbed by camp guards, gassed in mock shower rooms, shoved—still twitching with stubborn life—into huge ovens, while the unmistakable smoke and stench belched out of those blackened chimneys and spread across the green and guilty countryside. But the family also learned that thought simply cannot hold onto that much awfulness. The Liebers would never quite forget the dead, but they could not forever brood over them. In the end they absorbed those ghastly images as they had absorbed so much else in their years in America. They spent some restless nights, they reflected for a while on their own incredible safety and comfort and luck, and then—what else could they do?—they went about their business. What mattered most to them was that the war was over, Hitler was gone, and the factory on Bergen Street was again producing nut clusters and butter crunch and fancy cordials—those fragments of sweet delight they peddled to a bitter world. They knew, Sophie had taught them, how to relinquish the past and turn to the future. Anyway, their children were growing up, the family swelled and sprawled, and they could only hope, they *had* to hope, that the worst was over.

Then, in 1947, Dov Kalisher arrived in America.

This Dov was the youngest of the seven children of Sophie's brother Saul and, as far as the family could learn, the only one of the old-world relatives to survive the war. Out of the blue he got in touch with Asa Kalisher, an uncle he had never met, and Asa moved heaven and earth to secure him a visa and money for his passage. He sailed to New York in November. When the family heard he was coming, they foresaw a kind of gentle, large-eyed wraith, etherealized by suffering, but when they gathered in Sam's house on a Sunday afternoon to meet him, they found themselves in the presence of a short, fierce, and altogether substantial sort of fellow, who walked with a limp and spoke a loud, clipped sort of English that rang strange in their ears—he had acquired the language in a British field hospital, where he had been treated for a variety of ailments and parasites, and later worked as an orderly. He wasn't handsome; his mouth was curved down on one side, his complexion was mottled and patched, and he bore on his forehead a mournful scar that curved up to meet a blaze of whiteness in his dark reddish hair; but there was an intensity about him, a moody strength, that the Lieber women found disturbing. Every movement, every ounce of his tempered and burnished flesh, seemed calculated and purposeful and hard, as though he had achieved in the course of his survival an economy of being that made even the slender and efficient Sam appear profligate.

They would remember sitting with him in Sam's bright, plush, luxurious living room—which Essie had recently, for the umpteenth time, refurnished—while he talked about his most recent travels (an Atlantic storm, everybody seasick) and how happy he was to be, at long last, safe in America. He wore a lumpish gray refugee's suit, a white shirt with a frayed collar that was much too big for his taut and ropy neck, and old ill-fitting shoes, which gleamed sadly from recent polish. How odd it was to be with him, this survivor, this witness to history's most terrible truth, his memory no doubt crammed with pains and sorrows they could scarcely begin to imagine. He was part of their own flesh and blood—he had Sophie's chin and Asa's mannerisms—but he might just as well have drifted down among them from some alien universe. To be in his presence was incomprehensible and exhausting. They regarded him that day, and in the weeks and months that followed, as a kind of supernatural being, and wondered bleakly about the mysterious power that had sent him to them.

As the afternoon dragged itself along toward dusk, they could sense beneath the thin shell of his self-containment a force of unspeakable agony, and they felt increasingly on edge, waiting for the outburst that seemed about to occur. His dark eyes darted around, taking them in, and his hands drummed restlessly on the knees of his ill-pressed trousers. Certainly he was charming. He won the hearts of the children who were present by telling them tales of the dybbuks and demons that had lived in the old village, and by invoking for them the great-grandfather they had never met, bold and boisterous Yussel Kalisher, singing Yiddish folk songs while he worked, beating time with the thump of his cleaver. But perhaps even the children sensed in the man something vaguely sinister. How, everyone had to wonder as they listened and stared, had he managed to survive? Later, when they got to know him better, they would stop wondering, in fact stop thinking about it altogether, because there are some things it is better not to know, even if they are part of your history, your blood. He sat there finally with a plate of food on his lap, breaking through their nervous small talk to tell them in a voice so calm and cold it would recur in their nightmares that he was happy to be among them and that he expected never, never, to be hungry again.

For a moment their attention, which was usually so diffused and scattered that to be in a room full of Liebers was like trying to follow half a dozen different stories at once, focused fully on him, this cousin, this stranger, and while they may have been unable to express it for themselves, they were in the presence of a simple, harsh reality they had never previously known. The hush that fell over them was unbearable. Molly was so stricken by the moment that she burst into tears and went running to the kitchen. Walter felt an icy hand clutch his heart, and immediately began worrying about Jeannie (who was quietly dreaming her lucid infantile dreams in her carriage on the porch). Lou opened his mouth to utter a wisecrack, but even he was temporarily awed. Sam's Carrie, thirteen years old and utterly adorable, developed in that moment such a somber crush on the man that years later, safely and conventionally married, she would sometimes come awake in the middle of the night with the eerie sense that he had figured once more in her dreams. And Moe, who had recently transferred from medical school to dental school because he couldn't stomach the autopsies and dissections, and whose life had subsequently been all gloom, suddenly brightened with the thought that he was going to get to know, and perhaps understand, this marvelous man.

Moe, more than any of the other Liebers, more even than Walter (who had confessed to himself that his ambitions for Jeannie were a kind of antidote to Hitler), had been mesmerized by the details of the Holocaust. Even before the war was over, while he was still in uniform, Moe had started a scrapbook into which he pasted all the news stories and magazine articles he could find concerning the fate of Europe's Jews. It was a bulky thing with red leather covers and heavy black pages, and as the Allied armies "slogged" across Europe, it fattened with horrors. What for the rest of the family was a single insane event, impenetrable to thought, became for Moe a sequence of plans and atrocities and incidents, each dreadful one of which he felt compelled to envision and ponder. He memorized the grisly statistics village by village, ghetto by ghetto, country by country. He sated himself on eyewitness accounts of bizarre terrors. He could tell you the different modes of murder in the various camps, the particular functions of the SS and the *Einsatzgruppen*, the technical problems the Nazis encountered as they perfected the efficiency of genocide. He knew the names of the camp commandants and bureaucrats, the euphemisms, the links in the chain of authority. He knew the cynical motto of Auschwitz—ARBEIT MACHT FREI!—and the exact locations of those "recreation centers" where Jewish women lived as SS whores. Even in later years, never quite free of his obsession, he continued to gather books and articles on the "Final Solution," storing the stuff in cartons because he couldn't bear the thought of its sitting out in open shelves where his daughters could see it. Eventually he broadened his researches and studied the persecution of the Jews over the centuries, that whole familiar history of pogroms and inquisitions, forced conversions and massacres. He tried to imagine himself, just as he was, with his fears and his ambitions, inflicted with the sufferings his ancestors had endured. He conjured up all sorts of atrocities, his brothers killed, his sisters tortured, his wife raped, wondering how he would have borne them. Though he knew how perverse he was being, he felt cheated of the opportunity to measure himself against that other, somehow more authentic reality. That tortured history, after all, was part of his lineage, had been absorbed into his blood, and thus perhaps accounted for the moods and glooms that stirred in his restless heart. The medieval *shtetl*, the crude, drunken peasant mob on an Easter rampage, the fanatical priests working their pious cruelties, his superstitious ancestors huddling together in a dark cellar to carry on their rituals: there, among them, in olden days, he might have lived more deeply. But those things were measurable, drawn, as it were, to human scale, while the Nazis had gone far beyond. What held *them* so vividly in his mind was that they knew no limits. They had not only stepped over the line of the comprehensible, but gone so far past it that to imagine their minds and motives was like stepping off the earth. And always the question returned: what would have become of him—of his pride, his intelligence, his courage, his sanity—had he fallen into their hands?

It was inevitable then that Moe would be enthralled by Dov Kalisher, that they would enter into a kind of friendship predicated upon Moe's curiosity about the horrors Dov had survived. Two or three times a week Dov would come for dinner to the cramped, sparsely furnished apartment where Moe and Laura were living in those days. Laura would prepare one of those dainty meals of hers— "When Laura fixes supper, don't go hungry," the family used to say —and Dov would arrive, European-style, with a bottle of wine and a handful of flowers, and afterward the three of them would sit and talk about the old country, the family, a book they were reading, some new film they had seen—about everything, in short, but what was uppermost on Moe's mind. That would come later, after Laura had yawned and stretched and fallen asleep on the couch. That's when Dov would unburden himself, pouring memories which were as bitter as gall into the eager receptacle of Moe's morbid conscience. At last Dov would leave, and Moe would awaken Laura, and they would climb into their cold bed, and while Laura wheezed softly alongside him, Moe would lie awake in the foreboding darkness, feeling the talk of the night running like a harsh current through his thoughts. His shoulders ached. His limbs were taut and expectant. He was afraid to close his eyes lest he tumble into a nightmare from which there would be no escape. Even awake, he could imagine himself vividly—all too vividly—lying on rough wooden boards, peeking through a glassless window at the gun towers, the forbidden perimeter, the barbed wire, the chimneys that belched out their black smoke and stench all through the night. He would imagine himself roused up by vicious *kapos* in the first light of a frigid morning, assembling with the other ghosts in icy mud, in his own filth and rags and body smells, while the German soldiers with their ferocious dogs and burp guns wandered down the line of the helpless, smirking and shouting, dragging away to the ovens or the laboratories the sickly, the impudent, the weak. One night he rose up out of the miserable bed sheets and, sitting in a chair under the single odd light of a lamp, carved from a callus on his toe a sliver of dead skin, which he set afire in an ashtray, using a snippet of his own hair as kindling. He wanted to teach himself the odor of burning flesh, but the mild, sour, grilled-meat smell he produced was, he knew, a mere shadowy whiff of that elusive horror he wished so perversely, so sanctimoniously, to know.

Now at family get-togethers, as he had during his days at Columbia, Moe felt vaguely oppressed and enraged by the Lieber heat and ignorance and noise. Just as he had once viewed the family through Laura's eyes, and found himself appalled by their coarseness, now he tried to see them through Dov's. How impervious and protected they were, living their lives within a small and carefully defined space from which horror and tragedy, and thus beauty and joy and truth, had been excluded. Life, real life, the reality of the death camps, bounced right off them. They danced on the edge of an abyss and never bothered to look down. They shouted, laughed, whooped, argued, burst into sweat, turned red in the face, worried about money, stuffed their bellies, dreamed their dreams, and argued some more. No wonder the Nazis despised them. No wonder their old-world counterparts had let themselves be rounded up and shoved—still arguing, no doubt, still dreaming—into the gas chambers and ovens. But am I, Moe wondered, any different?

Certainly Dov was different. Dov had no illusions. Dov had been seared to a hardness, which Moe in his confusion felt obliged to admire. More than admire: to adore. He would close his eyes and touch his fingers to his temples to soothe what had become an almost perpetual tension, and Dov would materialize upon his inner eyelids, so clearly that he could see the thick dark hairs on the backs of Dov's

fingers and the peculiar texture of the scar that divided Dov's forehead. It was, he would later understand, a kind of madness that had
gripped him. He practically sleepwalked through his classes and studies. A constant acidity seared his stomach. In the minutes before Dov
was due to arrive for supper his heart would pound and heave, his
tongue thicken and dry. When he managed to sleep, he would have
strange dreams in which he and Dov struggled with each other
across a vague dark broken landscape until a kind of nervous discharge shocked him awake.

Laura, meanwhile, was feeling besieged. She didn't mind holding
down a job to support them while Moe went to school; she tolerated
the semipoverty in which they lived because she could foresee the
spacious luxury a dentist's income would afford; she had even
learned over the years to enjoy the occasional company of the family
—their "earthiness" was, she sometimes confessed to herself, refresh-
ing—but to come home from a day of case loads and office intrigues
and entertain Dov Kalisher was, she complained, too much for her.
Besides, she didn't like the man. There was something about him she
didn't trust. She kept reminding Moe that Dov had refused Sam's
offer of a job in the factory and Asa Kalisher's offer of a job in the
restaurant, and that he was paying for all the wine and flowers he
brought to supper, as well as his fancy new clothes and shoes, with
money he was "borrowing" from the family.

"And not just from Sam, who, God knows, can afford it," she told
Moe, "but from Molly and Evelyn and even poor Rose, which I
happen to know for a fact, and probably from all the others as well.
He's milking us all for what he can get. So he had a bad time in the
war. So lots of people had a bad time in the war. That doesn't justify
his being a parasite."

Her small reservoir of empathy had run dry. She hated the dense
cloud of suffering Dov brought into her house. She hated the way he
put his feet up on the furniture and the way Moe kowtowed to
him. She hated the fact that he took for granted the meals and the
hours they gave to him, and she was frightened by the way he sometimes gazed at her with his small, dark, steady eyes. She believed she
understood the meaning of that gaze, the hunger of it, as though she
herself were part of the dessert. Nor did it matter to him, apparently,
that she knew he was looking at her. Once she even tried to stare him
down—she was good at it; she had practiced in the office and the subway—but Dov kept his eyes fixed on her until flushed and angry, she

was forced to glance away. What could she do? If she complained, Moe would insist she was imagining things. He kept expecting her to learn to like the man. She suspected that Moe went out of his way to leave the two of them alone, as if—but no, she didn't dare think that. Still, Moe would invite Dov for dinner and then phone up to say he was going to be late, a casting to finish or a book to fetch from the library. On those occasions Laura would make herself busy in the kitchen, and Dov would sit himself down in Moe's easy chair, reading a newspaper, and the atmosphere would be all flutter and panic until she heard Moe's key in the door. She would have to struggle with herself not to look at Dov, afraid to discover that he was looking at her, and while some ghost from her childhood kept whispering to her that she was being rude, that she ought to be making conversation, she knew that if she opened her mouth, she would betray her troubled heart with a croak or a stutter.

Then one night Dov showed up, uninvited, in the middle of a snowstorm. Snow lay glistening on his hat and shoulders, and his face was damp and reddened with winter chill. Laura caught her breath and told him Moe was working late that night, and wouldn't be home for hours, and he looked at her, not smiling, and said he had talked to Moe, already knew that. What was she supposed to do? She had to invite him in, offer him a cup of coffee to warm him up.

They sat across from each other in the narrow living room, not saying much, waiting. Laura pretended to occupy herself with some knitting; but there was a tightness in her chest, and her clumsy fingers kept dropping stitches. The air around her seemed to hum with the echoes of dying screams. For a moment Dov closed his eyes and pinched the bridge of his nose as if he were fighting off memories too awful to endure. Then he got to his feet and stepped around the coffee table toward her. She felt stricken with that weakness his strong proximity aroused in her, and her neck cramped as she looked up at him, but she kept looking up because the alternative was to stare at the bulge in his trousers. She was aware of the diminishing space between her face and that bulge, and her heart almost stopped because she had already fantasized a hundred times the argument he might use on her—"The Nazis taught us that everything is possible, all is permitted!"—and knew she wouldn't say no.

"I have come especially to see you," said Dov, "to make a request."

"Yes?" she managed

"I—"

He hesitated. She lowered her face and stared into the abyss. A

216

kind of melting feeling came over her, neither pleasant nor painful, as she prepared to plunge.

"I want," he continued, "very much, to bring to your house for dinner a certain special friend of mine. You will understand that I seek to make a good impression."

"Oh," said Laura. "Oh, certainly!"

Not daring to admit to herself as they quietly discussed dates and menus, merely relatives after all, that what she experienced most poignantly for a moment, amidst the confusion, the guilt, the embarrassment, was a bittersweet pang of longing and regret.

In later years, at home in Great Neck, Moe and Laura would acquire the subtle art of elaborating and perfecting a small dinner party, but in those days the thought of entertaining a stranger in their house, particularly the sort of woman they imagined Dov would have acquired, put their nerves on edge. "He said, and I quote him, 'She embodies all my best hopes,' " Laura told Moe, and so with a tense curiosity that bordered almost on dejection, they prepared for the occasion. Out of the store of unused wedding presents came the pretty Irish linen tablecloth and napkins, the copper casserole dish, and that ornate silver tray that had been handed down to them as an heirloom from Laura's family. Moe tore himself away from his studies and his obsessions long enough to polish the windows and wax the floors, and Laura fought with the butcher to get him to slice the beef thin enough for stroganoff. The worst of it was the hour before the guests arrived. Things kept breaking, spilling, getting lost. Laura was close to tears and Moe's head ached with anxiety. He roamed the living room, turning lamps on and off, readjusting the chairs, abolishing specks of dust, and noticing—too late! the doorbell was ringing!—the toe of a single stray sock just visible under the couch. Guilty, furtive, jamming the sock into his jacket pocket, he climbed up off his hands and knees and hurried to admit his intriguing cousin and the woman who had come between them.

Her name was Pearl. She wore a silver mink stole over a garish green dress, her fingers glittered with gold and diamonds, her hair was bleached to platinum, and beneath a thick blaze of pancake makeup and bright lipstick, her face was rumpled and jowly and dotted with warts. She must have been forty, maybe more, a decade older than Dov Kalisher at least, and her eyes bulged, and her nose flared, and she trailed into the house a thick mist of perfume, and when she smiled, there was a smudge of lipstick on her false front teeth. She looked like a gilded frog. She was, in short, so gloriously vulgar and ugly that Moe held his breath as he contemplated her, compelled to amazement at his cousin's mind and motives.

What a depressing and endless evening that turned out to be!

Through the throb of a miserable headache, his jaw clenched in a ghastly smile, Moe had to sit and listen to the poor nervous woman babbling her most intimate secrets. She told them all about her first husband, "dear Morris," a wholesale jeweler, who had been trundled conveniently offstage the previous year by a bleeding ulcer, and about "Morris's little problem," and how as a consequence she was left childless and "comfortable" and alone, except for her cats—and what good is money, my dears, when you have no one to share it with, no one to love? She said that Dov was "a good angel" come into her life, and recalled how she had cried and cried when he recounted for her the sufferings he had endured. She told them she had heard from Dov all about his family, and she had been so looking forward to meeting them, and she hoped they would all be friends, and do you mind if we open a window, darlings, it's getting so warm in here.

Moe kept looking at Dov, and at last Dov looked back at him, so blandly, so inexpressively, that Moe's enthrallment to the man began to melt like a pat of butter; he knew, even as he sat there, struggling with his headache, breathing the warm richness of Pearl's perfumes, feeling the simple heat that shimmered up from her powdered and puckered bosom, that the stock of his illusions had been diminished by one.

Later, in bed, resting the burden of his headache on Laura's handsome breasts, wanting nothing more for the moment than a bit of comfort and release, enjoying the sensation of her cool fingertips on his brow, and feeling closer to her, more nearly in love, than he had felt in months, or even years, Moe was stricken by an unexpected memory of the days when he used to have to ride the subway from Park Place to Morningside Heights, prowling the train from car to car, seeking some perfect form and face that might answer to the fervent pulse of his desires. He didn't understand why that should return to him now—he missed the connection—but as he lay there, waiting for the blessing of sleep to come over him, he relinquished Dov Kalisher to the material fate he had chosen, that "simple ceremony" Pearl had mentioned, and, as it had so often in his life, his face burned with shame for all the foolish cravings of his hungry and relentless heart.

* * *

THE HIMMELFARBS MOVED TO MONTGOMERY STREET the day that President Roosevelt died. Deanna was just four years old then, but years later, in the midst of therapy, she convinced herself that she could dredge up from the murky bottom of her memory a brief glimpse of her mother bent red-eyed over the radio cabinet while abrupt moving men lugged in and planted all around her the furniture and cartons and lamps. Much more distinctly, Deanna could recall the eight-by-ten glossy photograph of FDR, which must have been purchased a couple of summers later on a family pilgrimage to Hyde Park and which hung through Deanna's childhood on the foyer wall, along with a pair of green ceramic boots and a certificate announcing her father's membership in the Magic Society of America. That view of the family's favorite President, grinning and waving from the back seat of a fancy touring car, with the famous cigarette holder clamped between his teeth, insinuated itself into Deanna's imagination. For a while she even believed that the man was one of her grandfathers, and in the darkroom of her fantasies she used to hold up that jaunty image—the car, the crowd, the pride, the radiance—against the equally familiar but far more troublesome image of old Jacob Lieber, with his fat book, in his sacred bower of artificial foliage.

She loved old photos. She adored the family album. On rainy days, bored with the drudgery of filling in spaces in a coloring book, she would drag the album out of the closet, where it languished among her father's trunk of tricks and the odor of mothballs, carry it to her bedroom (all pink frills and neglected dolls), and lose herself for a while among those marvelous blurred fragments of previous time. She was fascinated by the notion that a world of sorts had actually existed before she was born, and her nerves would start to tingle and ache as she rediscovered her relatives in the tightened flesh and old clothing of their former selves. For Deanna the past was like a theater in which her aunts and uncles and parents perfomed for her pleasure an amazing masquerade. That man on the beach, for example, with the mustache and the muscles, was actually her big-bellied and terrible Uncle Lou; and the giddy beauties perched on his shoulder were her mother and her Aunt Ruthie, trimmed-down and strangely illusive. She could remember being told that babies were "made" in their "mommies' tummies" (a disgusting thought, from which she concluded that they emerged from the anal tract), and she was teased, when she looked at old photos of her mother, with the thought that she was "in there," the little demon passenger tagging along for the ride. That there was once a time when she had no existence was a thought unfathomable to her. Nonetheless, a sharp pang of regret would jab at her as she fingered the heavy black pages, on which her mother had printed neatly, in white ink, notations such as "Prospect Park, 1933," "Our Florida Honeymoon, 1934" (with a fluffy pink bit of flamingo down stuck behind a snapshot of a lake), "Rockaway, Summer, 1936," "Ben's First Birthday Party," "Molly and Max," "Moe Graduates With Honors, 1940"—and her breath would quicken as she hurried faster and faster past these phantom figures toward the solidity of the wartime year in which she was born.

The album contained dozens of photographs, some of them professional, of Deanna at every stage of her infancy, her toddlerdom, her childhood. In later years the family would remind her how gorgeous, how absolutely gorgeous, she had been. Black-haired, dark-eyed, plumpish, with glowing cheeks the neighbors and relatives kept wanting to pinch, and a smile that widened gloriously every time a camera was pointed at her—"You were quite a ham," her mother would say, but as Deanna remembered it, it was the camera itself (the magic of a moment about to be eternalized) and not mere vanity that delighted her. Anyway, the impression of those pictures, that as a child she was always happy, was not a true one. Later, picking through the old bones and rags of her troubled psyche for her impassive and nonsensically optimistic therapist, she mostly recalled childhood moments of hurt and pain: the way her parents used to scream at each other, her father fighting with her rambunctious brother, how they bundled her off to her Aunt Ruthie's house the day her grandmother died, the many nights when she would lie awake in her bed and feel the lonely darkness around her pregnant with monsters, devils, witches, and, later on, burglars, maniacs, murderers, and her own thoughts vivid and aching with the noise and hurt of the family, and the wish that she could have been born something other than a girl.

She grew up in a limited world that was populated mostly by Liebers. Sure, there were Himmelfarbs, too, those polite, colorless relatives who belonged to her father's "side," but somehow in the scheme of things the Himmelfarbs didn't count. It was the Liebers, loud and ubiquitous, to whom she felt so inextricably and ambivalently attached. Later she would wonder why she knew so little about them, why their presence was so vivid while what must have been the real substance of their lives seemed to memory so thin and elusive. But of course, in those days she wasn't curious about them any more than she was curious, after a few initial explorations, about her breathing or her digestive system or the beating of her heart. The Liebers merely *were*. She inhabited a region bounded by their noise and expectations and supposed it to be the wide world itself. The family, the family, the family: in later years, self-involved, suffering symptoms of doubt and dread, she would get her mother or her aunts to talking about the old days and listen to their meandering and partial recollections as though her life itself depended on what they told her, sorting things out, discarding the irrelevancies, seizing upon those special stories that made her stomach flutter or her ears ring, rummaging through the flow of anecdotes and digressions and partial memories for some clue to her own aching and troublesome self.

"My family," she would tell her therapist, "you have to know about them, you have to add them up, because, in a sense, they are what I amount to."

The family, the family: maybe it was their collective existence that mattered most, the way they would gather themselves together in a living room to form a warm circle of hilarity and strife with a clear smell of chocolate lingering within. But memory could also seize them one at a time.

Aunt Molly, for example. Most of all in those days Deanna adored her Aunt Molly. Aunt Molly was fat and loud and funny, and sometimes she would lift Deanna up in her heavy arms and press her against her soft, humid breasts and whirl her round and round while she sang and spun and bounced, doing the Hucklebuck, balling the Jack. She would appear on Sunday afternoons, wiping the sweat from her neck with the scented handkerchief she kept balled up in her sleeve, and Deanna would search through her handbag, where there was always a lollipop or a pack of sourballs or a little mesh bag filled with chocolate coins. Deanna never forgot how those chocolate coins softened in the heat of her hand, the gummy chocolate sticking to the hard foil shell, which was gold on the outside and silver within, and how you would have to pry the thing apart and poke your tongue against the foil to get the chocolate off, and how if you chewed on the foil, it shocked your teeth.

In those days, between marriages, Aunt Molly lived by herself in a cramped and jumbled apartment with a bright cloth thrown over a daybed and a bookshelf filled with old "ris-kay" novels, some of which, in the course of time, Deanna would inherit: *Bachelor Girl, Green Hat, Jurgen, Flaming Youth*. It was fun to go visiting Aunt

Molly, especially when Aunt Molly became the first Lieber to own a television set. While the grown-ups talked, Deanna would sit on the floor with her brother and her cousins, watching the test pattern flicker on the small round screen, or the old cartoons and cowboy movies that were all they ever showed in those days. Once when she was watching a cowboy movie with her cousin Joey, her Aunt Molly erupted between them, laughing and shouting and calling over the grown-ups to point out her first husband there on the screen. Deanna knew that Aunt Molly had "gone through" several husbands, but it was typical of the family's reticence with children that she never heard anything about them. It was as though once you departed from the family circle, you ceased, even retrospectively, to exist. There were occasions—how often? never mind—when Aunt Molly would start crying and crying, while her mother and her Aunt Ruthie tried to soothe her, but Deanna was never allowed to know what those tears were about.

At Aunt Molly's apartment there was always a dish of chocolates to nibble, seconds from the factory, and Deanna was allowed to eat as much as she wanted because she rarely took more than a piece or two. Like most of her cousins, she was sated at an early age with the fine Lieber chocolate and much preferred the Life Savers and Dots and Chuckles you bought with your own nickels in the local candy store. Occasionally, not often, Aunt Molly might prepare a meal, but it was never any fun because, though everyone said Aunt Molly used to be an excellent cook, she had lost her sense of taste and Dr. Lipsky had forbidden her the use of salt; so her meals were dreadful huge heaps of dank *gefilte* fish and stewed chicken and watery mashed potatoes, and for dessert the apple strudel that had become a family joke, burned black and tarry on the outside, still raw and sugary in the middle. But that was easy to forgive. In fact, Deanna learned early the habit of forgiving her Aunt Molly everything, because, as the grown-ups used to say, the woman had no luck. Nevertheless, despite her smells and her obesity and her high blood pressure, despite her inexplicable rages and weeping, Aunt Molly was, of all the family, the most vivid, the most joyous. Her energy was intact. What a pleasure it was to let her teach you canasta, or to bounce on her lap, or to listen to her and Aunt Deborah arguing with each other—a strange concerto, all booming brass and drums on one side, a single sad violin on the other.

"True love is boundless," Deborah might say.

And Molly would start shouting at her: "A lot you know! Love, most of all, has its limits!"

Snapshots Deanna might have taken in those days, if only she had a camera: Aunt Molly and Aunt Deborah arguing; Aunt Essie ransacking her own kitchen, trying to find a treat for "my favorite little niece"; Aunt Rose in a black dress, blinking behind her thick glasses, lurching down the hill of New York Avenue, with Georgie, gapemouthed, his big gnarled ears jutting out, wearing a similar pair of thick glasses, lurching right behind her; Uncle Sam dozing in an easy chair, with his hat on and a precarious inch of ash dangling from the tip of his perpetual cigarette; Uncle Lou with his great mound of a belly squeezed up tight against the steering wheel of a furious new black and yellow Ford convertible which he maneuvered into three accidents the first month he owned it, and which years later sat rusting and bashed, without tires, propped up on old milk cases in the tiny garage behind the Grossman house on Crown Street; her cousin Carrie showing up at a family picnic in Highland Park wearing a billowing white cotton frock and a wide-brimmed floppy white straw hat with a fluttering green silk ribbon tied around it, so slender and pure and beautiful that Deanna's chest pulsed with longing and envy; her father eating his daily banana, with the peel draped in three neat folds around his fist, his lips breaking off a hunk of the sweet, soft, pale pulp—which would remind Deanna of how her grandmother, in the days when she occupied a hospital bed in the Himmelfarb apartment, used to be spoon-fed bananas with her pills mashed into it, and how Deanna wondered what it would taste like, and how when she made her mother feed her some, she gagged and vomited; Aunt Ruthie, standing in a housedress on the back porch, a *shmateh* around her head, holding at arm's length a dripping bag of garbage and calling frantically for one of her older boys, Jeff or Erwin, to come and take it from her; Aunt Sarah, in a gray man-tailored suit, sucking on a cigarette, which she held clamped between her pinkie and her third finger, and patiently explaining to a couple of indifferent nieces and nephews the political intricacies of the cold war; her mother and a couple of her aunts emerging from the back seat of her Uncle Sam's big Chrysler, carrying shopping bags filled with magazines and snacks for whomever it was they used to visit on Sundays in the big state hospital.

Well, whom were they visiting? They wouldn't tell her. She didn't know if it was a man or a woman, young or old, or what manner of

223

illness or infirmity kept him or her locked away in one of the big yellow brick buildings with the wire mesh on the windows. At first, they said it was "just someone they knew." Later, it was a "family friend" and still later, when she was too old for such vagueness, it became "a relative." The big mystery, the skeleton in the family closet. She used to wonder why her father never "went up" to see this person and why only some members of the family went—her mother and Ruthie and Deborah and Rose, but never Sam or Molly or any of the in-laws. All she knew was that on Sundays her father got up early and rode the bus down to Manhattan Beach to borrow her uncle's car; he would come home grumpy, having stopped along the way to pick up her Aunt Deborah and a bagful of rolls and jelly doughnuts, and they would have breakfast together—her Aunt Deborah nibbling at a half a roll with her little teeth—and by then Aunt Rose and Aunt Ruthie would arrive, and they would load the car up with their bags full of magazines and snacks and "presents" and drive out along the Interboro Parkway with the radio playing. She could remember how the radio signal would fade momentarily every time they went under an overpass, which she used to call a tunnel, and how she liked that road because it was filled with tunnels, and how the car would become shadowed for a moment and how the sun would explode in her eyes when they emerged on the other side. Then they would leave the highway and drive down a street past a Howard Johnson's and turn in at the big gate, where a guard stood waving the traffic on, and pull up at the entrance to the big yellow brick building, and her mother and her aunts would climb out of the car and go off carrying their bags full of magazines and pretzels and potato chips and boxes of Lieber's chocolates. She used to think it would be nice if someone brought all those "presents" to her, and sometimes she even wished she could live in one of those buildings: she could visualize so clearly the "presents" set out on a table next to a bed, while all around it was the blur of a room which she would never see and lacked the clues to imagine.

While the women made their visit, her father would take her and her brother and often her cousin Joey back to that Howard Johnson's for an ice cream cone, and as they ate their ice cream, he would show them tricks with coins and matches—the old routines she had seen so often that by the time she was seven or eight magic was ruined for her. Then they would drive back in the car, which, now that all the perfume and makeup had blown away, smelled rich with leather and sunshine, and park near a big grassy field where she and her brother and her cousin Joey could romp and play. Sometimes her father let them take turns sitting behind the steering wheel, pretending to drive. Joey particularly liked that. He would make motor noises and clench the wheel so hard the whites of his knuckles showed, and stick the tip of his tongue through the gap of his missing front teeth, as though he actually believed he was going somewhere and was in a hurry to arrive. Then they would return to pick up the women, who would emerge from the building empty-handed and subdued, and on the way home they would say to each other: "Well, he was better," or, "Well, he wasn't so good today." Not until she was a teenager did she understand that the place was a mental hospital, and not until much later than that did she learn that the "person" the family used to visit was an uncle, a Lieber brother, a man named Hymie, who filled the genealogical gap between Deborah and Molly, and whose madness, if that's what it was—"He wasn't so crazy, as I remember it," her mother would tell her, "he was just a little shy"—was another element in her rich and unpredictable and troublesome Lieber blood. Sure, a madman in the Lieber household: that, somehow, completed the picture.

The family, the family: later in life she would come to believe that they were all more or less attached to each other with invisible strings of feeling, and that the cavortings of any one of them could make all the others twitch and dance. They were superstitious about each other. Her mother believed that there was a kind of telepathy among them. How often, she used to say, had she picked up the phone only to find Ruthie or Rose or Deborah on the other end of the line? And thus, too, Aunt Deborah's premonitions. She claimed they were messages from the world of ghosts, but probably, Deanna would come to believe, they depended wholly on chemistry or electricity, some uncanny quality of the genes. The family: as though to share the old Lieber blood were a kind of destiny in itself, a fate from which, no matter how hard you tried, you could never be fully disentangled.

"No one's asking you to love your relatives," her mother used to tell her, "but blood is blood, so you might as well be nice to them."

Blood is blood. But what had she to do with Uncle Chaim, for example, who came to the house on Sunday mornings with his coat and his beard and his musty smell, and sat there in the kitchen, eating an orange off a paper napkin, talking to her mother in a language Deanna couldn't understand? Or Uncle Yonkel and Aunt Bea —Big and Little the family called them—who lived up on New York Avenue and seemed to spring to life only on Jewish holidays, when the Himmelfarbs would traipse up the hill for an hour of sponge cake and tea and polite, aching boredom, as though all the rest of the time they were packed away in trunks amidst the world's props and scenery? And why should she be nice to her Uncle Moe, the dentist, who always let you know how much better off he was than everyone else, and whose slick pomposity and phony smiles put her teeth on edge; or her Uncle Lou, who bullied and frightened her; or her Uncle Irving, who the family kept saying was making life miserable for her poor Aunt Rose? Be nice! Be nice! Oh, she was always nice enough. She didn't know how not to be.

She had friends, neighborhood children and classmates, girls who sat together for hours braiding each other's hair and tickling each other's arms, and boys with whom she played punchball and stoop-ball, and who let her into their ephemeral clubs during that phase of her childhood when she had become a bit boyish herself; but they were mere scratches on the plate of her memory. She would recall far more vividly the hours she spent with her cousin Joey, the third of her Aunt Ruthie's four children. They were the same age, and it was convenient for their parents to throw them together. It didn't matter that they didn't particularly like each other. On Saturday afternoons they used to go to the movies together and sit up in the front row, so close to the screen that the images (five cartoons and a chapter of "Crash" Corrigan or Rocketman along with the feature) blurred and crackled, sucking on jujubes or sharing the slivers of a Bonomo's Turkish Taffy bar that Joey had smashed against the metal armrest. Then they would go home and play cowboys and Indians, which was Joey's favorite game, and fight about who would be the cowboy and who would be the Indian and who would get to use the single cap pistol they had between the two of them. They used to play out in the alley behind Joey's house and when Joey had to pee, he would pull out his business and do it right there in front of her. She used to tease him about it because even then she believed that there was something profoundly silly about male genitals, and one time he got so mad at her that he turned and squirted her, and the warm gush of it trickling down her leg made her cry, and she went running toward his house, and he ran after her and caught her and threw her down hard on the gravelly pavement and said he would kill her ("I swear to God I'll kill ya!") if she told; and years later Dr. Steeben's eyebrows rose and rose when she resurrected that incident, because clearly there was something *significant* about it. But she knew it wasn't significant and didn't have much to do with her "case." It had more to do with Joey's case, because if she told, his father would punish him, and poor Joey hated his father and was terrified of him. Her own case, she was sure, was far more complicated than that.

Her case. Well, let's see. (The therapy didn't seem to be getting anywhere, but it was great fun anyway to pick through the memories and have all the old feelings shiver through the bare, ragged tree of her nerves.) Let's talk a bit about her brother. What is there to say? He built model airplanes out of balsa wood, filling the apartment with the odor of glue and dope. He collected baseball cards. He went to Ebbets Field with his friends and waited in the simmering dusk to collect autographs from the players who emerged wet-haired and ruddy from the locker rooms. He would get furious with Deanna when she touched his things. There was a time when he would stand naked in front of the full-length mirror on the closet door, admiring the black hairs that were beginning to mat his arms and chest and genitals. He was four years older than Deanna and spent the first thirteen years of his life shouting and whooping and getting into trouble—"a real *bondit*," the family said—and then, when he reached his puberty, as though a switch had been thrown, he turned in upon himself and became brooding and silent and successful, a good athlete, a good student, and eventually a good lawyer, a good father, and, in his way, a good if unfaithful husband, president of the B'nai B'rith, a "community leader" with his handsome face pictured in the township newspaper, a model life for a model Jewish boy. No, as far as Deanna was concerned, her brother didn't count for much, and figured only peripherally in her case.

Her parents, then. Oh, Doctor, I can't go on! Her favorite memory of her mother was when she would come home on a Saturday afternoon from one of her shopping trips, exhausted and flushed and happy beneath her bright burden of bags and boxes. She had expensive tastes. "Buy cheap, have cheap," she used to say. She would dress Deanna up "like a fashion plate" until Deanna rebelled against starchy frills and lace. She was determined that her hair, her clothes, her home, her children would be forever "in style." When Ben got a bicycle, it had to be a fancy Schwinn with chrome fenders and a dazzling array of lights and streamers and reflectors. No wonder that on Montgomery Street everyone believed the Himmelfarbs were rich. Even the family thought that Ev and Milton had money, though they

227

must have known better. Deanna's father went off to work in a tie and jacket, as if he owned a factory instead of merely working in one. Everything neat, everything tidy, everything in its place. For Deanna's mother, appearance mattered most. She lived like a fugitive with a sordid past: slip up just once, give the neighbor's an opening, and they would rush in and discover whatever mysterious crime she was hiding. But why, Doctor, why all the guilt, why the anxiety? What was she so ashamed of? Why was it so important to her to be just like —or perhaps a little bit better than—everyone else?

And her father. Now, perhaps, we are getting somewhere. Her father, with his moods and his magic. By the time Deanna was old enough to know about the magic he rarely performed professionally; but at family birthday parties and picnics he would entertain the cousins with his display of tricks, and occasionally the old vivid hopes would spring back to life within him and he would go off "on a job" for an afternoon or a weekend with his hidden pockets stuffed with coins and silk handkerchiefs and bits of rope and that sticky yellow gum that could, with a snap of the fingers, produce fire. But mostly he worked in the factory on Bergen Street and came home tired and grumpy and spent an hour or two on weekends studying the "Opportunities" listings in the newspaper. He dreamed of going into business on his own. He told people that if you had the right merchandise, you could start a business in a small way, working in your spare time, and build it into something substantial. In the years before the Himmelfarbs moved to Florida, he was always selling things: cosmetics, plastic kitchenware, costume jewelry, men's slacks, ceramic figurines. The stuff would arrive in crates which spilled excelsior all over the house when he opened them, and for a few weeks he would spend his free hours trying to be a salesman. But he wasn't very good at it. With a suitcase full of merchandise he was even more sullen and clumsy than with his bag of tricks. Sure, the stuff would slowly vanish, but there was always some portion left in the crates, the portion which, if sold, would have produced the profit. That he persisted in this round of humiliations, that he refused to abandon hope, was a measure, Deanna would later suppose, of how much he hated working for his brother-in-law in the factory on Bergen Street.

He was particularly moody in winter. He hated the cold, the ice, the slush, the heavy coats, the galoshes, the bitter wind tearing at his chest. He dreamed of warmer climates. He was always talking about his honeymoon trip to Florida: the sun, the flamingos, the white sand, the blue ocean water, the palm trees, the grotesque souvenirs carved out of coconuts had all blurred for him into a vision of paradise. In his fondest moments he imagined himself lazying away the daytime hours on the beach and performing at night—The Great Miltoni, a success at last—in the lounges and ballrooms of the big hotels. After supper he would go into the living room with his newspaper, and soon the newspaper would collapse and he would be asleep, dreaming and smiling, basking no doubt in the sunny warmth of his desires. Florida. Floridafloridafloridaflorida! Eventually he would get there, but Deanna was not yet ready to think about that.

Better to remember how her brother once took her to the candy store on Rogers Avenue for a banana split and how they sat and giggled over the mess of fruity syrups and whipped cream, closer to each other in that moment than they ever had been or ever would be again; or how she would listen to her mother and her aunts gossiping about the family, and how—because little children are all ears—they would switch to Yiddish when they came to the parts they didn't want her to understand; or how sometimes, just sometimes, her father would come home from work in a certain kind of mood and grab her up in his arms and rub his scratchy cheek against her face and whirl her round and round until the whirling combined with the smells of tobacco and sweat and chocolate to make her head spin; or how frightened she could be at certain radio programs, the creaking door of *The Inner Sanctum,* for example, or the all-too-vivid descriptions of "most wanted criminals" at the end of each episode of *Gangbusters;* or how in summer, at Rockaway, she would become so terribly frustrated when the pail of water she trudged up across the hot sand seemed to have in it nothing at all of the immensity of the sea. These were the sorts of things she could bear to remember: the froth of her childhood, mementos of her innocence, mollifying remnants of those good old days before she had to come to know what was wrong with her.

UNCLE ASA HAD DECIDED TO RETIRE. He must have been seventy years old, maybe more, and the family laughed when he said he wanted to travel a bit, see the world while he was still young enough to enjoy it,

But he wasn't kidding. He was running around with a woman half his age, a plump blond ex-waitress named Lena—the family always called her the floozy. As Asa explained it to Sam, he wanted to sell off the restaurant and his share of the chocolate business, and take off with Lena on a cruise around the world.

"Around the world no less," they said. "The floozy's putting *meshuggeh* ideas into his head."

He was amazing. That beacon of red hair which once had signaled to his sister through a mob of anxious immigrants had long ago faded to a thin glimmer of white; but the years had trimmed and hardened his florid beefiness, and now, lean, vigorous, solitary, proud, he tramped the streets of Brooklyn, brandishing, just for effect, an elaborate old cane with a carved dog's head for a handle. He still carried in his pocket that antique silver box, and he still loved to stifle arguments by exhibiting his mummified finger. When one of his cronies died, he would smuggle into the funeral parlor a piece of cheese Danish, wrapped in a linen napkin, and slip it into the coffin ("In case you get hungry on the way to Jerusalem!") while he was paying his last respects. The establishment of the state of Israel had rekindled in him a boyish enthusiasm, and he was always pestering the family to buy bonds and send money to Tel Aviv "so they can plant a few trees and make the desert bloom." On weekends the old restaurant with its wooden booths and overhead fans and wisecracking waiters, who might have bounced right off the Yiddish stage, still throbbed with customers, and there in the midst of the tumult would be Uncle Asa, clapping people on the back, dashing in and out of the kitchen, blowing his big reddish nose into a huge handkerchief, and tearing up the checks of radiant young lovers and blushing newlyweds.

The family used to argue about his age. They would add and subtract and make the appropriate allowances, but the numbers they arrived at never quite tallied with the image they had of the man established in the restaurant and already successful when Jacob and Sophie arrived in America. For Asa Kalisher the years apparently moved along at a separate, idiosyncratic pace.

"Seventy, eighty, what difference does it make?" they were forced to conclude. "The man will probably outlive us all."

The problem was that Uncle Asa wanted Sam to buy him out and Sam didn't have the cash. He was still paying off the banks for that new equipment he had installed after the war. To make matters

230

worse, the competition from the larger chocolate companies had grown and grown. The Lieber line of chocolates had been pushed out of the department stores and specialty shops by cheaper merchan-·dise which was thick with sugar and filled with preservatives, and even the nine retail outlets weren't doing so well anymore. It was the times. In the old days, when chocolate was for special occasions, people cared about quality; now, Sam complained, they would eat *dreck* so long as it left a taste of sweetness in their mouths.

"Why sell out?" Sam said to Asa Kalisher. "Hang on for a while. It's a good investment."

"General Motors is a good investment," his uncle replied. "The chocolate business I'm not so sure."

Despite the years of success, all Sam owned in those days, apart from the business, was the house in Manhattan Beach, a fund he had been accumulating for his retirement, and another fund he had been putting aside for his unborn grandchildren—he was anticipating the day when Rich and Carrie would be out of his hair and raising kids of their own. The rest of the profits had been spent (squandered, the family would later say) on automobiles and card games and after-noons at the racetrack and fine clothes and furniture and Essie's "hol-idays" and Rich's extravagances and the clamorous needs of the brood. But he wasn't worried. The good times had lasted so long, he believed they would last forever. Whatever little business problems came along, he would find a way to solve. You could always strike a deal. So for a couple of weeks Sam made the rounds of the banks, and spent long hours haggling with Dov Kalisher, and talked things over with some people who were "friends" of Murray Pinsky's; by the time he was finished signing all the papers he owed a lot of people a lot of money, but he owned outright seventy-six percent of Lieber's Chocolates & Novelties—Molly still held, as part of the legacy of Solly Poverman, the other twenty-four. Later he would remember how he brought a big bottle of champagne to the boat on which Asa Kalisher and the floozy were about to embark, and how they sat in the stateroom drinking the stuff out of water glasses and proposing hilarious toasts to each other. In recollection that seemed to him the moment when his life turned back upon itself and became that long, tedious process of loss he would eventually have to get used to. But he didn't know it then. In fact, a couple of days later he went and bought a new car. It was his way of demonstrating to himself, though he was up to his ears in debt, that the good times weren't over.

231

During the good times, you see, Sam bought a new car every year. He went through cars, the family used to say, the way Molly went through men. He favored Packards, Buicks, Oldsmobiles, Chryslers, in shades of blue that darkened as he aged. Most of all, it was the buying of the cars rather than the cars themselves that Sam loved, the luxurious pleasure of gallivanting into a showroom and feeling the plush carpeting rub along your soles and having the slick, eager salesman fawn over you. To caress the gleaming arc of a fender, to breathe the erotic air of new leather and steel and polish, to insert himself behind the steering wheel while the ample weight of his checkbook shifted in his breast pocket—such moments were, for Sam, the tokens of his success. It was like entering some enchanted garden and being allowed to pluck at whim the freshest flower, the ripest fruit. So what if later on, after the nicks and dents and scratches had appeared and the once-bright engine had blackened to a quivering hot heap of metal, he lost his taste for driving the thing? The year would roll around, another autumn would come, and like a little boy awakening to his birthday, he would hurry to buy a new one.

The good times. The comfort of familiar routines. The casual hours in the office when everything was functioning smoothly and he had nothing more to do than to tug gently at the myriad strings of his authority and absorb through his shoes the hum and beat of the factory machinery below, until it came to seem to him the music of his heart and blood. Or those long indolent afternoons in his box seat at Ebbets Field, cracking peanuts beneath a blazing sky and watching Jackie Robinson—"Oh, you beautiful black bastard you!" —bring to a kind of perfection the exquisite, slow, sporadic game of baseball. Or the evenings at the club playing pinochle or bridge for half a buck a point with the kibitzers breathing down his neck and the handless grandfather clock in the corner ticking and chiming the invisible hours. Years ago he had circumscribed a portion of the world and so defined his success. Fine clothes, expensive restaurants, vacationing in Florida or the Adirondacks, pulling out a wad of cash and peeling off fifties at the betting window at Belmont. An hour spent in a barbershop frequented by show-biz folk and racketeers. Parading Essie around the nightclubs so she could show off her new mink. Those family celebrations when he would plunk himself down in an easy chair and tug his hat brim over his eyes, pretending to doze, because in the space he thus created around himself he could taste more keenly, more sweetly, through the cries and tumult, the dependence of that whole uproarious mob on him. The good times. In the old days he had believed that the world, being what it was, was bound to steal away from him his luck, his money, his home, his health, everything; but that old mood of somber anticipation—his brooding sense that everything must change—had jelled into permanence. He had shaken off the legacy of his father and fallen so fully into the patterns of success that misfortune, when it finally came, would baffle him.

But it hadn't happened yet. Sure, there were problems—even the best life is filled with *tsurris*—but what problem couldn't be solved by striking a deal and writing a check? What you couldn't solve, you could finagle; and what you couldn't finagle, you could accept. Just as you had to accept accidents, enemies, a death in the family, a sick child, the creaks and ailments and sudden anxieties of middle age. Take Essie, for example. The years had formed her into a sharper, shriller version of her mother; she had the same pretensions, the same inanities; and there were times when Sam would sit in his own living room with his eyes fixed on that ornate pair of silver candlesticks they had inherited and feel himself for a moment back in the Schonwald brownstone, nodding and smiling and being polite, performing his best imitation of General Sharpe for his ghastly and resurrected mother-in-law. She was something, that Essie. She would climb into bed with her hair in curlers and her face shiny with cold cream, wearing a black sleep mask that made her look like some nightmare version of the Lone Ranger, chattering away at him and lisping slightly because nowadays half her teeth were left to soak overnight in a cup of blue dentifrice, and Sam would be amazed that over the years he had managed to tolerate her. Astonishing what a man could learn to accept.

Rich, too. It broke Sam's heart that the kid was too busy with his girl friends and shenanigans to study hard and go to college, but never mind, never mind: he would groom him to take over the business. At the age of twenty Rich was tall and handsome and loud and jovial, and dressed like a prince, and even though he was a spoiled brat, he had a good head on his shoulders, so there was no telling what he might be able to accomplish. "The kid has moxie," Sam used to say. He remembered the time when Rich turned sixteen and he gave him his own checking account with a thousand dollars as an initial deposit, and three weeks later, after a fight with Essie, Rich took his checkbook and moved into a hotel. Essie cried and cried, but

Sam was secretly amused. Why shouldn't the kid taste a bit of independence? He let him stay there, ordering his meals from room service and buying new clothes, until the checks started to bounce, and then he went and put his arm around him and brought him home.

"So, did you learn something at least?" he asked him.

"Yeah," said Rich. "A thousand dollars is *bupkiss*."

That's how it was with children. You had to learn to take the bitter with the sweet. They never managed, whatever your efforts, to enter into those paradisical realms you had imagined for them. Rich would come into the factory in his white suit with his blondish hair combed back upon his head and slap his uncles on the back and tease the girls on the packaging line, but he didn't know the difference between a criollo bean and a forastero, and couldn't tell you the function of the "conch." What he liked best was to plant himself at Sam's desk with his feet up and get on the phone with the suppliers and middlemen, mingling jokes and orders, kidding around, thinking he could move the world with nothing more than the jovial force of his personality. But he would learn, Sam told himself. Sooner or later he would encounter his share of miseries, and he would have to learn.

For Sam's fiftieth birthday the family threw him a big party at Asa Kalisher's restaurant. This was just a couple of months before Uncle Asa sold the place and took his floozy on that cruise around the world, so it was the last time the Liebers gathered there. They invited everyone, the brood and all the children, the uncles and aunts and cousins, from both sides, Essie's *mishpuchah*, even some of Sam's business acquaintances and his cronies from the club. Molly showed up with her latest "beau," a man named Izzy Kupperman, who was probably twenty years older than she was, but he was tall and bald and handsome and deeply suntanned, and later the two of them interrupted the hilarity of the occasion to announce their engagement. Uncle Chaim came, and so did Aunt Bea and Uncle Yonkel, who looked, they all said, "like death warmed over." (They didn't know that the poor man was carrying in his liver the cancer that would soon kill him.) Herb Spieler, the jockey, rode the train in from Saratoga, and Dov Kalisher arrived with his Pearl in their brand-new Cadillac, and the twins came from Philadelphia, and even Cousin Miriam showed up—that pale, sad spinster who "almost never went anywhere" since that day so long ago when she decided that to be in style she should cut off her gorgeous long hair (Debo-

234

rah used to claim that Molly put her up to it) and so lost the only boyfriend she would ever have.

They hired a band for the occasion, complete with a singer who stood behind the microphone, mopping his wet face with a towel and urging everyone—"Come on, even you *alteh kockers!*"—to dance. The music blared and crashed through the old restaurant, and when the mob joined hands and stomped through a hora, with Sam sitting on a chair in the middle of the circle like a bride, the floor shook and the overhead fans quivered. The waiters kept serving platters of hot hors d'oeuvres—*gefilte* fish balls, cocktail franks, stuffed cabbage, slices of *kishka*—and through the warm afternoon a gorgeous ice sculpture in the shape of a swan slowly melted until the neck broke and the head tumbled into the punch bowl. The presents were heaped on a table, a blaze of gaudy paper and bright ribbons, and they made Sam open them and pretend to be overwhelmed by all the shirts and ties and cuff links and monogrammed handkerchiefs he received. Then they forced him to make a speech. He climbed up on the makeshift bandstand with that greasy singer pounding him on the back, and for the life of him, he didn't know what to say. He stood there, all pride and embarrassment, mumbling foolish words of gratitude, and an old, old pressure heaved in his heart. For a moment his thoughts conjured up the cloaked memory of the night on the way to America when for reasons he would never understand he had been made to sleep in a forest, and then, supplanting it, the clearer memory of the time they shot Lefkowitz right there, at that table, where Dov Kalisher was now coolly cleaning his fingernails with a silver pocketknife. Somehow the bravado of the latter memory seemed to cancel out the anxiety of the former the way a city cancels out a wilderness. A more bookish man, Walter, for example, might have concocted a theory about that odd convergence, but Sam merely stumbled past the queasiness, fighting back the warm flush the memories brought to his face. He said a few final words into the microphone and ambled moodily back to his table, where he had to sit for another hour, enduring kisses from his sisters and shaking a lot of hands.

But in the weeks that followed his thoughts were roiled and his sleep became more fitful and sporadic than ever. He caught himself remembering the old days as though there was finally the need to make some sense of them. But how? What sort of sense? At times he would watch himself moving through the rigmarole of his daily routines and feel everything—the factory, the ball games, the restaurants, the nights at the club—becoming unfamiliar and new. He alarmed himself by staring, say, at Essie or Molly or Lou or Rose and seeing the aging faces of strangers. It was even disturbing to study himself, with his creases and his cropped white hair, in the morning mirror. Maybe it was because he was fifty now—the number itself seemed to contain an opening through which he was passing into an uncertain future. His life was rushing now 'round an inescapable circle toward the oblivion out of which he had come.

One Saturday morning, without thinking much about it, he got up early, put on a tie, and went to *shul*—or rather to that airy, bright, and somehow dispiriting Reformed temple his contributions had helped to build—and the ancient tones of the chants rising in that place he secretly despised momentarily soothed his nerves. But by the time he got home his mood had soured again, and he felt grumpy and chagrined. The night he slept in the forest. The time they shot Lefkowitz, with the blood on the table and the horseplayer dancing away to avoid the chair. He couldn't shake off the mystery of the one, the strange, bold, somber joy of the other. He was held for a while, caught in inexplicable tension between the two of them.

Through July and August, like some miserable summer cold, the mood lingered. "Change of life," said the family, as if the words contained an explanation. During that time there was no living with him. He was short-tempered and snapped at everybody. He would disappear from the office for hours on end, and people thought he was having another affair. Essie complained that he wasn't eating properly. He started keeping a bottle of Pepto-Bismol in his desk drawer. One night he even came home drunk from the club.

But Sam was not the sort of man who could go on wrestling forever with such *mishegoss*. By autumn he was distracted by more practical problems: raising the money to buy Asa Kalisher's share of the business; teaching Rich the fundamentals of the trade; arguing with Molly about her plan to marry Izzy Kupperman and move to Florida; dealing with Rose and Irving and their bitter quarrel about whether Georgie should be institutionalized. These were things he could handle, and handling them brought him back to the simple realities of the day-to-day. Eventually that mood, whatever it was, became just another memory, ever more faint and spectral as it dwindled into the past.

"It was nothing," he could tell himself. "I was just getting used to being old."

SIX

WITH HYMIE, you never knew what to expect. One moment he would be perfectly normal, the next he was in a world of his own. Fat, pinkish, bald, swaddled in a pale blue institutional bathrobe like some great overgrown baby, he would sit there on the sun porch, talking to you about the family, asking questions about the nieces and nephews he had seen only in those blurred snapshots he had taped to the wall above his bed, or reminiscing about the old days on Park Place, remembering how Sam would come home from work and take them all down to the candy store for an ice cream cone or a soda, or how Molly would fly into a rage when she caught anyone messing around in her drawers; and then, as though some inner switch had been thrown and all his thoughts and memories had been canceled, he would stare out bleakly through the wire mesh, agonized by the strangeness he saw. At such moments Rose would want to put her arms around him and comfort him as she had in the old days, the two of them wrapped in a blanket in front of Sophie's artificial fire. She still believed that if only the family had loved him enough, they wouldn't have had to send him away. But she also believed that she had lost the right to touch him. He belonged to the hospital now; his soft, mottled flesh exuded the sad odor of the place.

She dreaded having to visit him there. She feared the bland doctors and smiling orderlies and the acres of neat-trimmed grass, which no one ever got to use. On Hymie's night table she would see a half-filled water glass and an empty little white paper cup, and the sight would make her stomach knot and twist. She could imagine all too vividly the endless days and nights he had spent there, alone with his fear and suffering. She had heard him talk about patients who were violent and patients who were "filthy" and patients who maimed themselves, gnawing at their flesh or tearing out their eyes. He would force "presents" upon her, some childish clay ashtray or some pathetic potholder woven on a loom, and always, guiltily, she would end up throwing the stuff away because she couldn't bear the sight of it. Riding home to Brooklyn, while her sisters gabbed, she would sit in the back of the car, her eyes thickening with tears, and sense the old, mute, relentless anger that had been gnawing at her ever since Dr. Lipsky sent those men to the house to carry Hymie away. She had never forgiven the family for that; in her own quiet way, she was implacable.

After Georgie was born, she visited Hymie less often, her love and empathy being reserved now for her child. Between Georgie and Irving she had her hands full. Everyone marveled at her patience and endurance. At first, apart from a perpetually clogged nose, Georgie wasn't much different from any other infant, easier maybe, because he seldom cried. It was later, when he was three and four and five, and still not toilet-trained, and the apartment stank from his excrement, that the *tsurris* really began. Month after month, year after year, she had to go on washing him, and dressing him, and wiping his nose and *tuchis,* and feeding him, and carrying him around, and guessing at what hurt or hunger lay behind his uncanny howling. She spent hours and hours trying to teach him to feed himself; he would throw food around like a two-year-old, and she would have to sit there with him—"She has," the family said, "the patience of a saint!" —coaxing and smiling and talking to him, telling him what a clever little *boychik* he was if he managed to steer a spoonful of cereal into his gaping mouth. He couldn't walk until he was four, and then he would lurch around the apartment, an enormous and husky toddler, bumping into things and falling down and howling because he couldn't figure out how to put himself back on his feet. His "destructive phase" was endless. He broke lamps, dishes, even Rose's precious ceramic figurine of a swan, which Uncle Asa, perhaps remembering the story of the ugly duckling, had given her as a wedding present. Turn your back on Georgie for a moment, and there was no telling what he would get into. And you couldn't punish him; his condition gave him license. He just didn't know any better.

Nor, Rose used to tell herself, did Irving. Irving's mother had decided that Georgie's birth was a calamity and Irving agreed. They were ignorant people, the Malishes, stubborn and coarse and selfish, but the man was her husband, and Rose forgave him for everything. He refused to help her with the child. He would come home from work and if supper wasn't on the table, he blamed the kid. He grew ever more sullen and withdrawn. A child like Georgie needed doctoring, eyeglasses, dental work, medicines—but Irving flew into rages about the bills he had to pay. On Sundays he would go off to spend the afternoon with his mother and come back muttering about "decisions" that had to be made. Rose didn't argue with him; she let him mutter and rage. She understood that he was a weak and foolish man, and she believed to the end that she would manage to hold onto him.

Father, mother, child: in a word, family. As far as Rose was concerned, that was the natural order of life. There was a wholeness to it, a sense of completion, that Moe or Walter might have called aesthetic, but Rose didn't have that word; she had merely the mood, and that, for her, was enough. It had to be enough. During those first bewildering months after the birth and the *briss*, Georgie would lie in his crib, snorting and wheezing and choking on his own phlegm, and Rose would recall through her grief that old children's story in which a baby turns into a pig. Her face burned and her ears buzzed as her thoughts raced, against her will, to a dreadful conclusion—that maybe it would be better for the poor thing to die right away and so be done with its suffering. There were times during those sleepless, anxious nights when she imagined herself looming up, all hopeless love and sudden madness, to snuff out its pathetic life with a pillow. Father, mother, child: she would whisper the words to herself, turning them round and round in her mind, making of them an incantation against her own worst thoughts. Father, mother, child; Irving, Rose, George: believing the three of them, bound together in luckless agony, would somehow outgrow themselves, become something singular and beautiful, beyond all the pain, the ugliness, the limitation, the filth.

Thus she discovered that she could love the child. He was helpless and alive and altogether easy to love. He asked nothing of her but what she had to give: her time, her energy, her attention, her devotion, her feelings, her thoughts, her nourishing body, her comforting arms. She realized that it wouldn't matter to him that she was cross-eyed and homely; he would never stare, as even Irving sometimes stared, with vague disgust and horror at her glasses or her mole. He would never expect her to be anything more than what she was. She learned that it made her happy to sit with him in her mother's old rocking chair, holding him while he nursed and slept, touching his bald head, his small, stubby fingers and toes. She used to play a little game with him. She would give him her finger and he would clench it tightly in his fist—for the grasping instinct, Dr. Lipsky had told her, was strong in children of his kind—and then she would tug just hard enough to pull his arm upward, but not hard enough to jerk her finger away, and then relax again, tug and release, tug and release, until he fell into the simple rhythm. Tug and release, tug and release—it made him smile. And if he could smile, he could feel happiness. And if he could feel happiness, he was worth all her efforts and care. To make him happy: what better purpose could there be in her luckless and thwarted life?

Sometimes she wondered what the world looked like to him. He was immune to so much; his desires were so simple. She would hold him on her lap, talking to him, soothing him, and try to imagine her way into his visions and dreams. She would see the world dissolve into forms and colors and feelings, vivid and direct, uncontaminated by thoughts and words, by expectations and guilt. But he always proved to be more intelligent than she gave him credit for being. When he was five, they took him to an ophthalmologist, who probed his yellow-flecked eyes with beams of light (which made Georgie howl as though his soul were being violated) and produced for him a pair of thick glasses, complete with an elastic band to hold them in place on his head. Georgie loved them, after he overcame his initial fear. He went around the house staring at everything, humming his own little tunes to himself, because the vague world, with its furry blobs of shape and color, had now become clear to him. He even added to his small vocabulary ("Ah-ma" for "Mommy," "uhngee" for "hungry," and so forth) the word "ess-iss." He would come in on a Sunday morning to wake Rose and Irving up, hollering, "Ess-iss! Ess-iss!" until he learned to put the glasses on himself.

He learned to raid the refrigerator. Rose had to pack away carefully on the top shelves the food she was saving for meals; the bottom shelves she filled with fruits and vegetables and slices of American cheese, which he was allowed to *nosh*. He especially loved bananas. He would pluck one from the basket and bring it to her, mewling at her until she peeled it. It never mattered to him if there was a bruise or a soft spot. He had inherited the family sweet tooth. When Molly dropped in for a visit, he would come running to give her one of his wet, grunting kisses and to wait impatiently while she rummaged through her bag, teasing him, until she plucked out the candy he wanted.

"You're not so dumb after all," Molly used to say.

There were embarrassments, of course. Rose would be standing with him in the new supermarket that had opened up on Nostrand

Avenue and notice that his pants were drenched and a little puddle was spreading around his shoes. He would see some kid on the street with a toy or a candy bar and start howling because he couldn't have it. Once, in Walter's house, she left him alone for a moment with Jeannie, who in those days was half Georgie's size, and the next thing she knew Jeannie was crying and screaming because Georgie had taken it into his head to hug her—Walter never quite forgave them for that. But worse, this was just the sort of incident that Irving would throw up to her every time they started in on their old argument, for by the time Georgie was six or seven Irving had set his mind on having him "sent away."

No doubt it was his mother who put the idea into his head. It wasn't the sort of notion, Rose believed, that Irving would have dreamed up on his own. Mrs. Malish—that old misery!—loved to play the dutiful and doting *bubba*, petting the boy and feeding him sweets and bringing him toys and presents, but even Georgie could see that her heart wasn't in it, that she feared and hated him as if he were some nightmarish failure of her own. It used to rankle Rose, the way the old lady commiserated with her. "Believe me, darling," she would say, "I understand perfectly how hard it is for you." She pretended to worry about Rose's health and "peace of mind," kept noticing how "worn-out" her daughter-in-law looked.

"As he gets older," she told Rose one day, "you'll have to watch him like a hawk. After all, darling, with other children in the neighborhood, little girls—well, you know what I mean."

More and more openly, Irving campaigned to have Georgie institutionalized. He hinted, he cajoled, he reasoned, he demanded, he lost his temper and stomped around the apartment, yelling about how they no longer had a life of their own. He went through the family and got Sam and Moe and Ruthie and Evelyn to side with him. He enlisted Dr. Lipsky in his cause. Gruffer and huger than ever, but still the family doctor as far as the Liebers were concerned—even Laura let him deliver her babies—the old fellow would huff and grunt his way up the flight of stairs to Rose's apartment "to see how you're getting along" and leave in his wake, like scraps from a passing barge, leaflets and brochures describing various public and private "homes" for the retarded.

"They have doctors, nurses, teachers," he explained to her. "They can do more for the boy than you can."

Rose would have to bite her tongue, thinking: *That must have been, in Hymie's case, what you told my mother.*

She was stubborn. The whole world could come to her door with arguments and reasons, and that wouldn't change her mind. In the end Irving gave her a choice: she could keep him or she could keep Georgie, but she couldn't keep them both. And even that failed to move her. What choice did she really have? On the one hand, this silly, unpleasant, impossible man who jabbed so feebly and briefly at her once a week, and failed to penetrate, even after all their years of marriage, the empty spaces of her heart and soul; and, on the other hand, this helpless, stunted, goggled product of her own unlucky flesh and blood, and yet whose simple changing moods could fill her to brimming with misery or sadness or awe or—rarely, but it happened—a sense of wondrous and unexpected delight.

Later the family would say that Irving Malish "ran away from home," as if he had joined a circus or hopped a freight train or gone off with a *shiksa;* in fact, he merely quit his job at the factory, moved back in with his mother on Dumont Avenue, and started driving a cab. When the old lady died of apoplexy a couple of years later, it turned out that she had quite a bundle stashed away in various bank accounts and safety-deposit boxes and government bonds, and Irving inherited enough money to buy his own taxi and his own medallion, and every so often one of the Liebers would hail a cab and spend an uncomfortable ride staring at the back of Irving's thick head. He was always prompt in sending Rose her alimony and child support payments, sometimes with a little something extra, and occasionally he would call her up to ask how she and "the kid" were getting along. But he never came to see them, and she never talked about him, and as far as the family was concerned, he had deserted her.

"That Irving," they would say, "was a son of a bitch."

But that was only the overflow of their pity for Rose. In the weeks after Irving left, Rose's eyes behind the thick glasses were puffy and red from crying, and her pale face looked more harried and hurt than ever. She put on weight until her clothes no longer fit and her flesh bulged from a popped button or a broken zipper. Her ankles swelled up—water retention Dr. Lipsky said. She felt as though she had to walk naked and hobbling and embarrassed in the eyes of the world. She became increasingly nervous. She would sit up all hours of the night listening to the noises of the apartment house that surrounded her, trying to identify every creak, every footstep, aware that for the first time in her life there was no one in the house to protect her. Quick panic flashed at every sudden noise. Night sounds coruscated her frightened heart. She imagined burglars, murderers, rapists, fiends of every kind lurking at her door, climbing in the windows to put an end to her and her child. Sleepless, she would lie in bed listening to Georgie wheeze and snuffle in the other room, and if his nose cleared for a moment and he slept quietly, she would rush in to make sure he wasn't dead. It got so bad she thought she was losing her mind. She would remember Hymie sitting in the closet, and Dr. Lipsky's men arriving to drag him away to the hospital, and all the old taint of strangeness that ran in the Lieber blood, that curse of a grandfather she had never known. It could happen to her. Father, mother, child: that old incantation was no longer available to soothe her. Instead, she would press her face to the stony pillow and pray: "Dear God, dear God, for Georgie's sake help me survive!"

This was just a phase, however, a concomitant of divorce. She never fully got over her fears, but eventually she got used to being alone. She even discovered after a while that Georgie could comfort her. When she put him to bed, she would sit and hold him for a long time, rocking him back and forth in her arms, feeling his soft, clammy flesh and the steady pulse of his eternal childhood beating beneath, until the gentle rocking produced within him a kind of peace and silence. That peace, that silence, radiated back to her, calming her for the hours of night to come. Mother and child, child and mother: there could be, she discovered, wholeness in that alone, a perfection which made Irving superfluous. She would think of her mother in the years after her father died, or before, when her father was sickly and helpless and spending most of his time at *shul*. If my mother managed, she would tell herself, then so can I.

The family was eager to help her out. They invited her for meals, offered to do her shopping for her, drove her around town when she had to take Georgie to the doctor or buy him a pair of orthopedic shoes. They set up a system so that every night one of them would be sure to phone her. Molly sent crates of oranges and grapefruits from Florida until there was fruit piled and moldering all over the living room, and Sam showed up one night with a brand-new television, to which Georgie immediately became addicted.

"Poor Rose," the family would say in those days, intoning the words solemnly to each other as though they constituted a judgment. "Poor, unlucky Rose."

They never understood, as the years went by, that really there was no reason to pity her.

* * *

DEANNA WOULD LATER RETAIN, as a sort of primary emblem of Florida, an image of Izzy Kupperman sitting on the little dock behind his house on Biscayne Bay showing her how to bait a fishing hook with a piece of raw shrimp. She regretted that she had never been able to take a photograph of him as he was then, bald and tan and massive, wearing nothing but Bermuda shorts and sneakers in the warm Miami dusk, with lots of damp gray hair matting his chest, and clumps of black hair flourishing in his ears and nostrils, and several inches of fat, ugly cigar clamped between his yellow teeth. He was quite a character, this Uncle Izzy, and in a sense, he was responsible for everything. The way Deanna heard the story, he had made a bundle of money in the clothing business before he retired to Florida, and money creates problems. At the time of the wedding he had forced Molly to sign a lot of papers that were supposed to reassure the grown-up daughters of his previous marriage that she wasn't going to steal their inheritance. Deanna never met these daughters—the beauties, her mother called them— but she knew that Molly didn't get along with them. They resented the money their father was spending on her, and resented even more that Molly slept in their dead mother's bed. Anyway, after a year of bickering Molly got the notion that maybe she could placate the beauties by going into a business of her own, securing her own source of income, and so with a down payment that came out of her share of the chocolate factory, she purchased an all-night restaurant called The Red Mill (a flimsy pretext for a Dutch motif) and after a hectic six months offered Deanna's parents the opportunity to move down to Miami Beach and help manage it.

The Red Mill had a U-shaped counter—a horseshoe, Milton insisted on calling it—with forty-eight stools. It stood on a busy corner, and was open to the street on two sides. Only in Miami Beach in an optimistic age would anybody dream of building a restaurant which there was no easy way to shut down. Day and night the place echoed the hubbub of traffic and the buzz of neon signs. During tropical storms a fine mist of rain would blow in under the awnings to dampen the floors. On the inside wall, beneath a wretched mural of windmills and clog-clad Hollanders, was a jukebox with bubbles of opalescent light flowing up its sides, and Milton added to his stock of lugubrious anecdotes the story of the poor fellow who came in every night to throw quarters into the thing, playing "I'll Dance at Your Wedding" over and over again. In the cramped and overheated kitchen, on the big black stove, huge pots of soup and fricassee (a specialty of the house) simmered alongside the grill where steaks and chops and omelets were prepared. Deanna wasn't allowed into the kitchen. She was never told why. Maybe her mother believed that one of the cooks was going to molest her. Her mother was afraid of the cooks—that ever-changing sequence of tough-looking men, whose faces shone with sweat and whose ears were usually red from drinking—and so, Deanna later realized, was her father. His face would settle into a taut, furious expression whenever he had to fire one of them, and during the six months before Molly's marriage went to pieces and she decided, hysterically, to sell the restaurant, he must have fired a dozen. They came and went like moods. They stole food, they threatened him with knives, they doused the fricassee with their cheap booze, or they failed to show up at all.

"These *goyim*," Milton would complain, "they get a few bucks in their pocket, they don't want to work anymore."

Milton himself was prepared to work twenty hours a day to make a go of the place, not because he enjoyed the restaurant business—in fact, he loathed every moment of it—but because at last (at last!) he was living in Florida, far from Brooklyn, far from the chocolate factory. He loved the heat, the light, the scent, the palm trees, the dazzling stretch of sky. Molly or Evelyn would "spell him" for an hour or two in the restaurant and he would run to the beach to plunge and frolic. Though they were living hand to mouth, taking their meals in the restaurant, he increased his debts to buy a secondhand convertible so that occasionally he could take the family out riding over the causeways in the lingering, lemony dusk and feel the mild salt air blowing in his face. With the pride of an entrepreneur he kept track of the big new hotels that were rising along Collins Avenue; he loved to put on his best clothes and go wandering through their gaudy lobbies, as though the proximity of all that glitter and plush, those rich tourists, those gigantic chandeliers, assured his own success. He had brought down to Florida his trunk of props and tricks, but he had no time for magic, except for those occasions when he might entertain a customer at the cash register by manipulating coins and cigarettes. Never mind. For the while he thought he was in paradise.

Deanna disagreed.

"Florida," she would later tell her therapist, "is where my troubles began."

She was twelve years old, an awkward age, when they tore her up out of Brooklyn, dragged her away from the familiar comforts of friends and relatives and Montgomery Street. Her flesh was thickening and bulging and reshaping itself, and the first glum outbursts of the acne she would never quite be ride of had started to appear on what her mother still called "that gorgeous face." How disturbing it had been: those first letters back and forth, the initial touchy conversations between cautious mommy and eager dad, her mother taking Ben down to Florida "to look things over," and her father coming home from work at night to prowl and fidget while he waited for the phone to ring. One day he dragged her with him on the bus to her Uncle Sam's house, where she had to sit in the kitchen with her Aunt Essie while in the living room her father wheedled and begged and humiliated himself quitting his job at the factory and arranging a loan for the move. She would recall being excited, then airsick, then sleepy on the plane—a night flight to save money. She would retain an infusion of the Miami airport in the small hours of morning: twin drinking fountains ("White" and "Colored"), a melodious mob of Puerto Ricans weighing in for some even cheaper cargo flight up to New York, and an enormous yellow moon—a total stranger—floating in fragments amongst the palm fronds. And the next day she awoke, in ferocious brightness, to the shame and mystery of having stained with blood, there in her Uncle Izzy's immaculate house, a lumpy, alien bed.

It was awful. They had arrived in June, and all through the summer, until she was afflicted with Dade County schooling, she had no one to play with, nothing to do. The hateful sun dazzled her eyes; the overheated sky was an uncanny shade of blue, made of a foreign fabric—she had a hard time believing that the same sky stretched without interruption all the way back to Montgomery Street. One day, having tired of Izzy Kupperman's gruff hospitality, her mother took her out house hunting. They tramped until they were dizzy through a section of little pink and white apartment houses in the vicinity of the restaurant, avoiding the rainbow splash of water sprinklers everywhere, until some nice old blue-haired lady sat them down in her living room, poured them some iced tea, and informed them that they were obviously newcomers since they didn't have enough sense, though they were red in the face and on the verge of heat prostration, to come in out of the sun. It shocked Deanna to realize that walking the streets in Florida could be dangerous, but the place was proving to be rife with secret menaces. Her athletic brother returned from the beach one evening with furious red welts all over his back and shoulders, the aftermath of an encounter with a Portuguese man-of-war. In the purplish twilight vicious insects swarmed and stung. For a while Deanna passed some of the long disconsolate hours writing letters to her friends back home, but after the first round she stopped receiving answers. To fill the blankness of an afternoon, she would turn on the television and nibble candy while she stared at the soap operas, the kiddie shows, the test pattern. Long after bedtime her father would come home from the restaurant, and as she lay in that alien bed, touching herself—for she had already learned that the appropriate manipulations could blur her misery into a kind of damp pleasure—she would hear him arguing hopelessly with her Aunt Molly.

At last they found an apartment of their own. Her mother cried and cried as she scrubbed the walls, the closets, the cupboards, abolishing the previous residents' "unholy *dreck*." The air conditioner clattered and dripped, and their Brooklyn furniture, hauled out of storage, looked murky and dense in those pale sunlit rooms. In Florida weather, they were learning, food rotted quickly and fresh laundry acquired overnight odd blotches of rust and mildew. To cheer the place up, they went out and bought a bright blue parakeet, but a couple of weeks later someone left the cage by a window, and when they came home, it was lying dead of sunstroke amidst the gravel and droppings. She had always been a crybaby, Deanna's mother, but now she was becoming, in her own words, "a nervous wreck."

"How you talked me into this," she would scream at Deanna's father, "I'll never know!"

In September, plump and pimply, wearing a brand-new brassiere with a B cup, Deanna entered the seventh grade. They gave her some sort of test (Deanna liked tests) and found that she had the highest IQ in the school—anyway, that's what her mother would later claim —so they put her into the "special class" run by a Miss Fabian, a pert young matron with a shiny chin, and every other afternoon in that heyday of "progressive" education they went on a field trip. They visited bread factories, police stations, hotel kitchens, local museums devoted to insects or motorcars, a Seminole village in the Everglades (all mugginess and mosquitoes), and the Dade County mental hospital, where a kindly psychiatrist informed them that the inmates were "people like ourselves." On afternoons when they weren't climbing in and out of the school bus, they pulled their desks in a circle for discussions. One day they discussed why the boys were always picking on Deanna, why when no teachers were looking they would take turns holding her arms and pinching her breasts. Miss Fabian, flushing, told the circle of suppressed giggles that the boys simply hadn't learned the proper way of expressing their interest in Deanna, but Deanna knew better—knew that they hated her because they understood how much she despised them.

She was so bored and miserable that for the first time in her life, though she had been hearing for years from her parents and relatives how important education was, she started playing hooky. She and the only friend she ever made in Florida, a tall, pretty blond girl named Roxie ("That Roxie, she's a nut!"), would spend the afternoon on the beach or in the movies or walking up and down Collins Avenue, giggling at the tourists. From Roxie she learned, among other things, the art of stealing. They would saunter through Woolworth's and come out loaded down with all sorts of useless junk: Japanese fans, fishing lures, combs. One day they even lifted a couple of Brownie cameras, which they would wear around their necks on Collins Avenue in order to blend in—there had previously been a panicky moment when a police car slowed to a crawl alongside them while the cop looked them over. Spending-money (for pinball machines, limeades, whatever) was no problem, not after that telethon in the Miami Beach Auditorium, when they went down in the rain and made a contribution and received in return little plastic banks shaped like coconuts with the words "Cerebral Palsy" embossed on the front. Now all they had to do was go through the hotel lobbies with those banks and take up a collection.

Sometimes they went to Roxie's place. Roxie's mother—a sad, tolerant, well-tanned divorcée—ran the souvenir concession at the El Dorado Hotel and was never around. Deanna came to feel at home in that cramped two-room apartment with the big silky cushions and the blank walls. They would raid the refrigerator and sit on the floor among the cushions with the television blaring and tickle each other's arms and legs. They would play "dare-you" and "show-me" games of touch and feel, going further and further toward those squeamish, heart-thudding experiments which Deanna believed she had previously dreamed. Roxie's body, finally exposed, fascinated Deanna: those glowing narrow shoulders dusted with down; those big rosy nipples like skullcaps on her small white breasts; those long, slender, sunburnt legs—nothing at all like Deanna's own heavy *pul-*

kehs—with smooth, lovely incurves on the insides of her thighs; the funny little fringe of pale hair shading but not hiding the outer edge of her slippery pink oyster flesh, which enfolded a soft, salty, dew-damp little pearl. ("I just love to touch myself there," said Roxie, almost fourteen years old, worldly-wise. "Don't you?") The two of them, Deanna dark-haired and heavy, Roxie blond and nimble, bare on the blue shag carpet amidst the silky pillows, playing schoolgirl tricks with their fingers and tongues, and years later Deanna's heart would jam with all the nervous-erotic symptoms of arousal when she told her gentle therapist about it.

In matters of sex Deanna was ignorant. Her mother had muttered a few words about the mechanics of reproduction years before—Deanna could remember a tedious childhood book with lots of mysterious pictures of chicks and eggs—and had added a few more words on that first afternoon in Florida when they went to the drugstore for a box of sanitary napkins. She was probably saving the rest for Deanna's wedding day. Anyway, the act, as Deanna understood it, was disgusting. Who would want some stupid boy to stick his filthy *thing* inside you? Well, it turned out, Roxie for one.

"Wouldn't it be just incredible," she said one day, "if you were a boy and—"

She finished the statement by raising and lowering her shoulders, and Deanna's ears buzzed slightly because she was aware of how much, even while despising boys, she had always wanted to be one—how she used to pretend to herself that she *was* a boy, stolen away by a wicked fairy and hideously transformed. Boys were lucky, boys were special—where had she acquired such notions?—boys could be themselves, free and whole and complete.

"Well, I am," she told Roxie that day.

"Am what?"

"Am a boy. Only I keep it a secret. No one is supposed to know."

"My lips are sealed," said Roxie, running a hand across her mouth, and a few weeks later ("You see my crazy mother met this guy . . .") she moved to California and Deanna never saw her again.

That's how it was in Florida; people came and went. Deanna cried for a couple of nights, but she felt more relieved than regretful. With Roxie she had gone perhaps a bit too far. Now, alone again, with no one to tempt her, she stopped stealing, attended school more regularly, and put away for some later time the frothy chaos of excitement and perplexity that Roxie had aroused in her. To amuse herself, she bought some film for that prop Brownie and started taking snapshots of everything: restaurant customers, the cooks and waitresses, schoolmates, her father at the cash register, her brother in a baseball uniform, people playing pinball, orange juice vendors, lifeguards, tourists, strangers on the street. She experimented with odd angles, profile shots, the manipulation of shadows. She learned to wait for that moment when the automatic smile faded and a more authentic look of exasperation emerged on the subject's face. She pestered and wheedled and finally got her parents to buy her some darkroom equipment, which she could set up in the bathroom with a blanket hung double over the jalousie window. What fun it was to watch some image she had already stored in the precise file of her memory "come up" in the pan of developer, little fragments of a transient world, captured, caged.

By then Aunt Molly had left Izzy Kupperman and was living alone in a small downtown hotel, a cheap, dreary place squatting behind a sparkling signboard. Deanna would remember how she was sent over with a message one day and found the door open and her Aunt Molly asleep in bed in the heat of the afternoon, snoring outrageously, while an electric fan set up on a chair blew in hapless arcs across her pink, trembling, kimono-clad obesity. Evenings Aunt Molly would come to the apartment for long, loud, weepy talks with Deanna's mother. Then, all of a sudden, the restaurant was sold, and Aunt Molly was running a beauty parlor, and Deanna's father, betrayed, outraged, practically broke, was driving into Miami to work in a factory. For the rest of that year Deanna avoided the corner where The Red Mill was located because somehow, now that she could no longer sit herself down at the counter for a free meal or an ice cream soda, it had become a menacing, forbidden, guilt-ridden place.

After the restaurant was sold, Evelyn wanted to return to Brooklyn and family, but Milton was stubborn. He had waited so long to get to Florida that he was determined to stay despite the *tsurris*. He never stopped loving the heat of the tropical sun burning through his new flowery shirts and the salty-sweet smell of swamp that hung in the twilight when he took the family out on the causeways for an evening drive. Free of the restaurant, he found time to go "exploring." With the will of a man seeking redemption, he dragged his children to parrot jungles and monkey kingdoms and crocodile, or rather alligator, farms, where little dark men "wrestled" with the sleepy brutes— "Stand back," said the guide, "one snap of them jaws can cost you a leg." They drove south to the Keys and north to Vero Beach, so Ben could see the Dodgers in spring training, and west to the Everglades,

250

where they stopped at the same sad Seminole village Deanna had visited before. They tramped among flower gardens and orange orchards, fishing docks and coconut groves, and everywhere they went they felt hot and thirsty and betrayed, until Evelyn said: "Enough already. This weekend I'm staying home."

Eventually Milton scraped together enough money to buy a little souvenir and novelty shop around the corner from the fancy shopping district on Lincoln Road. He stocked all sorts of things: grotesque rubber masks, exploding cigars, kites, puzzles, little boats in plastic bottles (with a tiny plastic treasure box lying open in the fake sand), heads carved out of coconuts, rubber snakes, tiny crates of candy oranges, which they sent up north to the relatives, postcards, comic books, tourist maps. He sank his last penny into it, but he had high hopes. The plan was to use his first profits to put in a line of magic tricks, not the junk you sold to kids for a quarter, but good stuff, silk handkerchiefs, collapsing cages, and so on. He would build it up a little at a time and someday—who knows?—maybe he would become the major supplier of illusions to all of Florida or the whole Southeast. But his hopes didn't materialize. For a few months, while the "season" was "in swing," the store brought in enough income to live on. In May, however, the hotels emptied out and Miami Beach reverted to that sandy and forsaken strip of edgewater which at heart it had always been. Milton was lucky to extricate himself from that dusty and wretched little shop without going bankrupt—he found some other poor dreamer to take his place—and the Himmelfarbs, well-tanned and defeated, packed up their belongings, sold the convertible, and moved back to Brooklyn, back to the old neighborhood, back to Montgomery Street.

They returned to New York on a train because they couldn't afford to fly. It took twenty-four hours, afternoon, evening, night, morning, a miserable long ride. At dawn Deanna opened her eyes long enough to glimpse the Washington Monument gliding past the train window before a tunnel of some sort obliterated it. Then came the dim platform at Grand Central Station, where Deanna spotted her Uncle Sam smoking a cigarette in the hectic crowd, and the slow ride downtown through thick traffic past the factory lofts on lower Broadway—amazing how dark and grimy and old the buildings all looked; in comparison, the pale newish houses and hotels of Miami Beach seemed built of sugar cubes already melting in a retrospective rain.

She was in the front seat, squeezed between her uncle and her father, and her nose was filled with the male smell of them, after-shave and sweat and tobacco on one side, and on the other the more acrid odor of travel and desolation. Little bits of glitter were flaking off the dashboard knobs: Uncle Sam was overdue for a new car. A sudden jackhammer in the street made momentary black zigzags of her nerves. They broke free of the traffic and were on the bridge, the tires hissing over the metal grid, a subway train slipping slowly backwards alongside them, and halfway across her father stirred himself and said:

"You're in Brooklyn, Deanna. Still recognize the place?"

She didn't answer him; some ghost of Florida had sealed her lips. She felt herself caught between them, uncle and father, hating them as though they had inflicted upon her some obscure wound, and wondered—or, anyway, later believed she should have wondered—what on earth would become of her if she turned out to be, at bottom, just like them.

Back in Brooklyn, Milton consoled himself by dragging out his trunk of tricks, polishing up his act, and hounding the agencies. But there was still no money in that, and he had a family to support, so he searched and searched and ended up working for Barton's.

"You should see that place," he told Lou Grossman, "the way they've got it organized, the machinery—I don't understand how Sam manages to compete."

He made much less money working for Barton's than Sam would have paid him, but no matter how much Evelyn nagged, he refused to consider returning to the factory on Bergen Street. Somehow they got along. The kids were old enough so that Evelyn could go to work as an office girl, and between the two incomes they paid off their debts. Besides, he was stubborn in his way, that Milton, and after Florida, he knew he could no longer depend upon his in-laws.

EVERY SUMMER the family held a picnic in the park. All week long the women would be on the phone trying to organize the thing, rounding up the cousins and planning the menu, assigning salads to one and desserts to another, though in the end they always *shlepped* along much more food than they could possibly eat. What a sight it was to watch the Liebers converge upon some innocent picnic grove with their shopping bags and folding chairs, their coolers and portable grills, their Thermos jugs and watermelons and children. There were two sorts of Liebers, sun lovers and sun haters, and so the afternoon would start off with a great hauling and heaving of picnic tables into and out of the shade, and an uproarious flapping of tablecloths until they could be wrestled flat against the mischievous wind. Then Moe would take charge of starting the fire, with Lou Grossman hovering over him to kibitz; and Laura would start spreading some mysterious green stuff on crackers so everyone could have a taste; and Walter would vanish into the woods with Jeannie to see if they could match up the local weeds with those pretty pictures of wild flowers in their "fascinating handbook"; and Deborah would wander around in that patterned old sun frock she used to wear, nibbling carrot sticks and *kvelling* over the beauty of the clouds; and Evelyn, distraught, would start searching high and low for her "best sharp knife," which in fact was still lying next to the forgotten mustard jar on her kitchen counter; and Uncle Chaim would be comparing, in Yiddish, his aches and ailments with Uncle Yonkel (both, alas, would soon suffer no more); and Sam, a sun lover, would plunk himself down in a chair with his shirt off and a handkerchief tied around his grizzled neck, and spend most of the afternoon there, tanning himself and holding court. Meanwhile, the kids would be running wild, except poor Georgie, who was content to sit in the grass at Rose's feet, turning round and round in his clumsy hands a bright rubber ball, examining it intently, as though for him it contained a cosmos.

Someone would bring a portable radio to provide the background blare of the Dodger game; someone else would bring a kite, though by the time the tablecloths were well anchored with bowls of coleslaw and potato salad a muggy, kite-stifling calm would descend; and every year—this was one of the family rituals—Rich and Ben would bring along enough equipment to organize a hilarious softball game among the uncles and cousins. Except for the old people and the women, everyone played. Sometimes they let Georgie bat, and he would stand there grinning, holding the bat straight against his nose, until he lost interest and wandered away. Then—this was part of the ritual—Moe would drag his daughters up to the plate, even when they were practically babies, and while his impatient nephews jeered and complained, he would start solemnly explaining to his precious darlings the complicated fundamentals.

Joey, for one, hated those games. People kept moving the shirts they used for bases or running off the field to grab another hunk of watermelon, and after the first inning no one bothered to keep score. As far as Joey was concerned, there was no point to playing if you couldn't win. Back home in the schoolyard softball was serious business, and though he wasn't very good at it, he struggled and tried. But here they treated him like one of the little kids. Rich would start clowning around when Joey came to bat, pretending to throw a windmill pitch and then lobbing the ball softly toward the plate, and Ben would come loping in from the outfield and stand right on second, pounding his glove, daring Joey to hit it over his head, and Jeff would start teasing him, calling him champ and slugger, and all too often Joey would hit a soft pop-up or a feeble grounder, as if the bat had gone limp in his hands, and run to first base, already out, with his ears burning and his throat sore with rage and misery and humiliation.

Joey was the third of Ruthie's four boys, and the only one of them who "took after" the Liebers in any substantial way. The others, Jeff, Erwin, and even little Gary, were essentially Grossman, wiry, boastful, bullheaded, as darkly handsome and sullen as Lou had been back in the days when he was coming to the apartment on Park Place and everyone said that he looked like a "wop." But Joey had a tinge of Kalisher red in his dark hair, and a Lieberish *kopf* on his shoulders, and, now that his face had started to fill out, a pared-down version of his maternal grandfather's nose. Skinny, pale, bookish, alternately shy and belligerent, secretive, even a bit sneaky—"he's my sensitive one," Ruthie used to say—he lived among his more muscular brothers like a nimble and clever monkey among plodding young apes, absorbing his bruises when he had to, running rings around them when he could. For one reason or another Jeff and Erwin were always slapping him around, and usually he deserved it. He had a big mouth and he teased them unmercifully. By the time he was twelve or thirteen he would even loose his wicked tongue on Lou. For example, Lou was always plunking himself down on the leatherette lounger in front of the television and telling Joey to go to the kitchen and bring him "just a little something" to quench his thirst.

"You got two feet," Joey said to him one night. "Get it yourself."

Off came Lou's belt and there was howling pandemonium as he chased the kid through the house.

That was Lou. He was still bragging and bullying his way through

254

life, still scratching and *kvetching* and dropping cigarette ashes onto the rug. The older he got, the more careless he became. His legs were all bruises and welts because at work he kept banging them on the tables and machinery. The family still laughed about how he went out and bought a car after the war, and drove it around town with his big belly pushed up against the steering wheel, and how after a couple of months of accidents and "close calls" he was afraid to drive it. It sat rusting and bashed in the little garage behind the Grossman house, an emblem of Lou's splurges and *mishegoss*. The larger his failures, the more he boasted. He kept threatening to leave the factory and go into a business of his own until finally Sam said to him, "*Geh gesuntehayt!*" and then the only job he could find was in a candy-bar factory out in New Jersey. He had to leave at five o'clock in the morning to get to work on time and came home exhausted, grumbling about public transportation. His belly was bigger than ever. The doctors warned him about his blood pressure and diagnosed the onset of kidney disease, but he still poured gallons of beer and sugary soft drinks into himself. He also—this was typical of him—still had that gun he bought years ago when he was running his father's grocery store in Greenpoint. It was a black, ugly, stunted revolver and he kept it buried away in the little back room off the kitchen amidst his clutter of old newspapers. He saved newspapers from historic occasions. He believed that if he held onto them long enough, they would eventually be worth real money. He had newspapers headlining Roosevelt's first election, Pearl Harbor, D-Day, the bombing of Hiroshima, and the Berlin blockade. He had yellowing copies of the *Daily News* with gory front-page photographs of famous gangsters shot dead in restaurants and barbershops and telephone booths. He had an early-bird edition of the *Journal-American* announcing the election of Thomas Dewey. He even claimed to have an old *Times* from 1927 with a picture of the French crowd greeting Lindbergh, but he hadn't seen it in years and couldn't put his finger on it—it had vanished beneath a clutter of more recent events. When Ruthie complained about the mess, he told her it was "money in the bank," that he would sell the stuff in his old age to supplement his Social Security. Every so often he might spend an hour or two trying to sort it out, but he had no patience, no zest for order, and he would emerge grumpily from the storeroom with blackened hands and little flecks of paper like faded snow on his trousers.

With Lou and the four boys Ruthie's household was chaos. There was always a softball or a "Spaldeen" underfoot, and someone running or fighting or raiding the refrigerator for a bologna sandwich or a gulp of milk. To top it all off, Ruthie had to endure a dog—a big, dark, ugly German shepherd named King. Lou went out and bought the creature after a burglar broke in through a basement window and made off with Ruthie's pathetic jewelry box and a sum of cash that Lou had left lying around. It wasn't much of a loss—they probably collected from the insurance company a good deal more than was stolen—but it made Lou nervous. It violated some old sense of safety he had constructed around himself. Thus the dog. They kept it tied up in the kitchen because Ruthie refused to have its hairs on her rugs and furniture, and when anyone rang the doorbell, it howled and barked and pulled at its thick chain and dribbled gobs of saliva on the linoleum floor. Ruthie hated the thing, and pitied it, but what could she do? Once Lou got an idea into that thick head of his, there was no reasoning with him.

"At least," he told her, "you don't have to worry that some *shvartzer* is going to climb through the window and into your bed."

The dog was six months old and enormous when they got it, but not housebroken. Lou fixed that. Every time it messed the floor, Lou would fly into a rage; shouting, ranting, he would grab hold of its neck, push its snout into the puddle, and whack the poor thing a couple of times with his belt. It didn't take much of this to break the creature's spirit. Whenever Lou entered the kitchen, it would whimper and cringe, exposing its neck in a posture of submission that was programmed eons ago into its wolf's genes. Somehow Lou was pleased that the animal was spooked and neurotic. It barked like crazy at visitors, howled at cars passing in the night, and snarled when you tried to pet it. But it never bit anyone; its ferocity was all illusion and noise—"Just like the rest of my family," Joey later said.

Joey was the only one in the family who really liked the dog. He was the one who ended up feeding it and walking it and brushing the dirt and gnarls out of its thick fur. He enjoyed taking it to the schoolyard and letting it run. It was so big and fierce-looking that the tough Italian kids in the neighborhood were afraid of it. Joey liked knowing that they weren't going to start anything with him when he was walking the dog. Though he struggled not to show it—he would carry through life that proud, stubborn streak—he was shamefully afraid of the Italian kids. In fact, he was afraid of many things. A single relentless stream of anxiety flowed through his childhood and adolescence. At one time or another he was afraid of monsters, bogey-men, burglars, fire, heights, elevators, and subway trains. More recently he had become afraid of "the Bomb." In his darkened bedroom with the cowboy wallpaper, on the top level of the bunk bed with Gary asleep down below, and his old cap gun hung in its fake leather holster on the bedpost, Joey would lie awake listening to the airplanes going in and out of the city's two airports, thinking that any one of them might turn out to be a Russian bomber, eluding the inadequate defense of the DEW line and arriving to annihilate him.

He had foreseen precisely, with pounding heart, what it would be like, those last moments of his life: the high, sullen roar of the plane, the shrill, whining scream of the bomb descending, the blinding, killing sunburst. He wondered if he would cling to life long enough to know he was dying, to know the final agony of his atomized flesh. He suspected that he would, that consciousness must go on for a few moments after such a sudden death, even if disembodied—something along the lines of a chicken without its head. He imagined himself floating through the fireball amidst the boiling wastes of Brooklyn and slowly dissipating in the mushroom cloud. He understood the process. He had gone to the library and looked it up, and had seen newsreel footage from Eniwetok. $E=mc^2$. To achieve a nuclear explosion, all you need is a critical mass. Take two chunks of plutonium and hammer them together: *boom!* Fascinating stuff beneath the bright fluorescent lights of the local library, but at bedtime, in the dark, already *bar mitzvah* but not yet a man, it terrified him. And worst of all, the people around him, family, neighbors, friends, were too stupid to care, to worry, to understand.

To soothe himself, he would climb down after Gary was asleep, get the little clock radio off the night table, and bring it to bed—the cord just reached. Smothering with his pillow the click and the initial burst of static, he would turn it on, his heart leaping lightly with delicious sneaky pleasure. He kept the radio tuned to 1010 WINS, "your spot on the dial for Allan Freed's Rock 'n' Roll Party." Later in life, in his academic perch, he would spend hundreds of dollars on expensive stereo equipment and never quite resurrect within himself the thrill of those pounding rhythms flowing tinnily through a tiny speaker pressed up against his ear. Little Richard, Ray Charles, Bo Diddley, Chuck Berry. *Hail, hail rock 'n' roll! You're a thousand miles away-ay. A-WOP-BOP-A-LOO-BOP-A-WOP-BAM-BOOM!* The music would whirl into his mind, momentarily canceling all his outlandish fears and mute desires, insinuating itself along the precious routes of memory so that at school, at play, or in the midst of one of those agonizing fights with his father, without his having to grope for it, it would emerge again, loud and throbbing, from within the clatter and racket of his stirred thoughts—where not even his father could tell him to turn the damn thing off.

"Jungle music," his father called it, "nigger noise," as though for him it were the sum of all the baffled outrage and fury of his generation, the painful pulse of some old, dark, unknown life he thought he had escaped forever.

"Go ahead," he told Joey. "Listen to that garbage till your brain falls out. But God help you if *I* ever hear it."

There was no talking to the man, no reasoning with him. He was coarse and mean and indifferent, and Joey hated him. He hated him for mopey stock adolescent reasons—for the sting of the belt, the hours when he was made to stay in his room, the threats and the mockery—but he also hated him in a way that was singular and bitter and deep, hating him because there was nothing about him to like or respect or admire. There was no bond of familiarity between them. They lived like squabbling strangers in the same house. He despised the way his father talked, looked, ate, dressed. The only possession of his father's he envied was the clutter of newspapers in the back room. He loved to rummage there; a soothing magic could be found in that mess.

A historian in embryo, Joey spent hours absorbing the old comic strips, the advertisements, the sports pages, the squibs, the letters to the editor, because he had grasped the crucial principle of the thing, that the past was contained not in headlines, in "big" events, but in a multitude of small moods and tones and postures and fashions. It was the subtle texture of time that fascinated him, and he would read those old newspapers until his eyes ached.

One Saturday afternoon, rummaging, he found Lou's gun. It was in a cigar box shoved sideways between two stacks of newspapers, wrapped in a dingy, greasy rag, and the heavy cold feel of the metal, as he lifted the gun to eye level and stared out over its snubbed nose, amazed him, as though for the first time in his life he had gotten his fingers around a chunk of hard grown-up reality. He examined the thing, caressed it, let his hand become accustomed to its weight, looked into the barrel, and saw that it was empty. Huge, vague, threatening forms emerged in front of him as in a shooting gallery and—*pow! pow! pow!*—his excited imagination blew them away. "Finders keepers, losers weepers," sang some giddy childish voice inside his head. His stupid father, he assured himself, would never even notice it was gone.

He stuffed the rag inside the cigar box and the cigar box back between the newspapers, but the gun went into the waistband underneath his shirt. Later he would be amazed at how it seemed like such a natural thing to do. His father was in front of the television, probably asleep, in the living room. It would be easy to sneak it past him.

Enthralled, guilty, strangely happy with his guilt, with the gun cold against his belly and his face on fire, Joey stepped softly into the kitchen, where King stretched and yawned and stood up to greet him. He had to sidestep to avoid the damned dog and felt the gun slipping down into his pants. He slapped at it, but too late—it came to rest, cold and hard, against his thigh. Nervously, hurrying, he reached into his pants for it and missed; it slid farther down, and the only thing to do was to shake it out through his pants leg. He stamped, hopped, did a little dance, and the muzzle appeared at the cuff. He raised his leg and grabbed, but his hands were wet and trembling, and he was hurrying, and it eluded his grasp. He slapped at it, but his fingers had an aim of their own, and his heart bulged suddenly as he waited for the father-fetching thud against the linoleum floor.

That's when the gun went off.

The explosion came, not much louder than a cap gun, a sharp cracking *pop!* with a kind of resounding echo in it. For a moment that echo created a void within which Joey stood, astonished, heart-jammed, noting the distant glare of sunlight through the kitchen window, a few unwashed glasses in the sink, the big red second hand frozen below the nine on the kitchen clock. The gun had come to rest on the waxed yellowish floor—all innocence despite the wisp of smoke. Somewhere in another realm King barked once and snapped at his side as though an insect had stung him, then toppled and settled submissively into a sudden mess of blood. The ordinary world started up again.

The voice of Joey's father roared from the living room above the sounds of a baseball game.

"What the hell is going on in there?"

Joey said nothing—what was there to say? He merely thought: *now he's going to murder me,* and the thought somehow absolved him. He heard the heavy creak of footsteps and his father was there, looming, enormous, filling up the kitchen.

Stubbornly, almost belligerently, choking back bitter tears, Joey said, "I was looking at it and, and—it fell."

Lou glanced around, his features slowly congesting as he pieced things together: the boy, the wounded dog, the gun on the floor. Joey had never seen his father cry, didn't believe he was capable of crying, but Lou's face grew blotchy, and a bright line of dampness gleamed on the side of his nose.

"You goddamn little prick," he said, his voice thick with phlegm and rage, "you killed my fucking dog."

Then, more or less automatically, off came his belt.

Joey didn't think of running. Maybe it was the gleam of his father's tears that held him there, or some paralyzing guilt, or some old cautionary voice in his blood, urgent and implacable. In any case, he just stood there, stubborn and small, his lower lip jutting out, his heart torn between panic and pride, until the first lash of the belt stinging across his legs made him calm. Two, three, four times, with the dreamy kind of slowness that comes of high emotion, the belt hissed through the air, and he stood unmoving, letting himself be hit, and each time the belt stung him he felt himself absorbing power and courage and size. That's how he would remember it, as though it were all a question of magnitude: the room and his father were shrinking around him as he became large. It hurt, but not that much —he had become a momentary giant, and there was nothing he couldn't endure. He even managed a ghastly, challenging laugh.

Lou brought the belt up again and stopped, with a look of dull wounded befuddlement on his face as he realized that this laughing, stubborn, inexplicable son of his, grown monstrously willful, was prepared to accept much more pain than he, the good Jewish father after all, was ready to inflict. The old quarrel between them had been carried past a boundary of sorts, and he was not prepared to follow. He threw the belt down, gasping, almost howling with frustration. What a terrible place, this world, where sons are required finally to defeat their fathers.

"Damn you," said Lou, salvaging what he could of his authority. "Get over to Nostrand Avenue and bring back a taxi. And hurry!"

Between them they carried the dog in a taxi to a veterinarian. The bullet that Lou carelessly had left in the chamber had entered King's side in the area of loose skin in front of the flank, shattered bone and vital organs, then emerged intact to lodge in the plaster. The poor beast suffered an hour, and died. The vet—that bald, self-righteous, unreasonable little pipsqueak—insisted on calling the police, and so Lou and Joey had to concoct between them a flimsy story about Joey's finding the gun on the street. Later their little conspiracy was like new skin over a wound; it gave them something to smile about. Their quarrels continued; Lou went on railing at Joey's music and growling at Joey's disobedience, but it was all mannered and muted. Mostly they learned to keep out of each other's way. In his own blustering, sullen fashion Lou even came to regard Joey with something akin to awe and pride. But he never quite forgave him. He would remember his dog dying on the kitchen floor and say to Joey:

"Someday you should only know what a man suffers when he becomes a father."

HUMAN NATURE IS A FLUID THING. Change the surrounding and you change the creature. Maybe the past is all murder and misery, but the future—if we don't blow ourselves up—shines with infinite possibility. A dedicated parent can produce a superior child. Thus Walter believed, and on those beliefs he acted. You can never reach perfection, but that doesn't mean you shouldn't try. His own life was thwarted and impoverished, but Jeannie would have advantages he never had. He would give her music and clean air and proper stimulation. No one would ever warp her vulnerable psyche with superstitions and lies. Her best qualities, her most human qualities—imagination, empathy, memory, curiosity, love—would be encouraged, and gently, ever so gently, all old animal meanness, greed, anxiety, belligerence would be expunged. Give him time enough to form her soul and nothing in this world, not mediocre teachers or jealous peers or even her ignorant relatives could ruin her. She might turn out to be an artist, a scientist, maybe famous, maybe obscure, but either way an emblem of humankind's potential.

"And when she goes to the toilet," Molly used to kid him, "she'll shit jewels."

In fact, what Walter called the program—the enormous, gladdening, awesome task of nurturing his Jeannie—appeared to be working.

He had labored to create around her a suitable environment, and she had responded. At the age of six months, propped up in her crib amidst the Mozart and the mobiles, she had pointed an infantile finger at him and uttered her first word: "Dada!" At one she could walk without holding on and sit for half an hour with a book, turning the pages and looking so absorbed and forlorn you would have thought she was actually reading. By the time she was two he had taught her to count her fingers and toes, recite the alphabet in sing-song (which for some reason evoked in Walter an obscure recollection of his father), brush her own teeth, and mimic in comical deadpan that old version of "Big Rock Candy Mountain" he played for her on the Victrola. How adorable she was! Her eyes were dark and quizzical, and her face bore that expression of amused tolerance she would wear for the rest of her life. She had black hair and a pale face and a little red birthmark glowing like a fairy's thumbprint on her cheek. She loved to sit down, at four and five and six years old, and carry on long, precocious conversations with grown-ups. She was at the top of the scale in the standardized tests they gave her at school. She had started reading books without pictures in them and could amuse herself for hours on a rainy afternoon by assembling jigsaw puzzles with hundreds of little pieces. She had a capacity for delight and a generous soul. At the Met she had made friends with the Goyas and Breughels and Van Eycks. When Sarah got her to help out with the cooking and housework—this, too, was part of the program—she never complained. No one had to tell her to clean up her room or share her possessions with a visiting school chum. She loved, the little darling, those activity books Walter allowed her, with mazes and matching games and trick pictures of jungles, in which you had to find a dozen wild beasts lurking in the vines and trees and rivers, and horological charts from which she learned that her birthstone was ruby, her lucky numbers three and nine. Oh, Jeannie! Oh, Miranda! Oh, brave new world that will have such creatures in it!

Walter adored that child. He doted on her until he was afraid that his doting was a form of insanity. When she was a baby, he used to watch Sarah nursing her and feel beneath the surface of his fondness a pang of jealousy—he wished to be mother and father both, have his own plump and milk-heavy breasts for the child to suck. But madness or not, his life brimmed with simple and substantial pleasures. What joy to come home from the drudgery of work and have Jeannie rush up into his arms, or in bed, while he waited for sleep, to replay in his mind, instead of his old anguish and brooding, the hours they had spent together: the lessons he taught her, the clever questions she asked, the little sly jokes they created between them, the way she reached up with her white arms to give him his good-night kiss, and the feel of her hair, wet and sweet with the smell of shampoo, against his gruff, proud, paternal cheek. For Walter there were two Jeannies: the actual flesh-and-blood child and a second Jeannie, made out of wisps of memory and absorbed through his senses and pores, a marvelous little ghost child who would play forever in the magic realm of his hopes and plans and desires. This Jeannie, this fragile essence of her, was always with him.

The family used to worry about Walter, about the quality of his fondness and the pressure of his expectations. Common sense told them that to experiment with one's own flesh and blood was a sin. When she wasn't yet three and Walter was teaching her to read, they dispatched Sam to reason with him, which led to a brief, ugly fight. Later they plotted among themselves to give Jeannie a taste of what they considered a normal childhood. They invited her over to watch television, which was forbidden in Walter's house. They bought her dolls and jump ropes and pretty, girlish things. They took her to Coney Island and fed her cotton candy and hot dogs and let her go on rides Walter would have thought too frivolous or scary. But they saw that Jeannie was turning out to be healthy and happy and "normal" enough. Besides, as Deborah scolded them, Walter's doting was just an overspill of love, and as far as Deborah was concerned, no harm ever came from that particular excess.

There was nothing Walter didn't do for Jeannie. He dragged her all over town by bus and subway, to parks and department stores and suburbs and slums, so that she could "master her environment." He took her to a kosher chicken market to see the slaughterers at work because he wanted her to grasp "the simple ugly fact that we must murder to eat." For exercise—*mens sana in corpore sano!*—they went rowing and swimming and walking and (what a sight!) even roller skating together at a local rink. He sold off his stamp collection to buy her a violin and paid a dignified old Russian lady to give her lessons. Her musical talents proved meager, but it pleased him anyway to hear her scratch away at her scales. He bought a huge illuminated globe and the biggest atlas he could find, and together they roamed at random through the great outer world—Europe, China, Africa! What a natural and gentle teacher he was turning out to be. They polished off arithmetic and started in on algebra. ("Now listen, precious, this is like a treasure hunt, and *x* marks the spot, but the thing we're looking for is a number.") Every night, after Jeannie was bathed and combed, he would read to her, mixing into the commonplace broth of children's tales morsels of Dickens, Shakespeare, Plato.

"No idea that's worth anything," he told Sarah, "is too complicated for an intelligent child."

Moments to remember: Walter telling Jeannie, "No, darling, God didn't make you, your mommy and daddy did," and then showing her with the teaching aids at hand (a carrot and a powdered doughnut) the mechanics of the reproductive act. Walter and Jeannie swimming together at the pool in Brighton Beach, both of them using that economical sidestroke he had taught her, lurching through the riotous crowd, two happy fish. Walter choosing some inconsequential moment of mischief to spank Jeannie, so she might know what a spanking was like, and then crying himself to sleep that night ("*Oy*, what a world!") on Sarah's broad, freckled, patient shoulder. Jeannie asking Walter about "those people in the subway with chocolate skin" and Walter lecturing her on slavery and poverty and prejudice—"A disease I'm afraid some of your relatives have caught!"— and seeing to it, by scouring her kindergarten class, that her next birthday party looked like a poster for Brotherhood Week. Walter dragging Jeannie to a dermatologist to make sure that birthmark was benign. Walter getting furious with Evelyn for saying in front of Jeannie that Africa was a place of savages and "wild animals that can eat you up." Walter coming home with Jeannie from Great Neck, where Moe had worked and worked on her poor cavity-prone teeth, with Walter so silent, so somber, you would have thought it was his own mouth that tingled and ached.

He took special pains to cultivate her memory, which he believed was a sort of muscle to be exercised and developed. He taught her all sorts of clever mnemonic tricks for retaining dates and faces and names. He made her memorize, for the practice of it, chunks of poetry and prose. He would say to her, as she rowed them around the Prospect Park lake (in fact, they were moved more by the wind than by her huffing, sporadic, little-girl exertions) or as they stood together before the display of primate skulls in the Museum of Natural History (which turned out to be, for Walter, an oddly disappointing excursion): "This moment is precious, darling, so put it safely away in the bank of your memory and let it gather interest." He was always referring to some good time they had spent together or some "valuable lesson" she had learned, encouraging her to recall the minutiae of the moment, the colors and sights and smells, because detail was the key that unlocked the treasure box. He even found his own memory improving, as though the effort and routine of raising a child had opened old doors in himself. He caught himself inwardly comparing the phases of her childhood with recollections of his own. Occasionally in the private tangle of his thoughts he saw himself as father and child both, dawdling Jeannie on his knee and simultaneously—in some inner realm of timelessness—being dawdled on the knee of his father. Amazing the strong, sweet, resurrected love he felt for his sickly, foul-smelling, incomprehensible old papa. For the first time in his adult life he began to appreciate him.

His father had been a man of stern and primitive and superstitious beliefs, but he had acted on his beliefs as if they were knowledge—and who could condemn him for that? Out of the murk and misery of ancient ignorance he concocted his life, and so had suffered (only now did Walter comprehend just how much his father had suffered), but he acquired through his suffering a kind of grace; and with this thought Walter sensed his pulse quicken, and a sodden twilight joy warming his face. He wouldn't cry, there was no reason to cry, but oh! how vividly he remembered climbing up into his father's lap to explore the thick forest of his beard and being fascinated by the pale, smooth skin he found beneath it. He recalled how his father used to take him down to the bookstore and make him recite Talmud for the gaping *yeshiva buchers,* and there tingled again in his nostrils the dust and ink and paper that were, in a sense, the smell of his father for him. The world is a testing ground for a man's soul. Goodness is all. About that his father had been essentially correct. That goodness of his father, then, was what he must try to place into his daughter's open and vulnerable heart. And what a strange, uneasy pleasure it was to know that he could do a better job of it than his father had.

School was a special problem. Walter dreaded handing Jeannie over to "that conspiracy of ignoramuses." For five years he had nurtured the flame of intelligence and curiosity within her, and never mind his earlier opinion, he was afraid that in five hours they might snuff it out. He would have to fight a holding action against the armies of boredom and ignorance. He disliked her teachers. He was always running to the classroom to give them advice, but they still treated Jeannie like any ordinary little girl. He decided to enroll in

265

Brooklyn College at night, taking courses in education and child psychology so that he would be prepared to speak "their silly jargon," and though he complained that most of what they taught him was nonsense, and it made him uncomfortable to sit in a class full of prim, eager girls, he stuck with it. He was, after all, a student at heart, and Sarah encouraged him. She said he had a real knack for teaching, should even go on to get a license; she could imagine him in a classroom of his own, showing the world what a real teacher might accomplish. She also was able to breathe a bit easier when Walter was out of the house. She suspected that her husband and her daughter were forming a little closed universe from which, more or less inadvertently, she was excluded; so while she agreed in principle with "the program," it made her nervous, and she was glad if two nights a week Walter was diverted and she had Jeannie to herself.

Sarah also, incidentally, had her own obsession. She was terrified about what she called the Inquisition. At night, after supper, she would pick up the newspaper and read to Walter stories about their old comrades, who were being investigated, exposed, blacklisted, called to testify, thrown into prison, driven to suicide. Even milkwater liberals and vague academic social democrats were being harrassed. To make matters worse, though in Russia Stalin was murdering Jews, here the taint of anti-Semitism hung over the proceedings. This foulmouthed McCarthy was like the rest of the fascists. Any day now their turn would come. They would open the door one morning and there would be a polite, crew-cut G-man—"some damn, smiling, apple-pie storm trooper"—with a subpoena or a warrant for their arrest.

Walter scoffed at first. "They're after the big fish," he told her. "Why should they bother us?"

"Because," she said, "with those *momzers* anyone who think for himself is a threat."

It didn't take long before she had him convinced. More than convinced. Just as she had accepted his obsession with Jeannie's education, so he acquired her obsession about McCarthyism. But he gave it a particularly Walterian twist. He said he would welcome persecution. To be martyred for an idea, to be hounded and scorned, there was for Walter glory and truth in that.

Soon he was telling the family: "They'll try to make us name names, but we're not going to do it. We'd rather rot in jail." The way he said it, you knew that the thought of going to jail appealed to that old vague cloudy-brained side of him. He went around telling everyone the famous story about Emerson and Thoreau. Solemn, his voice bulging with significance, he would mimic their apocryphal conversation:

"So there is Thoreau sitting in the Concord jailhouse and Emerson looks at him and says, 'Henry, what are you doing in there?' And Thoreau, that brave and honest man, answers, 'Waldo, what are you doing *out* there?' " Lingering over the word "out," rounding his lips to prolong the diphthong and then dramatically spitting the final *t*, as though the word itself contained all the world's cruelty and injustice. That was Walter. He believed that, like Thoreau, he would be noble and indignant in prison, and that, again like Thoreau, time would vindicate him.

The only problem was, while he and Sarah sat in jail, who would take care of Jeannie?

He mulled over the possibilities. He knew that any of his brothers and sisters would be happy enough to take her in, but which of them could he trust with such a responsibility? He assembled them in his mind and examined their virtues and failings, a rather fascinating exercise, and in the end surprised himself by deciding that of all of them, out of the whole rowdy circle of his blood, it was Deborah he felt closest to, Deborah he most loved. Anyway, Deborah was partial to Jeannie. What was it she called her?—the child of the moon. She was always dropping in with presents or having Jeannie over for an afternoon of conversation and tea. And Jeannie was fond of her Aunt Deborah, liked the elaborate, old-fashioned manners she taught her and the "funny" words she used. There would be problems: Deborah had no sense of history, no passion for facts, and there was that craziness about the ghost. But Jeannie was old enough and shrewd enough so that a touch of gothic wouldn't harm her. Sure, it would be a sacrifice if they had to be separated for however long—a month? A year? More?—but sacrifice was the point. He would set for Jeannie an example of courage and high ideals from which she would benefit more (during what was, anyway, her period of latency) than from all the studies and nurturing.

Day by day the campaign against the "Commies" quickened. That poor Jewish couple from the Bronx, who were, Walter decided, probably people just like Sarah and himself, sat in Sing Sing and waited to die. In classrooms across the land millions of schoolchildren strained their powers of imagination to picture in full and terrible literalness something called the Iron Curtain. The Chinese entered Korea and the hysteria increased. People were saying that the U.S. Army, the State Department, even the PTA, had been infiltrated by traitors. But the routine at Walter's house went on as usual. No subpoena arrived. No apostate went before a committee to utter his name. No "security agency" investigated him. Their mail wasn't intercepted. There was no hollow echo in their telephone to tell them it was being tapped. No well-dressed strangers lurked on their street or followed Walter into the subway. Having already chosen martyrdom, Walter found this infuriating.

"What?" he would complain to Sarah. "We're not important enough for them to notice?"

It wasn't fair. They were robbing his radical youth of significance. They were depriving him of the noble sacrifice he was prepared to make. He speculated: perhaps their file had been destroyed or misplaced, some bureaucratic foul-up in the machinery of oppression. Perhaps some other Walter Lieber—it was not such an uncommon name—had suffered the fate that was meant for him. This thought made him gloomy. Was he absolutely *nothing* to them? He became irritable and restless. At work he misplaced documents and fouled the ledger. He would lie awake at night with his ears buzzing and his mind drifting toward some formless anxiety. His very obscurity, his failure to bring the evil world's attention down upon himself, was a dark chasm that could swallow him up. In the few hours that he slept, he dreamt bitter dreams and awoke with headaches.

A kind of insanity had gripped him, and Sarah caught it, too. Together they concocted an anonymous letter naming themselves as traitors and hinting they might even be spies; this item, scrawled in pencil on a piece of lined paper, they mailed to the FBI. They were sure the authorities would have to act. Sarah went out to Macy's and bought herself a bright red dress to flaunt at the hearing or arraignment, whichever came first. Walter got up each morning and showered and shaved his dark stubble with extra care and wore his best suit to work in case they came to the factory to arrest him. He also called up Deborah and told her to get ready for Jeannie. Sarah, meanwhile, washed all the windows and scrubbed the floors and dusted and vacuumed—"So the *goyim* shouldn't think we live in *dreck.*"

But nothing happened. Apparently they were to be persecuted by being totally ignored.

Walter decided to make one final effort: he applied for a teaching license. He assumed his application would jog the forgetful machinery, and was astonished when a week later he received in the mail a bland postcard telling him when and where to show up for the examination. In a high school auditorium filled with flushed co-eds, with his mood all a jumble of spite and curiosity and secret longing and pride, he took that exam—what fun it was to watch the pattern of pencil marks emerge on the answer sheet—and when the results were published, his name was near the top of the list. He couldn't believe a school would hire him; for one thing there would be the matter of the loyalty oath, which he would refuse to sign; nonetheless, every Sunday that spring, he investigated the Educational Opportunities section of the *Times* and sent off applications. It was, he claimed, another way of provoking the system. But those were the days of the teacher shortage and job offers began to arrive. Walter looked them over, picked out the least likely of the bunch—a "fancy-shmancy" private school in Brooklyn Heights—and arranged for an interview. He was going to face them, insist on his "record," and, if nothing else, have the pleasure of causing a scene. Sarah opposed his plan. Enough already: why go looking for trouble? But once Walter had made up his mind, there was no reasoning with him.

Later Sarah would tell the family how Walter came home from the interview with his face white as a sheet, how he walked in the door and stared at her with his eyes rolling and his mouth too dry to speak.

"So?" Sarah blurted. "What happened to you?"

"They hired me," he told her. "They said I was exactly the sort of person they had in mind."

And that's how Walter left the chocolate factory and went to work teaching social studies and math in the Peretz School, which was housed in a refurbished brownstone and supported by a Jewish millionaire with progressive leanings and agnostic tastes. Walter's salary, at first, was less than Sam was paying him, but the school had a special program for "gifted" children and Jeannie was entitled to free tuition. He liked being able to ride back and forth on the subway with her, and to see her with her classmates at fire drills and recess. He also discovered that he enjoyed teaching and was, as Sarah had predicted, very good at it. The children responded to his fervor, his honesty, his gentleness, his anecdotal style. They particularly loved those reflective moments when he would lean up against the blackboard and stare at the ceiling, and then, finding the elusive answer he had sought, turn to write it on the board, revealing the blurred ghost of an equation on his patient and good-natured back.

"As you see," he would tell them fondly, "things sometimes manage to work themselves out."

WHEN MOE FINISHED DENTAL SCHOOL, he borrowed money from Sam and his in-laws, bought a house in the suburbs, set up his practice, and started fathering daughters. They came one right after the other, five in all, bing bing bing bing bing, as though he had pulled a lever and won a jackpot. Every time you saw Laura she was burdened by a belly and *kvetching* about her swollen legs. With each pregnancy she became a little fatter, and between pregnancies she ran to health clubs and "milk farms" trying to lose weight. The girls all turned out to be pretty and brown-haired and dimpled, with Lieberish features that were softened somehow by their suburban upbringing and the admixture of their mother's genes, and when Laura decked them out in fancy party dresses, they looked, the family used to say, just like a row of flowers in a garden. They had been given perfectly conventional, girlish names, but they were always called by their boyish nicknames: Bobbi, Ronni, Micki, Toni, and Jo. Molly used to say that Moe had gone overboard in this business of children because he had set his heart on fathering a son; thus she could account for the nicknames as well as for that taint of gloom that, on occasion, soured Moe's mood.

Moe's girls, the family called them. How he doted! To listen to Moe, no one had ever had more beautiful, more talented, more obedient children. His big gray house on the green fringe of Great Neck was filled with dolls and stuffed animals and toy kitchen appliances and the framed results of their finger painting. At Halloween time Laura would create exquisite costumes, transforming the girls into adorable ghosts and witches and devils, and Moe would memorialize the scene with his expensive Japanese camera. They were big on holidays in that household and never passed up an occasion to celebrate. Valentine's Day became a glut of candy-filled hearts and gaudy flowers; the Fourth of July blazed with sparklers and flags and a ceremonial barbecue. They even got into the habit, at Christmas, of installing and decorating a tree, a Hanukkah bush they would call it—after all, why steal from the darlings, just because they were Jewish, those visions of sugarplums that danced in their dreamy heads? And for each occasion Moe had snapshots to pass around. It became a family joke, Moe's ever-present snapshots and the saccharine, self-congratulating pride with which he exhibited them.

If there is such a thing as the good life, said the family, Moe was living it. His practice was thriving; they supposed he must have been "pulling in" thirty or forty grand a year. He played golf at a country club and drove a sequence of automobiles that were bigger and shinier than Sam's. He went off with Laura on cruises to the Bahamas and charter flights to Europe, with some stranger hired to look after the children. His collection of early American pewter had been written up in a local newspaper. He dressed like a fashion plate, and tanned himself in winter under a sun lamp, and with his hair starting to silver at the temples, in the fullness of his handsome maturity, he certainly looked distinguished. At family occasions there would be Moe smiling and hugging the women and handing out generous presents to the brides and *bar mitzvah* boys. In short, he was achieving everything they ever wished for him. He set an example for them. They were constantly reminding their children how he had worked himself up out of nothing. True, he seemed to be drifting out of their orbit; they never got to meet those fancy friends he would tell them about, and he was too "busy in his workshop" to come to the phone when they called him on a Sunday morning; and he wouldn't visit Hymie no matter how much his sisters nagged him; and he found reasons not to join them during the Days of Awe when the family trekked out to the cemetery where Jacob and Sophie were buried. But they forgave him all this because he had fulfilled their expectations, he was a success. And they never found out, because he hid it from them beneath the smiles and the boasts, the snapshots and the fancy clothes, how dark and tormented his life had become.

He didn't have a name for the sense of pain and gloom that had thickened around him. He tried out words he found in books—alienation, nihilism, anomie, existential angst—but when he applied them to the particularities of his moods they seemed as ill-fitting and awkward as the shirts and trousers of his college days. He only knew that in the solitude of his mind he was struggling with something— call it a demon—self-born and implacable, as dark and inescapable as a tar baby, and the more he struggled with it, the more he was enmeshed. It had always been there, but now he could no longer hold it at bay. Everything about his life was troubling him. He was grumpy with Laura, for whom he had come to feel only familiarity —no passionate, no redeeming love. He was disturbed by his children; something in the bright fragile babble of those crystalline girls menaced him and set his teeth on edge. He hated the dreary routines of his profession. His stomach seethed and rumbled and sent bubbles of hot pain, in terrifying imitation of a heart attack, up into his chest. He was even—this was perhaps his grimmest secret—haunted by his face.

Seen straight on, dripping water, for example, in the simple glass of the medicine chest, it was not such a bad face; but in a clothing store, in the niche of the three-way mirror, he would catch among the myriad reflections unexpected glimpses of his profile, and these strange visions of himself inspired him with dread. The ugly thrust of his nose, the heavy, meaty droop of his lower lip, his hooded eyes, that little bulge of flesh at the back of his neck, a Lieber sign which barbers commented on but which he was seldom forced to see—these became for Moe the symptoms of his "problem," the visible appurtenances of the age-old ache and misery of his blood. That face, the face he was doomed to wear through the bustle and curiosity of the world, appeared alien to him, and vaguely hideous. His impulse was to scratch and mutilate it. He grew so self-conscious about it that he grew a mustache, a ragged reddish sprouting which Laura despised, and which only enhanced for him his masklike air. A space had opened up between what he was and the face he wore, and within that space, filling it, there was nothing but the demon—nothing, that is, but fear and agony and gloom.

It was always there. He would wake up some mornings and feel his whole body weighted down with the burden of it so that to drag himself to the bathroom was an effort. Sometimes it would manifest itself as a hot, itching pressure in his cheeks or a dull ache in his gums and jaws; sometimes it came as a headache, gathered into a tight, throbbing bundle behind his eyeballs. He could close his eyes and feel it unfolding within him, carrying him along toward some ever deeper misery, some dark, dangerous region of despair, and then, like a swimmer kicking up frantically from a great depth, he would have to force his eyes open and fasten them for safety on some bright, hard, comforting surface of the everyday world. No amount of sugar was capable of diminishing the bitter, metallic taste it left on his tongue. His stomach simmered and burned. Foods he loved in his youth —lox and herring and grapefruit—no longer agreed with him. During the day, while he busied himself with the necessary routines of dentistry and home life, it would withdraw to a mocking distance and squat there, lurking, waiting to surge back again. At night his dreams were hectic and restless; the eyes of the dreamer were the eyes of his maturity, but he was once more in the streets and rooms of his childhood, on Kingston Avenue and Park Place, with a shrill chorus of women in the background while he fought some furious battle of boyhood in the nonsensical armor of adult flesh. At times a sort of electrical discharge would tingle through him as if his nerve ends had exploded, and he would come awake, damp and terrified, in the middle of the night, with Laura sleeping, warmly, ignorantly, alongside him. He would want to wake her up, lay his head on her soft breast and find comfort, but he was afraid to tell her about it, afraid to admit his fear, afraid that in the telling the demon, that thing of shadows, would become more real than he could tolerate, would take on weight and flesh and overwhelm him.

He felt exposed, vulnerable, alone. He couldn't abolish from his thoughts the all-too-lucid fear of the taint of strangeness that ran in his blood. He remembered the stories he had heard of his mad old grandfather in some dismal muddy village driving his daughters to doom and clobbering devils with his walking stick. He would think about Hymie, that poor lost soul, sitting fat and silent and blank in the sunlight beneath the wire mesh, and he would tell himself: That's what can become of me. In his most dismal moments he contemplated suicide. The word more than any particular version of the act would bubble up into his consciousness and spread like a slow stain through the rippling circles of his thoughts. It was as though the wheel of his will was slowly turning against him and it absorbed all his strength to stop its terrible motion. He suspected it would take no more than an instant of madness for the word to become the deed. Suicide, suicide, sui generis, chop suey, two-on-a-side: grim play, because he believed that only by eradicating the word from his thoughts could he eliminate the deed from the world of possibilities. He wondered if death itself was the demon he feared. He would think of Dov Kalisher and the Nazi death camps, of all that muck and murder he once, in stronger days, had tried to imagine. Dov with his hunger and his money and his frog wife. Mad world we live in,

273

where the victim kisses the boot that kicks him. And what if Hitler was right, what if the Jews with their fear and their gloominess were a cancer on this earth? Survival isn't the only virtue. And thus—the wheel turning again—why not suicide? And it occurred to him in the pride of his misery, that the green lawns of Great Neck were just so much thin green skin spread preposterously over the abyss.

He led a double life. His face smiled and chatted, and behind his face, with fear and trembling, he cowered in a private cosmos of despair. He believed he had to keep it hidden, had to go on smiling and smiling, because the smile was a wall that held the torment in. To stop smiling, to expose his agony to anyone, would ruin him. "What is it with you?" Laura would ask him as he sat silent and sweating and blind in front of the television, or picked gloomily at some heartbreaking meal spread out in front of him on a restaurant table.

"It's nothing," he would tell her, reactivating the mechanism of his smile. "Really, it's nothing."

Then one morning he woke up with his stomach bloated and burning. He struggled through the day. refusing to give in to sickness, because he had an alumni function scheduled up at Columbia that night, a fraternity initiation, and he didn't want to miss it. He would remember riding the subway up from Penn Station with his belly radiating a blaze of fever that made him light-headed, and how at the Fifty-ninth Street station he saw a man he was sure was his double. He caught just a glimpse of the face, which was half hidden beneath a cheap hat of some sort, and maybe it was a sick man's dream, but he was certain that he recognized the nose, the hooded eyes, the thickness of lip. He was almost startled into shouting a greeting—this must be some long-lost cousin, some Lieber kin—but as he sat there tingling, the doors shut, the station surged backward in a blurred succession of pillars, and the moment was gone. However, the tingle lasted. He was feeling worse and worse. He arrived at Morningside Heights, and came up onto the crowded street, dizzy with pain and fever, seeing replicas of himself everywhere: behind store windows, in cars going by, vanishing into the dimness of the encroaching night, every tenth man was another Moe Lieber. He bore his aching belly onto the campus. The world withdrew to a hushed and respectful distance as a spasm of nausea and agony unfolded within him. There was a fluid feeling in his midsection, as though a hollow, a vortex, had opened up in the center of him and his innards were spilling through. For a moment he was reminded of the enemas his mother used to inflict on him. Then he collapsed. The next thing he knew (he never lost consciousness, but this is how he liked to tell it) he was coming out of anesthesia in St. Luke's Hospital, where they had diagnosed a bleeding ulcer and performed an emergency operation that saved his life.

When he left the hospital, his old clothes fit him and he had more silver in his hair. On doctor's orders, he drank lots of milk, stayed away from smoked fish, eliminated his evening and weekend office hours, and submitted himself—reluctantly at first, but later with a kind of dull acquiescence—to a course of psychotherapy.

His "shrink" was a bland, chubby, chain-smoking, lethargic post-Freudian named Levin, who fed Moe tranquilizers and antidepressants in diminishing dosages and listened, sleepy-eyed, while Moe contemplated the mysteries of his nature and nurture. That good doctor was certainly reassuring.

"Stop worrying," he told Moe right away. "For you depression is an occupational hazard. Whoever loves their dentist?"

Love was Levin's theme, love and its bizarre counterpoints, which once upon a time Moe had mistaken for hatred and envy. Love thwarted; love unexpressed; love which hid itself in shame and guilt, and thus turned acid and sour.

Moe was skeptical, but liked being able to talk openly about himself, and so, week by week, bit by bit, he re-created for Levin what he took to be the complications of his life. It was a dismal sort of fun to hold his life at his fingertips, every moment of it, with all its windings and crossings of deed and thought, memory and sensation. It was like working together the bits of a jigsaw puzzle, waiting for some large and significant pattern to emerge, though he understood that the puzzle of his life had too many pieces, and some of them were stolen, damaged, lost. There were even pieces mixed in of other puzzles, other lives, other imaginations and desires impinging upon his own.

Nonetheless, he made progress.

There was the business of his father, for example. ("Shall we talk about your father today?") Moe was thirty-three months old when his father died, old enough to have retained some traces of the man's influence, but too young to be able to evoke him in memory. All he could see of him was an old photograph, that absurd portrait with the book and the vines. He used to ache to peer through that photograph, believing that his father was beckoning to him like a ghost from the other side—and now in Levin's office, in the rushing swell of the hour, he pulled from the grab bag of memory or imagination (no telling which) a flicker, a sensation, a warm flutter of beard against his infantile cheek. It throbbed and throbbed, released at last, the pulse of Moe's oldest yearning. Had Levin actually summoned Jacob Lieber back from the dead, restored him to life and health and youth, Moe couldn't have been more grateful. Love. The strings of buried feeling that bound him to his family, and thus to himself. He was half a Lieber and half a Kalisher—the simple biology of it was written all over his face. This is what Levin, this new good father he had found, made him see, taught him to accept, and somehow, accepting, he had the illusion of feeling better.

The fellow who occupied the hour preceding Moe's was a tall, thick-featured type, probably a graduate student of some sort despite his oafishness. His neck was speckled with a rash that seemed to spread upward week by week, until it had enflamed his cheeks and forehead. Often he would emerge from Levin's office red-eyed and smiling, as though he had been delivered from anguish through a healing paroxysm of tears. Moe used to envy him those tears; his own came reluctantly, thick as glue, despite Levin's encouragements. He wondered whether the guy's problems were greater than his own, and thought perhaps he should strike up a conversation with him since they had Levin and *tsurris* in common; but he was afraid of that rash. It was a dreadful symptom, much worse than an ulcer. Maybe the fellow was truly insane and not just a blatherer, a worrier, a self-dramatizer like himself.

Moe also took an interest in the patient who succeeded him into Levin's office: middle-aged, bouffant, terribly neat, obviously repressed, forever on the verge of chewing her carefully crimsoned fingernail as she peered stiffly into her *Woman's Day*. He didn't want her to guess at his sorrows or think he was "sick." Absurdly, he tried to convey by his stance and gait that he was one of Levin's professional colleagues, just dropping by for a consultation or a chat.

Anyway, what he would remember most of his two years of therapy were the comings and goings, the long tense drive down the hill to Levin's office in Lake Success, and the return homeward, uphill, during which he would practice for himself—before having to try out on Laura—some new mood, some new image of self, some new strength that had therapeutically emerged. The rest, the magical cure that Levin wrought, blurred in time into a soothing vagueness like the gray wash of sky, with a solitary sea gull, in a hackneyed aquarelle.

He never told the family about Levin for the same reason that he never exposed to them his old turmoil: they wouldn't have understood. He wondered if they noticed the change in him, the new man that had grown up under the old skin. Probably not. He was sure that outwardly he was the same; it was only the inside, the old lurid theater of his mind, that had been rearranged. Even Laura scarcely saw it because he had kept so much of it out of her sight. He was closer to her now, had much less to hide, but in the "bad" days he had performed such a clever imitation of closeness that she hardly noticed the difference. The "bad" days. Funny, looking back, how outlandish he appeared. Depression, anxiety, identity crisis—the suitable words Levin had given him—that's all it was. What had been hell and torment then now seemed to the reasonable and ironic part of him a concocted, illusory, vulgar sort of despair. The demon had been unmasked, shown not to be a demon at all, but just some hungry, repressed, infantile rage—the child part of him throwing a tantrum in his brainpan. In recollection, in that cool light, what once was tragic had turned to farce. He believed it was better that way, better to accept the simple conditions of work and home and family, to accept one's limits and be at ease.

"That ulcer was a godsend," he told people. "It made me relax."

But occasionally a faint spasm of his old "symptoms" would shiver up through him, last, lingering echoes of muted gloom and fear, and he would experience a kind of nostalgia for his old anguish and strife. Not that he wanted to go back. No, it had been too awful. But he understood that he had paid for comfort by forfeiting grace. Nothing very large, good or bad, was ever going to happen to him. Firm lines of sanity had been drawn around him. He was "well," but he knew he would never be happy. He would have to go on feeling for the rest of his life the emptiness of the cured neurotic in the absence of his symptoms.

MILTON WAS IMPOSSIBLE. *The longer Evelyn was married to him, the* less she understood him. He drove her crazy with his moods, his magic, his constipation. To get a word out of him was like pulling teeth. Lately the only time he opened his mouth was to complain about her cooking or comment on the weather. It got to the point where she was picking quarrels with him just to hear the sound of his voice. Better yelling and screaming than that awful brooding silence of his. And with the kids gone from the house, with Ben out west in law school and Deanna living in the Village and attending NYU, Milton was worse than ever. He had converted Ben's room into a "study," if you please, packed up the baseball gloves and model airplanes, and moved in his magic tricks and paraphernalia, and after supper, if he wasn't dozing in front of the television, he would disappear into the study for hours on end. The only time you heard from him was when he came to the kitchen for a banana or ensconced himself in the bathroom. He was getting to the age where his stomach was always acting up, but the man would rather suffer than use a laxative. Evelyn kept telling him to see a doctor; the way he sat on the toilet maybe he had, God forbid, an obstruction, a growth; but Milton didn't believe in doctors. He said they were all quacks, and once they got their hands on you, you were finished. Everyone else in the world understood that medicine had become a science, but not Milton. He was still living in a superstitious age. Anyway, he argued, there was nothing wrong with him. A sluggish bowel was simply a Himmelfarb trait. His own father, may he rest in peace, had the same condition. So Evelyn would be cleaning up in the kitchen or preparing a fruit bowl for her Mah-Jongg crowd, and she would hear Milton all the way down the foyer, groaning and straining and muttering to himself, or, on rare occasions, as if the burdens of the world finally had been lifted from him, breathing a long, exultant, mournful *Ahhhh!*

Sometimes, just to heckle him, she would call out: "*Nu*, Milton, you coming off yet? I gotta go pee!"

At least if he would smile about it, laugh, tell a joke, but the man had no sense of humor. His whole life was his work, his magic, and his bowels, and he regarded each of them with the same sullen and stubborn earnestness. Evelyn had been married to him nearly thirty years, had raised two children with him, slept every night alongside him in bed, knew his quirks and habits, but more and more it was like being married to a stranger. He would come home, grumpy and acrid-smelling, with his face smudged with subway dirt and a newspaper crammed into his jacket pocket (she had told him a million times he was stretching the fabric), and she couldn't recognize in him—this sad sack, this *shlump*—the shy, ambitious young magician she had married. It nagged at her, that her life should be joined so thoroughly, so inextricably, to his. But what could she do? Leave him? Get a divorce? No sense even thinking such thoughts; they were beyond the circumference of her world. "You made your bed, now sleep in it," her mother used to say, and she would someday tell her children the same thing. Besides, all you had to do was look at her sisters to realize that when it came to men, the Lieber women had no luck.

So she kept herself busy. Being busy, Evelyn believed, was the solution to everything. She held down a good job in the accounting department of A&S, and with two salaries coming in she could pay for her children's education and still afford a few luxuries. Monday nights she went to meetings of her lodge; Wednesdays she played Mah-Jongg with the local *yentehs;* Fridays she and Milton got together with Ruthie and Lou and two other couples, friends from the old days, and either they killed the night playing gin rummy or they went out to dinner in a Chinese restaurant. Saturday mornings she had her regular beauty parlor appointment, and then Milton picked her up with the car and they did the heavy shopping for the week at Waldbaum's on Nostrand Avenue. Saturday evenings it was a movie or television unless they had some "function" to attend. Sundays she reserved for the family. If they weren't getting together in someone's house, they spent most of the day on the phone. She could talk for hours to Molly or Rose or Deborah or Essie. Sometimes she would call Sarah, though half the time, with the words Sarah used, you couldn't make heads or tails out of the conversation, and sometimes she would even call Laura to see how the girls were getting along, though she was annoyed that Laura seldom found occasion to pick up the phone and call her. In beween times, she cooked, she kept the house spotless, she worked on her needlepoint, or she read those fat books people were always recommending to her—*Exodus, Doctor Zhivago, Peyton Place.* If you kept busy, maybe you weren't happy, but at least you didn't have so much time to feel sorry for yourself, to brood about your *tsurris.*

One Sunday a month she liked to drive out to the Island to visit Hymie. It was, after all, a family obligation. But lately, with Milton, this, too, had become a problem. She had never learned to drive; she took a couple of lessons, but she got nervous when she climbed behind the wheel, so she had to depend on Milton to take her, and Milton was impossible. The older he got, the more he hated to drive.

After all these years he would still grumble about having to *shlep* across Brooklyn to pick up Evelyn's sisters. All week she would be on the phone making arrangements but Saturday night Milton would turn on the news "just to catch the weather report," and if, God forbid, they mentioned snow, or even rain, he called the whole thing off.

"I'm not driving that road in the rain," he would tell her. "It's bad enough in good weather, those curves around the cemetery. I'm not that young anymore."

That was Milton. He was in a hurry to get old. Maybe he thought old age would protect him from the threats and demands that haunted his life. It drove her wild.

"A little rain won't kill you!" she would tell him. "You're not going to melt!"

That would provoke a fight. They would shout at each other, and stomp around the house, and when it was about to subside, Evelyn, still frustrated, would make some comment that would start it up again. All the long bitterness of their marriage emerged in those fights. They would end with Milton, coughing and red in the face, running off to the bathroom or his study, with Evelyn shouting after him to get in the last word: "Stop already! You'll give yourself a stroke!" Sometimes she thought that they had done nothing but fight with each other all those years, that the fighting alone was what bound them together. But she didn't like to think about it because she didn't want to feel sorry for herself.

She had a great capacity for feeling sorry for herself. "The trouble with me," she told people, "is that I'm the emotional type," as though being emotional were a particular kind of disease. To make matters worse, she had recently entered upon her "time of life," and she was forever suffering from her "hot flushes." One minute she was fine; the next minute her face was on fire and her throat was parched and a kind of pulsing rhythmic misery was pounding through her. She would have to catch her breath, waiting for the sensation to subside, and in those moments, as she gasped and perspired, her worst thoughts came to her. That's when she knew that her life was nothing but a heartache.

Her children, for example, Ben and Deanna—how they aggravated her! When Ben was a kid, you couldn't shut him up, but now, the *gantze mensh*, you couldn't get a word out of him. "He's become the strong, silent type, like his father," she would tell people, but it wasn't funny. He was making out all right; after that summer of playing professional baseball in the minor leagues (a big waste of time, as far as Evelyn was concerned), he had gone to Rutgers on an athletic scholarship, and now he was out west and well on his way to being a lawyer—but why, why, knowing how she worried, couldn't the lawyer write her a letter or pick up the phone and say hello? And the girl friend, the "fee-ahn-say." Thank God she was Jewish—what more could you ask in this day and age?—but otherwise, she was no bargain. When you asked her what she did, she told you she was studying to be a hygienist. Fine, fine. But how could a girl be a hygienist and have such filthy habits? Every time Evelyn saw her—which, granted, wasn't that often—she had cheap makeup smeared on over an unwashed face, and her hair hanging as if it would kill her to take a comb to it, much less let a beautician fix it up for her, and everywhere you looked there was a torn seam, a food stain, an open zipper. For this she had brought Ben up to be neat and clean about himself, and dress well, and present a respectable figure to the world? This slob, not even pretty, with not even such a good figure, this is what a smart, handsome boy like her Ben brings home to her? *Feh!*

But what don't you do for children? She believed—had absorbed in the atmosphere of the family in her generation—that nothing was more important than helping the next generation be a little better off. When it came right down to it, what else did life have to offer? So you sacrificed; you gave up your own pleasures to build them a decent home; you changed diapers that made you nauseous from the stench and grieved over them when they scraped a knee or were mistreated by their friends; you nagged them about their homework—because at least they should be educated and have the advantages you never had—and you tried to instill in them a little sense, a little respect, a little knowledge of their traditions and the murky old world out of which they had come and to which, thank God, maybe they wouldn't have to belong (because for them, if they set their minds to it, the sky was the limit); and in the end, just to spite you, they were miserable anyway. Or if not miserable, selfish and ungrateful and too busy to remember that you were still alive.

You take Deanna. Okay, Ben would manage, he was smart, he worked, he had a good profession, but Deanna—*gottenyu!*—how had she borne such a curse? Bad enough in a daughter-in-law, but Deanna also was turning out to be a slob.

"Deanna," she would say to her, "you're in college now, so when do you stop already with the blue jeans and the filthy sneakers, when do you start dressing like a lady?"

But it was like talking to the wall. Deanna didn't care about her appearance. She was nineteen, twenty years old, and as far as Evelyn knew, she still didn't date. If you asked her, she claimed she wasn't interested in boys. Whoever heard of such a thing? Evelyn could recall her own girlhood, how at that age all she and Ruthie ever thought about was the next date and what to wear and who was going out with whom. She couldn't fathom Deanna's attitude. Was the problem that boys didn't find her attractive? Okay, so she had put a little weight on in high school—it was a crime the way the Lieber women, if they didn't watch their diet, ran to fat—and since she didn't wash her face carefully enough, she was plagued by a bad complexion. But she was a good-looking girl, if only she would care about how she looked. Not Deanna. She had cut off her hair because she said she didn't have time to comb it. And she had to go galumphing around like a *klutz*. She never just sat down in a chair; she threw her legs over the side and sprawled. And you could tell she wasn't happy. Something was eating at her, but she refused to talk about it. Evelyn knew, no one had to tell her, that Deanna was on the verge of flunking out of school, too busy to study, spending her time traipsing around Greenwich Village with the beatniks, becoming a kind of beatnik herself, if not worse. And the only time you saw her was when she was broke and rode the subway home for a meal and to ask for extra spending money, which Evelyn always doled out to her in the end because for children what don't you do? And because she could not look at her—never mind the cropped hair, the tomboy manners, the bad complexion that was like a map to goings-on in Deanna's life that Evelyn didn't want to think about—wihout seeing the gorgeous, glowing, happy, joy-bringing child she had been. That image, the image of Deanna in those professional, hand-tinted photographs that adorned Evelyn's vanity, interposed between them like a ghost.

So Evelyn suffered, and she suffered alone. She knew that Milton also suffered, but he was too stubborn to show it, too preoccupied with the business of his magic tricks. Ever since they had come home from Florida, the magic had become more and more like an obsession with him. The odd part was that recently, though he was spending more time than ever in the study, he no longer bothered to practice new tricks on the friends and relatives, no longer sought out weekend performances, no longer even sent away for catalogues and new paraphernalia. In the old days she had to put up with expenses and equipment cluttering the house, but now he was working with just a few small household items: coins, corks, spoons. She would pass by the study door and hear him talking to himself, as though he were communing with marvelous and tantalizing powers. She worried about him. Maybe the man was losing his mind. One night he came into the kitchen, set a glass of water down in front of her, and showed her he could make the water disappear. It seemed to slide right out of the glass as if it were running through a hole in the table. "Nice," she said, "very nice." She was not particularly impressed because she had seen him do better stunts before—the one, for example, where he smashed an egg in his pocket and showed you the pocket was empty—and she was surprised when her nonchalance upset him.

"Look," he told her desperately, "this really is a plain ordinary glass. There was no trick to it!"

She didn't understand it, but she would remember the look he had at that moment, haggard, wild, and secretly proud, his eyes flickering with mute appeal. But what was she supposed to do? For some reason he had taken it into his head to convince her that he really could do magic. But why? Did he believe it himself? Was he trying to please her? Or—a later suspicion—was he just setting her up for some final stunt? Years ago he used to claim he could read minds and move small objects by thinking their motion, but she had never taken this seriously, had accepted it as part of the sly mystification of his conjurer's trade, and eventually he had let it drop. And now here it was, as though he wanted to relive his youth, the same thing all over again. We get older, but we never seem to get any wiser, she told herself. He still had that old dreamy streak. She had never managed to convince him that the ordinary world, without magic, was enough.

She decided to humor him. When, a few days later, he showed her he could make a quarter stand up on its edge and roll off the table, she mustered her enthusiasm and said it was a wonderful sight. She was tolerant when he started—"with this force I have in my mind" —bending her best silverware. But the more she humored him, the more obsessed he became. He started staying up all hours of the night in his study, and when she yelled at him to come to bed, he would tell her to sleep without him. His face had become drawn and there were dark shadows under his eyes. If she asked him what he was doing in there, he would mumble something about "control" and tell her not to worry. But how could she not worry when he was acting like a madman, when all night long he went from the study to the bathroom, from the bathroom back to the study again, until she wanted to say to him: "Put the toilet in the study already and save yourself the trip!"

Then, toward the end, he seemed to give up on the magic. For two weeks he avoided the study, sat instead in front of the television, watching anything that happened to be on, not even bothering to change channels except when it came time for the weather. At first Evelyn was relieved, but he was so silent, so preoccupied, that it made her nervous.

"What's the matter with you, sitting there like a corpse?" she would say to him.

"I work hard all day, I'm tired," he would tell her. "Nothing's the matter."

"You were better off when you were always with the magic. At least you were doing something."

But she couldn't provoke him; he didn't want to fight.

That's how he was their last night together. He came home from work, ate supper, and plunked himself down in front of the television. He was still sitting when she came in to watch *The $64,000 Question*, which was one of her favorites. She would remember saying to him, to make conversation, that he should get himself on that program; his topic could be magic, and maybe he could make himself a little money. But he just scowled at her and pushed himself out of his easy chair, saying:

"Excuse me a minute, I got a rush call."

Later she swore that she heard him going down the foyer, heard the click of the bathroom door lock and the usual little groan as he eased himself down, with his aching bowels, onto the seat. Then she got caught up in the program. She would remember the little Italian shoemaker locked in the isolation booth answering questions about opera, making himself rich, and how she thought that here was a man who knew how to grab hold of an opportunity. They were handing him the check when she realized that Milton had not reappeared.

"Milton!" she shouted. "*Nu*, Milton, did you fall in?"

There was no answer.

"Milton?"

She jumped up, nervous and flushed. Later she would claim that she heard something, a sound that was hard to describe, like air rushing in to fill a space, a hiss and rush as when you open a can of coffee; she would say that she had a premonition, already knew the worst as she rushed down the foyer, calling his name. But it was only sickness she feared as she stood, hysterical, pounding on the locked bathroom door—a heart attack, a stroke, Milton lying unconscious and helpless on the cold tile. Somehow she calmed herself down enough to call the janitor; he arrived at last with a crowbar, that polite bleary-eyed black man she was afraid of, yanked once, and the door opened. He went in first, came out again staring at her.

"Don't know how it come to be locked," he bawled at her. "There be no one in there!"

A single small hard brown stool, Milton's last, floated in the yellow water. The toilet paper gizmo was empty, but there was no paper in the bowl. The little louvered window was locked from the inside. A newspaper lay neatly folded on the side of the bathtub. A few coins on the floor next to the toilet might have fallen out of a pocket. The illusion was perfect: it was Milton's greatest trick. And wherever he had found his end, whether dragged up into the magical void or beckoned down to Florida without the burden of wife and children to deprive him of paradise, whether he had authentically vanished or merely run away—whether, that is, life is a mystery or a muddle—no one in the family ever saw him again.

III

Here are your waters and your
watering place.
Drink and be whole again beyond
confusion.

—ROBERT FROST,
"Directive"

SEVEN

BROOKLYN WAS CHANGING. The *shvartzers* were moving in and the Jews were moving out. Sam saw it every day when he drove up along Flatbush Avenue on his way to the factory. Where Ebbets Field once stood they had put up a big blank apartment house—as Sam said, they had torn the heart out of the place. As soon as you got past Prospect Park, you entered the slums. The park itself was no longer safe. In the old neighborhoods you took your life in your hands when you walked the streets at night. Ruthie's Gary was attacked on Nostrand Avenue. They knocked him down and whipped him with radio antennas off of cars, leaving ugly, welted cuts all over his back and arms. The poor kid had to spend the night in the hospital. The police told the family that this sort of thing happened all the time nowadays, but there was nothing they could do to stop it. In the old days, when cops walked a beat, they knew who the delinquents were and could take them down to the station house and knock some sense into them, but now they rode around in squad cars, and everyone was a stranger. Anyway, they said, their hands were tied by the courts and the do-gooders. Children, little kids, twelve, thirteen years old, were already hardened criminals. According to the police, Gary was lucky, it could have been much worse. They told stories about kids being stabbed, shot, burned, mutilated, sodomized. There were neighborhoods in Brooklyn where even the cops were afraid to go. The place was turning into a jungle.

People were moving away, and you couldn't blame them. You wanted to be liberal-minded, but you had to live. Moe was out on the Island, Lou had put the house on Crown Street up for sale and was looking for a smaller place in Canarsie, and Evelyn, now that she was alone, had taken an apartment in Brighton Beach not far from Deborah—she said she would have moved out of Brooklyn altogether if it weren't for her job. Deborah herself, after all these years, was talking about moving to California. Among the next generation, no one wanted to live in Brooklyn. Rich, married and a father, bought himself a house in New Jersey and had to commute more than an hour each way back and forth to the factory. Ruthie's and Evelyn's kids had spread out across the countryside. Molly went up and down like a yo-yo between New York and Florida, trying to establish herself in a business. She opened restaurants, beauty parlors, dress shops, but nothing worked out for her. She was fatter than ever and pink with hypertension, and she had to stop to catch her breath when she went up a flight of stairs. Sam kept telling her to come back to the factory, maybe she would bring him some luck, but she wouldn't hear of it. She said the business wasn't big enough to support Rich and herself, that she loved that boy like a son, but she knew she couldn't work with him.

"Besides," she told Sam, "you don't need me there to add to your troubles."

It was true, business wasn't so good anymore. Most of the nine retail outlets were located in deteriorating neighborhoods, and even the Kings Highway store, which Deborah still managed, had been burglarized twice. Sam had to install sliding metal gates over the storefronts and steel double-bolted doors over the back entranceways, and still the thieves and vandals found ways to break in. Insurance premiums had become a major expense. At the New Lots Avenue store *shvartze* hoodlums had shown up, demanding "protection" money. Sam got in touch with his connections, but they told him they no longer operated in that neighborhood, there was nothing they could do. In the old days you paid the Italians and you got your money's worth, but how could you do business with *shvartzers*? The factory itself was located in the middle of a slum, and the workers were afraid to go outside for lunch. Shoplifting had become a problem. One kid would order a quarter's worth of salted peanuts while the rest of them were ransacking the counter. You couldn't safely walk the day's receipts to the bank. Instead, Sam or Rich would have to go around in a car to make the deposits. It was like trying to do business in a zoo.

The solution was to open new stores on the Island and over in Jersey, follow the old clientele, maybe even relocate the factory, buy new machinery, make the whole operation more efficient. Sam told himself he should have done it years ago when he still had energy, time, money. Now where would he be able to raise the necessary cash? When he went to the banks, they told him he had more debt than he could handle. He could run to the loan sharks, but he owed them money also, and was being bled by the vigorish. Then there was Dov Kalisher: Sam owed him a bundle. For years Dov kept saying don't worry about the money, it's a family proposition but lately he had been showing up at the factory—"keeping an eye on my investment," he said. The man was coldhearted and shrewd, and he had his fingers into everything. He would sit himself down behind the desk and start telling Sam what to do, and Sam had to grit his teeth. If Dov went into court with his papers, the judge would turn the whole business over to him.

Sam used to think that when you built up a business and made it a success, you could let it go on and on. But things kept changing. If you stopped for a minute to take a deep breath, everything started to slip away. Suddenly after all those years Sam had labor troubles. A man from the teamsters showed up, a sharpie, a real *gonif*, and the next thing Sam knew the factory was "organized." He didn't fight it. Why should he? All his life he had been pro-labor, voted for Roosevelt and Truman, came from a family of workers. He believed that when a man worked hard all day, he deserved a payoff. He tried to treat everyone the way he treated his own family, but the union was bleeding him. They made demands, and if their demands weren't met, they would shut him down and put him out of business. What good would that do them?

Then there was the *mishegoss* about the white chocolate. All over New York white chocolate had become the craze. The competition was turning out white chocolate cordials, white chocolate butter crunch, almond bark and peanut clusters and even nougats made with white chocolate. The customers apparently thought that white chocolate was some new kind of merchandise, that a superior white cocoa bean had been discovered. They didn't know that it was nothing but cocoa butter and sugar, with the cocoa itself, the very heart and soul of the chocolate, left out. Well, if it wasn't one thing, it was another. As far as Sam was concerned, white chocolate left a taste of ashes in the mouth. His stores carried a sampling of the stuff, but he refused to push it. However, if customers came into the store and didn't see white chocolate, they went somewhere else, and the business suffered. You could read the world's madness on the pages of the ledger. Meanwhile, the competition was making a bundle by wrapping their *dreck* in cellophane and shipping it all over the country. By the time you got it home it was turning gray around the edges, but people didn't care about quality anymore. The new generation was ignorant and had no taste. Dov would tell him to give them what they wanted, cut a few corners, build up the profit margin.

"Believe me," he would say, "you can make people eat shit and like it."

Sam wouldn't listen to such arguments. He was stubbornly attached to the old way of doing business. He believed that if your product was good enough, people would know the difference and would tell their friends. The best advertising was word of mouth, so in the long run, quality paid off. If anything, he was becoming increasingly fussy about the quality of his merchandise, spending hours in the warehouse, inspecting the shipments of the raw materials and entering into complicated lawsuits with the suppliers when their merchandise failed to satisfy him, throwing good money after bad by hiring lawyers and refusing to compromise. Even Rich knew that he was being foolish, and Rich, everyone agreed, had no head for business. He would arrive late in the office, claiming the baby had kept him up, and spend most of the day on the telephone kibitzing with his "contacts." Tall, loud, florid, essentially good-natured, he had the personality of a salesman and the heart of a playboy. Not once in his life had he ever gotten his fingernails dirty. When he went out of the office onto the factory floor, he looked awkward and out of place. The workers loved him because they could joke with him and call him by his first name and come running to him when they needed an advance or a day off. Sure, the whole world loved him; Sam loved him too—loved him as only a father can love his first-born son—and ate his heart out over him because he was sure that if it weren't for the business, Rich, along with his wife and baby, would go hungry.

Sam in those days was still hard and vigorous and quick-moving, with white hair that was cropped short and bristly, and murky green eyes that had set themselves into a perpetual squint. He still smoked what seemed to be a permanent cigarette at every moment of the day —it might have been glued to his lip the way it clung there with the bluish smoke rising up in front of his eyes and a precarious half inch of ash curling but never quite managing to fall—and he still wore light-colored suits and dark shirts and white shoes, with thick, luxurious silk ties. Rich would say to him:

"Pop, you look like a gangster on *The Late Show*. Let me buy you some new clothes."

"Sure, big shot," Sam would tell him. "With my money you want to buy me presents."

They teased and bantered and growled at each other all day long. Probably neither of them quite understood the mix of affection and hostility that lay beneath it. Rich had acquired Sam's extravagant habits. He wore tailor-made suits and alligator shoes; he ran to the racetrack and loved a good poker game; if you told him a hard-luck story, he would pull the last penny out of his pocket and worry later that the money didn't belong to him. A few years ago he had gone out to California to establish himself in his own business; that failed, but he came home with a girl named Rhoda, a sunburnt and dark-haired beauty with the figure of a movie star and big horsey teeth. Sam never liked Rhoda very much, didn't trust her smiles and exuberance, believed in the long run she would make Rich unhappy, but she had delivered into the family a little boy, a gorgeous, golden, smiling baby, upon whom Sam, the proud grandfather, absolutely doted. It was the greatest pleasure of his life when they brought the kid over to the house on a weekend and he held him up above his head and tumbled him to make him laugh. Then he could feel the flow of his blood running smoothly on into a joyous future—for a moment he could cast off the burden of his troubles.

But mostly he was tired; he was worse than tired; exhaustion had settled itself deep into his muscles and bones. All his life he had been an insomniac, but lately he slept and slept, a deep, blank sleep from which he awoke aching and exhausted. People would come into the office and find Sam dozing at his desk. He would close his eyes for a moment and the next thing he knew someone was shaking and prodding him awake. His legs felt waterlogged and heavy. When he had to drive for more than an hour, he would start dozing off at the wheel. For half a century he had been working; now he had no more patience for the day-to-day routines of the business. His thoughts veered away from the deals and problems. Even when he was relaxing at the club or the ball park, he was pressured and discontent. At home he would sit himself down with a newspaper and Essie, oblivious to his mood, would start chirping around him. He never bothered to tell her his problems; he assumed that she knew and didn't care. So long as she could run to the stores for new dresses and fancy perfumes and those French cosmetics which hid her wrinkles, and which lately had become a major expense. He could walk around without a nickel in his pocket and an empty checking account, but that didn't stop Essie from going away for a week to the Poconos. He didn't have the heart to tell her to stop spending. Money was her element; without it, he suspected, she would shrivel and die. When he tried to prepare her for the worst by telling her they might have to sell the house and find a small apartment somewhere, she just blinked at him and said:

"Then we'll need some new furniture."

That was Essie. He no longer loved her and he no longer hated her; he no longer felt much of anything about her except for a kind of comfortable, exasperated familiarity. Two heads on the same pillow, his mother used to tell him, soon become the same head. For himself Sam was prepared to face bankruptcy; some romantic streak in him even hungered after a barer, more fundamental sort of life. He could give up his house, his car, his clothes, his gambling, everything because he was nearly sixty-five years old, had surpassed his father's years, and had grown tired of luxury. He longed for that unburdening that would precede his death. But he had to go on struggling to save the business—for Essie, so that he could continue to support her in the style to which she was accustomed. Sometimes it occurred to him that he had squandered his life just to keep that idiotic promise he had been tricked into uttering by his shrill and hateful mother-in-law.

Things kept getting worse and worse. Dov Kalisher set a deadline for that loan to be repaid. In a philosophical mood, separated for a moment from his gloom and anger, Sam could admit that Dov's conniving was understandable; he couldn't forget that during the good times, while the family was living off the fat of the land, Dov Kalisher was starving in Auschwitz. But the man apparently knew no limits. He showed up at the office one morning accompanied by a lawyer, who started spreading legal papers out on the desk while Dov lounged in a chair scraping his fingernails with a pocketknife. It became apparent that Dov wasn't interested in the chocolate business; what he wanted was the land the factory occupied; in the background was some shadowy scheme involving millions of dollars for a public housing project. Evidently Dov had some influential politician in his pocket.

"Listen," he told Sam. "Business is business."

Sam wanted to throw them out of his office, but what could he do? If he didn't come up with the cash, he would lose everything. Money, *gelt,* moolah, dough, the almighty dollar bill. Have money in your pocket and you're king of the world; go broke and you're just another *shnorrer.*

In those days Sam still owned a one-third share of a cabin up in the Adirondacks. Years before he had gotten together with a couple of cronies to buy it as an investment, and every so often a bunch of them would drive up for a "fishing trip," from which they never brought back any fish. They would stay up most of the night playing bridge or pinochle and drinking Canadian Club with ginger ale and eating the corned beef sandwiches they brought with them from the city. Sam enjoyed the fake log walls, the ratty moose head, the smoky fireplace, and the occasional splash of some anonymous fish leaping at dusk in the nearby lake; he liked putting on old pants and a woolen checkerboard shirt, and not shaving for a few days so that his chin against the pillow felt manly and harsh, and tramping out into the woods to pee on the pine needles—for him this amounted to a return to nature. He would come home from one of those trips smelling gloriously rank and sour, and for a day or two afterward, caught up in momentary enthusiasm, he would have nothing but scorn for the harsh, hectic life of the city. It didn't matter that he couldn't tell a birch from an oak, or that the night sounds of the forest—the murmurous insects, the wind in the trees—could make his nerves tingle and his heart anxiously leap.

Anyway, in the midst of his crisis, while he was trying to figure out where he could raise the money to pay Dov Kalisher, Sam decided to take some time off and go up to the cabin. He had never been there alone before, but he figured he would take along a stack of mystery books, read all day and sleep all night, until he felt rested. Somewhere he had picked up the notion that a week of solitude would relax him, and that relaxed, restored, he would be able to deal with his troubles. In the meantime, Essie, Rich, the business, the family, could get along without him.

So early in October, in his four-year-old Buick, with a Thermos jug of strong coffee on the seat beside him to keep him awake, Sam drove up along the Hudson until the city was canceled and replaced by the orange and brown scenery he had in mind. Beautiful, he kept telling himself, beautiful, beautiful, as if he could create out of the mere prettiness of sunshine and autumn woods a cure for his gloom and exhaustion. But as the ribbon of the Taconic Parkway slipped away behind him, he became apprehensive. He could think of a dozen things he should have done at the office before he left. Besides, what good would it do him to run away? Did he suppose the problems, abandoned for a few days, would solve themselves, that he would come home to find Dov Kalisher repentant and a pot of gold on his desk? Turn back now, some part of him kept insisting, there is nothing for you up there, turn back, turn back. What would he do there by himself? What if, God forbid, he got sick? He could picture himself, the victim of a heart attack or stroke, paralyzed on the cabin floor with no one to help him, no one to care. He imagined himself dying in solitude, and remembered suddenly the words a Jew is supposed to utter at the moment of his death; he even mumbled them in grim rehearsal, arousing with the words old memories of his father and Rabbi Trauerlicht and the *shul* on Sterling Place, and something else, too—the night he slept in the forest, skimming up into his thoughts and vanishing again before he could grab hold of it. Never mind, he told himself, just keep going. It was all foolishness, all just a baffle for his fear.

During the last hours of that drive his hands were stickily clenching the steering wheel and his stomach was fluttering with nervousness and indigestion—the acid of all the coffee he had drunk. The car fought him and the road weaved and blurred; it was like driving through water. His forehead was hot when he touched it with his cold damp fingers, and his legs kept cramping. He wanted to pee, but all around him was wilderness, and he was afraid to stop. The trip seemed to take forever.

By the time he got to the cabin the sun was slanting through the windows, throwing elongated shadows across the dimming room. He unloaded the car, discovered that the electricity was out, lit a couple of Coleman lamps, and carried in logs for a fire. All the way up he had kept assuring himself that once he arrived, he would feel better, but now it was troublesome being there alone; everything—the lamps, the old furniture, the moose head—bristled with mysterious menace, and the silence made his ears ring.

Later he would recall a sensation of passage as the day vanished into night, as though he had been moving sluggishly along some murky path toward some unknown and alien place, and, almost there, his senses came alert as he hurried to reach it. Alone, with nothing to do and no one to talk to, he began to sense each moment, each pulse of his heart, as something distinct and palpable. It made him restless. He tried to read, but he couldn't focus his eyes on the page. He was too aware of the texture of the book rubbing against his fingertips, the stale taste of cigarette smoke in his mouth, the rub of his clothes against his body, the hiss of the Coleman lamp a few feet from his ear. His nerve ends seemed to reach out, tendrillike, to the world beyond his flesh, probing it as though it had become strange and new. What was happening to him? Was he cracking under the pressure, losing his mind? He closed his eyes and held them closed, shutting the world out, checking the drift of his thoughts, but for the moment he had no thoughts at all, no plans, no schemes, no problems, no memories, no wishes, no scraps of conversation, no voices, no messages for himself, no words, no imaginings—nothing but that tingling sensation of the moment in the moment that was passing. It was pleasant in a way, euphoric almost, but terrible, too. Time itself was blowing through him like a slow wind.

With an effort, proving to himself that he could move, he tossed the book on the floor, breaking its spine, pried himself up gingerly from the old armchair, and went outside, slowly putting one foot in front of the other, aware of every step.

Night had not yet fully come: over the treetops to the west the dark, star-pricked fabric of the sky faded into purplish gray toward some fading point of light beyond the trees; small night creatures, soft and quick, were moving through the forest. The air smelled of old rain; beneath the litter of dead leaves and twigs and pine cones, the rich, damp soil clutched at his feet. Anonymous, raucous insects clattered and buzzed and hummed around him, and as he stood there, wondering, the tingling of his nerves blurred into dread.

Remember, he was thoroughly a city boy, a stranger to stars and trees, insects and wild rodents, and the fact that his fear was vaguely comical made it no less real. Since he had no names, or even mental pictures for his surroundings—his mind cast in this environment no beam of its own—the forest was for him mysterious, threatening, and profound. For all he knew the lonely night was giving birth to beasts, savages, murderers, monsters, demons, ghosts. He might just as well have been standing then in the aboriginal wilderness at the haunted origins of time, struggling against some primal anthropoid terror. It occurred to him that he had felt this way before in some other place, perhaps even in some other life, this mix of fear and awe, with the same clear smell of damp woods mingling with the acrid odor of his own flesh. Where? When? It lingered on the verge of consciousness like a forgotten name or a snatch of melody; his senses brimmed full with the sensation of it; then, released at last by the darkness and the trees and the odors, he remembered the night he slept in the forest and started living it again.

They were on their way to America. He would recall how his mother had said they would have to pass through a miracle to get there. America! He was only five or six years old at the time and probably had never seen a map, or perhaps had looked at maps without those concepts of scale and distance you need to interpret them and so had seen nothing but meaningless shapes and colors. In either case, he carried no geography in his head—for him the world beyond the muddy nameless village of his birth was a blur. America could have been the name of another planet, a newborn world waiting in the heavens to be explored. He had no memory of leaving the village, but in a breathless bewilderment of recollection he could evoke a vague impression of a horsecart and a cart driver, whose legs were wrapped in rags, and an image of himself walking alongside his father, clinging to the flaring hemline of his father's big black coat, watching the slow, creaking spin of the wooden cartwheels. Then, because his small legs became tired, he was sitting in the cart with his mother while the infant Molly, wrapped in his mother's shawl, sucked and snuffled at a hidden breast. How long did that cart ride last? Hours? Days? It didn't matter. All that mattered was that at the end of it, in a kind of hollow space between that cart ride and other equally vague impressions of a train and a boat and his first glimpse of his Uncle Asa's red hair bobbing amidst the crowds of the immigration hall, came a forest and a night and a memory which had taunted him for years, and which he now had hold of at last. He had no idea where that forest was located. He could guess that it must have been close to the German frontier and that for this one night they were avoiding the villages and inns because they lacked the proper documents of passage or were afraid of the German border guards. He had been so very young, so ignorant of what was happening to him, that he couldn't be sure of anything, not even if that night was truly a memory or merely a dream; but it was vivid for him now, that other forest. He had even retained in his tingling nerves a jagged webwork of tree branches spread against the darkening sky and the emerging stars. They built a fire and sat around it. He was cold and hungry despite the fire and the meal they must have eaten, hungry and cold as though the fire cast no heat or light, threw nothing but scary shadows up into the darkness around him; but at the age of five or six he was expected to be *ayn klayne mensh*, a little man, and his mother had her hands full with the babies—he couldn't bother her—so he moved closer to his father, who sat bunched into himself, bundled in that big black coat, mumbling the evening devotions. Yes, he was seeing it and feeling it now, how he sat next to his father, listening to the quiet singsong of the prayers, and how, at last, still cold, he crawled into the warm space beneath his father's coat, and how his father grudgingly raised his arm to make room for him, and—yes, that was it, he could smell it, the smell of his father in the dark warm space beneath the coat, the same smell that soured his own flesh as he stood in the shadows of memory in this forest now and huddled in darkness in that other forest then, the two moments melting into one as he breathed, absorbed, took into himself, and made his own that rancid, bitter, unbearable stench—the unforgivable smell of his father's terror. He hated it; his nostrils and lungs fought against it; but he had to stay and breathe it beneath his father's coat just as he had to stay and breathe it sixty years later in the open darkness of trees and stars, because the smell of his father's fear had become his own smell, too, and there was no way to escape it. After all, when a father is so afraid, how shall his son learn not to be?

Fear. The fear of his father and his father before him, an inheritance of fear reeling backward in time for a thousand generations; and the fear of his children and their children to come for a thousand more. Sam was not the man to articulate this; he would not even try; but he had glimpsed the gloom of that old fearsome darkness against which men have built their towers and told their tales and flung their feeble light, and he understood, though perhaps he could not have said how he understood, that the darkness is held at bay by nothing more than habits and beliefs, customs and companions, the simple daily routines of work and pleasure. He lacked the words, but he had the feelings, the more-than-feelings, there in the midst of the forest, caught up in his memory and his mood. He saw that the darkness is never diminished, it is merely obscured, understood that sooner or later in this world of flux and loss the towers would topple, the light beams flicker and die. Eventually the stars themselves must blink out and the sky become black—even over America.

He shuddered, pulling himself back from the dizzy verge of his insight. Once upon a time he had drawn a circle around his life, and he could not go beyond it. A familiar warm, damp sensation at the tip of his business caught his attention, breaking the spell that memory had cast over him. Shuddering again, still smelling the sourness of his own sweat, he urinated against a tree, the long, hot stream carrying away with it his previous mood. Ah, that was better. As though a door had opened, his thoughts came back to him, some familiar portion of his mind talking to him urgently once more in his own familiar voice. Let's see now: how much money would he need? Say eighty or ninety thousand, good-faith money, enough, anyway, to go to the banks and renew those loans. Then he could pay off Dov, get him off his back. And where could he raise the eighty, ninety thou? Borrow it from the family, of course. God knows he had done enough for them over the years; let it be their turn to do for him. They owed him. And if they had to make some sacrifices to raise that kind of cash, hock their houses and cars and jewels, well that wouldn't kill them either.

He zipped himself up and went back into the cabin to wash his hands. His mind was occupied with schemes and plans as he kicked off his shoes and eased himself down onto the bed. The memory had receded; that odd nerve tingle had merged into mere excitement; and soon the excitement, too, began to recede. He was breathing steadily, dozing toward sleep, still in his clothes, still smelling himself, with the Coleman lamps hissing and glaring; and he could foresee the scene he would cause, the whole mob of Liebers gathered in someone's brightly lit living room with all their heat and noise, shouting and arguing about his proposal. Aching, grumbling, he turned onto his side, pulled his knees up, and slid his cold fingers between them. He warned himself to get up and turn off the lamps, but he was already half dreaming. Never mind, let them burn themselves out. The family would bellyache, but they would have to give him the money, they couldn't refuse. In the morning, after a good night's sleep, he would drive back and start figuring out the best way to approach them. Talk it over with Molly. Sure, might as well go home. There was nothing for him to do up in the woods by himself, and a whole week of it would make him *meshuggeh*.

One last fading echo of his dread sounded somewhere beyond the commonplaces of his drowsy thoughts, one last whiff of his father's ancient fear made him shudder once more and pull himself up even tighter into himself; then it was gone. He was almost asleep now, and they were all there with him, all talking around him at once, the whole inevitable noisy mob of his family. If only they would shut their mouths and listen to him, he could explain everything, he knew just what to say. But no, they wouldn't listen to him, they never listened, not them. They were too busy talking, too busy shouting and arguing, around him and through him, their voices loud and furious, selfish and expectant, joining and separating and joining again until it was all a chaotic babble within him—and they would go on like that, talking, shouting, arguing, until he was so utterly asleep that he no longer knew he was dreaming.

DEANNA'S FIRST LOVER, not counting Roxanne, was a girl named Nola, whom she met on the registration line her first week at NYU. It happened so casually, so easily, that later Deanna understood that she had been anticipating her initiation for a long, long time. Nola lived in a single room above an Italian restaurant on West Fourth Street. She had a pair of silvery, secretive cats, and a reproduction of Picasso's brooding portrait of Gertrude Stein glaring down from the wall. Her only furniture was a glass coffee table, a clutter of big pillows, and a small desk, where she wrote lots of sincere and jagged free verse, which Deanna pretended to admire. When it came time for bed, Nola pulled a roll of foam rubber out of the closet, opened it on the floor, and spread layers of bright purplish Indian cotton over it. For most of her freshman year, once or twice a week, Deanna slept with Nola on that makeshift bed. They never touched each other in the evening or the morning, but in the middle of the night they would wake each other up and grope together in the darkness. Light made Nola shy. She didn't want Deanna to see her naked. She had a boyfriend back home in Kentucky and she was planning to marry him. She liked to pretend she was a bride roused up on her wedding night, with Deanna cast as the patient groom, slowly, gently, lovingly arousing her. She would lie there passive and virginal and still while Deanna kissed her and unbuttoned her nightgown and touched her breasts, but when Deanna slid her fingers down between her legs, she would press her thighs tight together and begin to tremble. At that point Deanna was supposed to whisper love words and reassurances to her, kiss her some more, and stroke her long hair before Nola would finally relent. Moaning, still trembling, she would make the necessary adjustments, pulling Deanna down onto her, opening the warm wet center of herself, and then all hell would break loose—she would writhe and holler and scream and scratch, as though she were in awful struggle not with Deanna's careful, curious strokes and probes but with her own rising excitement. For those few moments she was all aching, ecstatic nerve ends. At first Deanna envied what she took to be Nola's extravagant sensitivity; her own flesh, in contrast, seemed sluggish and clumsy in response to sexual pleasure. Later she figured out that Nola was putting on an act for herself, that she had to feign the highest ecstacy to justify her shame, her surrender.

The artifice somehow made it easier for Deanna. She was still living at home in those days, riding the subway, but at three o'clock in the morning in that small, cozy, make-believe space of Nola's apartment, Deanna could believe that Brooklyn, parents, family, school, the rigmarole and conventions of normal waking life were far away. A circle had been drawn, an incantation uttered, a magical space invoked; and in that space Deanna could explore in relative safety the tortuous secrets of her desires and her nature. Nola's theatricality, the way she surrounded their gropings with pretense and darkness, as if they touched only in dreams, gave Deanna a sense of absolution. She didn't have to name, or even see, the things they did. They were like children at play in a secret playhouse from which they could emerge in daylight with their childish innocence more or less intact. Thus Deanna was amazed and wounded when toward the end of their friendship, during one of those earnest and terrible quarrels that eventually broke them apart, Nola screamed at her those words she would have to cough up later for her quizzical psychotherapist.

"You're nothing but a filthy lesbian, that's what you are!"

Amazed, shocked even, because that epithet was like a beam of light casting a shadowy form Deanna simply didn't recognize. Now she felt compelled to measure herself against that form, but no matter how much she turned and stretched, she couldn't make it fit. Lesbians were those squat, tough-faced, leathery women she saw marching their slavering dogs through the streets of the West Village. The very sight of them made Deanna's heart flutter in panic and a dull ache start up in the pit of her stomach. She couldn't imagine herself being akin to them. As far as she was concerned, they might have sprung up full-grown out of a different earth, created by nothing more than their own homage to a perverse principle, moving through their own mysterious and disconnected world. They seemed to trail no homes, no families, no childhoods in their hostile wake. No, they were a race of aliens, and whatever bizarre, unthinkable acts they performed upon each other on their stained and uncomfortable mattresses had nothing to do with her own vivid and unique urges. She was not a lesbian; she was, well, a thwarted boy trapped in the wrong flesh; she was the handsome baby prince cursed at birth by some hideous old witch and flung, with missing parts, into the coarse and unknowing and inescapable society of Lieberdom. Thus, for her, falling in love with girls was "only natural," while to let a boy touch her would be loathsome and queer. But it was girls, not lesbians, she wanted. Her heart was stirred by the sweetest, frailest, most wide-eyed and slender and absolutely girlish teenagers, the same sort of creatures her brother, at an earlier age, might have been attracted to. Her imagination pulsed with tender, gentle seduction scenes. Phrases out of the "blue" books that had been passed around in high school floated through the purple fog of her longing. In the months after her breakup with Nola she carried those phrases home to Brooklyn, home to her familiar bed, and there, in a flurry of "heaving breasts" and "pale thighs" and "soft love flesh" enfolding "throbbing members," she would stroke away her impossible cravings. During that time she had no bedmates, and her only friends were the sad, plump, sexless co-eds with whom she played bridge; for love she had just those dreamy, languid images of strangers, after-school beatniks roaming the Village streets, and like some shy, repressed, thoroughly nice Jewish boy, she was afraid to approach them.

She would tell her therapist that it was the worst period of her life, worse even, in its way, than Florida. Her mother would say to her, "So *nu*, are you meeting any fellows at school? You know, maybe if you put on a dress and wash your face and fix up your hair, one of them might even ask you out. A gorgeous girl like you, and you let yourself go this way and not care about your looks. What's the matter with you?" In fact, she did care about her looks, wanted to be handsome; but to be overweight, to have pimples on her face, to let her hair curl and tangle any which way excused her from the complications of a normal social life. The easiest way to deal with her mother's expectations was to let her go on thinking boys weren't interested in her. But it led to fights. Her mother would nag and nag until Deanna lost her temper; then would come those scenes of yelling and crying, of guilt and recriminations, with her poor father grumbling to himself in the background. It kept getting worse and worse until their anguish finally drove all three of them into a kind of unanticipated reasonableness; they sat down around the kitchen table one night and worked out a budget that would allow Deanna to continue school and live in a place of her own.

Thus she moved to the Village. She found an apartment near Bleecker Street, furnished it with family castoffs—tables and lamps from Aunt Essie, books from Aunt Molly, a well-worn couch from Uncle Moe—and settled in. Those were the days of coffeehouses and folksingers and cool, pale jazz wafting on a cloud of strange, sweet smoke from the dim-lit doorways of bars, and Deanna alternately loved the place and feared it. She liked gallivanting down Eighth Street past the bookshops and record stores and jewelry boutiques and hot dog stands, stared at by all the "square" sightseers who had left their bus around the corner as though she were part of the local color they had come to absorb. She liked feeding herself, and keeping her own hours, and striking up conversations with strangers in the grocery store, and walking back and forth from her classes—or not going to classes at all if such was her mood—freed from her mother's watchfulness and the loathsome subway. But sometimes at night, alone in her apartment, separated by nothing more than a cracked, dirty window from the loud, partying, moon-struck streets of the Village, she felt miserable and frightened. Out there anything was possible; out there her most hideous fantasies might spring to life; out there hard-faced alien shadows of no particular gender were waiting to catch her, seduce her into their nastiness, make her one of their own.

Later, when she had acquired theory and practice to explain herself, when she would march in parades of liberation and flaunt her "preference" in the eyes of the world, when she not only had come out of the closet but was trying to push her friends out with her, she would look back at those months of confusion and anxiety and wonder at the human capacity to confound desire with repulsion. But at the time she sensed that she was drifting between two worlds, neither of which was really her own. Some warped glassy space seemed to separate her from things. Out on the sunbright streets momentary configurations of light and shadow tormented her eyes; at night she would climb into bed and her heart would race and her breath would ache in her parched throat. She started taking in dogs just to have some simple, unproblematical, living flesh around her. Sometimes she would have to leave the Village altogether and go running back to her family. She would drop in on her Aunt Molly or her Aunt Ruthie, or ask her cousin Joey, who was up at Columbia, to meet her in midtown for a movie or a meal. Among her relatives she was more or less safe; their gossip couldn't hurt her.

Pensive, lonely, she tried to "find herself" as an artist. She painted pictures of clowns and matadors in bright acrylics on black velvet, framed them herself, and sold them on commission at a local tourist trap. When springtime came, she entered the arts fair and sat all weekend in Washington Square with her hackwork hung on the wall behind her. She had a certain facility of line, and a flair for contrasts, but she lacked the patience for authentic painting. She could copy, but she couldn't conceive, and she was too easily bored. She couldn't understand why anyone would want to spend hours and hours trying to capture the elusive image of an inspired moment. But she had acquired somewhere the easy notion that if she could make herself into an artist, everything else about her would fall into place. Art was the key piece without which the puzzle of her life would remain forever fragmented and unfinished. Art would justify her uniqueness, her isolation—if only she could figure out what sort of artist she wanted to be. So she dabbled, as though dabbling were the proper precondition for authentic work. Aside from the clowns and matadors, she acquired the knack of doing flowers—peonies and such—in thick slabs of primary color spread on the canvas with a palette knife. She made "cute" sketches of dogs with big, sad, human eyes. She bought a butane torch and soldered together nuts and bolts and bits of miscellaneous hardware to devise monkeys and acrobats. She ventured into silk screen and copper enameling, tie dying and ceramic pots. It was all imitative stuff, glossy and insincere, but it sold. This amused her. The tourists might just as well have been carrying home with them, to hang on their walls and set on their shelves, the indifferent parings of her fingernails.

Then there was her photography. She started accumulating reconditioned cameras and darkroom equipment, and when she was in a certain kind of mood, she would go around taking pictures of everything. To walk the streets with a camera gave her a sense of safety; the weight of it on her chest was like a talisman or a shield. She learned that when she stared at people through a camera, they would focus on it (mentally primping themselves) and forget about her—she might have been invisible. She could bring her camera to those family occasions at which her mother insisted she appear, and so long as she kept fiddling and focusing, her relatives left her alone and didn't ask embarrassing questions. Eventually she took down her paintings and put up enlargements of photographs that she liked—an old man, a fat man, a silversmith at work—but she still considered photography more fun than art, a continuation of a childhood hobby, a way of holding onto a piece of the elusive past. It occurred to her that photography was all that remained of the child she had been, and that between herself and her cameras there was a kind of gentle communion which nothing could disrupt. When she blanketed her windows and turned on the safelights and shut her mischievous dogs into the kitchen to keep them out of the chemicals, when her whole apartment had been converted into a big darkroom, a feeling of ease came over her; only then was her life not monstrously twofold.

During that time the family kept saying about Deanna that she was a "real kook," but that they "adored" her. They loved the way, when she dropped in on them, usually at mealtime, she could make them laugh. She was like Molly in the old days, they said, loud and brash and funny, hiding her *tsurris* behind her big mouth. And like Molly at that age, Deanna was wild. They had heard from Evelyn that there was no controlling her, that she lived among the beatniks and did as she pleased. She was still registered at NYU, but it was no longer a secret that she would never graduate; if you asked her what she was studying, she would laugh and say, "Bridge." She went around in denim shirts and paint-stained jeans as though she would never outgrow being a tomboy. Her eyes were red-rimmed from too little sleep and she had cut that gorgeous black hair of hers down to a mannish bob, claiming she had no time to take care of it. But what kept her so busy? Boys apparently didn't interest her. She mentioned friends, but you never got to meet any of them. The way she acted the family could imagine the craziest things. Moe, the *gantze* doctor, thought maybe she was on some kind of drug; Lou with his big mouth kept saying she was "a little butch," until the family shut him up. All they knew about for sure were her cameras and her dogs, and the dogs soon became a family joke. The number of them kept changing every time you talked to her. People would bring her strays and mutts and puppies, and she couldn't say no. When you visited her apartment—a privilege she reserved for only her few favorite relatives—her dogs would bark and leap and snap at your toes. Once, for a few weeks, she even had a monkey, who tore up her furniture and left little hard pebbles of excrement everywhere. The dogs, said Deanna, weren't pets; they were boarders. She tried hard not to fall in love with any of them, and when they were about to overrun her apartment, she would go on a campaign to find them new homes. The family laughed about how Deanna would call up out of the blue to ask if they wanted, or knew anyone who wanted, a "really fantastic little pup." She would show up in her battered old red Karmann Ghia with some pathetic, filthy rag of a thing quivering in a carton on the back seat. How could you refuse to take it in? Pretty soon half the Lieber cousins were raising Deanna's dogs. Every week she called up to see how the dogs were getting along and to give explicit instructions for feeding and bathing and grooming and shots, making you feel that she might swoop down at any moment to retrieve the poor thing from your negligent grasp. She spent so much time worrying about the dogs, the family said, she ought to go into the business. That was Deanna. Whatever she did, she was lovable and exasperating, and everyone knew that she made Evelyn eat her heart out. And all you kept hearing from Evelyn was how she wished Deanna would meet a nice boy and "settle down."

"Why," Evelyn would wail, "can't she be like everyone else?"

Well, she tried. Every so often she would meet some guy and strike up a friendship. She didn't hate males; she rather enjoyed their companionship, man to man, so to speak; but in the end she would have to make it clear that sex wasn't going to be part of the arrangement. Sooner or later every guy she got to know well took it into his head to "cure" her. She found herself involved in ugly scenes. Mild, pacifist poets in baggy pants and granny glasses, after eating the meal she had prepared and listening to her records, turned vicious and randy. The apparently effeminate fellows who ran the tourist traps in which she sold her craftwork would, upon getting her alone in the back room, start breathing in her ear and trying to feel her breasts. One time a guy named Paul, who later made a name for himself in a rock band in California, pulled out his nonsensical penis and waved it at her, saying: "Touch it, just touch it, I swear to God it will change your life." She had to become hard-boiled to protect herself.

Then she met Rita. More or less by accident they both reached for the same can of tomato paste in the grocery store, their fingers touched, and one thing led to another. Rita was twenty-six years old and formerly married, a gay divorcée with a sulky kid stashed away somewhere "back home," but stripped of her artsy layers of clothes and beads, she couldn't have weighed more than ninety pounds—and with her glossy blond hair pouring down her small shoulders and her gold crucifix hanging between her perfect miniature breasts, she looked more or less like the incarnate teenage temptress of Deanna's fantasies. That's what made their "arrangement" possible. Rita worked in some agency uptown by day and wove elaborate tapestries on a handloom at night. She had scars on her wrists, but had learned to "accept herself," and was wholly practical about her affairs. She introduced Deanna to massages amd marijuana and dildos. She gave her books to read which "explained everything" in protective jargon. Under Rita's tutelage Deanna added the word "androgynous" to her vocabulary of self-definition. She took Deanna to off-Broadway shows and out-of-the-way art galleries, where Deanna was astonished to find photographs hanging among the watercolors and oils, and introduced her to all the "right" places on Fire Island and in the Hamptons. She also taught her some marvelous nimble tricks involving fingers and tongues. But their best hours together were when they sat around naked after the brisk and efficient bed business and talked about things. Rita's big Italian family was a hilarious counterpoint to the noisy mob of Liebers, and so long into the night they would swap stories and anecdotes about their relatives, giggling until they were giddy. In a more serious mood Rita would get Deanna to do the talking—she had acquired among other things in her years of analysis the knack of "bringing people out." Rita might be girlish in bed, but during those moments she was comfortably maternal. She resolved that Deanna should conquer her fears by confronting them, and so she dragged her to "women only" bars, and taught her how to drink tequila sunrises and stare down "pushy dykes." Then they would go home and eat a midnight spaghetti dinner glistening with olive oil beneath candles stuck in wax-clotted Chianti bottles; or they would smoke a joint or two and raid the kitchen for a lemon or a bottle of vanilla extract, delighting themselves with the simple truth that a sensitized tongue can relish the sour and the bitter as well as the sweet. What fun they had! Rita was Deanna's good fairy, undoing some old witch's malignant spell. Until one day Rita said it was time for both of them to "move on" to other people and other experiences. Only then, in anguish, did Deanna realize that the word "love" had never been uttered between them.

That was in the spring of 1963, just a few weeks before Deanna's father disappeared. Deanna was to discover that consoling her mother was a way of consoling herself. Rita had untangled, among other things, some of the strings of feeling that bound Deanna to that hysterical woman. Eventually she would seek other lovers, but in the meantime, she would practice being "nice." Not that she had a choice. Her brother was more cut out for the job—her brother made a fetish of being "nice"—but her brother had decided after passing the bar to stay out west. He was married now and had a kid of his own to worry about; and anyway, his notion of helping was that their mother should move out there with him, to what he insisted on calling "the land of the big blue sky," as if the poor woman could possibly be happy away from friends and family and the routines of Brooklyn. Which left it up to Deanna. Three or four times a week she would call her mother on the phone and settle herself down on the couch with her dogs playing and nipping around her while she listened to her mother's latest tales of woe. Like so many of the women of her generation, her mother, in hardship, was turning into a crab. There had been times when Deanna used to wonder why her father had bothered to concoct such an elaborate stunt when, if leaving her mother was what he had in mind, he could have simply walked through the door; but in those months, with her mother playing like a virtuoso on strings of guilt and compassion, Deanna came to believe she understood the man. That woman was impossible. She ground every aspect of her life into undifferentiated misery. She started taking driving lessons at Deanna's urging—"Ma, you'll have to learn to be independent!"—but her instructor made her nervous, her feet didn't reach the pedals, and she was scared of left turns. She needed a new television set because the old one was all snow and ghosts, but Deanna's father had left her without any money, she cried, and never mind that everyone thought she was a millionaire. Her woe was endless. The neighbors in her new apartment played loud music all night long; her sister Molly kept complaining about a pain in her behind, but refused to see a doctor; next week was Bobbi's *bas mitzvah*, in some fancy place in Great Neck—how could she show up in that old *shmateh* of a dress everyone had seen before? It got to the point where Deanna would have to smoke a joint to get through the conversation.

"Listen," she would want to scream, "don't you think I have problems of my own?"

That's why Deanna didn't pay much attention when her mother started mentioning her brother Sam's business troubles, why, it scarcely registered through the haze of her preoccupations when she heard that Sam was going around the family, asking for money. She figured this was just more of the same old thing. Money, after all, borrowings and lendings, was the glue, Deanna believed, that held them together. For years the Liebers had been quarreling with each other, going round and round about something or other, but nothing ever broke the circle, nothing *serious* ever happened to them. As far as Deanna was concerned, her relatives lived in a closed, permanent world from which the significant events of the universe were excluded. Thus she was astonished one November morning to hear her mother on the phone not *kvetching*, not whining, but telling her in the calm voice of authentic misery that Sam was going into bankruptcy, the factory was lost, and, the worst part, he was so angry at the family that he wasn't talking to them anymore.

"Not talking?" said Deanna. "What do you mean, 'not talking'?"

"Not talking," her mother replied, and Deanna could perceive through her tone a vivid picture: her mother in a housedress without any makeup, with no eyebrows and flushed skin, chewing her pale lower lip, struggling against tears.

"Not talking is not talking. What more can I say?"

For a moment Deanna felt some force, some emotional gravity, tugging at her. Her impulse was to race to Brooklyn to try to talk them out of this craziness; but she pulled back against it, let it go. She had her own life to live, her own dark wilderness to explore, and she just couldn't see, in the final analysis, how what happened among the older generation of Liebers was any business of hers.

THE GREAT "BATTLE ROYAL," as the family later called it, took place in the autumn of 1963. It was as though an expert hand had rapped once along the fault line of some semiprecious gem and shattered the thing to pieces. For a time everyone was mad at everyone else. No one expected it, no one wanted it, but no one could do anything to prevent it. During those brooding, climactic weeks they were like puppets jerked and twitched by old strings of feeling tangled like a maze among them. Later, looking back, they would wonder how it could have happened.

"Money," they would say, "it was all because of money. Money and family don't mix."

But they must have known that it was more than the money, more than the demands Sam was making on them. So much misunderstanding, so much rage and bitterness, they said, could only be explained by the old taint of strangeness that ran in the Lieber blood.

It began amiably enough. Everyone knew about Sam's business troubles and no one was particularly surprised when Molly started coming around and making demands. The family had even anticipated that Sam wouldn't come himself; they understood how hard that would be for him, understood his pride and dignity. But they were annoyed that Molly claimed she was acting on her own initiative. No one could believe that. In those days Molly was living in a hotel room near Manhattan Beach. The family knew that two or three times a week Sam would pick Molly up on his way home from work and bring her to his house for supper—knew because Carrie had been calling her aunts and complaining about this burden on her mother. Okay, Molly was Sam's favorite, it was natural for her to act as his agent and confidante. But why lie about it, why go through such an elaborate charade? It turned out that Molly and Sam had even concocted between them a list of how much they believed each of the Liebers could afford to contribute, but at first Molly refused to mention numbers. Who did she think she was kidding? She would sit there in their living rooms, breathless and belligerent, explaining Sam's predicament and reminding them of everything they owed him. Shamelessly, like a blackmailer, she would drag up ancient history, all the jobs and loans and presents and favors, as if she believed that prodding their memories would send them running to Sam to surrender up their bank accounts, their insurance policies, their homes, their fur coats, their diamond rings, their pension funds, everything. She made it sound as though she were giving Sam her last penny and expected them to do the same. That irked people.

"What does she think?" said Ruthie. "That when it comes to caring about Sam she has a monopoly?"

You have to picture it. In those days Molly was fatter than ever—there was no telling how much she weighed. Pink, mottled flesh hung in great loose sacks from her upper arms and bunched in infantile folds around her wrists and knuckles. With her three or four chins, her face appeared to be resting on a stack of tires. It was alarming to see the obese and precarious bulk of her moving along above her smallish, almost dainty feet. She was always out of breath, always perspiring, always too hot, as though her massive flesh produced a radiant heat of its own. She would come in gasping and wheezing, settle her ponderous weight down on some poor creaking chair, and start talking a mile a minute, mopping herself with the handkerchief she kept balled up in her sleeve. Gold gleamed in the pink wet chasm of her mouth; her bright orange-tinted hair flared like a beacon; her green eyes—still beautiful, still ablaze with hunger and enchantment —would flash around seeking a soothing surface to settle on. Five ruinous marriages may have soured Molly's view of men in general, but Sam, as far as she was concerned, could do no wrong. If Sam said it, it must be so; his word was like law. Not even his own wife, she used to brag to people, understood him the way she did. So in his hour of need she was mustering all her vast energy to help him out. She even, at one point, went storming into Dov Kalisher's office without an appointment and spent half an hour talking, wheedling, arguing, shouting, while Dov sat there, cold as a fish, with his eyes fixed not on her face but on her massive bosom. That was Molly, still *die vildekeh* after all these years. She badgered and bullied and blustered. She made everything emotional. With Molly involved, what might have been discussed in an orderly way, with give-and-take on both sides, turned into chaos. No wonder that after her visits the family would get on the phone with each other to bellyache and spread rumors.

They told each other they were sympathetic; they were aware of their debts to Sam and would help him as much as they could; but there was a right way and a wrong way of doing things. Sam could have swallowed his pride a little, not sent Molly to do his bidding. Moe and Walter were miffed because Sam hadn't come to them in person, talked over his problems man to man. Ruthie and Evelyn complained that they were being asked to make sacrifices when Essie and Rich went right on spending. Why, even while Molly was making the rounds of the family, Essie was vacationing in the Poconos. The sisters were livid. It was like the old days, they said, when Essie settled herself like a princess into the apartment on Park Place and the whole family catered to her.

"Let him first hock Essie's wardrobe," said Evelyn, "then come running to us."

Soon the gossip around the family grew so bitter that Rose took it upon herself to talk to Sam. Dragging Georgie along with her, since she never went anywhere without him except when he was at the workshop, she marched herself into Sam's office and told him bluntly that sending Molly to the family was asking for trouble.

"What do you want from me?" Sam told her. "That I should come begging on my hands and knees? That I should humiliate myself in front of you? Molly's doing what I asked her to do—isn't that good enough?"

"No," said Rose.

She suggested that they hold a meeting, just the brothers and sisters, to clear the air. Sam didn't like the idea. Gather the bunch of them in one room, he argued, and there was bound to be quarreling and hard feelings. But Rose talked him into it.

"So," she said, "so we'll quarrel, we'll blow off steam. It won't be the first time. Look, Sammy, believe me, we want to help, we know how much we owe you."

So he agreed, and now Rose started making the rounds, trying to get everyone to settle on a date. That wasn't easy. First Moe and Laura went flying off to Europe on some kind of long-planned guided tour of Anne Frank's house and Hitler's summer retreat and various concentration camp sights—this, snorted Sam when he heard about it, was his brother's idea of a vacation. Next Ben's wife had a death in the family, so while she attended the funeral and sat *shivah*, Evelyn had to fly out to help take care of the baby. Then Deborah announced that she was going to California for a few days to talk to some people about a book she had written. The family had no idea Deborah was writing a book. Everyone got all excited. What kind of book, they wanted to know, a ghost story, a novel, maybe something about them? But when they asked her what it was about, she shrugged, as mysterious as ever, and said: "Things." Then, with typical lucklessness, Rose took Georgie to the doctor for a routine checkup and discovered he had a hernia. An operation had to be scheduled. Georgie was twenty years old, and weighed two hundred pounds, and when he looked at you through his thick glasses with that smile of his spreading slowly across his round face, you thought that he understood everything; but he still had the mind of a child, and Rose would have to sleep in the hospital with him.

Finally Sam lost his patience.

He called her up and said: "Look, you're arranging a meeting—so arrange! I've got a deadline to meet. This business can't wait forever."

That's when Rose blew her stack and let him have it.

"Business," she scolded him. "With you it's always business. Nothing matters but the business. The business excuses you from everything. Tell me, Sam, how come all these years you don't go out to visit your brother Hymie? You think if you pay the bills that's enough?"

Sam was stunned. "What does Hymie have to do with it?"

"Hymie," she said scornfully, "has everything to do with it," which finished the conversation.

The family finally agreed to meet on a Sunday in the middle of November. Now it became an argument about where they should gather. Molly said the obvious place would be Sam's house, but Ruthie complained it was too far away. "Let those who have cars do the traveling!" she said. Moe also objected. He argued that it would be easier to talk openly if they met on what he called neutral ground. Molly got furious with him. What was neutral ground? Did he think they should hire a catering hall?

"Imagine," she told Sam. "Neutral ground no less. This is what comes with a college education."

They went round and round about it, dragging the others in until Rose said they should come to her place. That would solve the problem of what to do with Georgie while the meeting was going on—she could move the television into the bedroom and plunk him down in front of it. But Sam didn't want to go to Rose's place; he was still sore about the phone call.

"For cryin' out loud," Molly told him, "let it be Rose's place, let it be anyplace, just let's get it done with."

She was disgusted with the whole bunch of them, including Sam, and as always happened when she was aggravated, she went on an eating binge. She ate so much chocolate that she couldn't move her bowels. For weeks she walked around with a pain in her behind, which kept getting worse. She raged and cried until Sam agreed to go to Rose's place. But the rest of the family wasn't finished with her yet.

All along it was assumed that just the brothers and sisters would meet; now, at the last minute, Lou Grossman opened his big yap to say that if he wasn't invited, he wouldn't allow Ruthie to come.

"Ruthie's a big girl," Molly told him on the phone, "she can do what she wants."

"That's what you think," Lou responded. "When it comes to the do-re-mi, I'm the one who makes the decisions."

That started another brouhaha.

Moe said that if Lou was coming, he would stay home. He might have to tolerate "that blowhard" on social occasions, but he had no intention of doing business with him.

Evelyn said she didn't care if Lou came or not—she would side with Ruthie either way. But if Moe didn't come, she added, there was no point to a meeting. After all, Moe was the one with the money.

Then Walter chimed in to say if Lou was going to be there, Sarah would be there, too. Fair was fair, and he was sick of Sarah always being left out.

"What do you mean 'left out'?" Molly asked him.

Which made it Walter's turn to explode. For ten minutes he harangued Molly about how all these years he had to live with the fact that his sisters disapproved of his wife, that they laughed at her behind her back and refused to accept her.

"And I know why, too," he said. "Because Sarah managed to get an education, and they're jealous of her!"

Molly could scarcely believe that Walter, the mildest of her brothers, was saying such things. All the hidden bitterness of the past was coming out.

"No one's jealous of Sarah," she told him.

"They're not only jealous of Sarah," Walter came back at her. "They're jealous of Jeannie, too."

"Walter," Molly said, "you're being an imbecile."

"I may be an imbecile," he concluded, "but at least I'm not an ignoramus," and he hung up on her.

Saturday came and no one knew if the meeting was going to take place. Everyone was trying to call everyone else and the lines were always busy. Lou was still being stubborn. Evelyn was having hot flashes. Deborah kept saying that they were all acting like a bunch of children, but anyway, it would be better not to meet tomorrow because the time was not "propitious." Rose took the position that it was her house, and as far as she was concerned, Lou was not invited.

"Did you tell Lou that?" Evelyn asked her.

"I've been trying, but I can't get through."

It turned out that Lou was on the phone with Sam. For half an hour they raged and argued.

"What are you going to do with me, Sammy?" Lou said at one point. "Take me for another ride?"

Rich happened to be at Sam's house that morning and got so mad at Lou that Sam couldn't control him. Half an hour later he went storming into Ruthie's house, shouting:

"Where is that son-of-a-bitch uncle of mine? I'm going to break both his legs!"

Jeff had come by that morning to drop off his kids so that he and his wife could go shopping for a new bed; he had no idea about the trouble in the family because even though Ruthie had told him about it, it hadn't really registered; all he knew was that the cousin he had always envied, this spoiled, backslapping, gladhanding showoff, was threatening his father. Words were exchanged. They stood bristling at each other like two hefty young animals. The next thing Ruthie knew her son and her nephew were tussling in her living room, threatening the furniture, while her husband was on the telephone shouting obscenities at her sister Rose.

To Jeff and Rich she said: "Cut it out! You're not so big that I can't still smack the both of you!"

To Lou she said: "Shut your big trap already and give me that phone!"

To Rose she said: "I'll be there tomorrow, by myself. Anything to get out of this madhouse!"

So the meeting took place with just the eight brothers and sisters. They could not recall another time when they had been together like that, with no parents or children or in-laws to come between them. It made them feel naked, exposed. Memories of old wounds gathered like ghosts in the overheated air, and the words they were uttering seemed almost superfluous. In one way they knew each other too well for words; in another way they hardly knew each other at all. They knew what they had been to each other in the days of their growing up, knew the old lines of relationship that the years had subtly altered, even torn. What they didn't know is what they were at that moment, and what they were already becoming as they talked at each other, their excited voices creating an imponderable future.

"Stop shouting!" Rose kept saying. "I'm sure we can settle this if we stop shouting!"

And Molly, at the top of her lungs: "Who's shouting? You're the only one who's shouting!"

And Moe, bitterly: "Oh shut up, Molly! It's you that's causing all the trouble."

"Me? Me? Oh, sure, I'm the one, sure!"

And Evelyn: "This is ridiculous. Between the two of them you can't get a word in edgewise."

And Ruthie: "Would you stop feeling sorry for yourself?"

"Who's feeling sorry? What are you talking?"

"Ever since Milton left, she walks around all day living on self-pity."

And Walter: "Let's get on with it, for cryin' out loud."

And Evelyn: "The delegate from Russia speaks."

And Molly: "Listen to her! And they call me the troublemaker."

"Who's calling you a troublemaker?"

"My baby brother with the college education, that's who's calling me a troublemaker."

"Calm yourself down, Molly."

"I should be calm? How can I be calm? You're all beating around the bush, and you call me a troublemaker. Have you ever heard of such a thing?"

"Stop shouting! I'm sure we can settle this if we just stop shouting!"

Round and round, back and forth, like waves battering a seawall, subsiding, gathering force out of dark hidden currents, rushing forward again until the seawall bursts.

"What are we fighting about? God in heaven! It's just money."

"Sure, when you've got it, it's just money. But when you don't have it, what are you supposed to do? Hock your life away?"

"And what if we lend Sam the money and the business goes under anyway? Then where are we? In six months he comes back asking for more?"

"And what about Rich and Carrie? How come they're not being asked to sell their houses and give up their cars?"

"From children you don't take. Children you give. When it comes right down to it, children don't owe their parents a damn thing."

"Sure."

"Easy for you to say because you don't have any."

"My sister has a mouth I wouldn't want to fall into."

"Look who's talking."

"I think you've all gone crazy."

"You know if Sam had half the money he spent on his wife, he wouldn't have to come running to us."

"Listen to her, the jealous sister!"

"This isn't getting us anywhere."

"Deborah's right."

"As far as I'm concerned, Sam can have everything I own. But what do I own besides the dress on my back? If it'll help, he can have that."

"Come on, who are you kidding?"

"Here we go again."

"Listen to him, my big shot baby brother. I haven't heard yet what you're going to contribute."

"I'll do what I can."

"Sure, we'll all do what we can. But what we don't have, we can't give."

"I'm glad someone finally said it."

"Look, as far as that goes, I'm prepared to write a check right now. But the timing is bad. I'm in the middle of redoing my office. My cash is tied up."

"Listen to him. If he's going to plead poverty, what do you expect from us?"

"I'm not pleading poverty—and I don't have to take that kind of crap from you."

"Come on, everyone knows you have more money than God."

"That car alone that you drive can save the factory."

"Okay, attack me as though it were all my fault. A lot of good that will do you."

"No one's attacking you."

"Leave him alone."

"Who's not leaving him alone?"

"If only we could stop shouting at each other!"

"Why doesn't Sam say something? He sits there, the quiet one, and lets everyone do his fighting for him."

"Can't you see you're killing him? What do you want him to say?"

"No one's killing anyone."

"And I wish you'd stop acting like you're the only one who cares about him."

"At least I've proved that I care."

"What? You don't think I've eaten my heart out over this? You don't think I was awake in bed all night eating my heart out?"

"Sarah Bernhardt!"

"Look who's talking!"

"Sam, say something already, Sam!"

"I'm sorry, but when it comes to loyalty, I have nothing to prove."

"So who said you did?"

"She did. My sister with the big mouth!"

"Sure, sure."

Sure. And when Mama was sick, who took care of her, who carried her bedpans and fed her like she was an infant and washed the shit

318

off her sheets? Who? Molly? No, not Molly. Molly was too busy. Molly had to find another husband."

"Cut it out, Evelyn!"

"No, I won't cut it out! Why should I? You talk about loyalty! As though we haven't made sacrifices. What about Hymie? All these years who runs to see him? Who sits there with him and holds his hand and listens to his *mishegoss* and comes home sick to the stomach about it every time?"

"No one forces you."

"No one forces me, she says!"

"Now wait a minute. Right is right. And don't think it hasn't hurt Hymie all these years that you and Sam don't go to see him."

"We're not the only ones."

"Oh, sure, that's a good excuse."

"Just listen to the bunch of you. You ought to be ashamed!"

"We're telling the truth. We don't have to be ashamed."

"Thank God Mama's not here to see this day!"

"Thank God is right!"

"And Sam sits like a sphinx saying nothing."

"Believe me, he's the only smart one."

"And you, too, Moe. You also could go see your brother once in a while. You and Walter, the great college graduates. As though we didn't work like dogs so our brothers could go to college, for all the thanks we ever got."

"Hey, no one stopped you from going to college."

"No one stopped me? Mama says, boys go to college, girls get married. What, you think I don't have the same brains as you, that you're so much smarter than me? So I spend my life married to a *shlump* and in the end have *bupkiss*, while your fancy society wife can't even pick up the phone and say hello."

"Stop already!"

"Just leave Laura out of it."

"Leave Laura out of it, he says!"

"You heard me!"

"Calm down, Moe! You'll give yourself another ulcer."

"I've never heard such goings-on. Can you please stop shouting!"

"I can't believe I'm sitting here listening to this crap."

"We're getting away from the subject everybody."

"Uh! A word from the peanut gallery."

"Oh, for cryin' out loud!"

"Calm yourself down, Ev."

"Calm? How can I be calm? I'm sitting here with hot flushes and they tell me to be calm."

"I told you, that's the way she's been ever since Milton went."

"I've got two words for you, too."

"This is not getting us anywhere."

"So why doesn't Sam say a word? This was his idea."

"Now wait a minute. It wasn't Sam's idea, it was mine."

"And you, too, Rose. You don't have to pretend to be such a saint."

"You're like a bunch of babies."

"We're babies and she's grown-up! That's a nice switch."

"Where's Sam going?"

"Oh, for cryin' out loud!"

"See, bigmouth?"

"Sam?"

"Where's he going?"

"Sammy!"

He was moving. It would have been better to walk directly out the door; but he had to go into the bedroom to get his hat and coat, and that made it awkward. Rose's living room was small, crowded; he would have to squeeze through them, stumble over their knees to get there. Then, the hardest part, he would have to come back through the living room to leave.

He chose a complicated path that took him outside the grouping they had formed, plotted it out in his mind so that he wouldn't stumble over a lamp or an end table, took a deep breath as if he were about to plunge into deep water, and went. Dignified, weary, showing no emotion except for the ruddiness of his burning face, he navigated the space between Deborah and Molly, circled around behind Moe and Walter, and stepped into the bedroom, his ears buzzing slightly in the suspended tumult his moving had caused. He would never forget how he found Georgie sitting on the edge of Rose's coat-heaped bed, with all that peculiar concentrated rigidity of his kind, his moon face jutting forward and glowing bluish in the light of the television. On the screen a man in a scientist's smock was dropping circles of grease into two plates of dishwashing detergent: in plate one the grease just sat there, but in plate two the circle exploded like the primal atom and was gone. Then Georgie jerked his head around, grinning his idiot's grin.

"Ugga Sam," he said joyously, "Ugga Sam."

There was an instant when all Sam wanted in the world was to sit down next to the poor bastard and watch television with him; instead, he reached out and rubbed Georgie's scalp, the unpleasant feel of the thin, dark, bristly hair somehow paying off an old debt; then he dug his hat and coat out of the heap, took another deep breath, and plunged back through the living room.

"Where are you going, Sam?"

"You don't have to walk away mad."

"Sam, you're being ridiculous."

"Someone stop him. Don't let him go off like that."

"I told you this would be the result."

"Sam!"

"Where's he going?"

"Everybody's got to have a temper."

"Well, if you ask me, he doesn't have to be so bitter."

"Sam!"

Old, tense strings of feeling tugged against him as he fought his way through the living room, down two gloomy flights of stairs, and out onto the hushed street, where instinct took over. He stood there for a moment, breathless, glancing around him for potential dangers —some kid with a knife, some madman with a gun, lurking in the shadows—before climbing into his car. In the dry, itchy bundle of his overcoat, shivering and self-absorbed, half believing they would come running after him, only half wanting them to, he sat behind the steering wheel looking up at the bland façade of the apartment building, trying to pick out Rose's window. Third floor, go left. All these years and he still wasn't sure which window it was. But it didn't matter: they were all blinded; behind each of them, equally, no one loved anyone enough. Well, he was free of them now; he had no more obligations to them; they weren't his family anymore.

He became cool and calm and silent. He fumbled through stiff layers of clothing for his key, started the motor, and drove off, driving at random through the grid of Brooklyn streets because it was too early to go home. He longed for an open road where he could drive and drive and never turn back, but at every corner there was a stop sign or a traffic light. Should he go back to Rose's place, get down on his hands and knees, and beg them for the money? Had he been so wrong to expect them to help? What did he ever do to them to deserve this? His anger was flaring again. He saw a gray, shabby, hunched old man come out of a bright candy store with a newspaper tucked under his arm, pull his head down into his collar against the cold wind, and shamble off into the shadows. He told himself he might as well go home. Essie would be waiting for him, probably anticipating, today being Sunday, that he would take her out to eat. On Sundays, routinely, they went to Sheepshead Bay for fish. He could foresee how he would sit there in the warm, glaring uproar of the restaurant, with no appetite, watching Essie peck at her food, and how he would have to shake himself out of his moody silence to tell her what had happened. She wouldn't understand. She would listen to him, she would try to look serious and sympathetic; but she wouldn't understand.

"So you walked out on them?" she would say. "Even before they had a chance to say no? *Oy*, Sam, was that really the right thing to do?"

She would finish her meal in endless small mouthfuls, hardly chewing, refusing to be rushed. Then she would want dessert. He could see her powdering her face and putting on fresh lipstick, puckering her lips at herself in the little round compact mirror until she was satisfied, and he would have to sit there waiting for her in all his shame and agony, with his pulse beating ferociously in his ears as it was beating right now. Essie, Essie, Essie. He might lose everything else, but he still had, he always would have, her.

IN THE EXHILARATION OF HER FRESHMAN YEAR, on the front page of her notebook, Jeannie inscribed the following:

> J. Lieber
> 333 New Hall
> Barnard College
> Columbia University
> New York City
> New York State
> USA
> The Earth
> The Solar System
> The Milky Way
> The Universe
> ?

But it was just a notion she had stolen from a certain novel she was reading for her literature class, and it failed to satisfy her. In the process of self-definition, she concluded, one had to consider time as well as space, perhaps even time more than space, since geography is a matter of choice or accident while temporality—the throb of history in every gene—is a matter of fate. To know what you are, you have to know what you come from: family, species, class, phylum. She was fascinated, for example, by the simple arithmetic of generation, that everdoubling line of progenitors forking and reforking backward through the murky past. Consider: she had two parents, four grandparents, eight great-grandparents, and so on. Thus the sum of her ancestors was an exponential function, a dizzy arc curving toward infinity. Go back ten generations, say three hundred years, and you could presumably find 1,024 human beings, male and female, fathers and mothers, all somehow surviving the plagues and wars of what dear Professor Rosen called "a century almost as ghastly as our own" to contribute sperm and ova to her making. And ten generations before that, let's say, while Dante was dreaming about Paolo and Francesca, her ancestors numbered precisely—she had actually figured it out with pencil and paper—1,048,576. Presumably there was an error somewhere in her logic because if you kept on doubling, the numbers became impossible; in Roman times, she calculated, there would have been roughly 20,000 *trillion* souls on the planet, all of them donating precious chromosomal threads to the warm stream of her blood, and this itself was still just a small splash in the whole hazy ancestral sea; but she was content to leave logic aside for the moment (foreseeing that the paradox unraveled only through hypothesizing a kind of crossbreeding or incest) and try to imagine them all, a superfluity of ancestors, more numerous than the stars, inhabitants enough for a billion different worlds, and all of them coming together in dire and passionate and sometimes beautiful spasms so that in the fullness of time, at this oh-so-ripe moment, one Jeannie Leiber might appear upon the earth. Why, it was as though infinity itself had bowed down to worship her. A blissful thought: and in the soft enchanted glow of it her expectations flourished.

Jeannie, the family used to say—much to Walter's annoyance—was Deborah all over again. She had the same fine dark hair, the same high, romantic forehead, the same small exquisite nose, which suggested a touch of old aristocracy in the Lieber blood. Even her birthmark, ruddy and round, had come to resemble those circles of rouge out-of-date Deborah was still smearing on her white-powdered cheeks. And like Deborah, Jeannie was old for her age and had a streak of dreamy abstraction. You would be talking to her and suddenly she was off on a tangent—behind the dark shine of her eyes her brain was tracing its own winding path to its own peculiar conclusions. No wonder that despite Walter's misgivings, there had developed early on between Deborah and Jeannie a special sort of closeness. For the rest of her nieces and nephews Deborah exhibited little more than polite curiosity; you couldn't even count on her to remember their names; but when it came to Jeannie and Jeannie's achievements—her skipping grades, her perfect exam scores, her science fair prizes, her entry into college (Barnard no less!) at the age of sixteen—she *kvelled* and doted. During Jeannie's childhood she was always showing up at Walter's house with books and presents, always inviting her over to her own apartment, which none of the other nieces and nephews had ever even seen, for an afternoon of talk and tea. She went around saying that Jeannie had a "spiritualized" nature, and that a place of honor, a throne of genius, was awaiting her in the world to come—a notion to which Walter would nervously respond: "Let them not be in such a hurry!" At times Walter brooded over the dark spell his superstitious sister might weave around his daughter's eager and perhaps too vivid imagination, but in the end he put his trust in Jeannie's rationality, that sunny bloom of skepticism he had so painstakingly nourished; and besides, as Sarah reminded him, he had to be sensitive to Deborah's solitude and hunger: she was, said Sarah, merely bestowing upon Jeannie all the generous and thwarted love which, in a better world, might have belonged to a child of her own.

Jeannie, in fact, used to treasure her visits to Aunt Deborah's apartment, where light and shadow mingled dimly in air that was musty and scented with the dust of dried flowers. As she stood there making the adjustment from the bright, practical outer world, her aunt would already be thrusting at her a fruit bowl filled with apples and oranges and bananas, which were freckled brown—"That's how they're sweetest," Aunt Deborah used to say. It was, that apartment, with its antique fixtures and ornate furniture, a wonderful place to explore. There were shelves of books with titles that were quite different from the ones at home, and an old gramophone on which Aunt Deborah would play arias by dead opera singers, and all sorts of cabinets and curio closets chock-full of ceramic figurines, paperweights, bits of glass sculpture, and lots of old clocks, each one of which told its own time. And when you grew tired of exploring, you could go to the window and peek out through the heavy drapes at the distant gaudy clutter of Coney Island and the dark green-gray ocean stretching away to a misty rise of land that Jeannie liked to pretend was the shore of Europe, the dark Old World where Aunt Deborah herself, and Uncle Sam and Aunt Molly, were born. Then there was Aunt Deborah's bedroom, or rather a heavy wooden door, beyond which Jeannie was not permitted to go, and through which, just once, she believed she heard a voice—*his* voice, the voice of Aunt Deborah's dead lover, though of course she must have been imagining it. But that's how it was there. The spiced lemony vapors rising up out of the teacup would fog her senses so that her father's version of reality would fade, and freed now from his hopes and lessons— which at all other times she respected, even adored—she could pretend to believe the marvelous things her Aunt Deborah would tell her, after swearing her to secrecy, about the supernatural world of ghosts.

It was like a game they played, the two of them, assembling the bits and pieces of information Deborah had been given, and then, like blind people, trying to perceive through groping and touch the contours of a foreign land. Reluctantly at first, but later with a kind of pedagogical zeal, Aunt Deborah told her about Ruben Stern and the eternal nature of love, and about the place where Ruben now dwelled, a place which, as far as Jeannie could make out, resembled some lovely insubstantial cojoining of a park, a botanical garden, an art museum, and a concert hall. She learned about galleries of painting and sculpture far more beautiful than any on earth, and spectral orchestras which filled the ethereal air with the breath of music, and endless fields of never-wilting flowers in divine shades of blue and purple, and lovely white fountains from which gushed the sparkling water which nourished the multitudes of the dead. She heard from her aunt ("just as I heard it from him") that no one suffered in the next world, not even the sinners, for there was suffering enough on earth; and that the only pain, and a sweet pain it was, was the longing for lovers that had been left behind. Because just like men and women on earth the ghosts joined themselves together to achieve pleasure and completion, and only those ghosts who are wedded to the souls of the living are driven back to earth to linger with, to wait for, their loved ones.

"So when I die," Aunt Deborah would say, "his spirit will enter mine, we will rise up together, and our destiny will be complete."

Jeannie was also fascinated to learn that ghosts, like their mortal counterparts, had doubts and arguments. Like creatures of flesh, they debated the purpose of existence, and whether there was a God or merely the democracy of souls with which they were familiar. They could not even be sure that they would go on living as they were for all time; though they had memories of their brief life on earth—at least as long as their loved ones remained in the world of matter— and were aware of themselves as pure spirit, they could never be certain that in the infinite run of time they wouldn't have to die again, step above their transcendent realm into a still higher reality, shed their spiritual substance (a kind of pure light) for something less tangible, more sublime. In eternity, Aunt Deborah patiently explained, all things are possible. So perhaps there were not just two realms, as the ancients taught, but many. Perhaps we must die in each realm only to be reborn in the next, rising higher and higher through ever-expanding spheres of timelessness until in the end we not only join ourselves to the ultimate, though infinitely receding, One Who is God, but become God ourselves, for compared to God, even the blessed spirits are as nothing; and—who knows?—perhaps at that moment of utter perfection, of final fulfillment, of—oh, never mind, we lack the words for such things—but maybe at that moment we come to understand the necessity of shrinking our omnipotence in order to create still newer worlds, and so on and so forth, a whole maze of worlds coming to life through an ever-expanding eternity in which the many are as One and the One becomes many.

In the full bloom of precocious adolescence Jeannie was enchanted by the romantic urgency of her aunt's passions and beliefs. It appealed to some dark secret part of her (as hidden from Walter as the far side of the moon), her hunger for things that were mysterious rather than confused, profound rather than merely difficult or complicated. Later her skepticism, her father's skepticism inculcated in her, would win out; ghosts exist, she would decide, but in the everyday world in which we have to live it makes a lot more sense to call them memories and dreams. After all, the fact that we crave mystery and profundity and immortality doesn't obligate the universe to provide them. Nonetheless, at the age of fourteen, fifteen, sixteen, she would climb into bed and the darkness would start beating around her like angels' wings and she would feel herself attached, through her Aunt Deborah's influence, to an ageless, spectral world of incredible joy and beauty, a world from which her poor father, for all his math and Mozart, was excluded. It made her feel squeamish; there was in such sensations a sort of betrayal; but she had begun to understand the pleasures that could be derived from secrets, from passion, from guilt.

She loved her father, loved him with fondness and humor and pride and gratitude, loved him despite what she already knew to be the self-indulgence of his "program" for her and the burden of his outlandish expectations, loved him because he was gentle and intelligent and bumbling and good-natured, loved him most of all, perhaps, because at bottom, whatever his faults, he really did love her—*and how many of her friends or classmates or cousins could honestly claim that*? There were times when she would have been content never to grow up, be his cherished baby forever. But she was beginning to sense the first pangs of separation. She knew that soon, all too soon, she would have to seek her own way, her own vision, explore her own world's hidden spaces—though even that was his idea. Those were the days when they were conspiring together over college catalogues, heaped up like threats on the kitchen table, and he kept saying that the time had come for her to be independent. He would remind her that he himself had been only twelve years old when his father died, and though it hurt, hurt terribly, hurt still, it had served to set him free. Some version of that sort of freedom, he told her, would be—"though I don't mean I plan to die for you"—his most precious gift to her.

Jeannie knew perfectly well that parents say such things to children when they are about to send them off to college, that graduation tears are tears of loss; but she also knew that her father would carry such a notion to a nonsensical extreme. Thus she was not surprised, she was rather pleased, when in those last weeks of summer, as she prepared to enter Barnard, her father became gruff with her, distant, almost mean; and though they both knew it was a pretense, though Sarah lost her patience with them—"It's just a subway ride away; she'll come home on weekends; don't make such a fuss!"—they both enacted right to the end that ritual of separation.

The day he delivered her with her stomach in knots to the small alien space of her first dormitory room, and stood there holding her suitcase, loath to let it go, he said to her, without even a hint of a wink to soften the cruelty:

"Well, I've done what I can for you. Now you're on your own."

Her only compensation was in knowing that his agony must have been greater than hers.

Those first weeks in college she studied hard, sought out friends, wrote poetry, protested an air-raid drill by standing in the rain on Broadway, went to foreign movies, discussed politics and predestination in the small hours of the morning, called her parents every Thursday night, felt homesick, and rode the subway to Brooklyn every other weekend to eat her mother's bland pot roast and get her laundry done. She realized that for all the talk of freedom she was doing exactly what her father had anticipated she would do. *Whom* was he kidding? She was still bound to him by her intelligence, her common sense, her "good study habits," her political idealism, all those things he had instilled in her early on. She would be talking to someone and hear herself mouthing her father's ideas, or taking notes in class and sense her father sifting the material, picking out the highlights, guiding her hand. "Between the idea/And the reality . . . Between the emotion/And the response/Falls the Shadow." And the shadow was her father. His intense, good-natured, cautionary voice interposed between her and the personal wilderness she sought to explore. In the process of self-definition— which was as good a formula for freedom as she could think of—she would have to burst through the limits he had set for her. And if the limits he had set for her were reason and intelligence, she could only overpass those limits, free herself, become herself, by doing something irrational, inane, stupid.

So she did.

"Lance" Rosen, assistant professor of English, was at least twice Jeannie's age, but he looked a lot younger standing in front of his class (Metaphysicals and Moderns) in his rumpled corduroys, fidgeting with a piece of chalk in lieu of smoking while he lectured, often brilliantly, on the significant resemblances between Burton and Joyce or Marvell and T. S. Eliot. Had he been authentically young and handsome, it would have been impossible, because then Jeannie would have called it love, and that would have frightened her. And had he ever made the slightest advance, had he ever looked at her with that warm, shrewd appraisal she received from men of every age on Broadway and College Walk, that, too, would have frightened her. But he was mild and abstract and apparently indifferent to her, and thus she was able to throw herself in his way. She started staring at him, pulling his eyes to hers, and then making him look away. She took to hanging around after class to ask him questions about the associative subtleties of a text. She wrote for him a vibrant paper, filled with suggestiveness, on the metaphysical connection between the verbs "love" and "die." In red ink, with a trembling hand, he wrote back that it was the most intriguing paper he had read all year, and asked her in to discuss it. In his office she pulled her chair up and leaned so close to him that she could smell the vague odor of his excitement. Never once did she pretend to herself that she loved him, nor that he was anything more to her than a talented teacher; it was just that, one thing leading to another, his classroom eventually expanded to include the rumpled bachelor's bed in his small, book-filled apartment on West End Avenue.

She surrendered her virginity to him without tears or complaints the way a few years earlier she had given up the last of her childish toys. She was interested, but not impressed, to know that her pale body, reflected in his eyes, was adequate to the purpose of their mutual pleasure. His body, with its freckles and pink plumpness, its small rolls of fat padding his hips, was not particularly appealing, but only silly schoolgirls worried about muscles and looks, and he had, anyway, a manner and a technique that a whole houseful of fraternity boys might have envied. Besides, it was primarily, to begin with, just a kind of experiment. The sensation of watching him drop his pants was akin to the anticipation she might have felt upon opening up some important book that people kept telling her she ought to read. The kissing was nothing special; with her father's glum encouragement, she had gone to high school parties and allowed herself to be kissed and touched, not without enjoyment, by nervous boys. What she was not prepared for, though, what nothing in all her wide-read, precocious knowledge had taught her, was the way her thoughts seemed to flow right out of her mind and down into the pit of her stomach when he moved his gentle lips from her neck to her nipple and reached between her legs to place his careful finger on the soft button of her sex. She was prepared for sensation of some sort; she had played with herself on occasion to investigate the symptoms of arousal, but she was not expecting such hot, damp, thoughtless urgency. Only later would she realize how very expert he was, that had she given herself (a silly expression, "taken him" would have been just as accurate) to some brash undergraduate, it might have required weeks or months or maybe even years to reach this sort of pleasure. She kept trying to remain detached and quizzical about the proceedings, to observe herself making love as she might have observed herself engaged in a conversation or reacting to a movie, but the more she tried, the more her thoughts drowned themselves in excitement; and when his tongue momentarily replaced his finger, when their reproductive flesh joined together, when she felt her own hidden nerve-rich center sliding up against his thoughtful, almost courteous thrust, it was as though a key had been inserted, a door flung open, a gleam of paradise revealed, and—

"Oh," she cried, "I never—I never—I never—"

For the next month or so, with single-minded dedication, she pursued what she still, in calm moments, called her experiment. Three or four times a week, assuring each other it was all for fun, that they would stop when it got "too serious," they would go up to his apartment and spend an hour, or a couple of hours, or eventually even whole nights, making love. It became a strange private joke they shared. They laughed a lot. He was gently amused by her eager curiosity and her neophytic shamelessness. She wanted to touch and taste everything. She was like a tourist let loose in a foreign land, running here and there, seeking out all the wonders that were marked with the flower of an asterisk in her imaginary guidebook. Earnestly, tenderly, she studied the physiology of the process, the initial heat, the sensitive zones, the skin blushes, the swells and partings, the fluids, the pulse of blood in the artery of his erection, the rush, the exhaustion, the sadness. She would investigate his used condoms, pouring his semen out over her fingers, sliding the slippery, pearly stuff between her fingers, amazed that it could contain so many potential babies. She was also fascinated by the slang of sex, and liked to whisper, sing, shout those words her father had once taught her ("Better they should come from me than the gutter!"), as though to hear them out loud in her own voice made them come to life around her and dance like merry imps in the warm, ecstatic air. How bizarre, how absorbing, how intoxicating, the primal process was.

During the month or so of what she would later call her first affair she did not go home on weekends. This was not policy on her part, at least not consciously; she had, for herself as well as for her parents, the handy excuse that assignments were piling up and she was strapped for time. Actually, she looked forward, or some part of her looked forward, to telling her father about her experiment; she foresaw, after they had gotten over the initial embarrassment, a long, cozy confessional conversation during which certain theoretical questions might be answered and her newfound freedom confirmed. She even imagined her father learning a few things from her report, since her feeling was (no matter what reason told her) that her parents never made love, had conceived her, perhaps, in a stupor or a dream. She just couldn't imagine her mother—that cold, distant, humorless, long-suffering, abstract woman whom she had never much liked— roused to passion or being anything more than troubled by her father's bumbling attempts at affection. Several times, talking to him on the phone, she was on the verge of blurting it out, but some other bit of news, some miscellaneous digression, or some unexpected jamming of her heart forestalled her. Anyway, her father was preoccupied in those days with some kind of quarrel that had erupted in the family. So she placed her experiment into her little stash of secrets, along with her Aunt Deborah's ghosts, and let it stay there, gathering interest, as it were, right up until that memorable Wednesday when Professor Rosen, with none of his usual eloquence or wit, stammered and sputtered and apologized and almost wept, calling their romance to an end.

It was, in retrospect, a hilarious scene. He thought he had to let her down gently, afraid he would break her heart. He said the whole thing had been an accident, a mistake, it never should have happened, he had only himself to blame, he loved her, he didn't want to love her, he was a fool, he was a beast, he would give her an A in the course, he would exempt her from the final exam, it was too risky, think of her reputation, think of his career.

"My God!" he howled. "Until I checked your file today, I thought you were at least nineteen! I had no idea you were so very, very young!"

She cried a little because he expected her to and because she felt bad for him, but she knew that in the story of her life he was a minor character, whom she would remember fondly, but never really miss. There would be others. And anyway, if she had to choose someone with whom she would whirl forever on the winds of eternity, it certainly wouldn't be Lance Rosen.

Two days later, unaccountably hungry, she walked into a luncheonette on Amsterdam Avenue for a late-afternoon snack and heard a fat woman with a huge goiter and rotting teeth bawling the news that the President had been shot to death in Texas.

She would remember drifting for a while among stunned strangers on the streets of Morningside, and seeing thick puffs of cloud hurry in shame past the darkening building lines, and expecting the buildings themselves to tremble and collapse in outrage at the awful, sudden, inexplicable event. The whole world, the gray pavement, the rush-hour traffic, the brisk November air blowing against the nerves of her raw cheeks, seemed terrible and new. It was uncanny. She could sense in those naked moments the hidden flux of life itself—not progress, not regress, not cause and effect, not circumstance or circularity, not accident, not destiny, but change, mere change, incessant change, things arranging and rearranging themselves in momentary patterns of illusion, as though they danced wildly to some primal rhythm, a heartbeat maybe, or the ticking of a clock. Years later, when she was living in Africa digging prehistoric clues out of the hard, parched earth, she would try to describe her sense of that occasion in a letter to her father.

"The future is always unknown," she wrote. "It is all a kind of wilderness, a place for haggard and amazed explorers who never know if beyond the next minute—the next treeline or mountain—they will stumble upon the bliss of an Eldorado or the desperation of a swamp. Which is why I have given myself over to rooting in the past. It's the only definition we have."

But that came later. On that broken-backed Friday, without thinking much about it, without even saying to herself: "I want to be there," she wandered down into the subway and rode to her parents' house in Brooklyn.

All that weekend the three of them sat watching the mournful shocks and ceremonies pass in shadows across the television screen, not saying much, not having to say anything, eating food they prepared together and cleaning up after themselves without any instructions having to pass among them, sleeping and waking again to that numb dreamy quality of the nation's grief, and the occasional hushed telephone calls from aunts and uncles—"Yes, we're watching it. Yes, it's horrible. Yes, Jeannie's here with us. Yes, it's a terrible thing." Again and again, until the images had wrung from them the last tribute of their emotions, they suffered through the motorcade and the veering camera, they admired the widow emerging from the airplane in her gorgeous bloody rags, they speculated about fascist conspiracies, they stared in awe at the book depository window and the hospital corridor and the Dallas jail, they recoiled at the gunshot that murdered the murderer, they followed the catafalque, the riderless horse, the drums, they stood in mournful vigil in the Capitol

332

rotunda, they wept, they actually wept, this household of radicals, for the beautiful, pathetic child saluting his father's grave—until the ritual was completed, the somber circle closed. Only then were they released from their civic obligation, allowed to return to their own private sorrows and joys.

Monday night, while her mother dozed on the couch, Jeannie went into the kitchen and found her father sitting alone at the table, a bowl of cottage cheese in front of him. With his big Lieber nose and his stringy neck, with his bony, black-haired wrists jutting from the rolled-up sleeves of his white shirt, he looked so angular and homely and earnest that she felt compelled to put her hands on his shoulders and press her lips to his coarse cheek.

"What a world," he sighed. "First my brother, and now this. I don't know what to feel bad about first. Well, it's history. Let's talk about something else. So what's new with you?"

She smiled compulsively, like some shy kid revealing her braces. Once upon a time he had taught her that to think clearly is to think bluntly, that euphemism clouds the mind the way perfume clouds the senses; she remembered that, and believed for a moment, despite the cautionary pounding of her heart, that she was going to please him.

"So *nu*," he was saying, "what have they taught you lately up there at your fancy college?"

And she responded in the clearest, plainest, most matter-of-fact voice she could muster:

"Fucking."

The events of this world are cradled in a web; touch one part and the whole must tremble; thus acts have causes you can never wholly unravel and consequences you can never wholly foresee. But these were just the abstractions that would occur to Jeannie later, after they had played out their painful little scene; at the time, some part of her immediately began pondering the vast mysterious tangle of her motives.

First came silence, like the silence of a theater as the curtain slowly drops and you await, breathlessly, the outburst of applause; and in that silence, even before either of them breathed again, she already knew, she could tell by the quick flush that spread across his forehead and the stunned anguish that flickered to life in his eyes, that she had miscalculated and blundered. She watched him struggling with himself, opening his mouth and pressing it tight again while he groped for some appropriate words to say to her across the distance that had opened between them. Her eyes misted and an apology came welling up thickly out of her clogged throat. Then the warm familiar space of the kitchen started wheeling slowly around her; in her giddy confusion she couldn't find anything upon which to focus her eyes; everywhere she looked was a question: *why? why? why?*

"I'm sorry," she heard herself saying, though she had no idea what she was sorry for or even if she was sorry at all.

Nonetheless, the apology swept her past the worst of the moment. Now she could look at him again as he shrugged, sighed, pushed away the cottage cheese, and lifted his hands, shaking his fingertips toward the ceiling in an ancient gesture of bafflement and supplication. His lips kept moving as he assembled a response in his mind, but he was still thinking it over, struggling with himself, examining his sudden wound and wondering how to apply to it the balm of reason and goodness; and such was the weird exposed tension of the moment that Jeannie almost burst into giggles. She clamped her teeth on her lower lip, hard, and at that instant—later she would call it an "epiphany," but it wasn't that; it was both more and less than that—some fundamental portion of her attention swerved away from him and toward herself. It no longer mattered very much what he was going to say. It was herself she was listening to, a small inner voice telling her quite lucidly:

You hurt him, you meant to hurt him, hurting him was the point.

But why? But why? She pushed her attention further inward, past that voice, probing gently, sampling the complicated clatter of her mind, but she found no answer. She had become all in a moment a mystery to herself. She sensed herself on the verge of a wilderness that was waiting to be explored. Out of a lush tangle voices and visions emerged, glimmered, vanished before she could grasp them. She pushed on further. She was in her Aunt Deborah's house, listening for a ghost through a heavy wooden door. She was in a rowboat with her father, straining at the oar handle, moving them slowly round and round a dazzling lake. She was piecing together a jigsaw puzzle. She was swimming in a pool, a little reptilian, salt water stinging her eyes. Somewhere someone was slaughtering a chicken. A telephone began to ring. She was in bed with her teacher, engorged with ecstatic strangeness, crying: "I never—I never—" A dead bird dropped a pink feather into a book. Too many sweets make you fat. It is now understood that subatomic particles swerve at random. On the big rock candy mountain the cops have wooden legs. Dada!

"—hardly what I expected," he was saying in a tone of gloomy pomposity, and she pulled back out of herself, reluctantly, to face him.

"I'm sorry," she said again, calmly, purposefully, to hurry them through the agony.

All she wanted was for the scene to end so that she could get on the subway and be alone with this wondrous new sense of herself. A whole world, cunningly made, awaited her. No, she wasn't sorry. If anything, she was glad, she was joyous, she was brimming with secret enthusiasm.

Unfortunately there was no easy way to make her father see how fine it was to have, in the process of self-definition, so very, very much to learn.

THAT WINTER SAM WAS SO BUSY selling off the factory and the house in Manhattan Beach, and hocking Essie's furs and diamonds and candlesticks, and haggling with Dov Kalisher—"that lousy *gonif*"—to salvage what little he could from the business, that he didn't have time to feel sorry for himself. Feeling sorry, the gloom and despair, came later, after the business was gone and he was living like a *shnorrer* in a small apartment on Ocean Avenue and had nothing to do but mope and grieve and complain and remember the bitterness of the family's betrayal. It got to the point where even Essie said he should go out and look for a job, anything; but he was sixty-five years old by then, receiving Social Security, and if the government wanted to pay him to retire, he said, why not retire? Besides, what sort of job could he look for? How could a man used to being his own boss and keeping his own hours work happily for someone else? No: better to grow old gracefully, live out his days in peace and quiet, derive what small pleasure he could from the visits of his grandchildren.

"Whatever we have will be enough," he told Essie, who had amazed everyone by giving up her luxuries practically without complaint. "Thank God I have no one else to be responsible for."

In those days he had cut himself off completely from Evelyn and Ruthie and Walter and Moe. He was not talking to them—*not talking!*—as though the sound of his voice were a gift he refused to bestow, a benediction he had chosen to withhold. As far as he was concerned, he said, the American-born Liebers weren't his family anymore. The only exception was Rose; he called her up when Georgie was in the hospital for the hernia operation; but even in that case there were hard feelings. When it came to the others, he didn't want to see them or hear about them, and he refused to go to their affairs. Invitations would arrive in the mail ("Send! Send!" said Evelyn. "We'll be the good ones"), but no matter how much they tugged at him, he didn't bother to respond. He missed Joey's wedding, Micki's *bas mitzvah*, Gary's engagement party, and three *brisses*, though he saw to it that Essie put "a little something" in the mail.

"It's the parents I'm mad at," he told her. "I don't need to punish the kids."

Family is family, he used to say. You could fight like wild animals one day, and you were still family the next. But now he wouldn't forgive or forget. Like a mother with a pitiable, misshapen infant, he nursed his grievance and wouldn't let go.

Things went from bad to worse.

In March, after weeks of hunting around, Rich landed a job as a salesman with one of the big candy-bar companies, and moved with Rhoda and the kids out to Chicago. This was a blow. Then Carrie announced that her Michael, who looked like a millionaire but had been drifting for years from job to job, had a "golden opportunity" in Florida, where one of his uncles was opening a big shopping center on land that was formerly swamp and needed a manager, so she would be packing up her family and moving down in the fall. Sam never told them not to go—how could he?—but you could see how much it hurt him. For years, through all the good times, he had distrusted the future, foreseen the end of his luck, and now, sure enough, blow after blow was falling on his head. All of a sudden he started looking old. Deep lines grooved his face. His back started to bend and he walked around slump-shouldered like an *alteh kocker,* dressed in old trousers and shabby sweaters. He went for days without bothering to shave, and to save a few dollars, he put off going to the barbershop until his white hair stood up like ragged bristles all over his scalp. He spent his time watching baseball games on television, or rereading his collection of mystery stories, or snoozing, or sitting at the window staring down through a haze of cigarette smoke at the clamorous little playground across the street, or following Essie around the apartment while she cleaned, trying to be useful. He learned how to make an all-day project out of changing a light bulb or unclogging the sink. The only thing that got him out of the house was when he went uptown to spend an evening at the club. At times he talked about quitting the club to save the dues money, but Essie understood the importance of his nights out and said she would sooner hock the clothes off her back and go hungry. She was really being wonderful.

Occasionally, on a Friday night or Saturday morning, Sam would go with Essie to services at the Manhattan Beach synagogue, where the names of his parents were engraved beneath the stained glass windows and stamped into many of the prayer books, and he would try to convince himself that the dread and emptiness the *davening* evoked in him, were manifestations of a kind of holiness. If he could see the hand of God at work in his misery, it would at least have some purpose. He would recall his father muttering against the world of vanity and illusion, and believe that at last he understood the spirit of that poor, anguished man. He had seen it in others and often suspected that he, too, might find piety in his old age. He would be called to the Torah, and he would stand there, flushed with sentimental longing, pretending to himself that the ancient and unfamiliar letters on the parchment were shadows cast by a mystery he might someday comprehend. Maybe God had taken away from him the things of this world, the burden of money, power, luxury, to prepare him for the world to come. Maybe even now his blessed ancestors were intervening at the Throne of the Almighty to save his impious soul. A pleasant thought: but no matter how many memories of his father and Sterling Place and Rabbi Trauerlicht he dredged up out of himself, he couldn't find comfort. At best he was merely haunted by the ghost of a dead religion. His life was not a scroll, but a ledger, splashed with the red ink of loss, and each morning, awaking to the gloom of another day, he had to wonder what he would lose next.

Then Molly got sick. All winter the pain in her behind had been getting worse and worse; she claimed it was her hemorrhoids flaring up, and was treating herself with ointments and suppositories and aspirin, but these weren't doing her any good. The pain got so bad that she couldn't stand up and she couldn't sit down. She spent long empty hours in bed, in a rapture of self-pity, watching soap operas and game shows on television in that morbid little hotel room, which Sam went right on paying for even while he scrimped on Essie and himself. What choice did he have? Molly had joined him in being mad at the family, so she had no one else to turn to, nowhere else to go. It was awful. He would come into the room and find her lying in a tangle of stained sheets, with her hair (all patchy gray and orange now that she could no longer get out to the beauty parlor) sticking in wet clumps to her forehead. She was afraid that if she climbed into the bathtub, she might not be able to climb out again, so she doused herself with perfumes and deodorants that turned acid on her skin and thus added to the harsh stench. She was fat and horrid; beneath the sheets her body was a formless mass of aching and rancorous flesh; without makeup her face was lumpish and pale and devoid of eyebrows; but memory had its own eyes, and Sam could see in her the gorgeous and passionate girl she had been. He still adored her. She was, despite everything, the same old Molly, crabby and stubborn, a never-ending heartache. He could talk himself blue in the face, he could send Essie over to beg and plead, but Molly refused to see a doctor. She was afraid of hospitals; all the doctors ever wanted was to put her on a diet; she didn't need some stranger poking around inside her; if Dr. Lipsky were alive—but Dr. Lipsky had been dead nearly ten years, how time flies! So she suffered. The pain, radiating, sent shivers into her spine. She was constantly nauseated and couldn't keep food down. Her gums were so sore they bled if she pressed her tongue against them. When she closed her eyes, she sensed something eating at the root of her, and told herself, with exquisite drama, that she was dying.

"Molly, I have enough without this," Sam finally said to her. "I'm calling a doctor."

"Let me die already," was her response. "You'll be better off when I'm six feet under."

There was no talking to her. The pain had nibbled away at the remnants of her morale. She made of her life one long tale of woe and guilt. She insisted on blaming herself for Sam's troubles. She said the business started going downhill with the death of Solly Poverman, for which, of course, she and she alone was responsible. Why, she had as good as murdered that poor man. Then, because there was no end to her selfishness, she had left Sam in the lurch to marry Max Gold, abandoning the factory for "that mental case." And now, with her big mouth, she had alienated Sam from the rest of the family.

"You're mad at the wrong ones," she told him. "Be mad at me. I'm the one who ruined you."

That was Molly. While they waited for the doctor to arrive, she was so terrified that she dug her fingernails into the back of Sam's hand, carving little crescents of blood, her face all pasty with sickness and fear, her lips so dry they cracked, as though the examination alone might kill her.

She went into the hospital in May and they cut out of her a tumor "the size of a grapefruit" and most of her rectum and colon. In those days Deborah was the go-between when Sam and Molly had news for the rest of the family—Deborah was the only one who was talking to all of them—but Deborah was in California at the time, about her book, so the family didn't get to hear that Molly was in the hospital until the operation was over and the lab report came back saying the tumor was malignant. They might not have heard about it even then if Essie hadn't put her foot down.

"Enough is enough," she said, and picked up the phone.

All that week the family trooped to the hospital one or two at a time, carrying gifts and boxes of candy, to see Molly and to play out, amidst the smells of sickness and disinfectant, little damp scenes of reconciliation. There is nothing like the proximity of death to bring a family together. Shy, nervous, apologetic, they tiptoed into Molly's room and forced themselves to smile while they absorbed the sight of her ("I thought she would look worse," they later said). They pushed forward their ritualistic peace offerings, and then, with hugs and tears, the insults and hurts were not so much forgiven as allowed to slide backwards into the soothing murk of the past.

"So how are you feeling?"

"I'm feeling terrible. What did you expect?"

Even Moe, who had his own bitterness, who wasn't talking to Evelyn or Ruthie, made the pilgrimage, and pressed his lips for a moment against the sticky cheek of this strange, fat, ignorant dying woman who was his sister. He felt so noble about the whole thing, so large-spirited, that when he went back out into the corridor and saw Sam arriving, he rushed to greet him. His smile forgave everything, he stuck out his hand—and had to stand there in shock and rage and humiliation while Sam turned his back and walked away from him.

Sam was unyielding. If he came to the hospital and one of them was with Molly, he waited outside. When they had to pass in the corridor, he looked the other way. It was something savage in him, something he didn't particularly like, but he couldn't see why Molly's sickness should change anything, and the fact that they expected a reconciliation made his silence more effective and gratifying. After all, to be not talking to people when you never got to see them was abstract and hollow, a theoretical state of mind; but to be not talking to them right there in their presence, in the yearning and expectant space of the hospital and Molly's sickness, was substantial and real. There was grim pleasure to be derived from snubbing them close up. His silence fell violently upon them. Let Molly make peace with them if she wanted to; they remained strangers to him.

Thus he allowed the opportunity to pass.

Meanwhile, Deborah came back from California and astonished everyone by offering to let Molly stay with her in her apartment while she "recuperated." That word, which they all used, was practically a euphemism since the doctors said it was only a matter of time —"weeks, maybe months"—before the cancer spread into her vital organs, but Deborah was optimistic.

"Molly's not dying so fast," she scolded. "She'll be married again before you know it."

Deborah was entering her days of glory. On her two trips out to California, where she had fallen among a group of kindred spirits, her long solitude was finally broken. She felt herself passing through a kind of mental door, like the door that lies between sleeping and waking—there came a moment when she actually yawned hugely and said to herself: "*Gottenyu*, how long have I been dreaming?" She became aware, as never before, of the incredible smallness of this world in the face of all time and space, but somehow that very smallness, that very insufficiency, subsumed within itself the possibility that eternity could be discovered in it. Thus, this world, too, was worthy of her attention; this world, too, could be bathed in truth and harmony, sweetness and light. So there was work to be done, work that she—freed at last from her obligations to the family business—was uniquely suited to do.

The book that she had been secretly writing for God knows how many years, and which ended up being called *Worlds to Come,* was published that summer by an outfit called Lunra Press; and even while the family was joking about it ("So tell me, where do I buy a copy of the masterpiece?"), full-page advertisements started appearing in the back pages of *The New York Times Book Review* as well as in a dozen or so more esoteric periodicals. What excitement there was to see in print a little round ectoplasmic photograph of Deborah floating like a silvery cloud above a blaring sequence of headlines:

Revealed for the First Time

** THE SCIENCE OF SPIRITS **

ETERNAL LIFE!!

"The Fate That Awaits You"

("But why," complained Evelyn, must she call herself Deborah Stern? What's the matter? Lieber isn't good enough for her?")

The book was printed on cheap yellowish stock with a purple cardboard binding that quickly came unglued. Later you could spot a copy of it on a shelf in every Lieber household, squeezed in, perhaps, between an ornate edition of the Old Testament and one of Deanna's books of photographs; but the language was dense and elusive, at least as far as the Liebers were concerned, and probably the only one who ever read it all the way through was Jeannie, Deborah's precious moon child. For complicated reasons, which Deborah would patiently explain if you asked her, you couldn't find *Worlds to Come* in ordinary bookstores or libraries; it was available only by mail order for $9.99 plus shipping. Nonetheless, it turned out to be a great success. Of human credulity there is no end. Deborah never mentioned numbers—in this, as in all things, she loved to be mysterious—but she made so much money from that book that she was able to pack up her gramophone and her clocks and move out to California. There she made even more money by conducting séances, lecturing on spectral topics at local churches and universities, and dispensing, for a fee, what she called "spiritual therapy," the crux of which was that if you knew how you wanted to be situated in the next world, you could make more sense of the pains and sorrows and frights of this one. Eventually Deborah became a minor celebrity of sorts, surrounded by an enchanted cult of pale, doting admirers. She bought herself a big old blue house in the vicinity of Los Angeles—an appropriately Gothic edifice with eaves and turrets and gables—and she still lives there, though every so often one of the Lieber cousins goes out to the Coast on business, pays her a visit, and reports back to the family that behind the white powder, the circles of rouge, the ever-black hair, the sapphire pendant, wrinkles have appeared: even Aunt Deborah is beginning at last to grow old.

Anyway, when Molly came out of the hospital that summer, she moved into Deborah's living room with her mess and her noise. Twice a week Sam drove her for radiation treatments, which made her hair fall out in clumps; she could no longer go to the toilet, but relieved herself through a tube attached to her lower intestine at one end and a plastic collection bag at the other; the various medicines she had to take left her dizzy and nauseated; you would be talking to her and her attention would wander, a cloud of puzzled yearning would darken her eyes, as though she had focused inward upon some twinge or spasm that was her death being slowly born within her. She was pregnant with death, but she still had moments of exuberance. The nausea would diminish for a moment and there would be Molly raiding the refrigerator or pot-wrestling in Deborah's small kitchen, making noodle puddings and apple strudel and potato pancakes, which she would send home wrapped in aluminum foil with her next visitor. One day she got out and bought herself a bright red wig, an outlandish thing which never quite fit, but it was better than being bald, she said. Another time Deanna dropped in with all her equipment to take some pictures, and Molly stood up, for old times' sake, and danced the Hucklebuck, clapping and singing and laughing so hard that tears streamed from her eyes. Long into the night she would sit and talk to Deborah about the old days, about her husbands and lovers, her pleasures and her ecstasies, the two of them closer to each other than they had ever been before, so close that Deborah came to understand that at bottom, spiritual or sensual, their hunger was the same.

"I'll tell you the truth," Deborah confessed to Sam. "I'm glad for the opportunity. All these years, and we never really knew each other."

Deborah was an angel. She bathed Molly, fed her, saw to it that she took her pills on time, cleaned up her vomit, and emptied her plastic collection bag. When Molly got depressed, Deborah would start an argument just to snap her out of it; and when Molly was frightened, Deborah would fetch her tarot cards and read in them the blissful destiny of Molly's eternal soul. Company would come with long faces, and Molly and Deborah would sit there glancing and smiling at each other, as if something, maybe dying itself, were a pleasant private joke they shared.

But even Deborah's goodness had its limits; Molly's condition deteriorated, and when she went back into the hospital for her second operation, Deborah started packing for the move to California.

Molly ended up in a nursing home not far from the street in Crown Heights where years ago she had lived with Davey Furst. The prognosis was ever more gloomy, but she clung with all her stubborn vitality to the fading glow of her life. Bald and ravaged though she was, with her teeth falling out and half her digestive tract removed, she once again found herself in love.

His name was Levitch—"No, not the same Levitch," she told Sam, "a different Levitch, but the coincidence brought us together." He must have been close to eighty, this Levitch, a tiny, shrunken gnome of a man with enormous hands and a big raspberrylike nose, but he was as sharp-tongued and vigorous and nasty-minded as a delinquent schoolboy. They were attracted to each other by their similar memories of tumultuous lives and their contempt for the resigned and enervated pieties of the old people around them. One corner of the sun porch belonged to Levitch; he would sneer and holler away trespassers; and soon Molly was sharing it with him. They would sit in adjacent wheelchairs, outdoing each other with ever more fabulous and hilarious accounts of their former affairs and marriages. If they had a moment alone, Molly would slip her hand under the blanket on Levitch's lap to "tickle his fancy," as he called it. His business was as soft and warm and withered as a piece of glove leather left lying in the sun, but never mind, never mind: their desires and their circumstances were practically adolescent. One night Levitch even wheeled himself undetected into Molly's room and hoisted himself into her bed, and there, in a slow, awkward, fumbling sort of way, he did for her what his predecessor had been unable to do years ago in what already seemed another existence, a reflection caught in a corroded mirror.

They were married a few days before Molly was sent in an ambulance to the hospital for her third operation. They didn't bother to tell the relatives; they just called in a rabbi and persuaded one of the doctors to give the bride away, because they were in a hurry, were afraid they might never see each other again. But Molly pulled through the operation, even rallied, and they had six more weeks together in the nursing home, doting on each other, inseparable, holding hands on the sun porch, a sentimental example for one and all, before they shipped Molly back to the hospital for the last time.

She weighed ninety pounds, was little more than a rattle of bones in an empty sack of skin, when she died.

The family went to Molly's funeral expecting that, finally, Sam would have to talk to them. If nothing else, they would exchange a few words of comfort and sympathy. It was now more than a year since the factory shut down, and as Evelyn told Ruthie:

"How long can you go on being bitter?"

Evelyn was planning to force the issue; she had lain awake half the night plotting and scheming, and foresaw in a gentle glimmer of anticipation a touching scene. She would walk right up to him in the funeral parlor and invite him to come sit *shivah* along with Ruthie and Rose in her apartment; she would tell him that at such a time a family should forget old quarrels and be together. Maybe he would refuse, maybe he would prefer to sit in his own place, but he would be so moved by her gesture that the moment would blur into hugs and kisses, with Molly's spirit smiling down on all of them.

However, by the time she got to the funeral parlor, in a taxi driven by a wild man through streets that were slick with fresh snow, a ride she would never forget, her face was burning and her heart was leaping with nervousness, and when she saw Sam sitting off on the side with Essie and Rich, with his hat pulled down and his chin on his chest, fending off the world, she didn't have the courage to approach him. She told herself she would catch him afterward and sat herself down with Ruthie and Rose and Georgie on the other side of the aisle. She scarcely heard a word of the service or of the stock eulogy that was delivered by a rabbi no one had ever seen before; she was aware only of Sam. She kept turning her head to look at him as though she were etching his profile into her memory; she even tried to plant through telepathy the notion of forgiveness in his brain. If only he would turn around! But he never once glanced at her, and by the time the service was over she was ablaze with indignation.

She got to her feet, struggled past a lot of knees ("What's her hurry?" she heard Ruthie say), and took up a position in the vestibule, determined to have it out with him once and for all. A man came up to her, put his hand on her arm, and tried to direct her into a limousine, but she shrugged him off, searched the flow of solemn faces for Sam's, spotted him, and moved.

"Sam!" she called, her voice urgent and loud, much louder than she wanted it to be, loud enough to interrupt the somber hum and movement.

A tableau: the funeral parlor vestibule, a few flakes of snow drifting through the open doorway, the diminished family pausing in silent array around Sam and Evelyn, everyone listening, everyone waiting to see what would happen, while Sam stared grimly at Evelyn and Evelyn, flushed with pent-up rage and humiliation, opened her mouth and closed it and opened it again, astonishing even herself when at last the words started tumbling out of her.

"Tell me something, Sam! Tell me one thing! Where the hell is it written that the world owes you a living?"

As far as Sam was concerned, she could have been saying anything, she could have been speaking a foreign language: the words didn't matter. For him the sensation was in the sound, the tone, the flare of emotion. She might have been clawing at him with her fingernails,

344

this shrill, hurt, angry, dreadful woman whose face he felt he could scarcely recognize despite those echoes of his mother in her nose and mouth and eyes. Nothing seemed to connect this manifestation— black dress, cosmetics, silvered hair—with the memories he had of a baby sister named Evelyn, whose smallest happiness was once his own delight. Whatever she had been, she wasn't now, such was the distance between them. And the others, too. They had faded to curious faces glimmering on the periphery of his vision, reminding him of people he used to love. He knew their names, but as if by accident, the way he knew the names of towns he had driven through once but could no longer remember: Schenectady, Potsdam, Coral Springs. Evelyn and Rose and Walter and Ruthie and Moe: they were nothing but memories, defined by memories; so if you withheld the memories, they ceased to exist. And at this moment, focused on nothing but this moment, he refused to know them—he just walked away, pulling his collar up around his neck as he hurried in despair and embarrassment across the sidewalk and into the limousine. climbing in behind Essie, another momentary stranger, who said shrilly to him:

"Leave it to Evelyn to create a scene."

As they drove to the cemetery; as he stood in rigid and willful solitude watching the machinery lower a coffin containing something he once called Molly, something he once loved, into a hole in the snow; as they drove back along barren parkways and streets; as he climbed the stairs to the unfamiliar apartment in which he lived, he had to wonder, since they were strangers, what shadowy forms he was struggling with, to whom really he was refusing to speak.

Over the next few months the family heard that Sam was deteriorating. They heard it from Rich and they heard it from Carrie and finally they heard it from Essie, who began calling them up for sympathy.

"He's making himself sick," she wailed to them on the phone.

He went around complaining of headaches and pains in the chest and indigestion. In the middle of the afternoon he would get ravenously hungry and go searching through the kitchen for odd snacks, pickles and herring and saltines and buttermilk, but at suppertime, when Essie put a meal in front of him, he had no appetite. He was always too hot or too cold, always fiddling with the radiators. Except for his nights out at the club, he didn't want to leave the house; he didn't want to do anything. He would sit for hours, smoking cigarette after cigarette, staring at the gray-blue patterns of smoke as though in their uncurling he might locate a significant truth. His silence made Essie frantic. She didn't know what to do for him.

Nor did he know what to do for himself. His brooding had grown so intense and mysterious that it frightened him. He would wake up in the morning with a taste of metal in his mouth and his limbs heavy and aching as if some ferocious force of gravity had been tugging at him through the night. Bizarre imaginings taunted him. He would close his eyes for a moment and see himself climbing through windows like a burglar to steal things, coins and lamps and utensils and plates of food, from his siblings. One night he dreamed he was murdering Hymie with a knife, a dream so vivid he could feel the mess of it on his fingers and hear the boy's vivid howling all the next day. He had moments when he found himself struggling to breathe; his throat would close up and he would start gasping and wheezing, with his heart beating in such wild panic he was sure it would burst. One minute he would be sitting with his mind empty, aware of nothing but the dreary space around him and the tingle of his exposed nerves; the next minute, as though a tap had been turned, a rushing stream of strange, partial memories would pour through him, memories of Pitkin Avenue and his father's bookstore and school and Asa Kalisher's restaurant, all jumbled together, unwilled and relentless, like the projection of a film made out of cuttings and scraps. He endured bouts of pathetic weakness, during which he couldn't rise to his feet or force his fingers into a fist, as if his energy had ebbed away from him. Often his hands would be icy while his forehead was burning. Like another Lou Grossman, he went around bumping into things, knocking things over, cutting himself, bruising his shins on chairs, and banging his head on cabinet doors. At such times he would recall with poignant intensity how at the age of five or six he would run crying to his mother with some childish wound which had resulted from his own mischief or naughtiness or disobedience, and how as he stood there in stoic agony while she daubed on the iodine or pressed a cruel ice pack against the pain, she would say to him:

"See, *tateleh,* God punished you!"

A tangle of vindictiveness and sympathy, an ancient web of love and guilt, the immemorial legacy of every Jewish mother to every Jewish child. You are the Chosen, you must obey, you must measure your life against the highest ideal; fail and God will punish you. That was the only sense he could make of his current suffering. He had failed and God was punishing him. Only how had he failed? Didn't the roots of the Liebers run deep into the dark rich American soil? Wasn't that the purpose he had been given? Besides, as far as he could judge, the terrible vindictive God of punishment did not exist.

Maybe, then, it was that he had outlived his purpose. Maybe every day, every hour, was just the empty gift of a nodding or malicious fate and there was nothing left for him but to die.

He fell to brooding over death, telling himself that it was going to happen to him soon, soon, and though he couldn't believe in any sort of immortality beyond the simple continuation of his seed in his children and grandchildren, he tried to convince himself, through the example of those hard-boiled detective stories he loved, that he was unafraid. But in practice, each erratic heartbeat, each jab of indigestion rising up into his chest, stung him with hot panic. There must have been a dozen times during those months when he was absolutely certain that he was experiencing the onset of the fatal heart attack that would send him spinning, in excruciating pain and bewilderment, into the final darkness. He would sense himself at times dropping into that void where life's last secret would be revealed—only to have the pain dissipate into a belly rumble and a belch.

In the end he grew so accustomed to these false alarms, felt so foolish in his fear, that when his heart actually clenched in sick agony, he refused to believe it was happening to him.

He was playing bridge that night, ensconced in the smoke and noise and familiarity of the club, the only place where he felt safe in those days, where his brooding thoughts didn't threaten him, where he could still joke and smile. Early in the evening the cards had been good to him, but later his luck turned sour, which was, he reminded the boys, the story of his life. He glumly sorted through hand after hand only to find a stray jack here, a lonely queen there, or perhaps a pathetic singleton king. To make matters worse, he had drawn Max Kalisky as a partner—Kalisky, the old fool, kept talking about his grandchildren until they had to tell him to stop the bullshit and play. Pain had been with Sam since suppertime, a smoldering behind his breastbone, but he kept assuring himself it was just another of those maddening bouts of indigestion, kept chewing Tums, kept pressing his palm against his bloated belly, waiting for relief. But the pain got worse and worse, like a fist slowly clenching at the center of him.

He was holding his first good hand in over an hour, a pretty string of eight hearts in a bower of black picture cards, when a flame flower suddenly bloomed in place of the fist and seared up into his neck and shoulders. He fought it off, struggling to concentrate on the cards. Eight goddamn gorgeous hearts, so never mind the pain; the problem was how to find out, with that moron sitting opposite him, who held the missing ace. He unrolled another Tums, chewed into it. Kalisky started with a club. Cohen passed. Sam opened his mouth, ready to investigate a slam, but what emerged was a thick gurgling groan.

This was no mere indigestion. His insides were blazing with agony. The green felt of the table, the cards he was holding, the smoke, the noise, the faces around him, everything was receding to an awed, respectful distance. Breathless, he fumbled to loosen his collar; the dangling ash of his cigarette toppled and spattered gray on his lap. He pushed free of his chair, got to his feet, struggling against intense pressure, as though he were trying to walk on the bottom of the sea. He was aware of everyone watching him, amazed and reverent in the proximity of death. Somehow he made it to the men's room. There was a kind of explosion, and when it was over, he was leaning against the sink, which was splashed with red vomit, and he had a bitter, vile taste on his tongue. It took him a moment to realize that the wet, pale, twisted, frightened face in the corroded mirror was his own, and he started staring at it. Perhaps it would contain some clue to the meaning of the awful burning, squeezing horror that raged inside him. His hand came up and spread against his breast pocket as if he were pledging allegiance to some final, gruesome flag. There were men surrounding him and he had the odd notion he was being attacked; for a moment he struggled against them; but then he knew they were trying to help him, and he yielded to their hands. Don't die, he kept telling himself, don't die, don't die. But there was nothing more he could do for himself and so he gave himself over to the pain and the fear and the hands, surrendering himself like a child, with his sour smell thick in his nostrils, yielding himself to the oblivion of what could have turned out to be, for all he knew, a silent and permanent sleep.

He would remember a dark space into which his body or mind or soul was cramped, against which he struggled in a dim, damp heat; then came a moment of uncoiling as he burst out toward some distant glimmer of light and heard around him a tumult of voices shouting and crying and wailing ancient prayers. He was in an obscure landscape, green and bright, near a grove of red-flowered trees, and he understood that he had entered the land of milk and honey, was moving through it, only he couldn't have said whether he walked or crawled or flew. He felt old and young, wise and foolish, expectant and disappointed, strong and exhausted, as though he were living simultaneously all the different ages of his life, and he kept moving through a vagueness of trees and grass and a shimmer of distant lakes merging at the horizon with the perfect bright blue of the sky, and he could sense the sky's brightness washing down upon him. He was looking for his father. He couldn't have said how he knew he was looking for his father, but the thought was clear: if he could find his father, he could make himself at home. In the distance vaguely familiar forms beckoned him, and there were voices behind him, some praying, some chastising him, still others offering him bits of advice he couldn't quite hear. When he turned his head to see who they were, the owners of these voices, he could catch only momentary glimpses of them as they slipped like shadows or ghosts beyond the periphery of his vision, and yet he was sure he recognized them. He hurried away, moving, the voices urging him on. Then he entered a building. He hadn't noticed it until he was inside. It was an old and ramshackle place with carved wooden doors and stained glass windows, a kind of synagogue. Certainly this is where his father would be. He went through room after room, searching for him, fleeing the voices, until he came to a place that was open to the brightness of the sky. His mother lay in a bed, white-haired and toothless and paralyzed, as in the days before she died. She smiled and beckoned him, and he went to her and set his face on her breast, noticing that she wore on her finger a familiar ruby ring, which he finally recognized as the one Molly had received from Solly Poverman. The bed started moving. He raised his face for a moment and saw the bright blue of the sky merging seamlessly into the darkness beneath him. Frightened, he clung to his mother, who stirred restlessly. She seemed to be growing larger. He could feel her breast plump and full beneath his face until she shoved her hand hard against his chest to push him away from her. She loomed up over him, young and beautiful, scolding him in Yiddish, lifting him up above her like an infant, scolding him in words he couldn't quite understand—though he would believe he understood her well enough later on, when he lay in a hospital bed remembering, after she had flung him away from her so furiously that he could still feel in his aching bones that sensation of flying, tumbling, falling that had brought him dimly back to life.

"You're not allowed to die yet," she had said. "First you must make your peace with the family."

A dream, a vision, a journey: he would never know which it was.

Later the doctor told him that for a few minutes during the night he had been dead on the operating table and that it took a shot of adrenaline directly into his stopped heart to shock it back to beating, so maybe he could believe that his soul had actually left his body for a while and glimpsed the world beyond. But it was just as easy to assume that he had simply hallucinated, in fading anesthesia and dawning pain, that bright landscape where ghosts walk and time doesn't matter. Either way, as he came awake and alive in the artificial light of an anonymous hour, attached to murmuring machinery, cocooned in the clear plastic of an oxygen tent, with his chest aching hollowly beneath bandages, he recalled with astonishing clarity a few fragments of that world, and sensed deep within himself the hidden shape and substance of the rest. Make your peace with them. He felt the weak ruins of his body pressed against the bed, but his mind was clear enough. He could imagine the night he had put them all through, the telephone calls, the running around, the hysterics; he could foresee how they would traipse to the hospital to visit him, with their gifts of flowers and candy. He understood Molly now, and smiled. His heart pulsed faintly but regularly in his ears. Whatever they had all done to each other, whatever darkness stained their past, whatever sin had been committed in their names when they were torn up out of the old country and brought to America, they had punished themselves enough. Family is family. Half dozing, at peace with himself, he began rehearsing the quiet healing words he was going to say to them.

EIGHT

―――――

DEANNA, LIKE SO MANY OF HER COUSINS, had spun away from the family into a space of her own. She was still living in the Village, though she had moved to a roomier apartment a few blocks uptown, and was working as a free-lance photojournalist, specializing in what was already being called the counterculture. Her subjects were hippies, flower children, radicals, college students, pacifists, protesters, musicians, drug users, faddists, mystics, and gurus: exhibitionists of every kind. She dragged her increasingly heavy bag of equipment through love-ins, campus strikes, antiwar rallies, draft-card burnings, rock festivals, happenings, communes, and slums. It was a glorious time to be a photographer because everyone in America seemed to have donned a picturesque costume and adopted an extravagant pose. One of her photos—a sweet-faced, lank-haired, barefoot girl handing out daisies in a swirling, indifferent Wall Street crowd—made the front pages of newspapers all over America and won a prize. People said it caught perfectly the space between the old and the new. Deanna herself came to hate that shot for its arrogant sentimentality, but it made her reputation. Editors badgered her; national magazines commissioned portfolios; the raw new galleries which had sprung up like bright weeds among the blackened SoHo factory lofts put her work on their walls; in the summer of 1967 UPI paid her way to San Francisco: her mother was finally able to brag about her to the family. Still, Deanna was discontent. In her jeans and her leather jacket, with a double strand of African trading beads around her neck and her hair "picked" into a substantial black bush, she could move invisibly and at ease through the outlandish, hopeful crowds of the "new generation," but she knew she was just masquerading. In her heart she was frightened and old-fashioned. Beneath all the giddy expectations of the day, she suspected, lurked the same old sour and hungry world, and it would take no more than a subway ride to Brooklyn, a metaphor for memory, to return her to it. Sure, it would be nice to break free of gravity, to float off into infinite sparkling space, but think of all the cumbersome paraphernalia you would have to tote along just to be able to breathe.

She clung, as though for safety, to her camera. Increasingly, when it came to photography, she was thoughtful, earnest, and ambitious. She could tell herself without irony that she was pursuing a calling rather than a career. She theorized, for example, that the trick of photography was the conjunction of intimacy and distance, and that, for her, distance was the easy part. Hiding behind her Nikon, contemplating through a long lens the ever-more-elaborate shenanigans of a frantic and outraged world, she felt separated from people, a cold eye snatching moments of alien life. She saw her subjects more clearly than they saw themselves, sensed the gloom behind their visions, and so was never comfortable with the talk, the slogans, the gestures, the dreaminess. Among her new acquaintances she sympathized but seldom empathized, kept her distance because she knew she could never really be part of them.

She struggled to find intimacy in the work she defined as art rather than commerce. She went through a phase of mistaking for intimacy the passions she felt for her lovers, and took pictures of them naked on chairs and windowsills or in bed, half draped in the rumpled sheets of their lovemaking. She accumulated dozens and dozens of these photographs, and tried to admire them, until one day, flipping through her files, pretending to herself that she was examining the formal contours of breasts and thighs and buttocks, and arousing herself at last to masturbation, she realized she could no longer remember all their names. Annoyed with herself, almost frightened, she took a piece of paper and started drawing up a list: Roxie, Nola, Rita, Sharon, Betsy, X, Nancy, Arlene, X . . . She wasn't promiscuous; she scrupulously avoided the tawdriness of one-night stands and told herself at the beginning of every affair that this time, maybe, it would last and last; but a week or a month would slip by and X would merge back into that fluid world of possibilities out of which she had come, and Deanna would find still another X to muse on. There was comfort, there was a momentary illusion of love to be had in that sequence of bumps and orifices, but not the intimacy she sought. As subjects for her camera her lovers failed because no matter how passionately she embraced them, they remained strangers.

She understood then that the African tribesman who believes the camera will steal his spirit has the right idea. She had been photographing faces, bodies, poses, and all the time, keeping it secret even from herself, she wished that eyes could be windows through which she could photograph souls. The conception excited her: eyes as windows! Over the next few months she actually tried it, executing a series of photos of nothing but close-ups of eyes: the eyes of a businessman, the eyes of a moron, the eyes of an infant, the eyes of an old rabbi, the eyes of a lunatic, the eyes of a bride, the eyes of a dope addict, the eyes of a boy on his *bar mitzvah* day, the eyes of a corpse, the eyes of a pregnant woman. She spent her time on the street, in prisons and hospitals, in churches and synagogues, in homes for the aged, in offices and banks, in toy shops and grocery stores, and finally at the mental institution where for all she knew her mysterious relative was still incarcerated, taking pictures of eyes. She became obsessed with eyes. She dreamed about them. She passed mindless minutes studying in a mirror her own eyes, which were muddy green, flecked with yellow the way her life was flecked with anxiety, with a kind of exaggerated redness of the canthus, from smoking marijuana, she supposed. Splitting in half an apricot, seeing the dark oval pit against the sweet fruit, she was reminded of eyes. One day she traveled all the way to Coney Island, to the aquarium, to photograph an octopus because she hoped to find significance in its single age-old eye. She would open the refrigerator and think the eye of the light bulb was winking at her when the mechanism, with a dim roar and power-stealing surge, switched on. Maybe it was a kind of lunacy, but it led to honest work, and in the end her eyes were a great success. Enlarged to gigantic proportions, peering out from the walls of the gallery, they mesmerized the critics. Gathered between soft covers and piled in heaps by cash registers, *The Book of Eyes* sold thousands. But Deanna was not satisfied. In her own terms she had failed. Eyes, after all, are not windows; in them she perceived not souls but only little spectral images of herself and her camera, myriad reflections of the artist caught dimly in a sequence of convex mirrors.

At the time she was between lovers, and despite her success, despite those ever-expanding circles of acquaintances, those journalists, photographers, artists, and lesbians with whom she felt bonds of one sort or another, she was lonely. She felt nowhere at home. Liberation had become the buzzword of the day, and Deanna told herself she was liberated indeed—except on Sunday mornings, when she was compelled to call her mother and listen to her complaints, or when there was a family occasion to attend and she couldn't cough up the usual flimsy excuse that spared her from attending. Liberated: but from what, for what purpose?

When it came to her work, she felt uninspired. Now that others were praising her talent, she began to doubt it. She told herself that her success was a matter of luck, that she had managed to produce a few good pictures by taking so many bad ones, that whatever quality there was in her work was random and uncontrolled. Even some hack of a commercial portrait maker, or a child let loose with a Brownie, might by accident catch from reality an intelligible design. Was she any different? Doubting herself, she came to doubt her instincts. She began studying art books, looking for ideas, notions, mannerisms. She went through a phase of photographing crowd scenes; she hoped they would be like Breughel paintings, but the world never offered such exquisite, spontaneous, appropriate order. Instead of the ingenious, revolving patterns of, say, "Children's Games," she would end up, in her studies of schoolyards, with a hectic, pointless mess.

Of course, she could still practice photojournalism; she could go out on assignment to a rally or a riot and bag the images her editors sought by viewing the world through their limited eyes, pursuing and simplifying into little pictorial anecdotes the confusion of people and events. She could remain detached, studying a world of surfaces: the sentimental pattern of rain-soaked roofs with a single pigeon rising from its nook; the metaphorical jumble of traffic signs, shopping malls, and billboards on a state highway in New Jersey; the sad totem of a dead child's tricycle in a suburban driveway. But she seemed no longer to see what she had once seen so clearly: the apish ambition behind a politician's bland smile, or the riotous webwork in a famous poet's beard. It was a matter of little things. As if the lens of her mind had fogged, she could no longer locate in a spill of water a glistening hint of beauty, or in the snatch of hair in her hairbrush a tangle of inexorable time. She had to trust her camera to take the world in, and meantime she waited, hoping to find again the lucidity of her sight.

The photographer learns to live in and for a moment; Deanna sometimes experienced, not unhappily, the sensation that she had come into existence full-grown and complete just a second ago, and that all the rest of her life, the hazing blur of memory, was a prankish and unimportant fabrication. She valued marijuana because it increased this sensation of vivid timelessness. If at every moment the

354

world was fresh and new, she could bring to it a childish, indeed an infantile wonder and awe. But lately she was haunted more and more by tantalizing memory. She could no longer examine herself in the morning mirror—now, as she was, with her hard face and her long teeth—without also seeing, superimposed, the "gorgeous" child she had been, and without glimpsing, like a shimmer of sunspots around her, the relatives and neighbors who had peopled her abandoned past. Rudely they shouted and bustled and shoved their way into her solitude. At night, alone in bed, with small muscles leaping and quivering in her shoulders and legs, she would close her eyes and try to breathe herself toward calmness, but then, with her guardian thoughts dozing, as though she were flipping through a pile of old snapshots, her memories would come. They frightened her because she couldn't control them. Her mind was like a blank theater in which some lunatic was flashing a familiar chaotic display of lights and shadows. Unendurable: that was the word she chose to describe such moments; unendurable: as though she had forgotten, or no longer wished to know, that she was made of the most durable kind of stuff, that she had inherited from her father patience, labor, and stubbornness, and from her mother sturdy clumps of tough Lieberish earth.

She entered a phase of crisis. Some old unknowable horror was encroaching upon her and she couldn't shrug it off. She put on so much weight that she had to go buy new clothes. Her complexion, always a problem, became red and ragged. Her stomach started acting up; she walked around bloated and full, but no matter how long she sat on the toilet, her jammed bowels refused to empty themselves. She had intimations of madness like flashbacks to an LSD trip. Her surroundings appeared to her a mere painted bowl through which she could pass, stepping outside of time and space, memory and personality, into eternity—but she knew that at the periphery of consciousness, the edge of the abyss, she would panic. Eternity wasn't for her, and so she clung ferociously, fearfully, to the wrack and refuse of material reality.

One day she found herself going around the living room smashing things, overturning the furniture, flinging magazines and newspapers, spilling a glass of wine, scattering the contents of ashtrays: she wanted to make the room a reflection of her thoughts, planning to take pictures of it. But when she was finished, exhausted and almost calm again, she realized that even the extravagance of violence had failed her. Through her expensive stereo equipment, which she had turned up loud and was careful not to damage, someone was singing a song about thirty thousand pounds of bananas, and the simple comedy of it tugged at her core of common sense. That clutter of paper, those overthrown cushions, the spilled wine soaking into the rug while her sympathetic dogs watched and wondered—what had any of it to do with her ambitions, her anxieties, her muddled gender, her tortured sense of self? She had produced not real confusion but simply a mess to clean up. She had succeeded only in giving herself housework—woman's work—to do.

Over the next few days she gleaned from various friends and acquaintances the names of several psychotherapists, and made appointments with three of them. The first, an elderly gray fellow named Engstrom, solemnly informed her that she had an artistic sensibility. The second, a younger man named Fish, offered to teach her how to scream. The third was a woman named Steeben, a maddeningly opaque Belgian with ankle-length skirts and horsey teeth and a strand of exquisite pearls adorning her ostrich neck; she listened to Deanna for half an hour and then murmured:

"Ah, you're hungry."

Deanna would have loved at that moment to rest her aching head upon Dr. Steeben's old bosom and cry and cry. She settled instead for spending two hours a week over the next couple of years submerged in the soft, frayed, gold-colored cushions of Dr. Steeben's easy chair, experiencing the sorrows of its previous occupants as a sensation of warmth on her backside, trying to conjure and exorcise all the noise and heat that had long ago insinuated itself into her psyche.

Time lies coiled in memory the way biology lies coiled in our genes, and you may choose to trace the whole of the tedious winding path or leap more blithely along the loops from moment to moment; either way, until you have comprehended the spiral, you cannot know what you are or approve of what you are becoming: this is what Dr. Steeben taught. The trail to the future must begin in the past. The object was to reconnect Deanna to her history, both personal and evolutionary, bringing her finally to an acceptance of it; then and only then would she be free to choose what she might become.

"Paradoxes and more paradoxes," Dr. Steeben would mutter. "You escape by embracing. You don't have to like it, but that's the way it is: you find yourself by losing yourself, merging into the all in all."

Thus Deanna was expected to resurrect inside herself first her parents, then her relatives, then the imprint of her ancestors on her troubled blood, moving retrospectively through ever-expanding circles of curiosity until she felt her connection to all that lives.

"Remember," the good doctor commanded, "the stuff we are made of was born in the stars."

In practice, though, Deanna never got much beyond her memories of the family. Hour after hour, week after week, she immersed herself in Lieberdom. How embarrassing it was to present them to the scrutiny of Dr. Steeben, to expose them to the glow of all that good sense and sophistication, to confess to this woman whose admiration she craved that she had come out of and thus belonged to what she considered a coarse, ignorant, greedy, commonplace uproar. What did they amount to, after all, a roomful of memories like a murmur of ghosts, a particular configuration of molecules imprinted on her impassioned nerves? How could evoking them help her? Besides, in trying to know them, to see them clearly, so much had to be guessed at, so much was a blur. Nonetheless, slowly, painfully, there in Dr. Steeben's permissive presence, they sputtered to life and threw their luminous shadows about the office. The way they shouted rather than talked: the way they heaped food on their plates; the way they laughed at their own crude jokes and hurried to hug and kiss each other despite their feuds and hatreds; her father's hapless magic, her mother's tormented aspirations, which had to be measured (Deanna came to realize) against the hopeful ignorance out of which she had come; her Aunt Molly's lovers, which she knew so little about; her Aunt Deborah's "ghost," materializing always in a shroud of quotation marks; the chocolate factory, the homes, the automobiles, the clothes, the money; Uncle Walter raising his daughter to be a genius; and pretentious Uncle Moe, with his scrubbed smile and his air of self-congratulation: like castaway toys, like forgotten birthday presents, they crept back into her thoughts, her life. She looked at them through Dr. Steeben's eyes and came to understand them, saw, for example, how they lived in a world limited by their fears and superstitions, realized how they had taught her long ago that there were boundaries in life, that beyond those boundaries she must not go, for to pass over the limits would bring as a consequence terrible punishment—saw this and knew that she had, through her art and her lovers, *overstepped,* and thus, without quite knowing it, was waiting for retribution, the wrath of the ancestral gods to descend. Like a handful of pebbles thrown into a lake, her thoughts became a multitude of rippling circles, and within the cool and tolerant aura of Dr. Steeben—this new "good mother" she had found—she studied, with dread and enthusiasm, all the complexities of their intersections, seeking some pattern or form that might become an emblem for her life.

"Stop struggling so hard against your family," Dr. Steeben kept telling her. "Relax into them. Blood is thicker than water, you know."

Until at last, bit by bit, she began to surrender her fear of being one of them.

Which still left the problem of photography. Distance and intimacy, intimacy and distance: the one was a matter of subject, the other a question of technique. For inspiration she emptied her file drawers and spread out all her old pictures in the living room and spent hours browsing among them, waiting for some instructive image to separate itself from the medley and leap to her eye. This didn't happen. But though it wasn't clear-cut, never hit her with the force of the revelation she craved, she found herself increasingly drawn to photographs of her relatives, the pictures she used to take merely to amuse herself when she was forced to show up at family occasions. Here was Uncle Lou through a fisheye lens, all bulbous nose and belly; here was Aunt Essie in fur and diamonds, scraping with the nail of her pinkie a bit of food from her upper tooth; here was her cousin Joey, incarcerated in a suit and tie, looking hopelessly at the ceiling; here was her mother, not posed, not striking a pose, but caught for a moment in a familiar gesture of impatience. Here was intimacy, far more intimacy than she could ever hope to fabricate in photos of objects, landscapes, or strangers. These images, like it or not, enthralled her.

She had previously dismissed these pictures, called sentimental the feelings they aroused, because she wanted the pilgrimage through photojournalism to art to be an outward journey, a movement away from the trite, familiar center of things toward some distant circumference. She had hungered for something she was not yet, and perhaps never could be. But now she sensed herself standing apart from her past, at the end of a tether, an elastic string that gently tugged her back. The family, the relatives (nice word that): even her first photos, the ones she had taken of her parents and her brother and her Aunt Molly in Florida, soothing herself with a stolen camera—

those little gray blurs she was forever on the verge of throwing away —were charged with intimacy, the simple naïve authenticity of snapshots in a family album. Of course, intimacy of that sort, intimacy in itself, is not enough. But what if now, from the distance she had achieved, grown, experienced, professional, liberated, with her perversions and her pipedreams, she returned to take pictures of, to immortalize the family?

She hesitated, toying with the notion. Once upon a time she had divided the world into the Significant and the Insignificant, and then, without really realizing it, had consigned her family (and thus your childhood, Deanna, your past, your own self, Dr. Steeben would have told her) to the latter category. Who that really mattered could actually be interested in *them*? They were not beautiful, not famous, not even bizarre or freakish; they were not among those who moved and shaped the world; they merely inhabited it, like dull beasts, eating and sleeping and stirring themselves on occasion to howl and frolic and reproduce themselves. Could she actually catch in all that dimness images that could glimmer and shine? Could she, without condescension, without mere irony or bathos, see them clearly enough to do them justice? Why not try? It would be, in any case, honest work to do.

So in her free hours—she still had to earn her money as a photojournalist—Deanna started going around the family, pulling her aunts and uncles and cousins out of the routines of their lives to take their pictures. It turned out to be great fun. When word of her project spread through the family grapevine, people called her up to ask when she was coming to "do" them. She heard from relatives she hadn't seen or spoken to in months, even years. Her procedure was cunning and simple. She would arrive with her equipment—her cameras, her lights, her lenses—and while she was setting up and choosing backgrounds, she would get her subjects to reminisce about the old days. In part this was a ploy to relax them, put them off their guard; in part she hoped to capture the bittersweet mood of memory in their faces and gestures, and thus record what was otherwise invisible and ineffable, the hidden force and faults of time and blood. But more and more she found herself authentically interested in the tales they had to tell. She began lugging around with her a portable tape recorder, convinced that she could hear behind the bland formalities and mild anecdotes echoes of the old family tumult. The story of the family was like a vast, unfinished puzzle and each of them was clinging to bits and pieces. No one portion might be complete unto itself, but in the accumulation of detail a rich and fascinating picture might emerge—in much the same way that Deanna's photographs of the family would finally be patterned not individually so much as in a web of juxtapositions.

She photographed her Uncle Moe in a leisure suit, with the silver hairs of his long sideburns swept back across his ears and a bit of toilet paper glued to a shaving nick on his chin, showing off his collection of old pewter. She photographed her Uncle Walter and her Aunt Sarah sitting across from each other at their kitchen table in what appeared to be a moment of silent and unbreakable communion. She photographed her cousin Joey, an academic cowboy, in jeans and a buckskin jacket on the library steps at Columbia, where he was teaching American history—and heard from him that day a bizarre story of how old Dr. Lipsky, whose huge gruff shadow loomed over the sickbeds of Deanna's own childhood, had once, to teach a lesson about playing with fire, burned Joey's finger with a match. She also heard during the afternoon she spent with her Aunt Rose and her cousin Georgie—coming away finally with an exquisite image of her aunt in an armchair in the background, all mingled pain and pleasure, while in the foreground, one foot raised off the floor, her cousin performed a kind of clumsy, childish dance—that Dr. Lipsky had "carried a torch" for her grandmother. ("How come," Deanna later complained to Evelyn, "you never told me these things?") Aunt Rose also told her about her Uncle Hymie, who, it turned out, was no longer in the hospital but lived, his symptoms controlled by some new miracle drug, in a halfway house on the Upper West Side. Deanna worked up her courage to visit him and found a fat, bald old man, half blinded by diabetes, squinting through thick lenses at the blur of a television set; he roused himself to ask a couple of questions to place her—"So you're Evelyn's little one!"—but mostly he just sat there, silent and empty, drugged into a sort of halfhearted sanity, listening to her talk, flinching whenever she aimed her camera at him, and producing finally out of the obsessively neat drawer of a battered vanity table a greasy, cracked old photograph of herself.

"Look," he said, "just look—this is you!"

She photographed her cousin Erwin, the accountant, in his New Jersey split-level, where he had established a huge pool table in the middle of his living room. She photographed her cousin Gary changing the diaper of his precious little baby girl. On a cool early autumn day she drove her Uncle Sam and her Aunt Essie to Prospect Park and photographed them there, by the lake, against a stark background pattern of docked rowboats, her aunt bundled in an old-fashioned fur stole and clutching her uncle's arm; her uncle, bareheaded, pale, tranquil, leaning firmly on the walking stick he had started using after his heart attack. She photographed all of Moe's girls: Bobbi, who had gone to Radcliffe and was already divorced; Ronni, the cellist, who was living near Columbus Avenue in those days with a very sweet, very gentle, very black-skinned ballet dancer ("No, my parents haven't met Antoine yet—you know how *they* are!"); Micki, a Bennington grad, cute as a button in her paint-stained denims; Toni, who was studying to be a doctor at Downstate; and poor, sincere Jo, who at the vulnerable age of sixteen had pounced upon a copy of the New Testament which "was just waiting for me there on the sidewalk, like a gift," and, all saccharine smiles, tried to convince Deanna to "let the light and love of Jesus into your heart." She even photographed Dov Kalisher—one of her most intriguing shots—mirrored like some picture playing card in his glass-topped desk, with his hair slicked back tight on his skull and a smile on his face that suggested steely satisfaction mingled with unspeakable pain, and his coat sleeve pulled back a bit so that you could see, if you looked closely, a single digit of the number the Nazis had tattooed on his arm; and three days after that unpleasant session, during which he was astonishingly abrupt and rude, Deanna heard from her mother that the poor man had been struck dead by a rushing taxicab in the middle of Fifth Avenue.

In those days much of the family seed was sprawled across the continent, so, in the spring, Deanna flew out to California to photograph her Aunt Deborah—later she had to resist the temptation of conjuring a ghost into the portrait through some cheap darkroom trick—and then zigzagged back homeward, gathering more pictures along the way. In Phoenix she photographed her brother and her sister-in-law and her three boisterous nephews posed around an elaborate plastic model of a sailing ship Ben had constructed—"The rigging's the hard part!"—and spent a night alone with Ben "on the town," during the course of which, in the purple fog of a gay bar he thought would please her (like most of her relatives, he had long ago guessed her "preference"), he confessed to having occasional doubts about his masculinity. In a Chicago suburb she found her cousin Rich doing very well as a candy-bar salesman ("My father's bankruptcy was the best thing that ever happened to me") and heard from him about her Uncle Lou's "chippies" and a hilarious account of the time Sam and one of his gangster friends took Uncle Lou for a ride. In Madison, Wisconsin, she caught a poignant image of her cousin Jeannie, who was finishing up her dissertation and planning in a mood of high excitement the fieldwork she would do in Africa, posed with a book against a tangle of vines and trees. (Deanna intended an element of satire in this, but afterward the family would say that the photo memorialized with precision Jeannie's hopefulness and beauty.) Then it was on to Florida, where she glorified her cousin Carrie in a blaze of sunshine; passed a maudlin morning driving around Miami Beach, stirring up memories, in a rented car; and spent two whole afternoons, though she had planned just an hour, with Asa Kalisher, who, vigorous and talkative, was living on Collins Avenue in one of those formerly swank hotels filled nowadays with old people. What fun it was to listen to him tell about the old days, her grandparents, the village out of which the family had come, the journey to America, his adventures out west among the Indians, the restaurant, the bookstore, her aunts and uncles as children, the love affairs, the origins of the chocolate factory—all the hidden, dark burrows of the past which this marvelous, ironical, energetic old man had explored and which Deanna yearned to hear about. She kept staring at the stub of his pinkie, posed him with his left hand against his face so that she could photograph it, got him finally to show her the famous silver box, as though his detached and mummified finger were itself the emblem of the mysterious ache he aroused in her. She thought she might like to stay with him forever, sit there with him in the cool, sun-speckled lobby until she had drained him of anecdotes, held close to him not so much by his words as by all the vivid lost life they implied; but on the second afternoon his tales at last grew tedious. She came away surfeited, thinking that though he had splashed bright colors here and there, he had withheld from her the fullness of the past—had, like everyone else, his own sorrows to conceal.

She arrived back in New York in a mood of exhilaration and went right to work in her darkroom, developing, printing, enlarging, cropping, touching up, reprinting, sifting, discarding, selecting. This went on for months. In those days she was living more or less permanently with a "friend" named Myra, and poor Myra, like a spurned wife, began complaining that she never saw Deanna anymore.

"That's what you get," Deanna teased her, "for choosing to live with an artist."

This Myra was brown-haired and plump and dark and astonishingly pretty in a soft, childish sort of way—Chocolate Pudding was Deanna's fond nickname for her. When they met, she was working as a technician in a film processing lab, but she wasn't very good at it, and hated the routine of work, so she quit and let Deanna support her. She said she was happy cooking and cleaning and fixing up the apartment. She was so scatterbrained and doting, so passive and compliant, so given to wet-eyed smiles of gratitude and longing, that Deanna's affection for her was practically paternal. Myra was gay— never more gay than when she turned herself inside out, so to speak, exposing all her sweet warm inner surfaces while they played yin-and-yang in bed—but in every other way this darling daughter of a Jewish pharmacist in Forest Hills was thoroughly conventional. She liked to entertain; she would cook elaborate French or Oriental dinners for Deanna's friends, who were more accustomed to receiving from Deanna a plate of spaghetti, a bottle of cheap wine, and something to smoke. Piece by piece she got rid of Deanna's Salvation Army furniture and brick-and-board shelves and replaced it with couches and armchairs and bedroom sets in the same fake Louis Quatorze style that Deanna's mother favored. She enriched Deanna's record collection (jazz, folk, rock) with syrupy Chopin and great creamy mounds of Streisand and Sinatra. Marijuana, she claimed, did nothing for her. She disliked the Village and wanted to move to a brownstone in Brooklyn Heights. She bought a butcher block for the kitchen and papered over the stained, cracked walls with some gold-colored "bargain" patterned with fleurs-de-lis in ruby-colored velvet. Finger towels sprouted like flowers alongside cute fruit-shaped soaps in the bathroom. As far as Deanna was concerned, it was all a bit tasteless and vulgar, but she didn't complain. She knew that what she felt for Myra wasn't love—it lacked some crucial element of equality —but it was, perhaps, the next best thing. Anyway, now that she had arranged the exhibit and sold the rights to the book called *Relatives*, she could afford to indulge her, and, as she told Dr. Steeben at one of her last sessions, this Myra, for all her ceremony and silliness, made her feel at home.

She even allowed Myra to meet the family. For years she had striven to keep her lovers and her relatives apart, protecting them from each other, she claimed, though dreading, in fact, the commitment—the authentication—such a meeting would imply. So long as they inhabited separate realms of her existence, she was safe from the bunch of them; but Myra pestered and nagged and rushed to answer Deanna's telephone, and Deanna brought her at last to eat supper at her mother's place in Brooklyn, and a week later to her cousin Stevie's *bar mitzvah.* She was amused and, after a moment's reflection, not terribly surprised that Myra got along well with her mother and her aunts. Myra could sit happily among them and gossip about clothes and furniture and recipes and fashions, just like a dutiful daughter-in-law. Among Deanna's friends she was often distant and intimidated, but among Deanna's relatives she became warm, lively, sympathetic. She invited them to dinner and sent them home raving about her cooking and hospitality. She kept track of birthdays and anniversaries, mailed out cards for the Jewish New Year, entered into a regular correspondence with Deanna's sister-in-law, spent hours chatting with Deanna's mother on the telephone. Deanna couldn't decide whether to be pleased or dismayed. What was she supposed to do with this bustling, friendly *haimisch,* coy, neurotic lesbian of whom her mother seemed wholeheartedly to approve, this sweet, clinging, affectionate, lovable *balabusteh,* who, in a less complicated world, might have made for Deanna a perfect wife. She had to wonder, as she watched Myra chopping and dicing and sorting out the ingredients of a Chinese meal, or running around the apartment with a *shmateh* on her head, polishing the windows and dusting the woodwork, or strenuously brushing her teeth and dabbing perfume into her armpits as she prepared herself, like a bride, for bed, into what sort of entanglement she had tumbled. There were times when Deanna was appalled by the way they lived, by their parody of conventionality; she would tell herself that soon, soon she would put an end to it and go back to her old freedom; but she couldn't disengage herself, and the longer it went on, the more she was bound to Myra, held in a warm endless embrace of custom and memory, obligation and guilt.

It was Myra who insisted on inviting the family to the opening of the exhibit. Deanna herself was of two minds. On the one hand, it would be amusing, she supposed, to have the flesh-and-blood models for those images on the wall mingling with the usual crowd of friends and critics and sophisticates; on the other, she was afraid of how they would react to the way she had exposed them, to seeing themselves so clearly portrayed with all their pores and creases and warts showing. She had struggled to hold in a cool suspension of irony the sentimentality implicit in the project, and had, for her own peace of mind, succeeded perhaps too well. It was never her intention to hurt them, and it nagged her that they might indeed be hurt. But she needn't have worried. They came, and they mingled, and they said silly things that were merely funny through the mild blur of marijuana with which Deanna had prepared herself, and the only one who went away angry was her Uncle Moe, whose smiling, defeated emptiness Deanna had aptly captured. All the rest were pleased enough to have been included, in any guise, as though Deanna had established them gloriously in a larger, more permanent world. As her Uncle Walter told her:

"I don't have to approve, but I do have to respect, your version of the way we are."

The punch bowl was emptied, refilled, emptied again. Platters of little cookies were gobbled up. The admiring crowd swirled slowly round and round the exhibit, talking and laughing and pointing fingers. The marijuana had worn off, but Deanna's head buzzed with pleasure. She was no longer distinguishing between critics and cousins, friends and family: they were all a single, jovial audience for her work. The eyes of fey Jon Kingsley, the gallery owner, twinkled with merry dollar signs. Arms embraced her; lips pressed against her cheeks; the air was warm and damp with the symptoms of success. She kept glancing at the pictures, hardly believing that she herself had created them. They appeared softer than she had imagined them, the harsh black-and-whiteness of them suffused, by some trick of her vision, with a faint bluish mist. Her body glowed with the pleasure of pride and accomplishment and the flow of her own warm blood. From across the room Dr. Steeben looked at her and smiled. Myra, in a delirium of self-delight, came up and hugged her, whispering love, promising ecstasy.

But it was too good to last. Her mother emerged from the crowd flushed with punch and reflected happiness, and stood there a moment waiting to be embraced. Deanna, then Myra, complied.

"Such a party," said her mother. "Such a crowd. I'm sorry your brother's not here. I feel like I'm bragging to people when I tell them I'm your mother."

Deanna, tightening, found nothing to say. Her mother's hair was swept up along the sides and sprayed with silver paint. Her dress was gold and gaudy. Dampness glimmered in the creases of her neck.

"I'm so happy for you," her mother *kvelled*. "My daughter, the success."

"I'm glad you're enjoying it," Deanna told her.

"I was talking to that Mr. Kingsley, a nice man, but I think he's a little *faygeleh*."

"Listen," said Myra, "let's go out to dinner together, just the three of us, someplace fancy."

"It doesn't have to be so fancy," said Evelyn. "Besides, you probably prefer being with your friends."

"No, really," Myra insisted.

"Sure, we'll celebrate," Deanna was compelled to say.

Evelyn was moved.

"She's a good-natured girl, your friend," she said. "The two of you, at heart you're both nice kids. I just wish the day would come when I'd see you settle down already."

Deanna experienced a familiar giddiness. "Mom," she managed, but her mother, oblivious, with an old idea rattling around in her head, plunged on.

"I know, you don't have to tell me, you're shy. But enough already. You can outgrow being shy. I'll tell you something. The world is full of nice fellas, and don't think they wouldn't be tickled pink to marry either one of you."

Myra, truly good-natured, just smiled at that; but Deanna felt the floor sinking slowly beneath her. This impossible woman. Would she never understand?

"Mom," she tried again, but her mother was invincible.

"Take it from me," she said. "I speak from experience. A woman doesn't sleep in peace when she doesn't have a man."

At which point Myra said: "You ought to try sleeping with another woman."

And Deanna almost died.

JOEY IN THOSE DAYS was just where he wanted to be, teaching history at Columbia, with a book and several articles published, a second book in the making, his wife finally pregnant, and his tenure practically assured. He was good at what he did, very good, and though the last decade had produced a superfluity of historians—of scholars of every kind—J. L. Grossman was becoming a name to reckon with. His specialty was the colonial period. His dissertation had proposed, through an impeccable analysis of demographic records, that the Puritans had actually played a lesser role in the birth of America than was commonly believed. He also maintained a personal and abiding interest in the conquest of Mexico, which he said provided the necessary hidden counterpoint to what he called in his lectures "the New England craziness, the expectation of Paradise on earth." The conquistadors had a simpler idea: grab the gold! There, according to Joey, was an authentic motive for braving a wilderness.

He gloried in contradiction, ambiguity, and paradox. Nothing warmed him more than an audacious, insincere argument. He could without undue discomfort take any side of practically any question. The correspondence section of the *New York Review of Books* was his notion of good clean fun. In the company of urgent student radicals he insisted sardonically on human depravity and the need for social order; among his more sober colleagues he fervently defended spontaneity, passion, and redemptive violence. Though at times he felt lost in the tangle of his disillusion, he held, nonetheless, as an article of professional faith, that the past was knowable through the murk and blur of time, and that even a random assortment of facts, meticulously collected, scrupulously observed, could provide a satisfactory image of sense and truth, the rudiments of a useful explanation. By way of demonstration he would assign to the students in his undergraduate classes the task of assembling their genealogies. They were supposed to salvage from their oldest living relatives the names and dates of their ancestors and as much as they could about manners, customs, religious convictions, political sympathies, philosophical beliefs. Next they had to interpret the assembled data—this was the point of the exercise—to determine how much of what they believed to be their own unique "world views" had actually come down to them, so to speak, through their blood. Joey conceded to his colleagues that as an academic experiment it was, perhaps, a bit simpleminded, but it contained the procedures of history "writ small," and besides, a recent best seller had made genealogical research practically a national obsession. Anyway, the students adored the research.

With his beard and his early baldness, his wire-rimmed glasses, his big Lieber nose, Joey at the age of thirty had come to resemble one of those topsy-turvy creatures you see in a child's book of games and puzzles: a face, and then upside down another face. The beard, to be sure, was just an experiment, a late-sixties accretion which he kept on, along with his denims and boots, in defiance of a more heartless and conventional decade. For nearly nine years he had been married sturdily, if not altogether happily, to a bright, handsome Vassar graduate named Annie, who had canceled her hopeless ambitions in the theater to go to work as a layout designer for a group of medical trade magazines. They had met in Manhattan, married in Great Neck (in one of those gaudy catering halls run by the Mafia, amidst a huge assemblage of relatives), honeymooned precipitously in the Catskills, rushed off to the grind and void of graduate school in New Haven, detoured for three wintry years in the cozy bleakness of a small liberal arts college in the upper Midwest (where they made each other miserable out of sheer boredom), and then, after his dissertation had emerged as a book, after the book had won a prize from a genial society of antiquarians, returned more or less whence they had come. They were established in a comfortable, old, high-ceilinged apartment on West End Avenue, surrounded by books and records and museum posters left over from their New Haven days, and the beginnings of a fine collection of pre-Columbian art. Summers when they weren't traveling they rented a house on the beach in Connecticut. The family wondered how they could afford all that, but Joey saw no reason why he shouldn't combine an intellectual career and left-wing sympathies with material success. He had delved with all his considerable shrewdness into the arcana of stocks and bonds, commodity futures and tax loopholes. For a while they had scrimped and saved, living on his salary and investing hers, and now they were collecting the dividends. They weren't rich, but someday they might be, and Annie's widower father, a Seventh Avenue furrier, was transferring funds to them as a way of evading inheritance taxes. So they had money enough to enjoy the usual luxuries of a smart, urban, childless couple. They took taxicabs to the theater and the cinema. They feasted in exotic restaurants and came home to try to duplicate—in a kitchen full of expensive devices—the subtleties of taste they had discovered. They belonged to a health club, where Joey played racquetball as a defense against what he called hereditary tensions and flab. They had a Sony color television which they used mostly to watch late-night mysteries and westerns in black and white, and an elaborate stereo system which filled their living room alternately with Annie's show tunes and Joey's rock 'n' roll, though Joey disciplined himself on occasion to the more intricate forms of music —Bach, Handel, Mozart—he felt professionally compelled to know about. In short, Joey had most of what he had set out to acquire when he was "just a working-class kid" in Brooklyn, and if he wasn't happy, he seldom believed that he ought to be.

He told himself that in the mad, random, ambiguous world in which we live, happiness is the condition of dullards and the dream of fools. His own nagging hunger and gloom marked him, he was sure, as a man of superior sensibility. To live is to choose; to choose is to surrender possibilities; thus life cheats us always. That he could walk across campus agonized by furtive, squeamish desires for some misty co-ed in the class he had just left; that he could stare out across dangerous Morningside Park and envy the furious life in Harlem down below; that whole days went by when his discontent gathered itself in lumpish aches at the back of his head, or made his eyelids twitch, or caused his hectic heart to stir and tremble; that he could gaze up at an evening sky and sense a faint exquisite terror at the emptiness between the stars: these were merely the concomitants, he believed, of his intelligence, his honesty, his introspective strength. He suffered, but that was more or less the human condition, and so he suffered stoically and with pride, congratulating himself for his refusal to sentimentalize his "tragic view" of existence. He interpreted his moments of despair as symptoms of grace. He lived the life of the mind. He had left behind him the superstitions and ignorance of Brooklyn and family. He had become what his hazy-eyed brothers and his brutish father (shrunken nowadays by heart disease and kidney problems to a mere dying shadow of himself) could never be.

Though he never said it out loud to Annie, he no longer believed in love or marriage. Marriage, he had decided, like civilization itself, was predicated awkwardly on restraint; and while he could recall with pleasure a moment early in his courtship of Annie, on a night enchanted by a lunar eclipse, when he had surrendered himself to bliss in the back seat of a friend's fogged car, he now suspected that love was just a social convention masking the basest of emotional hungers. People want to be in love, he had concluded, the way they want to go to heaven—soothing their fear of loneliness in the first case, their fear of death in the second. Nonetheless, his own marriage, for all its squabbles and wounds, for all its *philos-aphilos*, was a reasonably good one. Annie was decorative and smart; she didn't embarrass him; they fit comfortably enough together, and he had looked

369

forward rather blithely to raising a family with her. He believed in home and children, and had been eager for paternity. Long ago he had deduced the simple and obvious truth that one's primary obligation to life was to make more life. Life's fundamental quality, after all, is continuity; it's a seam without breaks, generation to generation, the passing on of those living molecules which are the filaments of a single thread reaching back through parents and grandparents to the first mobile flecks of jelly creating themselves in the primeval ooze. What other purpose could there be in life than the extension of that thread on into the imponderable future? *Be fruitful and multiply!* There, by Joe, was a categorical imperative.

But the years had passed in a succession of rubbers, foams, diaphragms, pills, and false alarms, while he and Annie established themselves in their careers and made themselves comfortable; and then more years passed while they plotted temperature charts and consulted doctors; and that spring, when Annie finally conceived, Joey felt neither joy nor fulfillment. He felt instead a kind of horror as if some glory had eluded him.

He feigned pleasure; he had to, had no right, that is, to trouble Annie, in her condition, with his doubts and fears; but during those initial weeks his nerves were frayed and his sleep ruined. He suffered through his classes and then walked home through the warming, lengthening evenings of early spring lost in confused introspection, oblivious to the motley crowds surrounding him, preparing himself for the smiles and hugs and kisses of reassurance he was obliged to bestow upon Annie, knowing that some necessary and crucial part of him had balked, and balked violently, at being a father. But why? For years he had held within himself images of a cute, dark-haired, fat-legged toddler tumbling with shrieks of joy into his expectant lap, of the good, wise, patient, doting parent he would turn out to be, of the pleasure of coming home to a rush of small eager arms and the sweet cries of "Daddy! Daddy!" But faced with the reality of it, with the authentic flesh of his flesh and blood of his blood doubling and redoubling in Annie's still-flat belly, he felt nothing but anxious revulsion and disgust. Why?

Haplessly, like a slow reader trying to piece together a fragmented narrative or an elaborate conceit, he sought clues to his condition. His usual ironic mode had failed him; he could no longer smile at his troublesome ambivalence; he would have to be, for once, conscientious and scrupulous. After all, inaction, too, has its consequences, was, in a phrase, action's despicable twin; and so a clock was ticking: baby or abortion, which was it going to be?

He never doubted that the choice was his, that he could say to Annie, "I don't want this baby, we made a mistake," and she would end the pregnancy. She might even be glad for the excuse, glad, though she was feigning a pleasure of her own, reading up on child-birth procedures and breast feeding, to follow his lead. Nowadays abortion was legal and easy. She would go to a clinic, they would insert a sort of vacuum cleaner, and the deed would be done. Neither of them had any strong moral objections. They both believed in the right to choose, in planning, in the obvious social good of not bring-ing unwanted children into the world. Even if you granted the claims of the anti-abortionists, conceded the silly theological squab-ble about when life begins and called the act murder, it was still, at worst, a kind of justifiable homicide. No theory or scruple made it impossible for him to consider that possibility—nothing but a qualm, a nervous shiver of memory (a dog bleeding to death on a kitchen floor) shadowing his thoughts as he contemplated it. But he could bear the guilt, as he had borne the previous guilt, if he could be certain it was what he wanted. Was it? How, in such a circum-stance, was he supposed to decide? He was trained to gather facts, sift through them, discard the specious ones, bring the rest together in a model of explanation—but what facts were pertinent to his strange case? What questions could he ask himself that wouldn't lead on, in ever-widening circles of consequence, to newer, more intractable questions? How, in short, faced with his bizarre reaction, could he understand himself?

He tried to be practical. He drew up a list of pros and cons. He could think of plenty of cons. The mess, the expense, the inevitable heartbreak children bring. The loss of freedom. The silly rigmarole of diapers and night feedings and pediatricians. The interruption of what was, after all, a satisfactory sex life. Annie's smooth, girlish flesh torn and ruined, her breasts pendulous and soggy, her stomach crazed with stretch marks. And in some not-too-distant future the little brat, grown to monstrous adolescence, defying him, hating him, murdering him in its seething, wretched id. He had watched his brothers and friends go through morbid changes after their children were born. They were haggled and beset; their conversation deterio-rated; they had to move out to the suburbs. A little pilot light of worry burned constantly in their brains, ready to flare at any moment into heartbreak and sorrow. Toys underfoot. Silly bedtime stories. Breakables put out of reach. Teenage baby-sitters, sometimes lovely, forbidden fruit to be conveyed safely home through the trembling, guilty, insane darkness. Arguments about discipline, television, household chores, money, he and Annie tearing at each other in the cage their marriage would become. And what if something went wrong, a congenital defect, a bad heart, fins instead of arms, leukemia, cerebral palsy, Down's syndrome—the kid an idiot like poor cousin George? How do you cope with that? How do you go on not merely living but doing, accomplishing, making your mark? To have children is to cage yourself within a small universe of drab and mundane miseries. All this—and on the other side nothing but sentiment and tradition and stupid instinct, balmy notions of blood and affection, and the fear of one's personal extinction masked by a vital theory.

These were practical arguments, but he had reasoned through them before. He had fought them out with Annie years ago when he would talk of babies and she would say to him:

"If what we want is something small and fragile to love, let's buy a puppy."

No, his mundane list of negatives couldn't really explain the hot panic her pregnancy had engendered in him. Then why? He groped in his own darkness trying to make sense of his torn mood.

Maybe it wasn't the pregnancy; maybe, rather, it was Annie who troubled him. He could confess to himself that despite his skepticism, some eager and hopeful part of himself had always imagined that someday he would find some other woman, leave behind him the complicated passions he felt for his wife and in new adoring arms enter a realm of unambiguous bliss. During his worst nights, when his equilibrium was threatened and skepticism didn't work and he felt himself drawn back toward the old mindless confusion out of which he had come, this was the dream that soothed him: some gorgeous golden-haired stranger, a mysterious spark of love flaring between them, the wholehearted intensity with which she would cherish and adore him. But to have a baby with Annie meant surrendering that dream forever. Once a child was involved, divorce would be out of the question; he would be bound to Annie forever.

Annie, Annie, Annie! How tangled were his feelings for her! Annie in a flannel nightgown descending the elevator on a Saturday morning to fetch, with ceaseless optimism, the morning mail. Annie ensconced on the toilet in the slow, sensual rush of polishing off a double-crostic puzzle. Annie protruding her lower lip as she pondered strange dried foodstuffs in an Oriental grocery store. Annie in a good mood, bursting into song. Annie in a bad mood, drawn up into herself on the couch as bristly and forbidding as a hedgehog. And now Annie quickened, burgeoning, carrying at long last their child. To tease, to argue, to tear at each other, these had become the procedures of their marriage. In some ways they understood each other too well, reflected each other back to themselves all too clearly. But in other ways they remained strangers.

He remembered how years ago, when they were spending a summer exploring America, they sat in a motel room near Yosemite Park and ate Irish soda bread and drank cold duck out of paper cups and watched, along with all the rest of the world, the arrival of the astronauts on the moon. In the books and movies of his childhood the possibility of that achievement had been the precise emblem of a hopeful future; but the future had come, was already slipping away into the past, and he realized, as he watched the spacesuits galumphing across the alien landscape and sensed Annie's fingers grasping for his, that whatever momentary elation or conviction the moment might bring, it would do nothing to change the course of his life. Men on the moon! For America the sky was no longer a limit. But the moon was a drab and familiar place compared to the dark craters and mysteries of Annie's secret soul. He understood that life itself, stretched to this new periphery, had in consequence become thinner, rarefied, and more vaguely insubstantial—and when he looked at Annie, she appeared to be floating through a void, far away from him, beyond his reach. What made it so terrible was that looking back at him, she smiled and beckoned, beckoned and smiled. Impregnate her then; let her have his baby; it was one way he might reach her.

So that was it. He stared at the memory and felt his thoughts rearranging themselves. Was it nothing more than the *triumph* of the pregnancy that was bothering him? If so, if he had been spooked by an unexpected tingle of victory in his nerves, then he could forget this nonsense about abortion. Why, he could no more wish to give up the baby than he could seek to erase those first human footprints from the lunar dust.

Anyway, he assured himself, nervousness was normal; all men, faced with the mystery of a pregnant wife, must experience such doubts and fears.

Thus it was decided, and with the decision, at least for a while,

Joey was able to relax. He sounded appropriately enthusiastic when he called up his mother to tell her the news and endured with a complacent smile the kidding he received from his brothers. He became increasingly dutiful about helping Annie with the household chores, and watched with pleasure the slow bulge of her belly and the swell of her small breasts. Sure, he had moments of doubt, and tight knots of tension still gathered in his shoulders and neck and temples, but the months hurried by and he was busy with his classes and papers to grade and those piles of index cards on which he had encoded his research. One day he stopped off at an import store on Broadway and blew twenty dollars on a silver baby rattle from India, the kid's first toy. It was an extravagant gesture, but it was worth it: for days afterward he felt lighthearted and complacent.

In June, with Annie's stomach grown to a substantial mound, they moved out to their summer house in Connecticut. They had estimated the birth date would fall in late September or early October, so they could enjoy one last childless summer and still have plenty of time to get back to New York to convert Joey's study into a nursery. In the meantime, to be on the safe side, they visited a local gynecologist and toured the facilities of the Yale-New Haven Hospital, just twenty minutes away, and started taking Lamaze classes on Tuesday nights. Joey was always happiest in Connecticut. He liked waking up to the sound of waves lapping gently at the gray, pebbly beach, and starting off his day with a swim instead of a shower, and in the brilliance of a summer afternoon hoisting the orange sail of his little boat and sliding across the gentle green waters of the bay, and then coming home for a gin and tonic on the deck. The pretty town of Hyton with its stores and winding roads and white steeples rising up out of a darkening hollow toward the ecstatic sunset sky; the long curve of the beach, where a few children and dogs might be at play; the multicolored roof of the boat club, a few late sails glimmering homeward through the dusk, and a distant lighthouse already throwing its practical beam in circles against the encroaching night—for Joey these were the tokens of richness and luxury, the assurance that he had escaped the concrete tawdriness of his Brooklyn boyhood. Here, more than anyplace else, he could feel himself at home. He had even considered leaving Columbia for Yale, buying a house in one of the old towns on the shoreline, one of those gray clapboard places with a shingle outside saying "1693" or "1709"—to live in a house full of history would connect him securely to the national past, make him a real American.

But that summer, with time and a pregnant wife on his hands, he couldn't settle himself, couldn't get comfortable, slipped back into the springtime's anxiety and gloom. He went wandering out for long, solitudinous walks that only increased his restlessness, and came back with his face burning in the questioning light of Annie's eyes. There were some good moments; Annie would occasionally take his hand and press it flat against her mound so that he could feel the kicking and stirring inside her, and they would share a few seconds of flushed anticipation; or they would drive home from those Lamaze classes giggling together over the solemn foolishness of the breathing exercises. But more often he felt worried and distracted. A kind of madness was being born in him. He had flashes of vivid, violent fantasy that left him damp and shaken. His memory, so precise in the matters of place and date and event that made up his profession, had become oddly dim about his own personal past, and this troubled him in a vague, Freudian sort of way. What was he hiding from himself? What unconscious message was he afraid to read? The various symptoms he was experiencing, the headaches, the restlessness, the fantasies, the occasional ringing in his ears—weren't they charges of repressed memory trying to break through? And if they were, what was he so eager to forget? At times he would close his eyes and try to visualize his parents, his brothers, the room he had grown up in, his teachers, the schoolyard, the world as it once had been, but it was all cloudy and blurred. People, places, bits of action would flicker in his thoughts and he wasn't sure if he was remembering or imagining them. He knew that if he followed this mood to its conclusion, he would begin to mistrust the whole basis of his life, and so tried to shy away from it, but his thoughts plunged ahead against his will. If memory is unreliable, if it blanks out some things, distorts others, entangles itself in dreams and illusions, then how can we know what we've been or what we are? What if his past was shot through with deeds and crimes he chose not to remember? One night, watching the late news, hearing a description of a man "wanted for questioning" in connection with a brutal rape-murder, he was terrified by the thought that the suspect of medium height, dark hair, curly beard the bland newscaster was describing was, in fact, *him*. Sure, it was just the free play of his overwrought mind, but for a few heart-clenching moments the game darkened into earnestness. How could he know for sure that he hadn't, in a fit of unrecalled insanity, done the horrible thing? Here, look, the picture of the victim, eleven years old, blond, a gold crucifix gleaming against the lace of her confirmation dress. The victim's father spoke earlier today to our Eyewitness camera.

"Oh, God," cried Annie, her belly huge, her face darkened and freckled by pregnancy mask, "why can't they leave the poor bastard alone?"

And there on the screen was the father, crew-cut, puffy, struggling against tears, recalling what a good obedient child his daughter had been while Joey's mouth went dry and his thoughts hammered and he felt himself in the distension of his throbbing nerves to be father, child, and criminal all at once, caught in a miserable overflow of imaginative empathy. He forced himself to his feet and hurried to the kitchen to find some ginger ale to drink, with Annie, always thirsty nowadays, calling after him to bring her some, too.

The rest of that summer was, in recollection, the worst time in his life. Beneath the threshold of his thoughts some ancient quarrel was going on, but the terms of it were obscure and the outcome undecided. All he knew was that he suffered. If it wasn't one thing, it was another, as though he were struggling to give form to some inchoate passion that was as dark and mysterious as a womb. He would wake up in the middle of the night trembling with the emotions of a forgotten dream. There were times when his head was so heavy he couldn't lift it from the softness of the couch cushion, other times when it was so light it tugged like a balloon at the root of his aching neck. Often his hands were damp and itchy, or his eyelids would start fluttering, or his ears would suddenly pop. He would go swimming and sense an urge like an undertow dragging him out into dangerous waters. He would be walking with Annie through a supermarket and feel a fierce erection bulging painfully, embarrassingly against his pants—and a few hours later, trying to make love to her, he would be soft and shriveled. He dabbled in self-analysis, came to various conclusions, which seemed momentarily to clarify his mood, and then surrendered himself again to thoughtless anxety. Some of this he shared with Annie, but mostly he kept it hidden, believing that he had no right, given her condition, to upset her. Meanwhile, with her usual efficiency, she was preparing herself for the event. She joined the La Leche League in town and brought home pamphlets for him to read about the wonders and benefits of human milk. ("Our generation is so neurotic," she once told him, "because our mothers didn't breast-feed us.") She was punctilious about taking vitamin pills and calcium pills, and avoiding medicines of every kind—even aspirin during the week when she was miserable with a summer cold—and practicing her breathing exercises and relaxation techniques. She started knitting a tiny sweater in yellow, and would sit in the evening, needles clicking, smugly communing with the life inside her, oblivious to his mood, as glowing and self-contained as a madonna. Maybe that was it, he would tell himself, mother and fetus form a closed circle from which he was excluded. Nature was busy inside her and he had become extraneous; there was nothing for him to do but to wait and worry and wonder.

He tried to keep busy. He went to the local library and brought home a pile of books plucked at random from the meager shelves, but his eyes blurred and ached when he sat down to read them. At a local tourist trap he purchased an expensive jigsaw puzzle version of Bosch's "Garden of Earthly Delights," and for most of a week he sat and assembled it on a bridge table, losing himself for a time in the fabulous intricacy and the subtly recurrent details of the thing. Occasionally he would kill an hour or two by putting on earphones, turning up the volume of the receiver, and letting the blare of rock 'n' roll fill the brooding hollow of his thoughts, but such was his state of mind during those days that the songs he used to love, the music he believed connected him to the dark primal rhythms of his life, repelled him and made him nervous. Taut, helpless, he would go out on the beach and toss pebbles in the air and practice shooting at them with the imaginary gun he had quick-drawn from an invisible holster.

Weekends they had company. Annie's pregnancy was like a magnet drawing his family to them. His brothers showed up in their big gleaming cars, with their rowdy children and their overdressed wives, to startle the quietness of his private beach. They had a visit from Deanna, with whom Joey shared a warm complicitous scorn for the rest of their relatives, and whose ever-more-obvious lesbianism troubled Joey in an unwilled sort of way; and from Annie's father, who left behind an embarrassingly large check "so you can buy a crib and stuff;" and, late in August, from Joey's parents along with his Aunt Evelyn, who had been cajoled into driving them up. His parents had news to announce; they had decided to sell off the old house in Brooklyn and buy a "condo" in Florida because the doctors had said his father's heart couldn't stand the strain of another New York winter. Evelyn was moving down with them, buying a place right next door.

"So when you come down to Brooklyn next time," his father said in a hoarse, strained voice, "I'll give you those newspapers I've been saving for you," and for the first time in his life it struck Joey with real force that his father, this impossible man, was going to die.

After lunch, while the women cleaned up the mess of corncobs and steak bones, the two of them went out to the beach, and when his father took off his shirt to soak up some sun, Joey was stricken by the sight of his soft, withered, womanish breasts and the sagging, empty bag of flesh that was all that remained of his once-huge belly. Formerly he had hated and feared this selfish, angry man; now with one small shove he could knock him down into the sand. A thought came suddenly, almost violently: all his life he had struggled not to be like him, to be everything he was not; but with Annie pregnant, with himself about to become a father, the struggle had been lost. He, too, would boast and rant and cheat and holler; he, too, in a flare of anger, would jerk off his belt and send his sons howling and hating through the startled house. He stood there watching his father cough and hack in the mild air, saw his yellowish skin and scarred legs and the ramshackle squalor of his shoulders and chest, and sensed his face start to throb and itch as though his lips and nose and cheeks were congesting somehow into the image of his father's features, were being pulled and twisted by his own coarse genes, by all the old ache and fury of Grossman blood. So that was it: he dreaded becoming a father because he dreaded giving birth to his own father within himself, dreaded not this sick dying old man who was essentially a stranger to him, but the enraged, cowardly, blustering, ignorant father who loomed enormous in the tangled corridors of his darkest memories. The thought splashed over him like a wave brimming into consciousness, cascaded, and slowly withdrew, drawing off with it the pebbly wrack of his confusion. He sighed with a kind of morose pleasure. It was a moment of profundity: an epiphany. But by the time they got back to the house, where Annie was impressing her mother-in-law with home-ground coffee and an array of French pastries, the mood had passed, and he suspected the moment had been just a meaningless surge in the chemistry or electricity of his brain. What is an epiphany, after all, but a commonplace insight charged with sick emotion, a revelation that leads you nowhere? Dramatics, self-dramatics, that's all it was, putting on a show for yourself in the private theater of your mind. Some profundity that is!

Still, he went to bed that night, after he had gotten rid of his parents and his aunt, with a residual heat warming the roots of his nerves—and was startled awake at two o'clock in the morning because there were lights on in the house and Annie was not by his side.

He found her in the kitchen drinking iced tea, working a double-crostic puzzle, and timing the cramps which had turned out to be more than her squeezed stomach rebelling against the three ears of corn she had eaten. She had called the doctor, who had told her that nothing would happen for hours, she should get some sleep. Joey checked himself over, expecting to find panic, but found instead nothing but grogginess and a small headache. He coaxed her back to bed, and for a long time they remained awake together in the darkness, hushed and awed by the simple actuality of the process, timing the contractions by the illuminated dial of the clock radio as they waited for the pains to fall into a strong pattern. She was doing her breathing exercises, and to help her, he matched his breathing to hers and put his hand on the bottom of her belly mound, feeling against his palm a bulge that he assumed was the baby's head pushing out toward the world, a child, his child, not willing, not eager, but forced anyway to be born. She cursed against the pain, and he kissed her damp forehead, feeling close to her, closer perhaps than he ever had, as though all that had come between them before, the long ambivalent years of marriage, squabbles, secretness, frustrated expectations, his own restless desires and moods, had been merely a prelude to love. He found himself whispering a confession to her, telling her that he wanted to be a good father and that he was afraid he wouldn't know how to be. "But you will," she told him, setting his head softly against her swollen and aching breasts, and he dozed off like that for a moment, with his cheek nuzzled against her maternal firmness and his hand touching her straining bulge, feeling for once all peaceful and silent inside, drifting through a dreamy, thoughtless mood more vital than knowledge.

Then they were up and dressing in the gray dawn, and searching for that tube of toothpaste Annie had bought to take with her to the hospital, with Joey's insides heaving and aching in sympathetic and envious response to Annie's labor.

Through the pink and purple dawn of what would turn out to be a steamy hot day they drove an empty road to the hospital, discussing names, settling on Jonathan and Jennifer, kidding each other that next time they would stay at home, call in a midwife, do it in the natural way. At the hospital they stole her away from him to "prep" her, and for almost an hour he stood and sat, stood and sat, waiting to see her again. Then, in the labor room, for what seemed an eternity, he sat by her bedside, holding her hand, letting her dig her fingernails into him every time a contraction came, feeding her chips of ice, and remembering with pompous solemnity all those Lamaze class techniques he had thought were so silly. She was sweating and pale and blue-lipped and swollen; he had never seen her so ugly or loved her so much. He even had to fight off an occasional rush of perverted desire; there were giddy moments when he wanted to have sex with her, there as she was, in all her agony, with the slimy crown of the infant's head showing through her dilated cervix. He was infuriated when the nurses would come in and smile at him, treating him like the cliché of the nervous father-to-be, but he had to admit to himself that that's what he was.

It was nearly noon when he followed Annie's bed to the delivery room. He was repelled by the pale green institutional walls, the white closets filled with syringes and bandages, the table, the grotesque metal stirrups into which Annie's legs were strapped—everything prepared and silent and ominous, as in a torture chamber. Fearful, sickish, trying to be curious, he stood by Annie's head, reminding her about the breathing exercises, watching the process in the mirror they had arranged for him. *Push, now push, now push. And relax. Now push, and push. And relax.* She strained and cursed, hating the pain. Her opening was shaved and cut and bleeding, had lost all sexual enticement and become a horribly huge and daunting thing. *And push. And push. Father! Encourage her! Push, push.* He wondered if he could ever have sex with her again, how his own puniness could fill that enormous doorway she had become. *And push, and push, bear down, harder, push, and push, and push, and . . .* It was happening, it was happening, first the slow head of it and then the rest, squiggling out of her, shoulders, arms, fingers, legs, penis, a boy—

> Not in entire forgetfulness,
> And not in utter nakedness,
> But trailing clouds of glory do we come—

a boy, a son, already crying as it would cry night after night for months, crying out its heartbreaking hunger and confusion, and the nurse was hurrying to wash it and wrap it as though she didn't want them to have to look at it that way; but he had looked, and had seen the whole mess of it reflected in the mirror, seen the fluids and the blood and the black slime with which it was covered and which he would later learn was its own dark excrement clinging to it like mud in the womb; had seen and thus had known that it is not glory, but blood and salt water and dark slime out of which we come. The simplicity of this truth shocked him and brought on a moment of anxious nausea: so it wasn't death or violence or madness or his father or his fatherhood or Annie or mere memory he was afraid of; it was this, life, life itself, the bitter mess and gore from which he had removed himself and was so eager to avoid.

"He's a darling," said the nurse through her mask, "he's absolutely beautiful."

She brought it, cleaned and pink and tiny in a white blanket, and handed it over to Annie. Annie was giddy, almost laughing as they sewed her up. She gave the baby her finger, *kvelling* at its strong grasp, making Joey lean closer for a better look.

"Hi, Jonathan," she said.

He was all right now. There had been a moment when it nearly got to him, but he was all right. He checked his emotions, felt appropriately warm and squeamish and relieved. The vile mess was gone; the baby was pink and puckered and beautiful. A boy, a son. He could imagine him at the age of four and five and six dressed like a cowboy or an astronaut, playing boisterously in the living room. Sure, have children; at least in them your continuance, if not your immortality, is assured.

He thanked the doctor, shook his hand, and bore with good grace the doctor's teasing about his greenness. Well, he, too, had labored and suffered, but he was all right, he was really all right.

Then they spirited mother and child away from him to let them rest, and he found himself roaming the hospital corridors, searching for a pay phone, groping in his pocket for the coins he would need to call his parents and tell them to spread the news. He was still all right; in fact, he was feeling rather wonderful as he rehearsed the conversation, bracing himself for their questions and excitement. Yes, he would tell them, it's a boy, another Grossman. Yes, he's fine, he's beautiful. Yes, Annie's fine, too. Yes, yes. Everything's fine. No need to worry. It was, after all, a perfectly normal delivery.

IN THE FINAL HOUR OF HER LIFE JEANNIE LIEBER, tall and tan, stood barefoot on the bank of an East African river enjoying the cool ooze of mud sliding between her long, monkeyish toes. At this place the river widened and slowed, becoming almost lakelike before gathering momentum around a bend and rushing westward to the falls. She had seen the falls that morning. Michael had driven her there in the Land-Rover, and they had climbed and gaped for nearly an hour, and then made love on a cloth spread over a flat damp rock, with the cascading roar in their ears and the mist rising up in a rainbow around them. A lovely moment, a moment of bliss, but the sun had given her a headache, and she was sore and grimy and uncomfortably sticky between her legs. So she had left Michael napping and come down to the river for a swim. The river water was green and murky, but through some trick of light and vision the surface reflected the brilliant impeccable blue of the African sky, enticing her in. She supposed that her khaki shorts and work shirt would serve well enough, here, for a bathing suit. She waved at a pesky fly and started breathing slowly, methodically, trying to soothe her headache and preparing herself for the cold shock of the water.

Behind her, a few hundred yards up a winding path, was Michael's little hometown, not much more than a village really, an ageless and ramshackle clutter of wattle-and-stick huts betrayed by the modern government office and school at its center. In front of her, across the water, a field of banana trees, the red and stunted fruit of which she had seen in the local market, rose through shimmers of overheated air toward some distant dusty green hills. Those hills interested her. Here and there, behind the blue blur, outbursts of tan rock broke through the greenery like eruptions of new earth, waiting to be explored. Site for a dig? She would have to discuss it with Michael. For now she was content to wriggle her toes deeper into the mud and contemplate the hills from a distance.

She had been in Africa nearly a year and was no longer startled by that quality it had of being somehow always ancient and new; still, it thrilled her. In Africa her inner clock was constantly resetting itself to new and unexpected scales of time. She could almost anticipate seeing a clan of long-armed premen, some vague form of *Eoanthropus,* pair-bonded and stone-armed, emerging over those hills, and she loved that pleasant, dreamy, timeless sensation. It was, in a sense, precisely what she had come to Africa to find. That iridescent fly and some newfound friend buzzed around her; absently, she waved her hand at them. If only she could stay and stay. Maybe when she got back to Laulu, the slow mails would have finally coughed up the letter she was expecting, renewing her grant and extending her leave of absence from the university. She wanted it so badly she could feel the pale blue tissue-paper envelope in her fingers, see the creases and smudges it would have acquired in its journey, and the canceled American airmail stamp—a small, reproachful sliver of home. Another year, and then maybe another. If the work went well, money could always be had. Certainly here she was closer to the center of her life than she had ever been in New York or in icy, boring, inconsequential Wisconsin. Maybe in the end her work, and Michael, would keep her in Africa forever.

Work for Jeannie in those days was paleoanthropology, which amounted to scratching fragments of fossilized bone out of the slopes of Laulu Gorge, a nasty gray gashed little wilderness set like a wound within the yellow savannas of central Kenya, some ninety miles from the more famous Olduvai. Her title was associate project director, but that didn't mean much since, except for Dickerson himself, all eight of the professional anthropologists at the site, including Michael, were associate project directors. Still, it wasn't bad considering that she was only twenty-six years old, and had squandered years of her education exploring the process of self-definition through literature, history, psychology, and art. The gorge was divided into three zones and they worked three to a zone, with a few local laborers and students to do the heavy digging. For comfort against the heat and flies and grime and exhaustion she would remind herself that since ontogeny recapitulates phylogeny, the mysteries of her own personal past lay buried there like primeval memories in the African earth, but mostly it was the bones of ancient herbivores they discovered, and she had learned to seek her primary reward in the slow, intricate pattern of the work itself. Nonetheless, sometimes, if she could fit a chipped flint into splinters of a wildebeest's femur, she could conjure up a vision of some ancestral forebear a million years ago, squat and filthy and brutish, sucking hungrily at rich marrow; and recently she had located, in fragments, not the skull she had hoped for, some shattered braincase that might indicate through inferred volume the intelligence of some new species of near-man, but a relic almost as interesting, the remnants of a hand. They spent weeks, she and Michael and pompous Dickerson, unloosing the fragments from the ground with toothbrushes and dental picks, and more weeks putting it all together like a jigsaw puzzle from which pieces were missing and the solution unknown; and ended up, after a bit of reconstruction, with three whole fingers, most of the palm, and the all-important thumb. It was one of the truisms of the discipline that intelligence can merely conceive a tool, it takes a thumb to form and hold it; and so the survival of an anthropoid depended at all times on a conjunction of hand and brain, of craft and intellect, and the coordination between them. That thumb spoke volumes—though it never told them what happened to the missing finger—and they were celebrating the find by taking a vacation.

Jeannie's notion of a vacation was to drive to Nairobi, check into some posh touristy hotel, take a long hot bath, eat an expensive meal in a restaurant, and make love to Michael in a huge bed, between crisp white sheets; but Michael insisted she come with him to meet his family, and she couldn't refuse without hurting him. Dear, sweet, gentle Michael. She suspected that what she felt for him wasn't precisely love, not if love meant certainty and surrender, but she knew that she didn't want to hurt him. She curled her toes and drew them back through the rich mud, watching the furrows she had made fill with water. She smiled. All those hours while they drove north toward the Ethiopian border along roads that became ever more narrow and rutted and ill-defined, past farms which gave way finally to brushland and patches of forest with a giraffe raising its slender neck on the horizon, he had been nervous and apologetic, worrying about what she would think of his family and what they would think of her. His eyes were murky; his face was as round and shiny and dark as a chocolate coin; little stiff curls of hair grew like peppercorns on his thick chest. As soon as they arrived in town, the usual swarm of dirty and half-naked children buzzed around her, laughing and chattering with their hands stretched out: "Madam, candy, give candy, madam," and though half of them were probably Michael's cousins, he was embarrassed by them and rudely shooed them away. Marry him? Give her parents a couple of coffee-colored grandchildren to brood over? With a squelching sound she pulled a foot out of the mud and stepped in further, wondering if she should consider the mud a threat or a grace.

Her headache was deepening to a warm throb of pain on the left side of her brow, nothing serious, just a hidden message from the right, wordless hemisphere of her brain, some small anxiety or sorrow she had repressed, probably something to do with her father. Poor Dada! Thinking about him evoked in her the melody of one of those old left-wing folk songs he would play for her when she was very young, and she hummed the opening bars of "Big Rock Candy

Mountain" before losing the tune and rhythm to some inner syncopation. A memory came, how he used to take her out to Prospect Park and rent a rowboat and let her steer them in lazy circles round and round the pretty lake—but why that memory, of all things, why? Never mind. She had learned the hard way that in the process of self-definition *Why?* was imponderable and involved you in illusion. Better to ask anything else—Who? What? Where? When? How?—rather than *Why?* Because if the answer to *Why?* was not a chaos, it was an order so complex it would seem a chaos to a finite mind, and between that sort of order and chaos itself there was no important difference. She started humming again, uncertainly, feeling the headache thicken. Poor Dada! Maybe when she got back to Laulu, there would be a letter from him.

His letters troubled her. He filled them with news of the family—the weddings and births and illnesses—and bits of political absurdity he copied out of the *Times* as if to avoid spilling the bitter secrets of his heart. He had such great expectations of her, and she was always disappointing him, always letting him down. She remembered how he came to the airport to see her off to Africa, and stood there, moping, in the rush and confusion, awkward and moist-eyed and bony, telling her to write often and take good care of herself, and how, after she had kissed her more placable mother and turned to embrace him, he confessed in tears that it was like seeing her off to war. He should have known better, but he couldn't help it: his image of Africa was compounded of Tarzan movies and newspaper headlines, and thus for him Africa lay in a dark terrible void, beyond the limits of his inner geography, was all a jungle where some half-savage terrorist might murder her or some wild animal eat her up. Oh, Dada! She wondered what he would think when she told him about Michael, and promised herself, as she had for months, that the next time she wrote she would mention him. But she could imagine all too easily the confusion it would cause him, the way he would have to struggle to align his enlightened principles with the primitive prejudices of his Lieberish heart. Uncle Moe had said, when he heard that Ronni was pregnant by a black man, that he wished he were religious so that he could go and sit *shivah* for her because now she was dead to him. Dada would be less melodramatic, and more sadly compliant in the end, but certainly he would suffer. *Dear folks, let me tell you about Michael. It's too soon to say that I love him, but he's an exquisite, gentle man, and very bright—in his way, a lot like you, Dada.* She imagined bringing Michael home to meet her family, the tables turned, herself just as nervous and apologetic as he was yesterday, Michael beaming sweetly at a mob of Liebers, and her father staring at him, seeing for the moment not the sweetness, not the gentleness, but those ceremonial scars, three on each cheek, coruscating Michael's face. Then trying to smile, and failing, so that his expression would become ghastly and torn.

Well, what have they taught you lately?

Fucking.

But really, she chided herself, you must write home about him. They have a right to know.

She took another step forward and watched the water play around her slender, tanned ankles, wondering how dangerous it would be to swim here. She noticed the current swirling and rippling around a jutting stick, thought about kwashiorkor and crocodiles. Michael had shown her a small crocodile that morning, dozing dirty dun green in the mud a few miles downstream, but the invisible worms of kwashiorkor worried her more. She examined the shoreline for snails: no snails, no kwashiorkor, she decided. Anyway, if she wanted health and safety, she could have stayed in Wisconsin, where the nursing homes were jammed with embittered old people with stunted and unexamined lives. Michael loved to tease her about the dangers of Africa. He told her stories about rogue elephants raging in the tall grass outside the town perimeter, of swarming red ants as big as your finger, of charging water buffalo overturning cars, of ragtag bandits who looted and murdered along the Kenyan backroads, of mysterious diseases which flared across the countryside like the scourge of a malevolent God—but though she was often frightened in Africa, she would not yield to her fear any more than she yielded to it in New York during the days when she had to walk at night alone in menacing neighborhoods. Fear was normal, fear was healthy, fear served an evolutionary function, but, she believed, fear like everything else had to be put to the service of intelligence, and her intelligence reminded her that fear was primarily a response to one's own inner workings: you impose upon the world the figments of your own worst dreams and desires, then struggle to protect yourself from your own imagination.

She turned quickly, hearing a sound, and saw some local women in bright rags, balancing large gourds on their heads, moving up the winding path toward the village. She waved at them and they started to laugh, showing rotted yellow teeth. She was determined to be nice to everyone she met here because there was no telling which of them might be Michael's relatives. For all she knew, for all Michael let her know, the whole town was one big happy family, the congregated spawn of Michael's splendid grandfather, who was the police chief, the judge, the postmaster, the government agent, and whose eyes, sunk deep in a face that was as wrinkled as a raisin, had never once stopped watching her during the family feast of the previous night. What had he made of her? she wondered. What would he say to Michael when he got him alone? What old drumbeat from another time moved his secret heart?

"You are welcome here," he said when he met her, and again, hours later, as he held her hand between his fingers, which were as soft and dry as pieces of chamois: "You are welcome here," with a mild placid question in his eyes as if he were measuring the length and substance of her for his own bed.

She watched the women move in single file up the path past a small boy lazily driving a few dung-caked and swell-bellied cows with a stick, envied the women their color and grace and rhythm, and was annoyed by how much sick prejudice there was in her envy. *Shvartzers*. Sure. It was in a rowboat in Prospect Park, on a hot summer day that returned to her with such peculiar force and clarity that she could see her father's white shirt sleeves rolled back to reveal the black hairs on his ropy arms, when she told him how she imagined the chocolate color would rub right off those brown people she had seen on the subway, and he explained to her in a tight strange voice that those people were called Negroes, and that they had been slaves in America the way the Jews had been slaves in Egypt, and that in this world there were people called *bigots*—he made it a spat and ugly word, bitter on the tongue—who through a kind of sickness hated and feared anyone who was different from themselves. He said she should always remember no matter what sort of ignorant talk she might hear, even from her aunts and uncles, that beneath the skin we are all cousins, all exactly the same. For years it nagged at her like a burr caught in a hidden loop of memory, not his little sermon on brotherhood, which was to be expected, but the sense she had even then, at the age of five or six, that her father for all his show of candor was hiding something from her, some inner darkness, some squeamish bigotry of his own.

Was Michael then some sort of test for him?

She didn't like that thought. It sharpened her headache and made her breath begin to heave dry in her throat. She wanted to run back to the village and look at Michael sleeping, as though only the physical proximity of him could help her wend her way safely through her confusion of feeling. The stillness around her began to hum with the voices of the Liebers complaining about what the *shvartzers* were doing to their old neighborhoods. The first time she made love to Michael she had waited for his breathing to steady itself into sleep and then got out of bed to examine herself in the bathroom light, had seen a brownish smear on her thighs and passed through a moment of lunacy before realizing that their exertions had brought on her period. Her headache was now a blare, and against it she started to hum again that old folk song, aware of the space between her humming and the song that was unwinding in her memory, the space between her memory of the song and the actual old recording of it, the space between the recording and the ideal music the singer, with his voice like honey and gravel, must have heard in his head. Those spaces defined her confusion.

You expect too much, she warned herself, touching the center of her headache, and then dipping her fingers into the current and dribbling lines of water down her well-tanned arms. You are like the rest of them, caught up in a delirium of expectations, turning in upon yourself, afraid through some lapse of attention you might lose the purity of your dreams, so self-absorbed, so hardened against hurt, that you have lost the capacity to love.

Those flies still buzzed near her face, and almost angrily she flicked her hand at them. The most heartbreaking sight in Africa was to see flies walking on the faces of little runny-nosed children who were too inured and passive to brush them away. The African flies were so bold you could close your hand around them and feel their vibrating life in your fist, crush them if you had the stomach for it, and inspect the ooze and crackle of them on your fingers. In the matter of flies the fossils held no revelations, but certainly the first humans were plagued by them. On a bright, clean, palm-lined street in Nairobi she had observed a pathetic beggarwoman nursing her baby at a shriveled, bare breast, wailing when she spotted Jeannie her ancient beggar's wail, with so many flies swarming around her greasy knotted hair you might have thought they were being born there. To love one must not expect too much; if you expect too much, everyone, always, will let you down. A fly swooped near her and she grabbed for it, but not determinedly enough, and it eluded her. She moved a few steps out into the river, her feet cautiously probing the slimy bottom which, the water being murky, she could not see. Were there river snakes here? She rolled her hair up into a bundle at the top of her head, found the barrette in her shirt pocket, and fixed it there, thinking that in this water she shouldn't get it wet. Come on now, in you go—but she still wasn't ready.

Strange how African sounds and odors and landscapes, precisely because they were so alien, sharpened her sense of home. Last night, for example, walking with Michael beneath the sprinkled salt of the stars up the hill to his grandfather's house, she was reminded of how her father used to take her to visit her Aunt Deborah, though later, as she sat on a grass mat drinking the spicy, honey-flavored local wine from a carved cow's-horn cup while Michael's grandfather stared at her and Michael's beaming rotund mother kept refilling her plate with food and some incredibly old, toothless crone, whose relationship to the family she never learned, cackled at her in the harsh tonalities of an unknown tongue, it was not Aunt Deborah's closed bedroom and antique clocks she recalled; rather, there was resurrected within her a lucid vision of the apartment where her Aunt Molly used to live—she saw clearly the mussed bed, the multiple rugs, the little television set, the tiny sink heaped with dirty dishes. Odd, quirkish, persistent memory: what biological function did it serve? How did it help the primordial *ur*-man survive in the vindictive wilderness into which he was born? And why that dreamy wash of nervousness which inevitably accompanies old memories, that dire sense of slippage and loss? Dickerson was out to prove that pair-bonding, with its concomitant of quotidian sex, preceded intelligence and toolmaking in the evolutionary tangle. Was it memory, then that called the hunter, after the frenzy of the chase, back to his hungry mate and babies? Memory that told his mate to admit only him to her rocky bed? Memory that bound us together—huddling in the dark, the shared warmth of bodies our only defense against the chill of a primitive night, the awareness of each other our only solace against pain and natural misery? Memory that set us on the course of family, clan, tribe, village, civilization? Memory preceding all? But if memory, then time. If a past, then a future, and the mind separating itself from the *now*. The first ape to lift its sluggish head and mark the course of the sun discovered time, and so became a man; and man's first uncontrollable thought, perhaps, was a memory of his lost apedom.

Slowly, indulging herself, she waded farther in, enjoying the cool, rippling, seductive creep of the water up her long thighs, shuddering and softly saying *Ooh!* when it touched her groin. Then she bent her knees and arched her legs so that the water flowed up around her loins and buttocks, loosening all the morning's stickiness and floating it away. *Ah!* She plucked her shorts loose where they crept up into her crevices and tightened her shoulders against the cool fingers of the water, sighing softly, while the sun's broken reflection chimed brightly around her and her head throbbed harshly against the sensations and the glare. Then, straightening, she swung both arms and splashed glittering diamonds of water up around herself. The two flies, startled, buzzed landward. Childlike and frolicsome, closing her eyes and opening them again, she crossed her arms to run her hands up into the sleeves of her work shirt, smoothing cool dampness along her goose-bumpy skin, shivering with the pleasure of it. Then she became self-conscious and turned to see if the women were watching her, but they had disappeared into the village and she was alone. Rules for swimming: wait one full hour after eating, swim with a buddy, no horseplay. The old world lingers in the depths of memory; the conflict between old and new, between what our parents made us and what we wish to be, produces our fear and our guilt. Sometimes her sense of her father, the way she could close her eyes and hear his voice inside her skull, chiding her for being less than he wanted her to be, appalled her. As though to embarrass him, she slid her hand into her shorts and touched herself underwater. At the touch her headache throbbed and vanished into a tingling excitement that rang in her ears. If only he could see her as she was now, standing waist-deep in an African river, in bright African sunshine, playing with herself, exciting herself past the murk of his expectations. Dada.

"We failed," he used to tell her. "My generation, I mean. We sought a better world, and we failed miserably, ignobly. Which is why your generation must succeed."

And what could she say to him but the simple, unutterable truth that in every way that mattered his generation and hers were precisely the same?

In the calculus, Jeannie had once been pleased to learn, an infinite series of determined points vanishes into the single smoothness of a curve. Thus in life it is a mistake to fix upon moments and ignore the curve of flux. The flow is the only reality that matters; we live along that curve. But occasionally, through stress or pleasure, a moment will close like a circle around us and we will come alive in it. Now was such a moment. She touched her secret nerve-rich center, momentarily eluding thought and memory and time, and sensed herself passing newborn into a new world poised between the water and the air, the hills and the blazing sun. Something, some small water creature, brushed against her foot, and the touch rippled up through her until her scalp itched. Now, now. She let go of herself and plunged, forgetting about her hair, swimming underwater with her eyes open against the green blur, and came up spitting and groping for the bottom with her feet. Shoulder-high. The bottom fell away faster than she had anticipated. Not that it mattered. She was a strong, graceful swimmer—her father had seen to that years ago in the saltwater pool at Brighton Beach. She gasped, caught her breath, and dove again, coming up, with her feet churning, in water that was over her head. She took a mouthful of water and spat it, imagined that she tasted cow urine and hippo dung, and didn't care. Water was her element. She cupped a handful of water and held it to the sunlight, watching the living motes dance within it: a billion years ago, earlier than time, sea broth radiated into life, and those bits of spiral thread still swim within our cells—how marvelous, how wonderful, to be part of all that. She dove and rose and breathed, dove and rose again. When she cleared her eyes and looked back toward the village, she saw someone she thought was Michael coming down the winding path. She couldn't tell for sure; he had a white shawl wrapped native-style around his head and shoulders to ward off the sun, and from this distance his face was just a little chocolate chip set in a marshmallow. Sweet Michael. She waved at him and he waved back. So it *was* him. In the exhilaration of the moment, watching him hurry down the path, she told herself that, yes, she loved him. Then, playfully, showing off for the man she loved, she kicked and dove and came up again, churning water with her feet and splashing with her hands, looking for him through the glitter of bright splashes she made. She spotted him coming down the path, waving a bit frantically, perhaps worried about her—just like her father. The two of them were brothers under the skin. She waved back, watching him, loving him, and loving her father, and all the rest of the world, too, and she was so caught up in the giddiness of the moment that she never saw the squat dark ancient form rushing up through the murky dangerous depths beneath her.

NINE

IN THE MONTHS AND YEARS after Jeannie's death Walter filled some of his emptiest hours by working up a family tree. He began by gathering notes on colored index cards, pink for Kalishers, blue for Liebers, green for in-laws, and so on. Then he went out and bought a set of calligraphic pens and three big pieces of parchment, which he sewed together to make a kind of scroll, and canceled the sad ache of many an evening by neatly lettering all the names and dates he had managed to collect. He said it was his way of thanking the family for helping him and Sarah through the darkest hours of their grief; people had flown in from all over the country to come to the funeral and offer what comfort they could; so it was a labor of love and, inevitably, given Walter's nature, a kind of obsession. He ran up enormous phone bills, interviewing distant cousins from both sides of the family, and calling up unknown Liebers and Kalishers, whose names he plucked from the library's collection of phone books, to ask if they might be related. Eventually he was able to flower the family tree with more than a thousand names, spread across six generations. He could tell you where most of these people lived or had lived, and how they made their money. He kept, along with the scroll and index cards, a series of subsidary charts for the various branches and offshoots from the main lines of descent, which on the Lieber side he traced back as far as his father's grandfather, a fellow named Avram, who was one of twelve children. For Walter in those days, as he mourned his daughter and approached his retirement from teaching, there was no better antidote for the gloom and pain of his life than to spread the whole mess of his research out on the kitchen table, add to it a newborn baby or two, and then ramble back and forth through the maze of generations, stopping here and there to ponder a missing name or an uncertain date. For him each entry was a life, each life a portion of his own rich blood and genes, and his sense of all those relatives growing up, finding husbands and wives, doubling and redoubling themselves on into the crowded future, momentarily sweetened the bitterness of seeing his own little twig, with its little closed bud, futureless and broken.

The work, the tree, the family—these were his best solace. There were even times when his spirits rallied and he talked about traveling to Europe to find the old village out of which the Liebers and Kalishers had come. There wouldn't be much left to it—Hitler and Stalin had seen to that—but by exploring the local archives and cemeteries, maybe he could extend the tree back another generation or two. Sarah welcomed the idea, said a trip might do them good, take their minds off their tragedy. Walter even talked things over with a travel agent. But when it came to setting a date and drawing up an itinerary, his heart sank. Jeannie's death—the bizarre and brutal fact of it—had canceled out too many of his hopes and dreams, too much of his capacity for expectation. He could go on with the routines of his life, he could teach his classes, he could eat his meals, he could shake his head over the latest political absurdities he found in his evening newspaper, he could rouse himself on occasion to write a sharp-tongued letter to the editor; but he couldn't plan beyond the day. How could he know, after all, what random horror the next hour might bring?

You can invest just so much in this world of ours, he told himself, because in the end the world takes everything away and you are left with nothing, nothing, nothing.

Nothing, that is, but bittersweet memories, and occasionally these, too, could comfort him. There were times when he could will himself back past the heavy closed door of Jeannie's death and she would come alive for him again, his own little ghost child at play in the hazy fields of recollection. Jeannie reaching up for him with her white arms to give him a good-night kiss; Jeannie bouncing and giggling on his back while he, on hands and knees, made a "horsey" for her; Jeannie at a birthday party in a rainbow of glowing childish faces; Jeannie at school (he is spying on her from the corridor) blurring her fingers at her teacher in the desperate happiness of knowing the answer; Jeannie coming home from college to discuss with him the sexual innuendos in the works of James Joyce; Jeannie scratching away at her violin: he could hear like an ache in his ears that dear failed music. At night, with Sarah snuggled up warmly against him (they had learned to go to bed at the same time, even if one of them wasn't tired, because the approach to sleep had become too treacherous to bear alone), he would be half dozing, smelling the faint sourness of his aging flesh, feeling the surrounding darkness creep slowly into his bones, and Jeannie would appear to comfort him, a gentle mind-made specter reborn out of wisps of memory and dreams and love. They would talk and tease each other the way they used to, play a few word games or tell each other riddles, and he could almost believe at such moments, as his sister Deborah did, that life is not cruelly bounded by death, but that some essence of us, a soul, a spirit, a thread of consciousness, something, something, lives on forever in a kind of lingering radiance. At such moments, half dozing, with his heartless skepticism half suspended, he understood Deborah's comforting superstitions; but no matter how hard he tried to surrender reason and good common sense, his stubborn and all-too-lucid intelligence kept insisting it was memories, only memories, which haunted him, that we can live just so long in this finite world of ours, and then no more.

Besides, memory could also be cruel. Some little things, the splat of rain on a window, an apple's brown bruise, a shout in the street, an airplane soaring overhead, the ringing of the telephone, might set him off, and he would find himself resurrecting not her life but her death; and then, in shame and agony, he would have to relive it all over again. Time might rub smooth the most jagged edges of it, cloak its full horror, but he knew he would never forget that ordinary night interrupted and shattered by a phone call from the other side of the world; the voice of Professor Dickerson squawking through hollow static the incomprehensible news (vaguely at first, but later on with all the gory details); the sensation, as he stood there listening in his own amazed damp heat, with Sarah clutching hysterically at him, of the floor pressing up against his feet, of his body drawn down as if the gravity of the earth itself had suddenly multiplied and tugged furiously against him; and Professor Dickerson telling him, as though it were a kindness:

"They recovered her body, and I'll take care of shipping it home to you; for what it's worth, I might as well tell you that they shot the damn thing."

But that was not the worst of it; the worst of it was still to come.

Between the news of a death and the burial of the victim, Walter was to learn, there is a dreadful spell of time when the mourners, against all logic, go on anticipating a miracle. Maybe this is a bad dream that will end; maybe the telephone call was a gruesome prank; maybe the doctors will work some magic; or the corpse, beckoned back to life by the sheer intensity of a father's grief, will get up and walk away. He had to wait forty hours for the coffin to arrive from Africa, and while he waited, while he writhed and suffered and thought about suicide and coped with Sarah—for whom a doctor had to be called in, a powerful tranquilizer prescribed—he clung desperately to such lunatic hopes. The phone might ring again, that voice might come back on the line to say sorry to trouble you, but it was some other man's daughter whose torn remains were flying to New York in a box. It could not be that Jeannie, his clever, lovely, loving, precious Jeannie, the best part of his own flesh and blood, had been dragged to death in a crocodile's jaw. It was too bizarre and awful to comprehend. He couldn't even bring himself, when he had Rose on the phone—for it was Rose to whom he entrusted the heartbreaking chore of passing the news on to the rest of the family; Rose who could best convey to the others the agony of his loss—to say it to her, to tell her the truth. So he lied, lied clumsily and stupidly because he had so little experience with lies, and so added to his other miseries the fear that the family would not believe the lie, would know right away that Jeannie was much too good a swimmer, had been taught too well, to die by drowning. Unless there had been something, some hideous brutal something, lurking there, waiting to pull her under.

But even that was not the worst of it, the hoping and the lies. The worst came later, at the airport, when the body arrived. The funeral parlor could have handled the formalities, he could have spared himself that agony; but he insisted on going. Perhaps he understood that the trip to the airport and the sight of the coffin would mark the end of his hoping, and during the forty hours of waiting, the hoping had become intolerable. So he went; he exposed himself to a hot, dreary ride in a hearse, to getting lost in the airport's winding maze of back roads until the stupid driver located the freight area, and to sitting in a dim government office with a huge oscillating fan puffing dust and jet fumes around him while over his head, beyond the low ceiling, life-laden planes roared up into the hot gray sky toward exotic destinations he knew he would never see, and no longer wanted to. He sat there, proud of his grim composure, and signed the papers, and then walked around to the side of the building to watch them wheel out the coffin, which was little more than a crudely nailed shipping crate, and load it into the hearse—four strong men lifting it as if it contained nothing at all—but he knew that it contained his Jeannie, and for a moment he thought his heart might fail him, so furiously was it pounding and thumping to the wild rhythms of his grief and amazement, so vivid was the image that blazed through his mind of her actual lifeless limbs and hair and breasts and eyes. If only he could rip open that horrible box and with his own hot breath and tears pour her spilled life back into her —he was on the verge of causing a scene—but he dug his fingernails into his palms and chewed to bleeding shreds the insides of his cheeks and kept hold of himself. He had to. Some old voice within him commanded him not to lose control in front of these strangers, these *goyim*. Then he was riding back to Brooklyn, conscious of the thick, pimply neck of the hearse driver and of the box resting silently on layers of satin behind him, and as they whirred through the hot shimmers of traffic on the Belt Parkway, he was wrung through by wave after wave of grief and woe, which gave way, when they left the parkway and started winding through the quiet familiar streets of Brooklyn, to a blessed numbness of exhaustion.

"That was the worst of it," he would tell the family. "I knew that if I could survive seeing that box, with the shipping labels still stapled to it, I could endure the rest of it."

And he did. He endured the anguished customs of choosing the casket and purchasing the burial plot (a triple one so that he and Sarah might someday go to rest with their child) and arranging with, Rabbi Neumann, who sat on the board of directors of the Peretz School and was probably as agnostic as Walter himself, a service that would honor the necessary traditions without insulting anyone's intelligence—endured it stolidly and grimly and good-naturedly because even though Sarah was tranquilized practically into a stupor, he was no longer alone. The family, with whom in recent years he had been so distant, came rallying around him, first the ones who still lived in New York, Rose and Sam and Moe and Deanna and Joey, showing up at his house to sit with him and run errands and fix meals and hold Sarah's hand and absorb the outbursts of grief and terror, and then the others, flying in for the funeral from California and Florida and Arizona and Vermont, from wherever the family seed had rooted itself as it spread across the continent.

For two days the telephone lines that connected the family

hummed and tingled with the mournful arrangements that had to be made; for two days Deanna and Joey kept shuttling out to the airports to pick up relatives and bring them to wherever an extra bed or couch or cot could be prepared for them. They all came, all the Liebers and Kalishers, along with a smaller showing of Sarah's relatives, drawn together by the old bonds of blood and memory and primal affection, as well as by the need to separate themselves for a while, in the face of such a bitter and unexpected loss, from the ordinary habits and routines of their lives; and since it had been years since they had been gathered together, there murmured beneath the solemn faces and quiet condolences a mood of nostalgia and reunion, almost, although Walter didn't feel it until later, an air of celebration.

He would remember coming into the funeral parlor with his arm around Sarah as she stumbled and swayed against him, and staring for a moment across the assembled crowd, and suffering through Rabbi Neumann's gentle and inconsequential eulogy, still seeing them, as if he had eyes in the back of his head, the whole *mishpuchah,* more vivid to him at that moment than they were even in Deanna's photographs, while the rabbi filled the mournful air with empty words and Sarah, tranquilized into a mere weeping shadow of herself, carved little bleeding crescents into his hand with her fingernails.

He saw Asa Kalisher, nearly a hundred years old, that shrunken and gnarled little nub of a man who had insisted on flying up from Miami for the funeral, sitting with his straw hat pressed down tight on his bald head and one damp tear line glistening in the crevices of his face like water squeezed from a stone. He saw Sam, pale and tired, hunched forward with his chin on his hands and his hands on his walking stick, with Essie in black on one side of him and Rich in dark blue on the other and, next to Rich, the handsome red-headed six-footer who was Sam's oldest grandson, his moody presence suggesting a kind of enlarged and simplified snapshot of Sam's younger self. He saw Deborah, who had materialized from California the previous day and had so far spared Walter the dubious consolations of her premonitions and communions; and Ruthie and Evelyn, practically twins with their silvered hair and their Florida suntans, surrounded by their respective broods; and Moe with all his women—his wife, his daughters, his granddaughters—that most luxuriously flowered branch of the Lieber tree; and Rose, puffy-faced behind her eyeglasses, squeezed in between Georgie and Hymie, for even Hymie, a perfect stranger as far as the younger Liebers were concerned, had come to the funeral; and, of all people, Aunt Bea, who by coincidence had arrived from Tel Aviv the previous week to visit the family and haggle with the government about her Social Security. They were all there, assembled for the occasion, and as he cast his mental eye around the room, he even imagined a few ghosts: his mother and father, and Molly with all her dead and vanished husbands, and Milton, and Lou Grossman, whose kidneys had failed six weeks after he retired to the good life in Florida. They had all congregated for him; for the first time in his life he was at their center.

He wanted to turn around and comfort them by letting them see how bravely he was bearing his grief, but he knew he mustn't—it would break the decorum—so he sat and spied on them through his thoughts, sensing their eyes on him while the rabbi droned on and on, filling the hushed gloom with empty words. "Everything to live for!"—that was the heartbreaking phrase people used, and now the rabbi said it: "Everything to live for!"—and something in Sarah snapped. Her body sagged toward Walter, and he put his arm around her heaving shoulders and let her weep freely on him, seeing her tears make little wet circles on his trousers, tasting on his lips the salty dampness of his own unbidden tears, and hearing behind him people crying or making quiet, clucking, sympathetic noises. He knew they were crying not so much for Jeannie or him or Sarah as for themselves—as they imagined themselves in his situation—and at another time he might have been annoyed with their hypocrisy. But they had passed beyond his criticism; there was now nothing about them he couldn't forgive.

At the cemetery, after the grueling ride behind the hearse in the funeral parlor's limousine and the dozen cars strung out behind it, running red lights as though death obviated the simple rules of the road, everyone formed a circle around the naked grave, crowding together as if some powerful force at the bottom of the hole were drawing them in. The eye of the hot May sun stared down mercilessly as the rabbi mouthed some more prayers and the grisly machinery lowered the coffin, the noise drowning out the distant hum of traffic from the Long Island Expressway and the even more distant chattering of birds. Sarah wept and wept, her supply of tears apparently endless, and many of the women wept with her, little quiet convulsions bursting out here and there around the circle; but Walter, though his eyes stung with empathy, had gone beyond sadness and grief. He stood there caught up in a taut and heightened mood, a kind of clarity of mind that was awkward and exhilarating. He had never felt, despite himself, so fully alive. This was the same cemetery where his parents were buried, and he was conscious of their nearby graves, and of Molly lying a hundred yards away beneath a double headstone that said "Levitch," and of Uncle Chaim and Uncle Yonkel and Lou Grossman, that preposterous, coarse man. A shadow of his boyhood passed over Walter and chilled his soul. The Hall of Primates, the commandment implied: Love them! The sun was burning hot on the back of his neck, and he hated its glare, knew that he belonged—like Deborah, like his father, and perhaps like Jeannie—to the pale unsatisfied glow of the moon; and with this thought there was released within him a bitter joy, a sweet misery, an emotion that was neither hope nor despair, but some final mingling of both. So we die. All that fuss, all that tumult, and then we die. The coffin settled against the earth; Sarah howled and subsided; mechanically Walter threw down the ritual handful of dirt and heard the dry patter as it sprinkled across the coffin. Deborah was at his side, saying:

"She's gone to a better place now."

His temper flared, but he bit his tongue and forgave her. Because we are all, in our own separate ways, doomed to expect too much.

It was evening. The family had come back from the cemetery and crowded together in Walter's living room to initiate the ceremony of sitting *shivah*. Walter wondered why he was submitting to it, why the previous night he had nearly quarreled with Sarah to get her to accept it. He remembered how, when his mother died, he had set aside his atheism for a few days, sat with the others, and found some comfort in it; but it was more than that—it was that his family anticipated the ritual, had come together to be part of it. Anyway, by the time he got home, Rose, having skipped the cemetery, had laid out platters of hard-boiled eggs and bagels and lox on the kitchen table, and the funeral parlor had delivered a couple of wooden benches, and when Walter escaped the crowd long enough to run to the bathroom and empty his aching bladder, he discovered that someone had draped a towel over the medicine chest mirror. So be it, he told himself. He would mourn in the fashion of his ancestors, crouched on a hard bench, with ashes in his hair and his clothes symbolically rent. At such a time even a hollow ceremony is better than no ceremony at all. Jeannie, infatuated with the past, would have understood; and

Sarah, at least for this one night, was too numb and exhausted to complain.

He returned to the living room mopey, secretly proud, wondering what would happen next.

He would never forget that night. That night was, perhaps, the most astonishing part of all. People came and went—friends, neighbors, Sarah's perfunctory relatives, distant cousins—but his own immediate family stayed, held in unspoken anticipation of things to come, drifting off to the kitchen to eat something and then returning to the living room to rejoin the circle of borrowed bridge chairs that had formed around the sofa and the *shiva* benches. A couple of memorial baskets arrived and were opened, the fruits cut up, the boxes of chocolates passed around. Deborah remarked that no one nowadays made chocolate the way the Liebers used to, and Sam smiled, and Deanna told the hushed dimness that she loved visiting the factory when she was a kid. Outside, the pale spring evening slowly gave way to night and the windows darkened. Laura switched on Walter's reading lamp, which threw vague shadows around the room. Sarah's eyes were closing, so Walter coaxed her to bed, sitting with her until she began to snore. When he returned to the living room, Evelyn was telling how Asa Kalisher had flown all the way to New York with her and Ruthie, talking about the time Jeannie had come to Florida to visit him and take his picture and listen to his stories about the old days, until at last it dawned on them that the old man had confused his grandnieces and believed it was Deanna who was dead. That reminded Sam of the time Uncle Asa sent him to deliver a payoff to a gangster named Waxy O'Brian, and how he walked with his heart in his mouth into that Irish clubhouse—this was when he had just gone to work in the restaurant—and how, after he handed over the sealed envelope, O'Brian put his arm around his shoulder and said to his cronies: "Boys, this lad is Asa Kalisher's nephew, and he's got plenty of moxie. You see him around, you make sure no one is bothering him."

Something on Sam's face as he told this story, some old surviving boyish pride as he recalled that odd benediction, lightened the mood of the room. Even Walter had to smile—and a few months later, after Sam suffered another heart attack and was gone, that's how Walter remembered him best, sharing anecdotes with the family and grinning at the small glories of his past.

The conversation turned to Aunt Bea. Everyone was flabbergasted at how young and vigorous she looked. They remembered that when she moved to Israel twelve years before, she was so feeble and asthmatic they expected she wouldn't have long to live. Sam said maybe she had found in the Holy Land a fountain of youth; if so, he would move there tomorrow. Then Rose recalled the days when Aunt Bea and Uncle Yonkel would come to the house for a visit and Molly would run down the hallway, shouting, "Big and Little are here! Big and Little are here!" Which reminded Deborah of Aunt Bea's cousins, the Zalman boys, who had been horse thieves in the old country and when they arrived in the New World turned to stealing automobiles. One day, she related, Mishie Zalman parked one of his stolen cars by a fire plug in front of his house on Decatur Street; he woke up the next morning, looked out the window, and saw a cop, his foot up on the running board, writing out a ticket. So Mishie threw open his window and shouted down: "Wait a minute! I'll move it!" And that's how they caught him.

"It's not funny," concluded Deborah, raising her voice against a burst of laughter. "The poor man spent two years in jail."

The talk grew louder, the laughter more easy, as they sat and ransacked their memories to find anecdotes to counterpose against the mood of the funeral. They hadn't forgotten the sadness of the occasion—but how much can you grieve, how much can you cry? Like the fruits and chocolates they nibbled, their stories served to sweeten and momentarily diminish the ashy taste of death. Everyone joined in. Everyone had memories to contribute.

Ruthie told one about Moe, seven or eight years old, picking at a mosquito bite on his hand until it got so infected blood poisoning set in and red lines started creeping up his arm.

"When Mama saw it, she boiled up a pot of water and shoved his hand in, and you could see the red lines drawing back. *Oy*, how he screamed!"

Moe denied the story, but Ruthie said he probably still had the scar, and, sure enough, there it was on the back of his hand, a little patch of dark, irregular skin. They made him walk around the room to show it to everyone, and the mood became giddier.

They told the one about Levitch coming to the apartment and Jacob thinking it was Deborah he wanted to marry; about Dr. Lipsky falling in love with Sophie and trying to cure Hymie by taking him to a whorehouse; about Deborah staying out all night with Buster Stern while Sophie sat by the window eating her heart out; about

Walter at the age of eleven, a little *yeshiva bucher*, deciding to grow *peyiss* and Sophie saying if he did, she would cut off his ears; about Sam taking Lou Grossman for a ride—

"And I was mad as hell at Sam then," said Ruthie, "but I have to admit it did my husband some good."

To impress Deanna and Joey and Gary, who were sitting in wide-eyed reverie, they recalled the ice storm that had hit Brooklyn years ago, and how for two weeks you had to get down on your hands and knees if you wanted to go outside; and the time they were sitting *shivah* for their father and Deborah saw Uncle Chaim coming from the bathroom and thought it was a ghost; and the one about Evelyn dating an Italian fellow whose father was in the meat business, and how he showed up at the house one night with a present for the family—ten pounds of pork sausage in a paper bag.

"It didn't take Mama long to put an end to that," cried Ruthie, and everyone howled.

To get even, Evelyn told one on Ruthie: how she was being courted by two beaus and accidentally arranged a date with both of them for the same evening. According to Evelyn, they arrived at the apartment at the same moment and kept looking at each other as they walked up the stairs—"and practically had a fistfight," Evelyn concluded merrily, "over who would get to ring the doorbell!"

The room grew warm. The men shed their jackets and the women fanned themselves with whatever was at hand, wiping their damp faces with handkerchiefs, caught up in the hot buoyant tumult of their tale-telling. Even the terrible and sad things seemed funny in the mood of hilarity that enveloped them. They told so many stories that Walter had to remind himself that they were, they had to be, more than a collection of anecdotes.

Sure, there was something ghoulish in it, Walter later realized, to sit there laughing at such a time, to kibitz and whoop on Jeannie's fresh grave; but for the moment it was enough that Jeannie's death had brought them together, gathered in a circle to dispel a tragic darkness. Alone they were merely fragments, hungry and fearful, but together, joined by the bonds of their blood, sharing their memories against the dreariness of time, they could feel themselves even in the face of death to be sufficient and complete. Outside, a car with a damaged muffler roared to life and sped away into the darkness, and Walter, separating himself from the giddiness for a few seconds, followed it in his mind as it rushed across Brooklyn beneath the bands of streetlamps. He could imagine the noise of it disturbing a thousand quiet apartments where—who knows?—maybe no one loved anyone enough. Jeannie, Jeannie. His eyes burned; his heart heaved solemnly for all his ruined dreams. He wasn't over her death. It would remain forever terrible for him; he would go on mourning for the rest of his days. But now, returning his attention to his family, immersing himself again in that strange, holy air of celebration they had concocted out of nothing more than their memories of their own strong, stubborn, thwarted lives, he experienced a kind of secret joy.

Sam was telling about his father buying the bookstore and bringing home for the children a box of stereopticon cards because he couldn't fathom why anyone would buy "two pictures exactly the same." Which reminded Deborah of the time she stayed up all night cutting and pasting red cardboard and paper doilies because Sam wanted to decorate the bookstore with hearts for St. Valentine's Day, and how she had to hide what she was doing from their father. Somehow that launched Sam on a long, vague story about the family, on the way to America, spending a night in a forest; and Deborah swore she didn't believe a word of it, because she would have remembered it if it had happened; and Essie said mysteriously that she could recall only one time in all the years that Sam ever lied to her; and Deanna stepped in with a memory of how her Aunt Molly used to let her search through her purse for the little sack of chocolate coins she kept hidden there; and Joey remembered Aunt Molly bursting in upon them when they were watching television to show them her first husband in a cowboy movie; and Deborah teased Walter gently about the time he wrote a letter denouncing himself to the FBI; and then they got started on Georgie's *briss*, with Rose, laughing through tears, saying, *"Sha! Sha!"* to shut them up while Georgie sat there grinning, his thick glasses glittering, as though he understood every word they said. But she couldn't shut them up. Moe remembered Milton at the *briss* performing his famous trick with the egg in his pocket, and Laura confessed to being "nervous as hell" the first time Moe took her to Brooklyn to meet his family, and that started Sam on an anecdote about meeting his mother-in-law—and they went on and on, long into the night, until they had exhausted themselves with the telling and retelling, the laughter and tears. Walter would always remember how at last, one by one, they stood and stretched themselves, recalled to the solemnity of the occasion, murmuring a few final words of condolence to him as they prepared to go home; how the circle broke reluctantly, apologetically; how he stood holding the door open for them, telling them, while they hugged and kissed him, and wished him well, that he would never be able to adequately express his gratitude to them; and how in the end when they offered to stay with him, not leave him alone, he had to insist that he would be all right now, really he would—a man learns to live with anything—and besides, it was late, it was nearly morning, it was time for them to go.